Lighthouse Beach

Also by Shelley Noble

Lighthouse Beach
Christmas at Whisper Beach (novella)
Beach at Painter's Cove
Forever Beach
Whisper Beach
A Newport Christmas Wedding (novella)
Breakwater Bay
Stargazey Night (novella)
Stargazey Point
Holidays at Crescent Cove
Beach Colors

Lighthouse Beach

SHELLEY NOBLE

WILLIAM MORROW

An Imprint of HarperCollins*Publishers*

LIGHTHOUSE BEACH. Copyright © 2018 by Shelley Freydont. All rights reserved. Printed in the United States of America. No part of this book may be used or reproduced in any manner whatsoever without written permission except in the case of brief quotations embodied in critical articles and reviews. For information address HarperCollins Publishers, 195 Broadway, New York, NY 10007.

HarperCollins books may be purchased for educational, business, or sales promotional use. For information please email the Special Markets Department at SPsales@harpercollins.com.

FIRST EDITION

Designed by Diahann Sturge

Chapter opener art © Sherry Zaat / Shutterstock, Inc.

Library of Congress Cataloging-in-Publication Data has been applied for.

ISBN 978-0-06-267596-5

18 19 20 21 22 LSC 10 9 8 7 6 5 4 3 2 1

To all those who keep the light burning and help guide us home

Chapter 1

The moment Lillo Gray pulled up to the Atlantic Yacht Club and Hotel, she began to sweat. Okay, it was summer in Maine, which could get pretty hot, but it wasn't that. It wasn't even that the battered VW van she'd borrowed in order to get there had no air-conditioning or that it was totally out of place among the new, high-end cars in line for valet parking. Valet was the only way to park; she'd checked.

It was everything. The sundress and shoes she was wearing were borrowed from her friend Sada. Even her wedding outfit was on loan from Barbara Carroll's consignment store.

Who wore someone else's clothes to a wedding? The shoes were too big, the sundress was too short, and the back of her thighs had stuck to the scratchy seat the whole way from Lighthouse Beach.

She should never have left the small island where she lived—and would probably die. She just shouldn't be here, especially not for a wedding—and yet here she was.

Because Jessica Parker was getting married.

Lillo barked out an unintended laugh. The line moved forward. She jumped when the car door swung open and a young man in khaki trousers and polo shirt greeted her with a smile—a smile that almost hid his chagrin. He'd get razzed for being the one who had to park the old VW.

She smiled back, a smile just as forced as his, and tried to unglue her thighs from the seat while sliding gracefully to the pavement. An epic fail. He had to catch her arm as one foot slipped out of the backless shoe.

By the time she'd returned her foot to the shoe—not an easy task without bending over while keeping her skirt down—a bellman was already placing her luggage on a shining brass cart. At least her luggage was her own. A present from her parents when she went off to medical school. Another epic fail.

She followed the man inside to a large reception area of white wood and expensive carpet. Across the back, a panoramic view of the bay and ocean was bisected by a trumpet-shaped staircase that led to a balcony where bridesmaids and groomsmen would line up for photographs. The bride would stand on the staircase looking dreamily at the camera, or maybe triumphant, her white train artfully spread out on the descending stairs. All for a white leather album that no one really wanted on their coffee table. Or maybe they wouldn't even print the photos out, but put a digital album on display that would slowly flash pictures one by one until the cycle began again. On and on and . . .

"Lillo!"

Lillo turned toward the voice and saw a tall, model-thin woman hurrying toward her, something she accomplished easily in stiletto heels. Lillo smiled tentatively as she scrutinized the shiny designer hair, the big round eyes, the overbright smile. She didn't have a clue.

"I can't believe you made it."

The woman, about her own age—late twenties, early thirties—stopped in front of her and did one of those shoulder-lift, face-tightening gestures of excitement and delight.

It was a reaction that Lillo remembered well. Still . . .

"Jess?" she asked tentatively. The last time she'd seen Jess Parker was when they were two unhappy fifteen-year-olds at fat camp. Both unhappy, but not for the same reasons. Lillo's parents owned the camp, and Lillo, skinny as a rail mainly from doing nonstop chores, was resented by most of the campers because she was so thin. Jess was a chubby, depressed rich kid, full of self-loathing. She was far richer than the other campers, arrived in a limo, under the supervision of a servant, overweight enough to send to camp, but not fat enough to fit in.

They'd been drawn together from the first summer Jess had attended. She'd been ten to Lillo's barely nine, but they recognized in each other something special. Misunderstood by their parents and the world, they'd become best friends for three months of the year, and wrote to each other during the rest of the time until they'd see each other again. Every summer Jess lost weight; every winter she gained it back and her parents kept sending her back to camp. During the school year, Jess dreamed of coming back, Lillo dreamed of getting away and becoming a doctor like Doc Clancy, or like Ned Hartley would become someday. Year after year they met again—until that disastrous last summer.

Now Jess was the really thin one, svelte, almost gaunt, and the happiness in her eyes and smile seemed frantic.

"Wow! You look wonderful," Lillo said. Her arms went instinctively around her friend. Because somehow they were still friends. Lillo could feel it arcing in the air between them. Was that why Jess had not only invited Lillo to the wedding, but had sent a separate e-mail begging her to come?

"Let's get you checked in, then we're sneaking off for happy hour." Jess hustled Lillo up to the registration desk. When Lillo opened her wallet to get her credit card, Jess stopped her. "Comped." She handed the bellman, who was standing at the ready, a bill and told him to take Ms. Gray's luggage to her room.

"You don't need to go up, do you?"

Lillo glanced down at her car-wrinkled dress.

Jess took the room card from the desk clerk and handed it to her. "You look fine. You look great. If you have to pee, you can pee at the restaurant."

Lillo didn't resist when Jess steered her toward a side door and onto a lawn, wide and green enough to belong to one of the mansions along the coast road. To their right the bay sparkled all the way to the sea, from behind them laughter and the tinkling of glasses drifted down from the balcony bar.

Lillo glanced up to see a crowd of exquisitely dressed people at the rail.

"Don't look," Jess warned. "It's Mother's cocktail hour with the invited guests. They might see us and invite us up."

"Are those men in white—"

"Arab oilmen. The governor is flying in tomorrow along with a senator or two. Mother is in her element."

"Shouldn't you be up there?" Lillo asked as Jess steered her across the drive, away from the hotel.

"No. Tonight's our night."

Jess stopped to pull off her shoes, motioned for Lillo to do the same. As soon as Lillo picked up her shoes, Jess grabbed her free hand and they ran across the lawn toward the parking lot. Lillo was super aware of the crowded balcony bar. And was hit with the same jolt of excitement and anxiety she'd felt when, as girls, they'd skipped out on the camp activities to escape to the secluded beach, where the trees and boulders hid them from view and judgment.

At the edge of the parking lot, they stopped to put their shoes on.

"You can park your own car?" Lillo asked.

"God no, how utterly middle class." Jess gave her signature eye roll. Lillo had always envied those eye rolls. "Anyway, we're not driving. We're drinking."

They wove through the parked cars until they were out on the road. Across the way, a few houses and stores made up a picturesque postcard of a New England village. Picking a moment when traffic was heading toward them in both directions, Jess hustled Lillo across the street. Honking ensued.

"Jeez!" Lillo exclaimed when they were safely—barely—on the opposite sidewalk.

Jess merely grinned and kept walking.

"Where are we going?"

"To a bar. Don't worry. We have a reservation. It may be a little trendy for you."

Lillo wanted to say she could do trendy, but Jess didn't slow down. "There's nothing but trendy around here. Or else extremely homegrown with terribly authentic ambience." She stopped suddenly. "Is the Corner Luncheonette still on Lighthouse Island?"

Lillo shook her head. "Burned down several years ago."

"Oh, that's too bad. I loved that place. They didn't build back?"

Lillo grimaced. "Not worth it, I guess. The owners left the island. Lots of people have. Hey, where's this fiancé of yours? Will he be at the restaurant?"

"No. Girls only, with my other two besties. I hope you love them."

"I'm sure I will." This was beginning to sound more like girls'-

weekend-away than until-death-do-us-part, Lillo thought, suddenly wishing she were anywhere but here. What had she been thinking?

As they made their way down the narrow sidewalks of the little shopping district, Jess talked about her friends. "We were all in the same sorority. Diana pledged us. She and I became great friends and ended up working together in Manhattan. Allie married right out of college. Owns a ginormous vineyard in California."

The escapades they'd been through as undergrads. "We were crazy. I don't know how we survived college."

And what they looked like. "Diana's tall, thin, totally urban, you'll like her, though. Allie's petite. Sweet. But tough in her own way. She's had to be."

All this while Jess practically force-marched Lillo down the crowded sidewalk. Not once did she mention her fiancé. No "I can't wait for you to meet James." No "He's made me so happy." Not one question about what had been going on with Lillo since high school. No explanations for why Jess hadn't stayed in touch. Or why she'd been so adamant about Lillo attending her wedding.

Jess barely slowed down when they reached the glass doors of MoonBeam, a lantern-illuminated part pub, part bistro that seemed confused about its place in the culinary world. The specials board was an eclectic mix of seafood, vegan, and taco bar.

Jess waved off the hostess and made a beeline for the enclosed porch at the back of the building, steering Lillo with a tight grasp on her elbow.

Lillo barely had time to acknowledge the two women seated at a corner table before Jess thrust her into a chair and collapsed in the chair beside her.

"Lillo, meet Diana and Allie."

"Diana," the woman sitting across from Lillo said as she stood partially to reach across the table and shake Lillo's hand. She was one of those tall, well-dressed, sophisticated women with an expensive haircut. A powerhouse. Definitely fit Jess's brief description and definitely belonged at a posh wedding like this one.

Unlike me, Lillo thought.

"And Allie," said the shorter, blond woman to Lillo's right. Her hair was pulled back into a messy bun and it made Lillo relax a little. "We've heard so much about you. I'm so glad to meet you at last."

Lillo nodded and smiled at both of them, wondering why they should have heard all about her when she hadn't even heard from their mutual friend in years.

"I'm so glad you're all finally here," Jess said. "Now everything is perfect."

And she burst into tears.

Diana and Allie were on their feet and coming around the table to Jess before Lillo even realized what was happening. She turned in her chair to frown at Jess. "Is this nerves?" she asked. "Or are you unhappy?"

Diana and Allie stopped in midsoothe. Both heads swiveled to look at Lillo. Jess locked eyes with her.

Jess sniffed. "Same old Lillo."

"You expected me to be someone else?"

"Evidently not," Diana volunteered, looking at Lillo with an intensity that made her want to disappear. "And thank God for it. We've been wondering what was going on since we got here."

"I'm fine, fine," Jess said. "Really. It's just nerves, and the stress of all this planning and dress fittings and cake tasting and guest lists. I don't even know half, maybe three-quarters,

of the people invited. It's all just a bit much. And now they're
forecasting rain. And we may have to move the ceremony inside
and everything will be ruined."

"It's not going to rain," Allie assured her.

Right, thought Lillo, who was facing the window. If those
weren't storm clouds, she wasn't a lifelong Lighthouse Islander.

"And if it does," added Diana, "it won't last until Saturday.
Everything will be dry in time for the wedding."

"It's going to be a beautiful wedding to a wonderful man,"
added Allie. "Lillo, do you know James?"

Lillo shook her head. "But I can't wait to meet him."

"Everything is a go, rain or shine," Diana said. "So you don't
have to worry about anything."

"You're right. I was just having a moment. I'm fine now." Jess
huffed out a sigh. "Waiter, girlie drinks all around."

Allie patted her shoulder and returned to her seat.

Diana exchanged looks with Lillo. Either she had more to
say, or she was signaling Lillo that something was amiss. Or
something. Lillo had been so reclusive in the last year that she
was afraid she'd lost the ability to actually communicate with
others, verbally or otherwise.

And as far as what Jess was feeling? Was it normal wedding nerves? Or was something much deeper bothering her old
friend? It had been a long time, a really long time, since they'd
even seen each other, much less talked or shared secrets.

Even so, Lillo tumbled into the time warp where nothing
had changed. It was the little telltale signs of distress she had
always recognized. That tight little shrug, the grasp on her elbow, the brave forced smile as Jess made excuses for being late,
for being fat, for not being lovable.

Lillo huffed out a sigh. She was exhausted already and the
festivities hadn't even begun.

They started with martinis, dirty for Diana, pomegranate for Allie, and lemon drop for Jess. When it came to Lillo, who was a beer drinker, she floundered and ended up ordering a glass of white wine.

A discussion of the menu followed. What Lillo noticed first were the prices. Just about everything started at thirty dollars. It was going to be a long weekend. And it would take a serious chunk out of her sporadic income.

"Bride's treat," Jess announced as if she'd read Lillo's mind. And Lillo blushed, even though she knew Jess hadn't actually read her mind.

They ordered small plates for eight large people, a pitcher of sangria, and a gigantic order of nachos that Diana, Allie, and Lillo dug into with gusto while Jess picked out the tomato chunks and olives. Both friends were animated and funny, and in spite of Jess's seeming preoccupation, Lillo began to think she might actually have fun. Diana manipulated the conversation and the tone of the evening with the finesse of a good cruise director, though in reality she turned out to be the CEO of her own start-up app company.

"She's amazing," Jess said as she lifted the pitcher of sangria with both hands and sloshed wine and several pieces of fruit into her glass. "Two years and she's doubled her employees and her revenue."

"Aren't you glad you got in on the ground level?" Diana quipped.

"And how. You make my portfolio sing," Jess said, and took a healthy gulp of her drink.

"We'll all be singing at the rate we're going," Diana said as she filled Allie's glass then her own. She pushed the pitcher across to Lillo, whose glass was still almost full. She topped it off just to be polite.

"I think I'm getting a buzz already," Allie said with a lop-sided grin.

"That's because you've gotten spoiled on your own expensive wine." Diana turned to Lillo. "Allie is a California vintner. Acres and acres of potential cabernets and merlots."

"It's my husband's family's vineyard," Allie said. "Since 1874."

A momentary silence washed over the table and Lillo wondered what she was missing. But since no one enlightened her, she just sipped her sangria and waited for the conversation to begin again.

"And what about you, Lillo?"

Lillo nearly bobbled her sangria. She put her glass down. She'd known she'd be asked this question, and she had a nice answer prepared.

"Oh, I'm sorry," Jess said, rousing herself. "Lillo and I were besties and we've kind of lost contact in the last few years—my bad."

"Not at all," Lillo said. "E-mail works both ways, we just got busy. We're here now, that's what counts." She cringed at her own duplicity. She had no idea why Jess had invited her or why she'd actually come.

"I know you went to medical school. Are you finished? Are you practicing in Lighthouse Beach?"

The questions were rapid-fire. They all laughed.

In her enthusiasm, Jess didn't seem to notice. "Lillo always wanted to be a doctor, right? She was always taking care of birds and turtles and stuff, and practice-bandaging. I was the guinea pig." She sighed. "Some of the best times of my childhood." She reached for the sangria pitcher.

"Did you specialize?" Diana asked politely.

Lillo froze. They'd bypassed the whole introductory part of her explanation of why she wasn't a doctor. So she just jumped in.

"Actually, I'm a landscaper." If gardening for local folks who weren't able or didn't have the time to care for their own little plots of green could be called landscaping. She also helped out at the community center, nonpaying. And the lighthouse gift shop, lower than minimum wage. She got by.

"Landscaper?"

The drink Jess was holding started to tip. Lillo caught it just before it spilled over. "'Fraid so."

"But what about medical school?"

"I went." Lillo shrugged. "It just didn't work out."

"Why?"

Oh God, why had she come? "Too much blood," she said, and forced a laugh. *Just too much damn blood.*

"Oh."

"Well, I've always been envious of anyone with a green thumb," Diana said. "If I ever get out of my apartment and into a penthouse with a roof, I'll call you for sure. Allie, too."

"Right," Allie agreed. "Thousands of acres of green. I can't keep a poinsettia alive."

Lillo smiled and laughed throughout the rest of dinner, but she was wondering if Jess had invited her thinking she was a doctor. And if it mattered that she wasn't.

It obviously didn't matter to Diana and Allie, and by the time they wove their way back to the marina they were acting like old friends—very stuffed, slightly tipsy old friends.

It was late, after midnight; the road was empty of traffic, and with the exception of Lillo losing her shoe again, they made it to the other side without mishap. Music and laughter echoed across the parking lot from the marina balcony. Things were still in full swing there. Lillo started thinking about her bed.

The four women picked their way between cars and SUVs

and the occasional motorcycle and were halfway across the tarmac when they heard a moan.

Lillo stiffened, alert, ready for any surprises.

"What was that?" Jess asked, looking in all directions.

Another moan, louder this time.

Lillo moved in the direction of the sound.

Diana held her back. "Let's get out of here."

"But if it's a mugging . . ." Allie began.

"It isn't." Diana swept her arms around Allie and Jess and urged them toward the marina.

Another high-pitched moan, closer. Instinctively, everyone stopped and turned in the direction of the cry.

"Oh shit." Diana began pulling Jess away. Allie's mouth dropped open. Lillo stared. A couple was clenched in a standing embrace up against a Mercedes that shone silver in the security lamps.

"Do you think she needs help?" Lillo asked.

"Oh baby, oh baby, yes."

"Oh, really," said Diana.

"I guess not," Lillo said. "Who cries 'Oh baby, oh baby' anyway?"

The four of them had stopped, and like the witnesses of a train wreck, compelled to look, they stood, slightly tipsy and weaving.

Allie giggled.

"Oh God," Diana whispered.

Jess reeled. "Oh my God, is that—"

"No," Diana said, and thrust her toward Allie.

Allie jolted into action and threw both arms around Jess, but Jess pushed her out of the way. "You cretin!" she screamed. "You—" She was cut off by conjoined cries from the couple.

Jess lunged forward, but Diana grabbed her by the waist.

Allie latched on to her arm and the two women trundled their struggling friend away.

Lillo took a quick look back. The man had collapsed over the woman, leaving her pinned against the car, but she didn't seem to be struggling to get free. The couple in their tumble over the top were oblivious to their audience.

In fact, they both appeared to be relaxed in postcoital recovery. Ugh. Kind of stupid, but not worthy of Jess's reaction, unless . . . Lillo was beginning to have a nasty suspicion.

Jess heaved a gut-wrenching cry. "You bastard."

"Let's get her back to the hotel," Diana ordered.

She and Allie each took an arm and they pulled Jess away.

Lillo turned to follow the others inside and realized they hadn't been the only observers. Two valets leaned against a nearby car, arms crossed, enjoying the show. Above the door to the hotel, the crowd at the balcony bar stood at the rail, all looking out to the parking lot. And at the very front was a couple she recognized, older than Lillo remembered them, but just as distinctive. And just as judgmental and demanding as they had been years before. The Parkers.

"Hurry," Lillo said, and added her body in an attempt to shield Jess from curious eyes. Too little too late, she knew as they guided the sobbing Jess across the lawn toward a secondary door away from the gawking crowd. Diana held the door while Allie pushed Jess inside.

Lillo stopped Diana from following them. "Was that who I think it was?"

"You said you wanted to meet the groom? Well, you just did."

Chapter 2

"Let's get her upstairs," Diana said as she steered them down the hall toward the corridor with the elevators. "This way."

Allie pulled up short. "But that goes right past the bar. What if someone sees her?"

Jess's legs crumpled beneath her.

"Well, we can't parade her through the lobby in this condition."

"Diana's right," Lillo said. "I'll go ahead and try to run interference." She stepped past them, searched the hallway, and then motioned them forward. They'd gone several yards when a man burst through the doors to the bar, which swung back, nearly hitting the woman who was close on his heels.

"Mother of—" Diana swore, and attempted to turn Jess in the opposite direction.

"—the bride," Lillo finished. She held her ground. She knew those people. They were older, but there was no mistaking them. They swept past her like she wasn't even there.

"Jessica Braithwaite Parker. Stop this instant."

That voice. Just as demanding and cold as it had been the first time he'd dropped his daughter off at camp. And his wife cowering behind him as usual. Never once had Lillo seen the woman stick up for Jess. Not even tonight.

Lillo's stomach turned sour.

Jess stopped, turned, already slipping away from her friends, even though she could barely stay on her feet. And Lillo wondered if it was because of catching her groom in flagrante delicto in the parking lot before a crowd of people, fear of her parents, or because she was just weak from starving herself for the wedding.

Diana and Allie immediately repositioned themselves at her side.

"I know you're upset," Mrs. Parker began.

"Upset?" screeched Jess.

"Keep your voice down," Mr. Parker snapped. "Do you want the whole world to hear you?"

"Like they just saw her fiancé bonking another woman?" Diana said. "That just wouldn't do, would it, Mr. Parker?"

Parker moved into them, took his daughter's arm. "We'll take you to your room. After a good night's sleep, without these outside agitators, things won't seem nearly so dramatic."

"Ha!" said Diana. "That's a first. I've never been called an agitator before."

Parker shook his finger at her.

From the way Diana looked at it, Lillo was afraid she might take a bite out of it. She did absolutely nothing to stop her.

"Your father's right," added Mrs. Parker. "Your big day is almost here and you want to look your best."

Lillo's brain fritzed out. How could they still expect her to marry that ass?

Diana was the first to react. "Wait a minute. Her big day was when she graduated magna cum from Wharton business school. Or when she almost single-handedly turned CPF Global around. You think marrying James Beckman's family fortune is her big day? Yours maybe. But it will suck for her."

"Of course we're proud—" her mother began.

"This is not about you. And you can't expect her to walk down the aisle with that ass in front of everyone knowing what just happened."

"Oh, grow up, Diana. Boys will be boys." Mr. Parker tried to push Jess toward the elevators. But her feet seemed nailed to the floor.

"That's why women marry 'men.' Maybe you should postpone the wedding until he grows up. Which, if you ask me, will be never."

"You girls are making a mountain out of a molehill."

"And upsetting our daughter," his wife added.

"Ha," Diana said. "I think James Beckman has already managed that on his own."

Mrs. Parker grasped both of Jess's hands. "Things will be fine on Saturday, as long as you quit crying, dear. You don't want everyone to see you tomorrow with puffy eyes and a big red nose. We want this weekend to be perfect."

Jess pulled her hands away and ran her index fingers under her eyes, but it was a hopeless attempt. She sniffed, then looked straight at Lillo. For an eternity, their eyes held.

And Lillo understood in that instant why Jess had begged her to come to her wedding. She still couldn't stand up for herself, not even after all these years.

"I can't. Please call it off. I can't walk down the aisle with everyone laughing at me."

"Don't be ridiculous. It'll be forgotten before you return from your honeymoon. Go to bed—things will look different in the morning."

Jess hung her head.

Lillo threw her good sense to the wind and stepped in front of them. "No, they won't. They'll only be worse. How can you ask Jess to marry someone who would do that to her anytime, but especially tonight of all nights? If she doesn't want to get married, then she isn't going to."

Mr. Parker turned on her. "Who are you? I don't believe you're anyone we know."

"Lillo Gray."

"Gray," he echoed. "Gray. I don't recall . . ." His eyes narrowed; the storm clouds descended. "Good God. You're the girl whose parents ran that camp where we sent Jessica for those summers, not that it did a speck of good. What are you doing here?"

"Jess invited me."

"Well, you can uninvite yourself. And you other two can take yourselves off to bed; we'll see to Jessica."

The three women didn't move, but Lillo could feel Allie's resolve weakening, a woman who didn't like confrontations. Neither did Lillo, and yet here she was. This wasn't a few months at camp or college. This was a life choice. And Jess was no stronger tonight than she'd been at ten or twelve or sixteen. Maybe it was hopeless to try to help her.

"You'll cut this nonsense out this minute, Jessica," Mr. Parker said. "You will walk down that aisle on Saturday and do it with a smile on your face."

Jess gripped her stomach and caved. "Do you hate me that much?"

Mrs. Parker took her by the shoulders. "We love you and we want what's best for you."

Diana barked out a laugh. "By making her marry a sleazebag who can't keep it in his pants even at his own wedding? Sorry,

Jess, but it isn't the first time, and knowing James, it won't be the last."

Jess moaned.

"You," Mr. Parker said, actually pointing a finger at Diana, "can mind your own business."

"She hasn't had as many opportunities as you have, Diana," Mrs. Parker said. "For all the good it did you. And she may not have another as good as this, if she gets any."

"Jeez, what century are you living in?"

"We just want her to be happy."

"By making her marry that creature?" asked Lillo. "That's going to make her happy? You never did get it, did you, or have you always consciously tried to undermine Jess's self-esteem?"

"How dare you!" Mr. Parker exploded; his face turned so red that Lillo feared for his health.

"We've always encouraged her to be better," Mrs. Parker said.

"Like the way you encouraged her year after year at fat camp? We didn't miss the little gibes. The smiling condescension. You must really think kids are stupid. Well, they're not. And it hurt. And she wasn't even that fat. Well, it stops now. Jess never needed to be better, she just needed to be herself. And you wouldn't let her." Lillo sucked in her breath, horrified at herself. She'd spent the last year trying to erase herself and now—

What had she just done? She didn't know what Jess wanted. She didn't even know what she herself wanted.

Diana and Allie were staring at her. So were the Parkers, and even Jess, who straightened slightly.

Mr. Parker took a threatening step toward her. "I want you out of here, tonight."

"I'll happily leave . . . when Jess tells me to."

"If you're not out of this hotel in the next hour, the manager will help you out." He turned his back on Lillo, arrogant as always. He thought she was afraid of him, but nothing could be further from the truth. Bullies didn't scare her in the least.

If she'd had a weapon handy, she might have tried to kill him. She stepped back, horrified at her own thought.

"I suggest you other two girls return to your own rooms. Jessica, your mother and I will walk you to your room."

The three friends took an unconscious step toward Jess.

She gulped. "It's okay. I'll see you in the morning." She grasped Lillo's wrist, whispered, "Please don't leave. I'll talk to them." Jess stepped away from them and walked down the hall, cutting between her parents as she passed, neither slowing down nor glancing at either of them.

With another quelling look, Mr. Parker took his wife's arm and propelled her toward their retreating daughter, catching up to her and flanking her as they turned the corner to the elevators. Not two parents offering comfort and support but two guards taking her to face her life sentence.

"Whew," Allie said. "You were fierce, Lillo. No wonder Jess was so determined to get you here."

"I just hope I didn't make things worse. Do you think she stills wants to marry him?"

"I don't think she ever wanted to marry him," Diana said. "Not really. They just brainwashed her into thinking no one would ever marry her if she was left to her own choices."

"That's terrible," Allie said. "I can't believe any parent would do that."

Lillo and Diana exchanged looks. "They would," Lillo said. "Some people really are that despicable, no matter how much they try to convince themselves otherwise."

Diana sighed as she looked into the empty space of the corridor. "And I thought I had controlling parents. This is so wrong. I swear, if I ever have children, which is looking like it's pretty much not happening at this point, I will never use them as pawns in a power struggle or for empire building. And you can quote me."

She started off down the hall. Allie and Lillo ran to catch up.

"So where are we going?" Allie asked.

"Well, I'm not going back to my room," Diana said.

"And I'm not leaving. Jess begged me to come. I didn't really want to. I didn't understand why after all these years she asked me, but now I get it. I just don't know what, if anything, to do about it."

"None of us are going meekly back to our rooms," Diana said. "We're going to follow them upstairs, and when Jess is alone, we'll make a stealth invasion."

Allie's eyes rounded. "Are we going to kidnap her?"

"Now there's an idea." Diana stopped at the next corridor and peeked around the corner to the elevators. "Safe! Come on. We don't have much time." She hurried ahead of them and jabbed the up button so hard Lillo half expected the building to shake.

STEALTH INVASION INDEED, Lillo thought as they crept along the corridor to Jess's room. Skulking along like she didn't belong here. Which she didn't.

Farther down the hall, a room door opened.

"Quick," Diana warned, and ducked into the ice-machine alcove.

The three of them pressed against the wall until the people passed. Diana held Lillo and Allie back and peered out. "It's them. We'll give them time to get in the elevator, and then it's Operation Wedding Fail."

Lillo frowned. It was almost as if Diana was having a good time.

They scuttled down the hall and huddled around Jess's door

like the three witches in *Macbeth* while Diana tapped on the door then stuck her face in front of the peephole.

Lillo had decided Jess wasn't going to let them in when the door opened a crack. They all pushed inside. Lillo shut the door behind them and put on the chain just for good measure.

"Are you okay?" asked Allie.

A silly question, Lillo thought. Jess was definitely not okay. Not okay, but resigned. Lillo remembered the look. And she knew Jess had capitulated. She'd be marrying James Beckman this Saturday.

Lillo could only stand back and watch as Allie and Diana sat down beside Jess, attempting to heal a hurt that had begun long before she had ever met James. And Lillo knew all the talking in the world wouldn't cure the pain.

"They're right," Jess said, and sniffed. "I won't get a better offer."

"Really?" Diana asked. "You want to walk down that long aisle to marry a man who cheats on you and say 'I do' to God knows what kind of life you'll be dished out?"

She snorted, stood up. "Come work for me. That's a real offer. Not 'Will you marry me so I can continue to act like the ass I am, help myself to your family's assets until you get so fed up you divorce me, pay me, give me alimony, stock options, anything I want just to get rid of me.'"

"Diana, that's not helping," Allie said.

"Then what do you suggest?"

Confronted, Allie only shrugged.

"It's my own fault," Jess began. "If I'd been more—"

"Oh God, I can't believe this." Diana stalked off across the room to stare out the window.

But Lillo could. Nothing had changed. She couldn't help Jess. Hell, she couldn't even help herself. Then why had she come?

She didn't owe Jess anything. But Jess had wanted her here, so Lillo had come, like a moth to a flame she had come.

Jess was the same old docile, malleable girl she'd always been, except for being ridiculously thin. She would swallow the dregs of her self-esteem and do what she always had done. Make apologies for her shortcomings, promise to try harder, and do whatever would please her parents.

At first, all those years ago, Lillo hadn't understood Jess's insecurities. The Parkers might have been richer, more prominent than most of the other parents who brought their kids to Camp Beacon. But basically, they were just like all the rest, sending their kids to camp for their own good because they loved them too much to let them mess up their lives by their own bad habits—or to reflect badly on the parents. And ended up driving most of the kids further into the same habits they were trying to break.

Of course, Lillo hadn't realized how insidious all that parental caring was until much later, in one of her college psychology classes. She'd never had those kinds of problems with her own parents; they were loving, not terribly organized, but always supportive of their only child—and yet she had delivered them the ultimate betrayal. She should never have left the island—then or now.

But you did.

She crossed to the bed and stood directly in front of Jess, looked down at her so intently that finally Jess had to look up.

"Do you love James?"

"Yes, of course."

"Why?"

Allie's head snapped up. Lillo was aware of Diana turning to look at her.

The room was completely silent. It was such a simple question, but they hadn't even thought to ask it.

"Well, because he's . . . handsome and—" Jess squeezed her eyes shut. "And . . . and everybody's so happy for me."

Lillo's heart plummeted. If that's the best Jess could do, things did not bode well for her future happiness.

"Maybe tonight was just a one-off," Allie suggested. "You know, wedding jitters?"

No excuse, Lillo thought. "Has he cheated on you before?"

Jess's mouth twisted. "Of course he has. He doesn't love me. Marrying me is good for business."

"Is there any reason for him to stop now?"

Diana strode back to the others. "Why are you even asking her about this? She can't marry him. He'll make her miserable."

"He already has," Allie said, her eyes tearing.

Lillo shook her head. What a mess. Until a few hours ago, her life had been so . . . uneventful. She'd worked really hard to make it that way. She'd gotten used to it. That balance. The calm. Yeah, the calm you feel while balancing on a log going down the rapids. She let out a long breath, took another.

"Do you want to marry him? For yourself? For your own happiness?"

Jess covered her face with her hands. "What have I done? I've ruined my life, embarrassed my family. Poor James."

"Poor *James*?" Diana said incredulously. "He was fu—"

"Diana!" Allie exclaimed.

Diana pursed her lips and clasped her hands to her stomach. "Having his way with a waitress from the hotel bar."

"She was a waitress?"

"Jeez, she was still wearing her uniform . . . most of it anyway."

Lillo focused on Jess. "What do you want to do? Truly want

to do?" She took a breath. Ignored her final *Don't get involved.*
"But make sure you make the decision you can live with."

At first Jess said nothing. Diana shifted on her feet. Allie was
sitting ramrod straight. They were messing in someone else's
life. They could make Jess do what they thought best. She would
cave. She always caved to the stronger person. And there were
three of them right now. But that might not be the best choice
for her. And they would be responsible for that, too.

"No. No, I don't want to marry him. I never did, really. He
would never have asked me if he hadn't been coerced into it by
his parents."

"Didn't take much to twist his arm, if you ask me," Diana
said.

Lillo shot her a look, but Allie surprised her. "Well, we didn't
ask you. Don't try to make her decision for her."

Diana blinked and for a moment Lillo thought she would
explode. But she merely smiled, the kind of smile Lillo thought
she might use in a boardroom when she'd just received insider
information. "You're right. Whatever you decide, Jess, we've got
your back."

"I want to get out of here, as far away as I can."

Lillo grimaced. "Doesn't really solve the underlying problem."

"It might," Diana said. "Things might be clearer in hindsight."

"I think we've already entered hindsight," Lillo said.

Diana's smile morphed into a full-out grin. "I was thinking
the kind of hindsight you got from a rearview mirror."

"We are going to kidnap her," Allie said. "I knew it. We'll be
in so much trouble."

"Not kidnap," Diana said. "Road trip."

Jess hiccuped and wiped her eyes. "Could we? If I could just
get away for a while, it would give me time to figure out what to
do, once my family disowns me."

"They won't disown you," Allie said reassuringly.

"They won't," Diana agreed. "They'd never give up her trust fund." She held up her hand. "Sorry, but it's true. The more they have, the more they want. They'll just have to get over it."

They all looked at Lillo.

"Don't look at me. It's up to Jess." Lillo could send them off on a road trip and she could go back to Lighthouse Island, where she belonged and where nothing unsettling ever happened except for the weather.

Jess stood up. "Can we go now? They'll be guarding me like crazy tomorrow."

Diana, instead of jumping on the bandwagon, frowned. "Just one little problem. Allie and I both flew in for the wedding, and you came up with your parents. There are no available rental cars for the weekend. I already tried to get one."

"Lillo has wheels," Jess said.

"Me? But it's an old VW."

"It doesn't matter. It runs."

"Barely."

The other three looked expectantly at her.

"But—" Lillo's stomach went south. She started shaking her head before the arguments even reached her mouth. She couldn't be responsible for three fleeing women.

"Call valet parking for your car," Diana said. "We need to be out of here before James arrives to beg forgiveness, which he no doubt will as soon as the Parkers can get him zipped up."

"Oh God," Jess moaned.

One look at Jess and Lillo picked up the phone.

"Okay," she said a moment later. "They're bringing it around. Now what?"

"Go get your stuff and the car and meet us out on the street." Diana reached into her purse, brought out her room card, and handed it to Allie. "I'm in 315, just grab my toiletries out of the bathroom and throw them in the suitcase. I never unpacked. Garment bag in the closet. You and Lillo take everything downstairs and move the car to the street. Jess and I will sneak out the far-side entrance and join you. You have five minutes."

"But what are you going to do?" Allie asked.

"Pack her clothes and leave a note."

"But where are we going?"

Diana frowned, looked to Lillo.

Lillo shrugged. She didn't have a clue. But she knew where she couldn't take them.

"I know right where to go," Jess said, suddenly showing a sign of life. "They'll never think to look for me there."

"Where?" asked Allie.

"Where?" demanded Diana.

Oh please, no, thought Lillo.

"Lighthouse Beach. It's perfect."

Chapter 3

Diana pushed Lillo and Allie into the hallway, shut the door, and turned to look at Jess. "Well, it didn't take much for Prince Charming to turn into a toad, did it?"

Jess's mouth twisted. "You knew, didn't you? All about him."

Diana nodded.

"And you knew that I knew."

"Yes, dear. I did."

"But you didn't try to warn me against him."

"That never works. You'd just hate me for saying it." And didn't she just know all about that. "I was hoping you'd come to your senses."

"Well, I did, in spades, in front of the whole world. I'll never be able to face those people again."

"No loss, if you ask me. Now stop being mopey and let's get you packed up. Only essentials—and hurry."

Jess just stood there.

"Or if you're changing your mind, I can just leave without you. But I won't be a party to this travesty."

"No!" Jess ran for the bathroom.

Diana sighed and headed for the closet. She hauled out a suitcase and threw it on the bed. Went back to the closet and rifled through the clothes hanging there. Useless for a road trip. She picked out the least wedding-looking dresses, slacks, and blouses and tossed them into the suitcase.

Jess came out, cradling a mountain of toiletries in her arms.

Diana quickly looked for a carryall of some kind, spied the shopping bags of wedding favors stacked in the corner of the room. She picked the sturdiest-looking one and dumped the favors onto a nearby chair.

Jess let out a squeak of protest.

Diana shot her a look—fight or flight, do or die—it was a look that her employees were used to; it was a look she and Jess had exchanged many times as they climbed the ladder of a corporation neither of them wanted to work for. But they had been fierce, and if one started to cave, the other gave her the look.

Then Jess started dating James Beckman and Diana quit to start her own app company. Things had blossomed for Diana and gone south in a major way for her friend.

She held out the bag and realized that Jess was staring in horror at the dumped gifts.

Diana rattled the bag.

Jess dropped the toiletries into it. Diana moved on to the dresser and rummaged through the underwear, a combination of bikinis, thongs, various styles of bras . . . She scooped them up and tossed the whole bunch across the room to the suitcase.

The next drawer held camisoles and frilly nightgowns. "Unbelievable." She shut the drawer, opened the next. Picked out whatever would fit in the suitcase. And shut it with more energy than was necessary. She was suddenly annoyed at Jess for getting herself into this situation, for putting Diana and her other friends in the middle of it. They were wrecking a huge amount of preparation and expense and upending people's travel plans, not to mention the embarrassment. There was bound to be fall-out. Diana had planned to take a week off. That week called for a weekend wedding, then a relaxing spa at a four-star hotel in downtown Boston where she intended to touch some of the major players in the app development industry when she wasn't packed in mud, being massaged and manicured and generally pampered while she worked.

Well, how bad could Lighthouse Beach be? There was a beach. And what else could she do but help Jess?

She lugged the suitcase off the bed.

"What about the closet?" Jess asked.

"I already went through it for something casual; the rest is wedding stuff. You won't be needing it. Really, I've never seen so much frou. Didn't you bring anything more normal?"

"I was supposed to be getting married, not going to a girls' weekend away."

"Well, now you are. We'll shop when we get to Lighthouse Beach. Now come on, time's up." Diana stopped Jess at the door. "Seriously. Is this what you want?"

Jess bit her bottom lip. Nodded.

"Then use the hotel stationery and leave your parents a note."

"What do I say? They'll be furious."

Diana suppressed a sigh. "Say you need time to think and please cancel the wedding."

"I can't do that," Jess said.

"Then stay here and get married."

Jess dropped her bags and went to the desk, opened the drawer, and pulled out a sheet of stationery and a pen. "Please cancel the wedding and . . ."

"You love them and you'll be in touch."

Jess finished writing. Placed the note carefully on the bedside table and stood looking at it.

"What are you waiting for?"

"This." Jess pulled the engagement ring off her finger and placed it in the center of the note. "Let's blow this joint."

She grabbed her bags. Diana cracked the door open, looked out, then pushed Jess through the opening. They ran down the hall away from the elevators, took the stairs to the first floor, and left the hotel by a door that led out to the far side of the hotel. They crept along the hedge until they reached the street.

There was no car waiting for them.

Diana put down Jess's suitcase and looked up and down the street. Nothing. Headlights turned out of the marina. After a second of panic when she thought the Parkers might already be after them, she realized it was just a delivery van from the hotel. But no Lillo and Allie.

Where the hell were they? Their absence was bound to be discovered soon. Diana didn't think for a minute Mama Parker intended to let Jess spend the evening alone. And she would certainly be holding a bedside vigil to keep Jess's friends away. And if Diana knew Papa Parker, and she did, he'd be dragging "poor" James upstairs to make whatever excuses he could come up with.

Where *were* those girls? This is why companies failed. When something needed to be done ASAP, people dragged their feet, let inconveniences get in their way. Diana should have gone for the car; she would have grabbed the nearest valet by the shorthairs and force-marched him to the parking lot if need be. But Lillo and Allie were probably standing politely waiting with their dollar tip while the valet took his sweet time getting the car.

The delivery van made its way slowly up the street. Diana

tapped her foot in consternation. The rusted old clunker stopped right in front of her. Not a delivery van but an old VW bus. The driver's door opened and Lillo jumped out. She ran around to the back and opened the hatch while Diana stared in disbelief.

"I told you it was old," Lillo said. "Are you going to get in or not?"

LILLO STOWED THE bags, pushed the two newcomers into the back seat, and jumped back in. Well, at least she wouldn't have to spend her weekend in uncomfortable shoes, she thought as she guided the van back onto the street and north toward Lighthouse Beach.

She wouldn't have to talk to people with whom she had nothing in common while trying to juggle a champagne flute, finger food, and a purse with nothing in it. Why did you need a purse at a wedding anyway? Maybe for tissues if you were inclined to cry. Which Lillo wasn't. She hadn't cried for months. Didn't intend to start up again over a wedding or the lack thereof.

She shifted gears and pulled into the lane. No one spoke; maybe the calamity of what they'd just done had begun to settle in. They were kidnapping the bride from a ridiculously expensive wedding, with hundreds of guests left wondering what had happened—though if they'd been in the bar that night, they might have a clue.

Lillo glanced in the rearview mirror. Jess was huddled against the door. Diana sat upright, looking straight ahead. She caught Lillo's eye and Lillo guessed they were both thinking the same thing. They might just have a disaster on their hands.

For starters, what was she going to do with these people? She liked Allie and Diana, and Jess needed them, but Mac would need her van back, and Lillo didn't have the room or the inclination to play hostess. She was used to living alone and her place was little. Well, it had three bedrooms, but they were tiny and one was filled with her old life, boxed up and never looked at.

They could stay there overnight. If the Parkers didn't find Jess or Jess didn't cave before the next day, they could get a rental car from the mainland. Jess, Allie, and Diana could go on their trip and Lillo could go back to her life.

The first raindrop fell as Lillo turned onto the entrance ramp to I-95 North. Within minutes, the drops turned to sheets. Lillo turned the wipers to high and hunched over the steering wheel to see the road as the old van was buffeted by intermittent gusts of wind.

Jess started crying again.

They were one of the few vehicles on the highway and miles went by before Lillo saw the blur of taillights ahead. A car had pulled to the side of the road to wait out the storm. Lillo didn't relish stopping the VW on the road. She didn't relish stopping anywhere but home. She should never have left in the first place—*the very first place,* she added grimly.

They all grew silent as the enormity of what they'd done crept over them; at least Lillo guessed that's what it was. She was feeling pretty guilty. Not because she helped Jess to get away, but because she might have swayed Jess's decision to leave. She'd spent their childhood watching her best friend yo-yo between other people's opinions. Trying to please, to be loved. Lillo didn't want to become one of those people now. But Jess, for all her quiet crying, hadn't once suggested she wanted to turn around and go back.

"How about some music?" Diana said from the back seat.

Allie reached for the radio.

"It doesn't work," Lillo said. "Sorry."

Allie settled back, Lillo hunkered forward, and the night grew darker.

Allie let out a yelp when rap music broke the silence.

"It's my phone," Jess said, the words trembling out as she spoke them. She rummaged in her purse. "It's my father. What am I going to do?"

Diana looked back at her, then to Lillo. Lillo shrugged. The phone kept rapping.

"Well, decide soon." Lillo took the exit for I-295.

Diana let out a huff of air. "You'd better answer it. If you're going to give in, best to do it now before we get any farther."

Jess scrambled to take the call.

Lillo could hear Mr. Parker's voice from where she sat. He was livid.

"I left a note," Jess said.

Lillo doubted if he even heard her, he was yelling so loudly. *What an awful man.*

"Dad. Dad."

Mr. Parker didn't slow down.

"You never listen to me. I'm not marrying James. He humiliated me in front of all the guests. I won't do it."

Beside her, Diana fist-pumped the air.

"I'll have those girls arrested."

Allie gasped. Lillo glanced at Diana in the rearview mirror; she couldn't see Jess.

"I don't know what you're talking about. I took a cab to the train station. I'm going home to Boston. I don't want to talk to you or anyone. So don't call again." She ended the call.

"Can he really have us arrested?" Allie asked.

"Of course not," Diana said. "It's just more of his usual intimidation—threaten, coerce, sue . . . Bully tactics, annoying and sometimes financially costly, but he has absolutely no grounds to have us arrested."

"Can he?" Allie asked Jess.

"No, but he can make everyone's life miserable. And you were just trying to help me."

The rap song started up again. "Dammit. Stop calling me!" Jess sounded hysterical. With Jess, hysteria could quickly turn to defeat.

"That's it. Let me talk to him." Diana reached for Jess's phone.

Jess snatched it out of her reach and clutched desperately at the door.

"What the hell are you doing?" Diana screamed.

Suddenly they were all pelted with stinging rain. In one violent gesture, Jess tossed the phone out of the window. She quickly rolled the glass up and fell back on the seat. "God, it's wet out there."

"Jeez," Diana said, staring at her.

"What?" Jess asked. "You thought I was going to jump?"

"What *did* you do?" Allie asked, leaning over the back of her seat.

"I tossed my phone. You can believe they already got a reading off the GPS. I should have thought of that. This way they can't follow us. I may be a dummy when it comes to choices in husbands, but I know my electronics." She sniffed. "And I know myself," she added in a much quieter voice.

"I should have thought of that, too," Diana said. "I just wasn't sure we'd get this far."

Jess shot her a fulminating look. "Be sure. For better or worse, I'm out of there."

Diana rummaged in her purse. "Does this box of bolts have a light that works?"

Lillo reached up and turned on the overhead light.

Diana began to dismantle her cell phone.

"What are you doing?" Lillo asked.

"Deactivating GPS, then shutting down locations so they can't trace us. When we get to some real light—hopefully sometime tonight—I'll migrate over to one of my dummy numbers. Don't look so startled. I have to change numbers all the time. Industrial espionage. Hacking. Apps are big business. I'll need yours and Allie's, too."

"I need my phone," Lillo said.

"You'll have it, but I have to turn off our GPS or they'll be flying up to wherever we're going and beat us there."

"It's in the side pocket of my duffel."

"A duffel," Diana mumbled under her breath. "The mind boggles."

Lillo drove down the empty interstate with the interior light on, which made the night black as pitch while Diana deactivated everyone's GPS. "Just a stopgap. We'll do something permanent tomorrow."

A half hour later they turned off the interstate and onto a county road. "Are you okay back there?" Lillo asked after a long silence from the back seat.

"Yep. Just peachy," Diana said.

"How much farther?" Jess asked.

"In this storm and in the dark? A little over an hour."

"Too bad we didn't think to bring something to eat or some water bottles," Allie said.

"True," Diana said. "I'm feeling a double grande mocha latte about now. Or a Courvoisier. Or both."

"Or a warm baguette and Brie with a mellow, smooth-finish pinot noir," added Allie.

"Or chips and dip," Jess said. "I have to pee."

Allie turned to look at the others. "Maybe we should stop at a motel for the night."

"That might be a good idea," Diana said.

"You should have thought about that before we turned off the highway," Lillo said.

"I knew it. We're in the middle of nowhere."

"No, we're in the middle of Maine and not even in the middle. The ocean is a few miles over on your right."

"And there are no tourist places?"

"Well, yeah, but not like Jones Beach. They're little and sleeping since it's almost two A.M."

"What's that?" Allie asked, pointing to an orange-and-green haze up ahead.

"Remington Tavern."

"Maybe we could get a coffee and a bite to eat just to wait out the worst of the storm."

"Sounds like a plan," Diana agreed, and leaned over the front seat to see.

Lillo put on the blinker and slowed down, looking for the entrance to the parking lot. They weren't the only ones with the idea of waiting out the storm; the parking lot was packed— mainly with trucks and motorcycles.

"It's a biker bar," Allie exclaimed.

"Sounds like fun," Diana said tentatively.

"It could be dangerous," Jess said.

"You're the one who has to pee."

"Not that bad."

Remington's was the only eating-drinking place for miles, so people learned to get along, for the most part. Not always. Four wedding refugees dressed in their finest casual chic were bound to cause a stir and maybe some come-ons.

"We can't go in there," insisted Jess. "Terrible things could happen."

As if seeing your fiancé screwing a stranger in a parking lot while your guests watched wasn't horrible enough.

"I think you better keep driving," Diana said.

Lillo flipped off the blinker. She didn't need convincing. She just wanted to get home, even if that home was going to be crowded for a few hours. She arched her back, rolled her shoulders, and hunkered down. A few minutes later she turned the VW onto the road that would eventually take them to Lighthouse Island.

"It's so dark," Diana said. "Are those trees? I thought you lived at the beach."

"I do. It's just that there are forests before you get there. In some places the trees—"

A loud pop exploded in Lillo's ears. The van lurched to the side, and Allie screamed. Diana yelped an expletive as an all-too-familiar *thud, thud, thud* echoed beneath them.

Blowout.

Lillo wrestled with the steering wheel and gradually managed to bring the van to a stop on the side of the road, where she hit the emergency lights, then leaned against the wheel gulping in air until her heart rate gradually subsided to normal. Then she turned to the others. "Everyone okay?"

"Yeah," Diana said, climbing back on the seat. "Should have kept my seat belt on."

"What are we going to do?" cried Jess.

"Change the damn tire," Lillo snapped. "Sorry, just a little adrenaline rush. You guys just sit tight. I'll get us fixed in a jiff." Of course the spare and the tire iron and the rain ponchos that Mac kept in the back were all under a pile of luggage.

She pushed the door open and was immediately pelted with cold rain. Tucking her head into the wind and rain, she hurried to the back of the van. No easy feat, since the grassy shoulder had already turned to mud, with the skid marks left by the van's tires rapidly turning to puddles.

She opened the back, looked at the pile of luggage, and squinted the rain from her eyes. When she opened them again she was looking back at Allie, who had exchanged places with Diana and was pulling the top suitcases out from the back onto the back seat. A second later Diana joined Lillo at the back of the van.

"You're going to get soaked," Lillo said.

"Already am. Let's do this."

Between the three of them, they managed to get the area free enough to uncover the jack, lug-nut wrench, and spare.

"Got a flashlight?" Diana yelled over the splashing of the storm. "Never mind, I see it." She yanked an emergency lantern out from under a tarp that covered various and sundry tools.

Lillo unscrewed the tire cover and tugged it out. It wasn't a full-size tire, but with a little luck it would get them home. "Really, you're going to ruin your outfit and shoes," she told Diana, who stood beside her holding up the lantern like the Statue of Liberty welcoming the huddled masses on a really nasty night.

"I'll live. I don't know shit about cars but I can at least hold the light."

Lillo assembled the jack and reached back in for the lug wrench. A roar in the distance made her turn around.

"What was that?" Diana asked, her eyes suddenly round beneath her expert makeup.

"I don't—" A glow appeared in the darkness and the rumble became louder, grew to a crescendo as a band of motorcycles roared past them, leaving only a ringing in Lillo's ears and a faint red after-halo of taillights.

The rumbling dropped out; the bikers were turning around. The back door of the van swung open.

"Get in the car," Jess yelled. "Get in the car quick."

Lillo shook her head. She had a job to do, and whether it was busting heads or changing a tire, she was going to do it and get home before her life got any more out of control.

NED HARTLEY HIT the brakes. He knew that van. But what the hell was Mac doing out here in the middle of the night?

He waited until the others slowed down then motioned them to turn around. It took some maneuvering on the narrow country road. So much for a warm bed and a couple of hours' sleep before work began in the morning.

They rode back to the van, stopping the bikes as close to the shoulder as possible, facing the van, their headlights acting as spotlights.

Ned took in the scene. Hatch open. Doughnut tire propped against the van. *Flat tire.*

He climbed off the bike, ready to read Mac the riot act for being out in this weather, this late. And scaring the crap out of him. There was someone with her, but he or she was hard to see in the pouring rain and his visor was poor help against the elements. It must be something catastrophic to send Mac out in the middle of the night.

While Roy and Nando set out flares behind them, Ned strode to the van but stopped abruptly when he saw that not only was Mac not alone, it wasn't even Mac. Two women wearing drinks-at-a-trendy-restaurant dresses and heels stood at the back of the van.

One of them was clutching the lug wrench like she might be considering bashing his head in. He had an overwhelming desire to hold up his hands and intone, *We come in peace,* but that was just wrong. She was probably frightened. Being surrounded by a motorcycle "gang," even though there were only seven of them, could be intimidating. Even though they were decent guys. And then he recognized her.

"Lillo?"

No response, just a tighter grip on the lug wrench.

She probably hadn't heard him. "Lillo," he said louder.

She jumped. Hunched toward him. Then relaxed.

He lifted his visor.

She didn't lower the lug wrench.

"Great," she said, but she sounded more resigned than glad to see him. "For a minute I thought you were the Creature from the Black Lagoon. It's the poncho." She pointed the lug wrench to indicate his rain gear.

"Keeps me dry." He pointed toward her dress and sandals.

She looked down. "I didn't know I'd be changing a tire in the rain."

And what were they doing standing in the downpour hurling barbs at each other?

"Get in the van and I'll finish up for you." He reached for the wrench.

She didn't let go. "Thanks, but no need for you to get held up."

Really, he should just leave them to fix the flat themselves. That would make Lillo happy until tomorrow when she realized how stupidly she'd reacted then would castigate herself for the rest of the day or week or however long she thought she needed to punish herself for not being perfect.

"We're not in a hurry." He pulled the wrench, she held on; she always got stubborn when anyone tried to do stuff for her. "Dammit, just give me the wrench."

The van's back door swung open and another woman jumped out of the car. She rushed toward them, grabbed the wrench out of their hands, and lunged at him.

Reflexively, Ned stepped to the side and the woman prat-fell into the mud.

Ned winced.

Lillo groaned. "Really?"

"Sorry." Ned leaned down, but when he tried to help the woman up, she started flailing and screeching. Ned was acutely aware of the guys behind him. A couple of them were new this trip. And it didn't matter how old you got, or how much good stuff you tried to do, a guy just never got past not wanting to look like an ass to his compadres.

He finally managed to drag the woman to her feet and passed her off to the silent sidekick who was standing next to Lillo.

Lillo had picked up the wrench, which was now covered in mud. He tried to take it from her.

Which set off the mud-splattered harridan again. "Leave us alone. Just get out of here. Allie's in the car and she's calling the police." She tore away from her friend's grasp, let out a cry of pain, and sat down in a puddle.

The second woman pulled her to her feet. "Sorry; she just got out of a bad relationship. I'll tell Allie to cancel the call if you could please help us. Thank you." She took the screecher by the waist and helped her back to the car, stopping only long enough to pick up the shoes she'd lost on the way.

With his luck they'd be bringing her into the clinic first thing tomorrow.

"Doc," Roy called out. "You gonna change that tire or just talk to these pretty ladies all night? We're getting wet back here."

"Can I please have the lug wrench? The guys all have work scheduled for tomorrow and the clinic opens at eight."

Lillo handed him the wrench. "Thanks."

He took it and knelt down by the back tire. Lillo didn't get in the car but stood over him like an avenging something. Clancy rolled the doughnut over. And after a brief "How's it going, Lillo?" he and Ned changed the tire with the same precision they showed in surgery.

Clancy threw the old tire into the back of the van and slammed the hatch shut.

Ned stood. "You'll have to get a new tire. That one's busted."

"I figured that."

"I saw the van and I thought you were Mac. What are you doing out here? Besides changing a tire?"

She just stood there getting wetter. "Is this an interrogation, Doctor?"

"No, just curious. How've you been?"

"Good. You?"

"Good. I didn't see you last time I was in town."

"I was up the coast."

"Avoiding me?"

"Nope."

Ned bit his lip to keep his mouth shut.

Clancy stood off to one side, patiently shaking his head. "So, Lillo, what are you doing out here in the rain, changing a flat tire and wearing a dress?"

"Coming back from a wedding."

"Ah. Is that where you picked up these ladies? Friends of the bride?"

"One of them *is* the bride."

"If that ain't something," Clancy said. And pushed his visor down.

"You've got the bride in the van," Ned said. None of this made any sense.

"If you must know, we sort of kidnapped her, but it's a long story and we're all getting wet, and your gang is getting restless."

"It's been a long day. It looks like you're going to need a push to get out of this mess. Get in, and when I yell, put her in first. See you while I'm on the island?"

"Probably. Thanks for the change and the push." She got back in the van.

Ned and three of the others gathered at the back bumper. The men pushed, the wheels spun until they gradually gained the pavement. "Now!" he yelled, and the VW shot forward.

Ned saw Lillo's hand sticking out the window and waving in the rain. He held up his own hand, even though he knew she didn't see him. She wouldn't have even looked back to see if he was still there.

Chapter 4

At least that was over, Lillo thought. Facing Doc Hartley was what it must be like facing an old flame, not that she had anything that had ever flamed for long. Her flames incinerated everything in their wake and turned everything to ash.

Still, he was the last person she wanted to meet anywhere, especially not now, not here, with her looking and acting like a fool. He was one of the few people who could shatter her well-constructed serenity. And she resented him for it. Not his fault, but there it was.

That road trip was sounding better and better. Maybe she'd go, too.

"It was lucky those guys were able to help," Allie finally said from the passenger seat.

"Yeah," Lillo agreed.

"They could've been dangerous," Jess said.

"They could have, but they weren't," Diana said. "But thanks for trying to save us from them."

"You're laughing at me."

"No, not at all, though I think, Lillo, if we might have some heat back here . . . I know it's absurd but Jess's teeth are chattering."

Lillo turned on the heat. It wasn't as absurd as Diana thought. It sometimes got cold in Maine. Even in the summer.

Gradually the heat suffused the interior of the van and her passengers drifted off to sleep. Lillo blinked against the mesmerizing *swipe-swipe* of the windshield wipers and wondered if she'd ever get back to the right side of normal.

The rain began to let up about the same time the pitch black of the sky turned to deep gray, and the passing shadows morphed into recognizable landmarks.

Lillo's eyelids were getting unbearably heavy when she drove over the narrow bridge to Lighthouse Beach. The rattle of the crossing brought her fully awake. The others began to rouse, and by the time they passed the WELCOME TO LIGHTHOUSE BEACH, LIFE WILL NEVER BE THE SAME sign, everyone was awake.

"Are we there?" Diana asked.

"Yep."

"It's totally dark."

"It's nearly four in the morning. You were expecting a strip of nightclubs?"

"No, but a streetlight would be welcome company."

"We have six but we turn them off at ten."

"Oh brother," mumbled Diana, and slumped back on the seat.

Jess peered out the window. "I can't believe we're here."

Allie said nothing, just looked forward as if she could see what none of the others could see. Lillo had been wondering what her story was ever since she'd sat down at the bistro this afternoon. Maybe she'd have the chance to find out.

Except she was sending them on their way as soon as they had rested.

She pulled the van to a stop in the large parking area in front of the keeper's house and the jetty out to the lighthouse. To the right, behind a whitewashed fence, Lillo's cottage was perched on a triangle of soil, wedged between the jetty and a rocky outcropping that almost separated her tiny patch of sandy beach from the public beach that gave the town its name.

"We're home," she sang ironically. She had no idea where she was going to put them. What had she been thinking?

Allie was the only one who seemed at all alert. She got out of the car and opened the back door. Diana yawned and climbed stiffly from the back seat.

Jess followed her, but even more slowly. "Where are we? This isn't your house."

"Yeah, it is. I tried to warn you. Mom and Dad sold the old house and the camp when I went to college." Actually, they'd sold it so she *could* go to college, but she tried not to think of that. "I told you it was small. Hope you're not too disappointed."

"No. Just surprised. I can't believe they'd sell."

Neither could Lillo, but they had, and by the time she found out, it was too late. Fortunately, the house and outbuildings had eventually ended up in the hands of the island's veterinarian.

Allie and Diana grabbed their luggage and followed Lillo through the gate and down the stone walk to her cottage. Jess brought up the rear, stumbling along with her suitcase wobbling on its wheels and the bag of toiletries dragging along the ground.

Lillo unlocked the door and reached inside to flick on a light. Nothing happened.

"Lights are out," she said. "Happens a lot when we're having weather. I'll just get the lanterns."

They all pressed in behind her and stopped. They didn't seem too anxious to further their acquaintance with her humble abode.

Of course, they might be even more disconcerted once they could see it in the light.

Lillo dropped her duffel bag and pushed them farther into the room, then she felt her way to the hallway closet, where she kept an array of auxiliary lighting and the odd towel and washcloth.

She gathered two big lanterns and three smaller flashlights for her guests to use and took them out to the sitting room, where they were huddled in front of the large picture window, staring at the towering shadow that loomed in the semidarkness beyond.

"Lighthouse Island," Lillo explained. Deposited the lanterns on the wooden table where she ate, wrote, and worked numerous crossword puzzles, then handed out the flashlights.

"Wow," Allie murmured.

"Well, it's unique," Diana said, and took a flashlight from Lillo. "Daunting, and not sleep inducing, but unique."

"It's charming in the daylight."

"Shouldn't its light be flashing or something?" asked Allie.

"Please tell me you have light-blocking shades," Diana added.

Lillo gave Diana a look, but had to admit she was beginning to enjoy her dry take on absolutely everything.

"The coast guard retired it years ago. Now it has a gift shop in the house next door and the light keeper runs tours to the top when the tide is out."

Allie turned to her, frowning. "What happens when the tide is in?"

"The causeway is covered in water and the island becomes a true island." *Mac's own private sanctuary.* "You'll probably meet the keeper tomorrow. Miriam Mackenzie. But everybody calls her Mac."

She returned to the closet and pulled out bed linens and as many decent towels as she could find and carried them to the two back bedrooms. Then she joined the others where they sat on the couch, flashlights beaming in no particular direction and looking like the ghoul family at the bus station.

Lillo smothered a laugh. "Okay, here's the deal. I have three bedrooms but one is being used for storage, so it's off-limits. I figure Jess can have my room. It's the one at the end of the hall."

"Oh no. I'll be okay on the couch or anywhere."

Lillo gritted her teeth. "No, you won't. You've had a rough day. And let's face it, it's not going to be all martinis and nachos for the next few weeks. So rest up while you can."

"Whoa," Allie said under her breath.

Diana smiled at Lillo. In the lantern light, she looked a little demonic.

"You two can have the second bedroom. It has twin beds if you don't mind sharing a room."

"I'm fine with that." Allie looked at Diana.

Diana shrugged. "Sure, why not."

"Only one bathroom, I'm afraid. And it's small."

"We'll make do," Allie said on a yawn.

"Jess, my bed actually has clean sheets, so why don't you use the bathroom first and get to bed while I make up the other room . . . Jess?"

"Okay." Jess pushed off the couch with a grunt.

"Are you okay?"

She nodded.

Lillo frowned. "Did you hurt yourself when you fell tonight?"

Jess shook her head. "Good night."

"Good night," Allie and Diana said.

Jess went into the bathroom and shut the door.

The other three made up the beds in the second room by lantern light. When Lillo came out into the hall, the bathroom door was open and her bedroom door was closed.

"Bathroom's free," she announced. She grabbed the last blanket out of the closet and walked past the third bedroom to the couch. It wouldn't be comfortable, but it was better than sleeping in the unused bedroom—if she could even find the bed beneath all that junk, that history—the detritus of her former life.

She lay down, carefully avoiding the uncoiled spring that always managed to stab her in the back. She punched the throw pillow, pulled the blanket up to her neck, and stared out at the lighthouse as a string of golden light stretched across the dark horizon.

God, she was tired. She stretched, yawned, and nestled into the soft cushions. The spring stabbed her in the back, and just as she fell into sleep, the lights came on.

AT LEAST THE porch light was on, Ned thought as he stowed the Harley under a cow bower at the side of Ian Lachlan's house. Ian was the local vet—animal whisperer, horse boarder, family therapist, and special educator. They'd met at a peace rally, both just out of college on their way to vet and med schools, both out to make the world a better place. Their enthusiasm was matched only by their naïveté. Fifteen years later they had reconnected, both changed, but still friends. Ian was probably the only person in town besides Lillo who called him Ned.

He climbed the steps, pulling off his helmet and rain poncho. He dropped them on the porch floor and opened the door. Ian never locked his door, which was strange considering the life he'd led.

Ned suddenly felt bone-tired. A wet ride, running into Lillo, then depositing the two new guys with their hosts before finally calling it a day.

"Perfect timing," Ian said, coming down the stairs. "The lights have been out all night; they just came back on."

"Sorry I woke you. Just no way to silence a Harley."

Ian shrugged. "Wasn't asleep."

Doc nodded. *Physician, heal thyself.* Easier said than done.

Ned dropped his duffel. They shook hands and slapped each other's back.

"Want coffee? Or a bed?"

Ned shrugged out of his leather jacket. "Bed. We didn't mean to get here this late. We had to wait for one of the new guys, who got held up in traffic on I-95. Assam. You'll like him. He can fix just about anything, from locks to air conditioners. Then the rain held us up."

"You better get some shut-eye. Time nor tide nor the residents of Lighthouse Beach wait for the beleaguered M.D. Bed's made up. Even washed the sheets since the last time you were here."

"Thanks. I appreciate that. Any dire cases I should know about?"

"I haven't heard anything. Anna McLennan is getting weaker. Her children came down last week, they were talking about hospice, but Ike held firm. Swears he can take care of her. Mac and Lillo help out where they can, but . . ."

"Speaking of Lillo, I ran into her about ten miles out of town. She was driving Mac's van with three other women. They'd had a flat tire. Said they were coming from a wedding." He yawned.

"She drove to Kennebunkport, some friend who went to camp here when they were kids. Which is odd enough. But the wedding isn't until Saturday."

"Weird. I think she said she had the bride with her. But I was so tired by then"—and shocked at seeing Lillo—"I could have been mistaken."

"Bound to be a story there. You'll find out the particulars in the morning, probably with your first patient. It took the whole town to get her on the road. I've never met a girl so stubborn and so . . . I don't know."

Neither had Ned, but if he hadn't figured it out in all the years he'd known her, he wouldn't figure it out tonight. He would have a busy day tomorrow; for the rest of tonight he, unlike Ian, would sleep like a log.

BETWEEN GETTING UP to turn off the lights and turning over to avoid the rising sun, Lillo managed to get about four hours of sleep. It took her a few groggy minutes to remember she was home, had houseguests, didn't have a thing to feed them, and that she was the only one awake.

It wasn't until she was on her feet that she realized all her wearable clothes were in the closet of her bedroom, where Jess was asleep. She didn't want to wake her; she needed to talk to Mac first and figure out what to do. There were clothes in the third bedroom, but she wouldn't wear them; she didn't know why she kept them, as a reminder maybe. She crept into the bathroom, which was barely large enough for one much less three extra women, two of whom were surely used to the best. She wasn't sure about Allie, but what she'd witnessed of her so far, she would most likely make do without much comment.

She reached into the hamper and pulled out a pair of wrinkled khakis and a grease-smeared tee. They would have to do. After a quick splash of water on her face and hair, mainly to wake herself up, she went outside, quietly closing the door behind her.

It was a sunny day. Sort of amazing when you considered how stormy it had been the night before. Everything looked intact. She hadn't heard any wind during the wee hours, though she doubted if she would have heard a freight train outside her window in her exhausted few hours of sleep.

She walked barefoot out to the sand and took a few minutes just to breathe in the sea air and relax to the expanse of the waves. Why had she ever left this place? The world was cruel, even weddings were cruel. The sea could be cruel but without malice. It was everything she needed.

But at the moment she had three extra people asleep in her cottage, and she'd need to consult Mac on what to do with them. She backtracked and walked across the parking lot to the gift shop. It wouldn't be open yet, but Mac lived in the back and would have a pot of coffee brewing.

The flowers in the little bed along the front and side of the clapboard house were vibrant in the morning air. The peony blooms from the bushes that lined the walk had taken a beating in the rain and were so heavy that Lillo had to press against the fence to pass by. They'd have to be tied up again. Maybe this afternoon.

The small square plot of land in back of the shingled house was crammed with vegetables and herbs. Originally laid out in neat squares but already overflowing into a tangle of promised bounty. Mac had a green thumb as well as a refined New England palate. Her lobster stew was famous.

Lillo knocked on the paint-peeled back screen door. As always, it rattled with each touch. Mac's "C'mon in" echoed from inside.

Lillo brushed her feet off on the old lobster rope doormat and stepped onto the storage porch. The porch had been added on during the last century and the kitchen windows opened onto it. She could see Mac, short and muscular with a crop of gray hair, standing at the stove. She was talking to someone.

Lillo hesitated. Clancy Farrow sometimes stayed with Mac when he was in town, and Lillo knew he was in town. She'd seen him last night. Maybe she should come back later, but if she waited she might not be able to talk to Mac alone.

She stepped inside to the smell of fresh-ground coffee. *Home.*

She was expecting Clancy, and wasn't prepared for the shock or the irrational proprietary feeling that jolted through her when she saw Jess sitting at the kitchen table.

"What are you doing here?" she blurted.

Jess cowered back against her chair. And Lillo backpedaled. "I mean . . . I thought you were still asleep. I didn't hear you leave."

"I didn't want to wake anyone. So I came over to say hello and see if I could beg Mac for a cup of coffee."

"I'm telling ya, ya coulda knocked me sideways when I opened the door to the runaway bride," Mac said. "Had to tell me who she was. Woulda never recognized our little Jess in a million years."

"I guess she told you what happened."

"Between her and Clancy, I got a pretty good picture of what you gals have been up to. Let me see . . ." Mac looked up to the ceiling. "The shenanigans of the groom in the parking lot, the parental oppression, the flight from Kennebunkport, the flat tire, and the motorcycle gang. Sounds very exciting."

"Sounds like you need to get out more," Lillo said.

Jess hiccuped, groaned, and cradled her face with both hands. "Ouch." She immediately sat up again.

"Jess, your wrist," Lillo said.

"I'm all right," Jess said, lowering her wrist to hide it underneath the table.

"No, you're not. It's swollen and black and blue. Why didn't you say something?"

Jess just shrugged.

Lillo didn't need to ask. Some things never changed. Jess trying not to call attention to herself, trying to disappear. Maybe that's what the not eating was about, attempting to physically disappear. Lord, what had Lillo gotten herself into?

"I think," Mac said, sliding a mug of coffee toward Lillo, "that you better—"

"—take her over to the clinic and have it checked out," Lillo finished for her. "They can rule out a break or possible hairline fracture." Seeing Mac was about to comment, she hurried on. "Speaking of the clinic, where is Clancy? Isn't he staying with you this trip?"

"He's been here and gone. Mary Alice Grotsky's boy got an attack of appendicitis a little after dawn. Had to convince Mary Alice to call an ambulance to take him to the county hospital." Mac shook her head. "She begged Clancy to do the surgery right then and there. Poor woman hasn't had insurance since Ethan died. Can't get Medicaid 'cause she owns a business and their own home—such as it is."

"I'll be fine. Really," Jess said. "Maybe you can just wrap an ACE bandage around it."

Sure she could, like an ACE bandage could solve all Jess's problems. Could stop her from needing all the people she couldn't depend on. It couldn't. Not now, not all those years ago when Jess had hidden a broken rib from her counselors so she wouldn't miss the hike around the lake. So she could prove that she could make it.

She'd come to Lillo. They'd wrapped an ACE bandage around her then. She'd struggled to keep up. Everyone complained that she was taking too many rests, that she was holding them up. And she wouldn't let Lillo tell.

That hike ended in a trip to the hospital.

So, no. An ACE bandage wouldn't do.

"Lillo?" Mac's voice.

"Huh?"

"I said you can take her to the clinic after breakfast." She turned to Jess. "Now sit down and drink your coffee before it gets cold."

"Please, Mac. I don't want to be any trouble."

Mac crowed a laugh. "Trouble? You're worried about being a trouble because of a sprained wrist when you just left the groom at the altar, three-hundred-some-odd guests holding empty champagne glasses, a gigantic hotel bill, and two irate parents? Honey, I'm nominating you for president of Cold Feet Anonymous." She chuckled. "Ya gotta love her."

No. You didn't. *Unfortunately*, Lillo thought, because under all that mucky, mushy, indecisive surface was a compassionate, loving human being who deserved love. But then again, life dished out shit indiscriminately, didn't it?

Jess struggled out of her seat. "It's not too late to go back."

"Is that what you want?"

"No, it is not," Diana said, coming through the door, Allie on her heels. "Sorry, we would have knocked but the conversation was just too good not to interrupt." She zeroed in on Jess. "Do you want to go back and marry that—James?"

Allie reached across Diana and extended her hand to Mac. "I'm Allie Lusano; this is Diana Walters. We're friends of Jess's and Lillo's."

"Mac Mackenzie." They shook hands, Mac leaning over Lillo to reach across the table.

"How did you find us?" Lillo asked.

"Followed our noses to coffee," Diana said. "Actually, I heard you leave and watched from the window. Figured you might be having a strategy meeting and we hustled over here to be part of it."

Allie nodded.

"In the clear morning light—beautiful day, by the way—I realized that maybe we had been a tad too adamant last night, so I roused Allie and we came over to give Jess a chance to renege before it's too late."

Lillo's mouth dropped open in disbelief. They practically kidnapped Jess last night and now they were wigging out? "What the—"

Across from her, Jess looked gobsmacked.

"But I changed my mind on the walk over. I think we made the right decision, but I just want to make sure we didn't strong-arm Jess against her better judgment."

"Now you think of that," Lillo said.

"Actually, it was Allie. I know we did the right thing."

"I'll just put on some more coffee," Mac said, and headed for the sink.

Allie came around the table and sat down beside Jess. "Did we make you do something you don't want to do?"

"You didn't."

"Well," Mac said, drying her hands on a dish towel before tossing it on the counter, "while you girls discuss it, Lillo and I will get out some breakfast things from the pantry. Allie, you're in charge of coffee. It beeps when it's ready."

Lillo rolled her eyes, but Allie merely said, "Yes, ma'am," and got up to watch the pot.

Mac lifted her chin and Lillo followed her to the back porch and an adjacent walk-in pantry where shelves of preserved food, the deep freezer, and the second fridge lived.

As soon as they were in the pantry, Mac switched on the light and turned to Lillo. "What's going on with you, girl?"

"Me?" Lillo asked, surprised. "I went to a wedding that I didn't want to go to, then got lassoed into abducting the bride-to-be because I was the only one with transportation. And now they're thinking about going back?"

"You forgot the part about the flat tire."

"Yeah, we had a flat. I had to stand out in the rain to change it—"

Mac dipped her chin, her pants-on-fire chin-o-meter: the lower the chin, the bigger the lie detected. Mac's chin was practically resting on her chest.

"Okay, Ned and his band of merry do-gooders stopped and insisted on finishing the job."

"After he had to wrestle you for the lug wrench, the anorexic runaway bride attacked him with the damn thing, and all he got was a wave good-bye."

"It was raining. I guess you heard all this from Clancy before he left."

"Ayuh." Mac opened the fridge and pulled out a dozen eggs, bacon, and a gallon of orange juice and set them on a chopping block next to the fridge.

Lillo eyed the food skeptically. "I think you might be overly optimistic with all that breakfast stuff. Jess's practically anorexic. Diana, big business person from Manhattan, probably only eats free-range egg whites, and wouldn't be caught dead near a carb or fat or salt or—" She stopped. "Though she did make quick work of an order of nachos . . . was it only last night?"

"Can you see what preserves are up on the top shelf? I think I still have some strawberry and maybe some blackberry. Strawberry season is almost upon us again. Now, where's that butter?" She reached back into the fridge. "You know, Lillo. This would be an excellent opportunity to . . . oh, I don't know . . . break out of this rut you're in. Ah, there it is." Mac added a container of hand-churned butter to the growing pile.

"I'm not in a rut."

Mac's chin-o-meter went to work.

"The way I live is my choice."

"And a bad one, if you ask me."

"Well, I didn't."

"Oh, don't get all huffy. Just give it a try. If they decide to stay, enjoy the weekend. Sit out on the beach. Talk about whatever women your age talk about these days."

It sounded so normal. "I have no idea what they talk about. Diana designs apps."

"What's that?"

"You know, for your phone."

"Oh."

"Allie is a vintner."

"I know what that is. So make some app—etizers and drink some wine. Have a blast."

"And if Jess wants to go back and marry that jerk?"

Mac shrugged. "You'll have to drive them back. But I hope they talk her out of it. He sounds like a real donkey's backside." She began stacking the food on Lillo's outstretched hands. "It'll do you good."

"No, it won't. They can't stay with me. They all have money, lots of it. Diana was going to spend the next week at an expensive spa, Jess was going to Aruba for her honeymoon, Allie lives on thousands of acres in a huge house. Instead they're here, staying at my cottage, which if it were any smaller would be a tiny house."

"It's just what the doctor ordered."

"Don't mention him. One tiny bathroom, hardly enough room for Thumbelina, much less four adult women with cases of makeup and beauty products . . . well, three women with beauty products, I have shampoo and soap."

"I'll leave the back door open. They can use my bathroom.

Having them here will do you good. And I'm thinking it will do them good, too. For sure, it will do me good. You're not the only one trying to figure out the meaning of life."

"Oh, give me a break."

"Well, what else do you want to call it?"

Lillo hesitated. "I don't know."

Mac repositioned the butter on top of the food Lillo was holding. "How 'bout . . . starting over?"

"Mac."

"Ayuh. It'll be just like the old days. People filling the kitchen, hungry for food and conversation."

And safety, thought Lillo. And here they were again. "And what if, like the good old days, the Parkers descend on us with goons and a lawsuit?"

Mac turned a crooked-tooth grin on her. "Oh, they won't. The camp no longer exists, your parents have moved to Florida, and no one here knows your whereabouts, especially not this weekend when the whole town knows you've gone to Kennebunkport."

"Until someone sees me skulking about town."

"O ye of little faith. What do you think living on this island is all about?"

Mac took the eggs and carried them out. Lillo followed, turning off the light switch with her elbow and closing the pantry door with her foot. She should have joined the circus as an acrobat instead of wasting all that money preparing for a career that would never be.

Lillo and Mac literally ran into Diana coming out of the kitchen. "Hey, I came out to the porch to see if I could get cell reception," Diana said, sounding like a cruise director and dressed like she was ready for drinks in the Hamptons.

"Uh-huh," Mac said. "I have a landline you can use."

"Thanks, if this doesn't work . . ." Diana moved over to let Mac pass, but when Lillo followed, she herded her off to the side and to the far end of the porch. "I think we'd better make a trip to the clinic," she said in an urgent whisper. "Jess is in a lot of pain and I'm afraid she's about to cave and go home."

"Great." Why was Lillo not surprised. Jess had never been able to stand up to her parents, or anybody else, for that matter.

"I assume that was a satiric 'great' and you're not happy about it."

Lillo blew out air. "If she's going to cave, it would be better to cave now and get her back in time for the wedding."

Diana took Lillo by the elbow and Lillo had to juggle the jam, the bread, the bacon, and the butter to keep from dropping them.

"Look, Jess has her problems, I get it. She can be a big pain in the butt with her lack of backbone, but she's a loyal friend. I don't want her to make the biggest mistake of her life, because once she marries that fu—oaf, she'll never get away from her family or her lack of self-esteem. She'll live in total humiliation and she'll take it because she doesn't know how not to.

"She called you because she needed you. Not me or Allie. We would have come anyway. We were sorority sisters. At college, she wasn't like this. She studied hard, she had ambition; a passion, if you will. We were on our way up in the corporate world. Then the parents got on to the marriage thing. Totally blew everything she'd worked for."

Allie's head appeared in the doorway. "Mac says she needs the bacon."

"On my way," said Lillo, and tried to sidestep Diana.

Diana followed her, saying into her ear, "Please. Give her one more chance."

Lillo stopped, stared at Diana. Really studied her. She wanted to ask, *What's in it for you?* Successful, obviously rich, and comfortable in her own skin. Why did she want to help Jess Parker, rich, spineless, harmless—

Why did Lillo?

"I wish we were sisters."

"Me too. I could come live in your mansion in Boston and have lots of clothes."

"No, we could live here in this comfy house at the beach, and your mom would make French toast."

"Burned around the edges."

"That's my favorite part. My mother never makes French toast . . . or anything else."

"That's stupid. You have a cook that can make you everything you want."

"Not everything. Especially not French toast." And Jess had cried.

Lillo swallowed, as if that could stop the memory—the remorse of that memory. The sick burn of wishing she had been more understanding, even then.

To a chubby, unloved girl, French toast was the embodiment of someone loving her. Even burned French toast. Lillo hadn't understood then. She did now. "Okay. What do you want to do?"

"Let us stay here for a few days, maybe a week. I know it's an imposition and you don't really want to be stuck with us. But I need time to de-brainwash Jess again and then get her to come to work for me. Once she's back on a normal track, making her own money again, she'll be able to see the future more clearly."

Lillo wasn't optimistic; she'd spent several summers bolstering Jess's self-esteem only to have her return the following year, back to being the same human pincushion she'd been before. It was tiring. And yet they'd had wonderful months together. Explored nature and the nature of their hearts. Hormones and heartaches and hopes for their futures.

Together they'd made great plans, shared deep secrets, and enjoyed their girlhood. But apart . . . Jess never escaped her family's demands and expectations. Lillo's parents gave up everything for her to go to medical school. Two ends of the spectrum, and they'd both failed miserably. Jess still couldn't please her parents, and Lillo? Lillo had totally betrayed hers.

"So?" Diana had stepped back, almost as if to give Lillo space for her memories.

"Okay. But first we'll make sure this is what she really wants, and that she wasn't just swayed by our desire to help her."

"Deal."

Chapter 5

Ned's eyes were gritty when he stumbled downstairs after too little sleep. He'd been so tempted to ignore the alarm and take another hour or two. As it was, he'd set the snooze button twice. He didn't allow himself a third twenty minutes. There would be people waiting before the clinic even opened. And if you started behind, you got worse behind before the day was over.

There was no sign of Ian; either he was out with the animals or finally sleeping. Seemed like nothing ever changed with him, nothing got worse or better. Ned snagged an apple out of the basket on the kitchen counter. It was bruised and probably mealy, and on its way to the horses.

Well, Ned would be sure to thank them later. He took a bite out of it. Yep, mealy, the end of the winter's store. But it would go a ways to quelling the pangs of hunger assaulting his stomach. It had been a long time, several beers, and a rainstorm since his last meal.

Hopefully Agnes would have the coffee on. He'd ask her to send out for a sandwich or something. Kyle at the pub would

have someone send it over. And Mac would be making her lobster stew for tonight. She always invited him over the first night
the guys came to town. Later there would be a clambake or
something for all of them. His stomach growled.

He clamped his teeth on the soft apple while he zipped up
his windbreaker, and shook the moisture off his helmet before
shoving it on his head. Finished the bite of apple as he trotted
down the porch steps.

By the time he stowed his bag in the hard case on his Harley,
there was nothing of the apple but the core. He thought, *What
the hell,* and ate that, too.

It was chilly under the trees surrounding the clearing in front
of Ian's house. When the Grays owned the house and camp,
you could see the ocean from the front yard. And a swim was a
short run down the hill to the beach. But Ian liked his solitude
and he'd let the brush grow wild.

Doc shook his head and climbed onto the bike. Ian liked
his solitude too much. But what could you do? He started up
the Harley and headed down the drive, breathing in the fresh
after-a-rain air.

He wouldn't have this if he worked in an office, kept regular
practice hours, and spent several days a week doing surgery.
There were plenty of those doctors. The people of Lighthouse
Beach and people like them needed health care. And it was a
mite easier to bring the doctor to them than try to get them to
travel to the nearest health-care facility.

He rode into town and down Main Street, all two and a half
blocks of it. Town was bustling. Old Man Rafferty lifted his
hand from the rocker on the porch of the general store. Barbara
Carroll made sure to be standing in the doorway of her consignment shop.

He lifted his chin to several other locals, and a block later turned onto a narrow street of shingle and shake houses. A crowd had already formed outside the door of the two-story fisherman's house that served as the clinic. News traveled fast in Lighthouse Beach and it looked like it was going to be a busy day.

Doc rode the Harley around to the back and parked in the narrow strip of dirt behind the house. It looked like he'd beaten Clancy to work, but the back door was open. Good. Agnes had already arrived. He jogged up the steps to what had originally been the kitchen but now served as both kitchenette and storage overflow.

The chaos was less than when he'd last been here. Agnes Tucker had been busy. Receptionist, soother of owies, and holder of nervous hands, coffeemaker and cleaning lady, Agnes ran the part-time clinic like a benevolent drill sergeant. And never accepted the smallest token of payment from the day she was "hired."

"It's every man and woman's duty to help out where they're needed. You and Clancy Farrow know that and so do I." How could they argue with that? Even when they tried to share the lobsters, the jars of homemade preserves, the heads of cabbage that people brought in payment, she'd politely refuse. She did hang the drawings of the children they treated on the walls. She saved every single one and soon the waiting room walls were so filled with pictures they had to continue them into the hallway.

Not only was it a nice gesture on Agnes's part, but also a brilliant move, because it kept anxious children busily employed looking for their pictures and those of their friends while they waited for their appointments.

Coffee was made and smelled fresh. He poured a mug and went out to tell Agnes to open for business.

He was savoring his first sip of strong Maine coffee when he opened the door to the waiting room and stopped dead. The room was packed. He could see the line of people waiting outside through the window.

"Good morning, Doc."

"Mornin', Doc."

"Welcome back, Doc."

"Good to see ya."

Agnes waved to him from her desk. She scooted her chair back, took a stack of folders from her desk, and brought them over to where Ned stood in the doorway, coffee mug lifted halfway to his mouth.

"Full house this morning," she said brightly. She handed the folders to him. "And Doc Farrow called to say he had to go over to the mainland with Mary Alice Grotsky. Her boy's got appendicitis and she wouldn't take him without Doc going along."

"When will he be back?"

Agnes shrugged. "As soon as he can. You'll have to handle things until he gets here." She smiled out at the sea of faces. "Mr. Amancio. The doctor will see you now."

No one spoke much while eggs and bacon and toast made the rounds. Everyone had a hearty appetite except for Jess, but Lillo wasn't going to push her to eat. She wanted to stay out of that particular power struggle at all costs. When Jess got hungry she'd eat.

"They're whoopie pies. Mrs. Glasgow just made them from scratch and she gave me two."

Jess shook her head. Bit her lip. "I can't."

"Come on. They're delicious." Lillo shoved one of the whoopie pies

toward her friend. She could hardly wait to bite into her own. They were still warm from the oven and the filling was oozing out the sides. It was everything she could do not to lick the edges before giving it to Jess. "One whoopie pie won't make you fat."

"Fatter."

"You're not fat. Here."

Jess practically snatched it from Lillo's hand. While Lillo savored the first taste of chocolate-and-cream bliss, Jess devoured her pie in three bites.

"Hey, Lillo."

Lillo jumped. "Sorry?"

"Can you pass the milk over to Allie?" Mac asked.

"Sorry." Lillo shoved the pitcher across the table.

"Having deep thoughts?"

"Nope, making a grocery list."

Mac gave her a look. "You concentrate on snacks and booze. I'll take care of the rest."

"Mac, we don't want to impose," Allie said.

"No imposition. I never have enough people to cook for. And it's something I love."

"And she's good," Lillo added. "Wait until you taste her lobster stew."

"Sounds like a plan," Diana said. "But not all the time and we'll pay for the food. No arguments. We've descended on this little village like three harpies and I for one don't cook."

"I always help in the kitchen at home," Allie volunteered. "I could be the sous-chef. And maybe you'd give me some pointers on making your famous lobster stew. Only . . ."

"Only what?" Diana asked.

Jess looked alarmed.

"I have a flight back to California Monday. I don't know if I can stay away longer than that." Allie turned to Mac. "I have a little boy who I left with my in-laws. He's only four. I haven't left him very much."

"No pressure," Mac said. "Stay as long as you feel comfortable then go home. The only rule around here is to enjoy yourself for whatever time you're here. How about you, Diana?"

"I took off the whole week from work, so I'm available to set the table and do dishes."

Jess looked from one to the other and burst into tears.

Great. Allie was missing her kid. She'd probably get on that plane. Diana would have to get back to work sooner rather than later. You didn't start a company and then go on vacations.

And Jess would either return to her parents to be humiliated for humiliating them or she'd stay with Lillo. Just the two of them. For how long?

"So what do you say, Lillo?" she heard Diana saying. "You okay with a girls' long weekend away?"

Lillo looked up from the piece of toast she'd been holding halfway to her mouth for way too long. Mac was right. She was in a rut, but it was where she wanted to be.

On the other hand, a girls' weekend away might be fun. She used to love them. She pushed away the niggling voice that said, *This is a bad idea—it will unravel your life and it won't be pretty.*

"That's settled," Mac said. "So finish breakfast, take Jess over to the clinic and get some relief for her wrist, put on your swimsuits . . ." She squinted out the window. "And maybe a sweatshirt, and enjoy your time here."

Jess clutched Mac's hand. "I don't want anyone to get in trouble because of me."

Mac snorted out a laugh. "Trouble? We got so much trouble

already, what's a little more?" She held up the pot. "More coffee, anyone?"

LILLO WASN'T THE only one with ambivalent feelings about the coming week. Diana was used to a cutthroat world, a creative exchange of ideas beset by hackers, backbiting competition, out-and-out theft. She wasn't sure how much she could take of the old homespun "salt-of-the-earth" lifestyle. She was having trouble wrapping her head around the fact that she'd given up her first vaca in months to stay in a primitive, overcrowded shack, probably subject to hurricanes and tidal waves, with three other women as diverse as friends could possibly be.

She cut a sideways look at Lillo, who seemed to be lost in some serious thought. Well, they *had* just appropriated her home for their long weekend away.

She was an odd bird. A year younger than Jess, which would make her about thirty. But weird. Not country, not cosmopolitan, she'd obviously seen some of the world, but she lived like a hermit.

Diana had no doubt that Lillo wished she'd never brought them home with her and that it was Mac, not Diana, who had convinced her to let them stay. For one sane moment, she thought of her four-star hotel in Boston, the spa day she'd reserved. Then she cast her plans to the wind.

This was bound to be more interesting. And actually, she didn't care if the Parkers did find them. She'd been waiting to give them a piece of her mind for years.

Mac insisted on doing the dishes, but Diana made her promise to text them a grocery list before the day was out. A few minutes later they were all piled back into Mac's van and headed toward the Lighthouse Beach clinic.

They drove down Main Street past quaint New Englandy–looking shops, most of which seemed to lean precariously to the left. There were quite a few people on the street.

"It looks just like a Maine fishing village."

"It *is* a Maine fishing village," Lillo said. "Though there's not much fishing going on these days. Too many corporate outfits nosing out the independents."

"Lots of tourists, though," Diana said. "You have a good liquor store?"

"I wouldn't say good, but adequate."

"So, any fun things to do?"

Lillo laughed. "Not much, I'm afraid. Visit the lighthouse. Sailing. Hiking. Sunbathing. Hanging out at the pub."

"Does it ever get warm enough to wear a bikini on your beach?"

Lillo flashed her a grin. "It's warm enough today. You have to inure yourself."

"Ah."

"But having a little bit of land behind and the jetties on each side cuts out a lot of the wind—and other people, if you want to lie out in the altogether. Just only at high tide, please, when there won't be families with children walking out to the lighthouse with their binoculars. The insurance is astronomical as it is."

"Who pays the insurance? The coast guard?"

"Therein lies the rub, as they say. They sold it to the town years ago and retired Mac. The town has been paying for the insurance since the lighthouse is the only thing that draws any tourist trade. With fishing being what it is, we need all the outside cash we can get. The only problem is paying for the escalating premiums."

"Is that what Mac meant when she said they had so much trouble they wouldn't notice more?"

"That and unemployment, poverty, the usual."

"Gotcha." Diana had researched the demographics of dying towns as a part of her economics studies. But the thought that a quaint little town right on the ocean could be one of them . . . news to her.

Lillo turned off Main Street and onto a narrow side street called Shandy Way. Two blocks later she stopped the van in front of a weathered shake-shingled house.

"This is the clinic?"

"It used to belong to the Gregorio family, old-time lobster people, then they moved on and the Devon family bought it. Dr. Charlie Devon lived here and had his office downstairs, then Charlie Devon Jr. had his practice here, and when he died without finding someone to replace him, he left the building to the town to be used for the next doctor or as a free clinic. So far we don't have a local doctor, so what we have is a part-time clinic."

"So you only can get sick on Tuesdays and Thursdays?"

"Pretty much. Only we haven't even had that since the beginning of spring, when the nurse practitioner who was running it moved away. So, until we find a replacement we depend on visiting doctors and the emergency room on the mainland.

"Though we're lucky. The clinic is open for the whole week. So you guys go in, tell the receptionist, Agnes, you're my friend. And I'll pick you up when you're done."

"Aren't you coming?"

"Uh, no. I have a few quick errands to run. I'll meet you back here. Just come out when you're done. Or have Agnes call my cell."

"Right." Diana opened her passenger door just as two men came out and down the walk.

"Mornin', Lillo. You back from the weddin' already?" asked the younger man.

"Find any fella to say 'I do'?" asked the older, and broke into a fit of congested coughing.

"Too many bad jokes gonna kill ya, Dad."

"Ayuh, 'spect they will. But if Lillo don't choose soon, I'm gonna take her home with me."

"I'm gonna hold you to that, Jacob," Lillo said. She waved as the two men walked off down the street.

"Friends of yours?" said Diana with a jab of holy-crap-what-have-I-gotten-myself-into.

"Most people are friendly here."

And how's that for dodging a question? thought Diana. "Shall I use your name to get an appointment?"

"Nah. It's much looser than that. Just give your name to Agnes; she'll take care of you."

Allie helped Jess out of the van. Lillo shifted gears.

"Wait. What about payment? Will they take Jess's insurance or do we have to pay up front?"

"Don't worry about it. See ya in a few."

Diana climbed out of the car and barely had time to slam the door shut before Lillo was driving up the street.

Diana, Allie, and Jess, holding her arm close to her body, watched her drive away.

"That is one strange lady," Diana said. She meant it. At first she'd thought maybe Lillo had high-functioning Asperger's syndrome or something. But it wasn't that. Diana usually got pretty fast impressions of people, even though she worked in computer code all day. But not Lillo Gray. She would eventually. She just needed a few days.

They moved slowly up the walk. Met a mother and three kids coming down the steps. Stepped aside when a teenager holding his hand in a towel rushed past them. Allie ran ahead and opened the door for him.

The kid mumbled a thank-you and hurried inside.

Diana was ready to insist that they see to the kid immediately, but when she stepped inside the kid was gone. The waiting room, however, was packed. People standing, sitting, chatting, kids running around, pushing battered plastic trucks across the floor. Chairs and what looked like church benches were crowded into any space they would fit. The floor was wood, painted white, and looked like it had been through hell.

Nothing screamed hygienic. Fortunately, Jess didn't have any open wounds, and if they could manage not to touch anything until they got back to Lillo's and Diana's cache of Purell, they should all survive.

Needless to say, the pandemonium stopped as soon as everyone became aware of the newcomers. A woman sitting in a chair nudged the teenager next to her, and he and another boy got up and went to stand against the wall. She motioned Allie to bring Jess over.

Diana made her way over to a battered desk where a gray-haired lady sat arranging a mountainous stack of manila folders.

"Can I help you?" the woman asked, more curious than concerned.

"We're friends of Lillo Gray." Diana wasn't surprised when the conversation nearest them cut off to a whisper. It was a gamble. Lillo could be the most notorious, hated member of the community as far as Diana knew. But she didn't really believe it. And it only took a second for the receptionist to prove her right.

"Oh, you must be the girls from the wedding."

"Yes. We are. Our friend hurt her wrist. We just need an X-ray to make sure it isn't broken?" Diana was aware that she'd ended her statement as a question like some gawky teenager, but she wasn't sure the clinic even had X-ray equipment.

"Well, we'll just have Doc take a look and see what he thinks. Have a seat. We're a little backed up this morning."

Diana signed Jess's name. The receptionist handed her a clipboard with a ballpoint pen attached by a string. "Just have your friend fill this in." Diana took it back to where Allie and Jess were sitting.

"Heah, take my chayah," the woman next to Jess told Diana.

It took her a second to translate "take my chair" and by then the woman had already stood. "Weay'll be goin' in soon."

Diana thanked her and sat down. She handed the clipboard and pen to Jess.

"Wow. This must be a really popular doctor," Allie said under her breath.

"If he's the only act in town, this could take a while."

"Maybe we could just see the nurse practitioner," Jess said.

"If there is one, I'm sure she's pretty busy, too." Evidently they hadn't heard Lillo's explanation of the precarious state of the clinic. Diana decided not to enlighten them. No reason to worry Jess any more than she already was.

"Are you in pain? Should I ask for an aspirin?"

Jess shook her head. Diana looked around for a free magazine. Normally she would just pull out her phone and do business or open the newspaper app. But the sign over the door to the office said NO CELLS. And there were no cells among the waiting patients. Not even surreptitious e-mail checking. These people didn't mess around.

There wasn't a free magazine and the ones she saw other people reading were months old. So Diana stared at the only other things available. Pictures drawn by children. Joey and his broken leg. "Thank you, Dr. Hartley" scrawled in awkward letters. Mindy and her measles. "I love you, Doc." The thank-yous filled the walls, mostly written to Doc, or Doc Hartley, a few to Doc Harley, and others to Doc Clancy. Popular guys.

The door opened. Everyone in the room looked up. The kid who had run past them on the steps came out. He looked quickly around the room, ducked his head, then scurried across the room and out the front door.

"Mrs. Spencer?" The receptionist waited for the older lady to rise from her chair and edge her walker toward the door.

"Lovely day, Agnes. So glad to have the doc back."

"Yes, it is, now watch yourself getting through the door."

Diana heard the doctor welcome Mrs. Spencer before the door closed.

One patient at a time. This could take all day. No wonder Lillo hadn't wanted to stay. Diana had half a mind to hit the local stores and see what she could find in the way of girls'-weekend-away provisions. Maybe she and Allie could take turns staying with Jess.

Time didn't march, but crept inexorably on. Half hour. Hour. When one person came out, another went in. When they left, they were replaced by others.

"I wonder what he looks like," Jess said.

"Who?"

"The doctor. I think he must have white hair like those television doctors. All crusty old New Englander but with a heart of gold." Jess sighed.

"Good heavens," Diana said. "She's hallucinating."

"No, really. Haven't you noticed, everybody's so friendly."

Until someone mentions religion or politics, thought Diana. "Well, I can hardly wait to meet this paragon of Yankee medicine. Evidently from a long line of crusty New England doctors whose offices also were housed here. I just hope he doesn't retire before he gets to us." She glanced at her watch; they'd been there for over an hour and the room had continued to fill.

She actually jumped when Agnes announced "Jess Parker" and the whole room turned to watch them maneuver their way across the floor.

"Miss Parker," the doctor said as soon as Agnes ushered them into the nether regions of the clinic. Just a hall with several doors, probably the same doors that had led to bedrooms in a former life. "This way, please."

Before Diana got a good look, he turned and walked through an open door. They followed him into a room that was barely large enough for a desk, a medicine cabinet, and an old examination table.

He turned around. "I'm Dr. Hartley." He surveyed the three women and zeroed in on Jess. "Looks like you've hurt your wrist."

Jess said, "Uh."

Allie and Diana exchanged looks.

"I take it back," Diana said under her breath. The doctor might be a New Englander, but he wasn't crusty by any stretch. No wonder his waiting room was packed. The guy was strikingly handsome in an unaware kind of way. Tall, sturdy, with darkish brown hair long enough to curl at the edge of his shirt collar. Looking about as delicious as a crusty old New England doctor could possibly look.

"Your wrist?" he repeated, smiling at Jess.

"Yes. I think I sprained it."

"Climb up on the table." The doctor helped her to sit and Diana and Allie tried to press themselves into a corner to make room.

He began to gently manipulate Jess's fingers. "Does any of this hurt?"

Jess shook her head.

"You're not from around here?"

"No. We're visiting a friend. Lillo Gray."

He hesitated. Looked at all three of them as if reconfiguring his first impression, then he smiled. "Ah, the wedding party."

"How did you—"

"It's a small town. Your reputation preceded you."

He turned Jess's hand over, eliciting an intake of breath.

"Why is he smiling like that?" Allie whispered.

Diana shrugged. It was a pretty weird bedside manner. Smiling was one thing—it could set a person at their ease. But Dr. Hartley looked like he was about to burst out laughing.

"So how did this happen?" he asked.

"I fell in the mud."

"No. How awful."

"It was."

"Does this hurt?"

"A little."

"And what were you doing in the mud?"

"We had a flat tire. And we'd stopped to change it when these bikers—"

"Here?"

"Ow. Yes."

"I hear bikers can be very dangerous people."

"Yes, I was afraid for our lives."

"You don't say."

Diana began to get a strange sensation. Like the doctor had already heard about their flat and the Good Samaritan bikers.

"I thought the head guy was attacking Lillo, so I tried to stop him and fell, that's how I hurt my wrist."

"Hmm."

"They were actually very helpful," Diana explained, "but Jess—"

"Just got out of a bad relationship," the doctor finished. "Understandable."

Jess's eyes widened.

Allie slapped her hand to her mouth.

Diana just nodded. That would explain all the misspelled pictures to Doc "Harley." He hadn't just *heard* about their run-in with the gang . . . he was the leader of the pack.

Chapter 6

How on earth did Lillo hook up with these women? Doc wondered as he wrapped the sprained wrist.

"Do you happen to ride a Harley?" the brunette asked. Doc glanced up at her. Tall, slender, very well put together, clever looking, and expensively dressed. Fish out of water here in Lighthouse Beach.

"As a matter of fact."

"What?" Jess asked suspiciously.

"I'm the scary biker who changed your flat."

"No way. He was huge and . . ."

"Scary," Doc supplied for her. "But it was me. I have the marks to prove it." He held out his left hand; two of the knuckles were scraped where he'd had to take off his gloves to pick up the lug nuts.

The brunette leaned over to see for herself. "Sure you weren't in a bar brawl to get those?"

With a sense of humor. "Almost positive."

Jess blushed. "You've been laughing at me."

"Not at all. I'm sorry we frightened you. And I'm glad you're a loyal friend. Not everyone would take on a threatening group of bikers to protect someone else."

His patient looked like she might burst into tears. Now what had he said? Was this the bride, maybe? Hadn't Lillo said she had the bride with her? And this one had just gotten out of a bad relationship. Just weird. Leave it to Lillo to pick up a bunch of nutcases and bring them home.

"So you're all here to visit Lillo?"

"For a few days," the brunette answered, moving slightly closer to the seated Jess. A protective move? What the hell had Lillo gotten herself into?

Doc pinned the end of the bandage. "Ice for the next forty-eight hours, keep it immobile as much as possible, and take ibuprofen for discomfort if needed. The swelling should go down in the next few days. If you develop a temperature or sore joints, come back to the clinic. Regardless, see your own doctor when you get home." He held out his hand to help Jess from the examining table. She took it and slid to her feet.

"Does she need to keep the bandage on?" This came from the third woman, blondish-brown hair, tanned, looked like the outdoorsy type. "We plan on spending some time on the beach. Can she get it wet?"

They were planning on swimming. Right. They probably had their in-ground pools set to sauna degrees.

"Sure. Stop by the pharmacy and get a second bandage to alternate with it. Just have Lillo rewrap it when need be."

"Thank you, Doctor." Jess shook his hand.

"My pleasure." He walked them to the door. "Where is she, by the way?"

"Lillo? She dropped us off."

"I see."

"She had some errands to do."

"I bet she did." He hadn't meant to say that aloud. Lack of sleep, lack of food, lack of a second pair of hands.

The brunette was watching him too closely for his peace of mind.

"She's a busy girl—woman." He walked them down the hallway and nudged them through the waiting room door.

The brunette paused in the opening. "We'll tell Lillo you said hello."

"I didn't."

"What?"

"Say hello."

"Ah, I see. Good day, Doctor."

And good riddance. He smiled, nodded, turned to find Agnes standing beside him. "I'll just send out for some lunch." She handed him the next folder.

"Mrs. Olsen, the doctor will see you now."

LILLO SAT ACROSS the street from the clinic wondering if she should go inside to check on the progress of Operation Sprained Wrist or just sit in the van without a book or even a car radio.

She should have thought to get everyone's cell numbers, then remembered they probably shouldn't be using their phones. Having houseguests was turning out to be more complicated than she thought. She'd stood in the local market trying to remember the last time she'd stocked her kitchen or made dinner for more than herself, or Mac and her. It hadn't been that long, but she just couldn't remember. So her cart resembled something from a teenager's slumber party. Fortunately, the grocery was only a five-minute walk from the cottage. They wouldn't starve. But they might complain about her choices.

She hadn't really resigned herself to having a girls' weekend away. She used to enjoy them back in her other life.

For some reason she couldn't leap over the concrete wall of her epic fail to the time before. The time when the future was exciting and she was self-assured—too self-assured as it turned out—convinced that she was about to take the world by storm.

Now what was she? Someone who had kidnapped a bride from her destination wedding. Trundled three women out of a hotel and into a van, drove them to an unknown location. It was a terrible, reckless thing to do and yet there had been times when she caught herself smiling. Laughing at the bistro before the great reveal. Jess and the lug wrench were priceless. Fortunately, she didn't think the wrist was broken. Diana asking her about bikinis on the beach. For an instant here and there she'd felt like a . . . a . . . girl again. Carefree. Optimistic.

But the feeling was gone now. Sitting out here in front of the clinic when she could have been inside.

She pushed that idea away. Instead she thought about the sound of the waves, the shadow of the lighthouse, the wind whipping through the trees in the woods. Her breathing slowed, her heart returned to a steady beat, and three women walked down the front steps of the clinic.

"Go okay?" she asked as they climbed inside. She started up the van.

"Did you know the doctor was the car mechanic on the Harley from last night?" Diana asked.

"Yes. That's how I knew the clinic would be open today. They were on their way to Lighthouse Beach."

"You could have warned us," Jess said. "I felt like such a fool."

"Oh, stop it," Lillo said. "No self-esteem issues are allowed on girls' weekend away. I didn't tell you because I didn't think about it. That's all. My bad."

She pulled onto the street.

"I picked up lunch stuff—sandwich meats, chips, and things like that. I didn't know how Jess would feel."

"And dip?"

They all turned to look at Jess, even Lillo, though she used the rearview mirror.

"Just wondering."

"We can certainly stop somewhere on our way back to Lillo's," Diana said, settling back in her seat. She looked across at Lillo.

Lillo winced. "Onion soup and sour cream?"

"Both," Diana said. "Now tell us about this Dr. Hartley."

This was why she hadn't told them about Doc. She didn't want to explain stuff and get tangled up in the history of Ned Hartley in Lighthouse Beach. "Let's see. He and several other biker types spend the summer going along the coast to the smaller towns that need stuff done; they have a couple of doctors, sometimes a dentist, handymen, mechanics, it's always different. Whoever is free at the time."

"Are they members of some organization?"

Lillo thought about it. "Not that I know of. I think it's just something Doc started a few years back. He lived here for a while as a teenager. I guess he came back to visit, saw a need, and filled it. He works at the hospital in Portland part-time and travels around to remote communities under their aegis."

"The waiting room was continually packed while we were there, but I don't think I saw one person pay even a copay. How do they support themselves?"

"Not a clue. I've only been back myself for the last year. I haven't seen him too much to ask." In fact, she avoided him at all costs. Last night had been an unfortunate fluke.

Lillo turned the van onto Main Street. "Do you want to stop for more food? And dip? The local grocery store is on the next block and the liquor store is right next door. I don't know how good the selection is. I don't drink that much and usually only local beer."

Diana leaned over the back of her seat. "Jess, can you hang on while we make a liquor run?"

"Definitely."

Lillo maneuvered the VW into a parking place right in front of Beach Liquors. She parked and they piled out of the van, except for Jess.

"Any special requests?" Diana asked.

"No, but here." Jess handed over her credit card.

Diana just looked at it.

"What?"

"You threw your phone out the window but you're going to use your credit card?"

"Oh, I wasn't thinking."

"No, and it's okay. This is your time to be nutso. So don't feel bad. I have cash, and when that runs out we'll figure it out." She cut a look to Lillo.

"Not to worry. I stopped by the bank this morning. So we're solid." Lillo had stopped by the bank, where everyone wanted to know why she wasn't at the wedding. Then she returned the unworn wedding outfit to Barbara Carroll at the consignment store, where Barbara asked even more questions. She explained just enough so that people wouldn't speculate and wouldn't answer questions about Jess's whereabouts to anyone but the police.

She hadn't returned the sundress to Sada. She was afraid it had been ruined by the rain.

"You'll be okay?" Lillo asked Jess.

"Yes. I'm sorry to put you in the middle of this."

"Hey. You and me, like the good old days."

Jess tried for a smile. "They were awful."

"Pretty much. But we got through it, didn't we?"

Jess hesitated. "Did we?"

"Yes, now don't worry."

Lillo shut the door and hurried after Diana and Allie. They'd gotten through those days, but what the hell good had it done? Jess on the lam with a murky future, and Lillo with not much of a future at all.

Diana grabbed a cart and Lillo led them to the back of the store where the wine and better spirits were shelved. It didn't take Diana long to fill the cart with mixers and vodka and rum and gin. Though she did turn up her nose at a couple of the labels. Allie's palate was more discerning, but she did manage to come up with several "drinkable" reds and a "so-so" pinot grigio and two magnums of "acceptable" champagne.

"We only have to use cash for the next couple of days and then it will be too late to get her back in the most tasteless expensive wedding dress you've ever seen." Diana reached for another mixer that was so pink, Lillo imagined it glowing in the dark.

Lillo winced. "Insult to injury."

"In spades."

"You know, if you guys are planning on continuing your road trip, there are better stores with cheaper prices on the highway."

"True," Diana said as she read the label. She looked up suddenly, catching Lillo off guard. "Getting cold feet?"

"About what?"

"Having us thrust ourselves on you for the weekend?"

"I thought we settled that."

"We did unless you're having buyer's remorse."

"I'm not. You're welcome to stay. Though I have to say, if you want to avoid the Parkers you might be better off staying mobile. They're probably out looking for Jess now. I mean, they must be worried."

Diana put the pink mixture into the cart, added a second bottle. "I don't know about 'worried.' Maybe once they get over being angry and mortified. And dealing with the caterers, and the hotel and irate guests and—"

She grinned. "Sorry, but they're toxic people. And I'm sure once they realize Jess is not in Boston, they'll send their minions to find her. And quite frankly, I'd like for them to find us so I can confront them in friendly territory."

"Whew. All right, then. We'll prepare the ramparts."

"Exactly."

Not a very comforting thought for Lillo. She'd withstood the brunt of Jess's parents more than once over the years. The last year, when they threatened to sue the camp, had been the worst because it had included her parents, who were the most caring people in the world.

But once again she couldn't desert her old friend. She didn't hold out much hope. She'd known Jess longer than Diana and Allie had, and she knew that sooner or later Jess would go back and eat crow and be miserable. Allie and Diana would go back to their lives. And Lillo. Things would go back to normal . . . whatever the new normal would be.

They purchased their supplies and Lillo ran into the grocery next door to get the ingredients for dip. When she came out, the van door was open and Jess was striding up the sidewalk looking like murder.

Lillo hurried over to her. "What's happened? Where have you been?"

"Ugh, there was a group of boys acting like little asses."

Lillo looked down the sidewalk where a group of four boys was swaggering down the street, pushing each other, making noise. "Oh, Tommy Clayton and his gang. If you can call eleven and under a gang. School is out. They're unsupervised and all hell breaks loose. It's the nature of small-town living."

"Well, I think it's awful. The things they were saying about this poor kid. Making fun. I don't know, it just got to me."

"Brought back fond memories?"

"Ugh. It makes me so angry. Why doesn't someone do something?"

"Like you? Were you going to chase them off and beat them with your soft cast?"

Jess lifted her chin in a way she used to do when she was trying to be brave. "Maybe. Not one person tried to stop them. Two of the kids they were harassing managed to get away, but one didn't or couldn't run. They just kept taunting him and pushing him. I guess it all just came flooding back, and somehow I was out of the car and chasing them. Me, of all people. Then the guy from the newsstand came out with his broom. Didn't faze them."

Lillo took Jess's good arm; Jess actually seemed to have forgotten about her sprained wrist in the adrenaline rush. "Well, until somebody figures out what to do with them all summer, it's a problem that won't go away. They've never really hurt anyone, physically."

"Yet," Jess said.

"Yet. Now get in the van. We have onion dip."

They were back at Lillo's cottage by three, but Lillo was already exhausted. As soon as the drinks and food were packed into the fridge, Diana announced she was going to the beach.

"Who's up for a swim?"

Lillo smiled to herself. It was June; the water was really cold.

"Why don't you and Allie go ahead. Beach towels are on the bottom shelf of the linen closet and there are chairs on the deck.

I'll get Jess settled on the couch, and then we'll all have drinks before we go over to Mac's for dinner."

Diana nodded. "You guys have a lot to catch up on."

Did they? *Whatcha been doing all these years?* There was nothing in her life that Lillo wanted to discuss. But she did want to know why Jess hadn't contacted her in all these years, and then suddenly invited her to her wedding.

Lillo piled up pillows behind Jess's back and put another one under her arm for good measure. "Did Doc tell you to keep compression on and then ice?"

"Yes. He gave Diana instructions. He said I could soak it in the ocean for twenty minutes when we were at the beach but I just wasn't up to it right now."

Lillo wouldn't be either. The water temperature was worse than an ice pack. "Do you want a drink? Or tea. I usually have a cup of tea about this time of day."

"Tea would be great, thanks."

Lillo went into the little kitchen to put on the kettle. It was small and efficient but might not hold four women all making coffee at the same time. Fortunately there was a breakfast bar and pass-through that would keep things from getting too crowded. She rummaged for a selection of tea. "Constant Comment okay? It's either that or Sleepytime herbal."

"Constant Comment is fine."

When the tea was steeped, Lillo filled a plate with cheese and crackers, put it all on a tray, and carried it over to the couch.

Jess was looking out the window at the lighthouse, lost in thought.

Lillo pulled an end table to where Jess could reach it, deposited the tray on it, and sat in her favorite reading chair.

Jess took her mug of tea. "Remember when we used to sneak

over the jetty to the lighthouse to see Mac? And she'd make us tea and some of those hard cookies she called biscuits?"

"I do. She still serves them with tea."

"She looks older."

"So do we all," Lillo quipped.

Jess sighed. "They mean well, my parents."

"That's not an excuse. It never was."

"I know. I wish you had known me in college."

Lillo looked up at that. "Why?"

"Because you would have liked me then. I think."

"I always liked you. I like you now."

"No, I mean I was different then. I was good at being a college student. I wasn't the wreck I was when you knew me and I wasn't the wreck I am now. That's where I met Diana and Allie."

"Diana said you were good at your job, too."

"She did?"

"Yeah. And are we beginning to see a pattern here?"

Jess didn't answer for a few moments. "Because I was away from my parents. I have to believe they do have my best interests at heart. But all their best interests just make me miserable. And when they're around me I just revert to the jiggling mass of humiliation I was as a kid. I can't seem to help myself."

"Well, at least you recognize it for what it is. So now you can change it." She might not have any other options. George Parker could be vicious, even to his own family. "So why did you invite me to the wedding?"

Jess put her mug down. Hugged herself like it was cold outside. It wasn't.

"Instinct? I'd like to say I wanted to see you again. That I wanted my best friend for years to celebrate my new life with me."

"But?"

"But that would be a lie. When Mom and Dad pulled me out of camp and wouldn't let me come back, I hated them. But then I went off to college, and things were better. I was merrily working my way up in Manhattan when my parents reared their ugly heads with a fiancé in tow.

"I'd successfully—I thought—built a wall between me and my past."

"And as we all know," Lillo said, "walls don't keep anything out for long. But they do keep your weakest parts in." God, had she really said that? Was that what was happening to her? One more attempt at a platitude and she'd smack herself in the face.

"Exactly. Mine only kept out the good parts of my past, the parts with you in it; but the bad stuff found a way through.

"I knew I was trapped, and I knew Diana and Allie would never understand how I got to this point. Diana knows James. She never liked him, but she stuck by me all the way to the yacht club and would have stuck by me all the way down the aisle.

"And the horrible part is, I don't even like James. He's an egotistical, entitled rich boy. I guess I'm entitled and rich, but having those two qualities in common is hardly the grounds for a good marriage."

"Then why did you agree to marry him?"

"I was in it before I knew what was happening. No. That's a lie, too. I just let it happen to me. It was just like it always was, with my parents coaxing and manipulating, yelling, threatening— God, it was awful, so, like always, I gave in. When I finally came to my senses, I knew you were the only one who would really understand and that if I could just get you there, I might figure out a way to deal with it. And I prayed that you remembered me and would forgive me and come help me one more time."

And then what? Lillo wondered. Would Jess drop her again

when she was no longer needed? She wasn't sure she liked being used that way. But it was too late to be angry now. She shrugged it off. "Well, you extricated yourself and you did it without even needing me to intercede."

"You're wrong. I did and do need you. To be a friend, and I want to be a friend back. It was sheer good—humiliating—luck that we caught James at it in the parking lot. I'm sure he did it on purpose, maybe not consciously, but quite frankly he doesn't like me any better than I like him. Oh God, how did I make such a mess of my life?"

Lillo laughed. She couldn't help herself. Because boy, could she relate. She may have been the tough one when they were kids. The resilient one. The one with a plan for the future. But she had failed just as miserably as Jess and she had no one to blame but herself.

"It isn't funny."

"No. It isn't. I'm sorry."

"I know this is hard to believe, but I'm good at what I do. I'm smart and effective in finance and organization. I know how to get things done. I'm not greedy and hard-hearted like my father, but I know how to manage, and the best part is, I care about people. Most of the friends I've made and my work associates don't know that I'm a bullied, humiliated mess. Because I'm not. Really, not anymore. Just to my family, and I can't seem to break truly free from them."

"Well, you may have burned that bridge, and quite frankly, good for you. You always said you were going to do something good one day."

Jess sniffed. "So maybe now is my one day."

"Do you have a plan?"

"I—"

The door to the deck slid open. "Holy shit, it's cold out there."

Diana stood dripping just inside the door. "Light a fire, make coffee. Wrap me in a blanket."

Allie, laughing, pushed her farther inside. "Such a wuss. This is nothing compared to the Pacific. *That's* cold. I claim the shower first." And she took off down the hall.

Lillo and Jess watched them drip across the floor and disappear. Fortunately, the mood of intimacy had been broken and it didn't return when the bathroom door closed behind them. Lillo didn't think either of them wanted to do any more soul-searching tonight.

NED DIDN'T LEAVE the clinic until almost five. He'd worked nonstop today and he knew tomorrow would be just as hectic. The days after that would be calmer as the acute patients were replaced by the yearly physicals and the chronic sufferers. He sure as hell hoped Clancy made an appearance soon.

There was no sign of Ian when he reached the house. Ned raided the fridge for something to eat and a beer, even though they would be eating at Mac's in a couple of hours. He found a beer, but the fridge was pretty empty. He did find a box of crackers in the pantry. They were stale, but at that point Ned would have picked mold off them; stale was a godsend.

He went upstairs to shower and change; when he came back down, he found Ian sitting at the kitchen table nursing a beer. He was still wearing his work clothes and the smell of the stables.

"Hey, shake it. We're due at Mac's in a half hour and I'm starving."

"You go on ahead."

"But you're coming to Mac's, right?"

"Not tonight."

"Man, your cupboard is bare."

Ian shrugged. "I'll make do. I'm just not in the mood for people tonight."

"You never are."

"I'm tired of it—the anger, the violence, the ignorance . . ."

Ned sat down across from him. "Rough day?"

"Yeah. Had to put down Frank Duffy's horse. He wasn't happy. He tried to stop me. I warned him time after time that he was abusing the animal. Cheap feed, overwork, untreated sores. But he just railed and blamed everybody but himself.

"I tell you, holding that syringe . . . well, forget that. I put the horse down, then he yelled at me for not carting the carcass away. I called Animal Control. I don't trust him not to just dump him in the woods somewhere."

Ned listened. He couldn't know the depth of Ian's feelings. They'd been pushed to the max. These days he pretty much held himself in check. But it took its toll.

"I don't think you'll run into any of that at Mac's. And she's making lobster stew."

"Thanks, but I wouldn't be very good company. I'll send over a bottle of wine for dinner by way of apology."

"Mac's stew calls for good beer."

"From what you've said about Lillo's friends, they're not beer drinkers."

"You haven't even seen them."

"It's the way you described them."

"Dismissive?"

Ian shrugged.

"Well, I got to know them better today."

Ian looked up.

"They came into the clinic. It turns out the runaway bride was the one that went after me with the lug wrench. She sprained her wrist in the fall."

"Lillo brought her into the clinic?"

"Nope. Lillo dropped off the other three. She didn't come in." Ian shook his head.

"Pot and kettle, my friend. Pot and kettle."

"Maybe, but I'm still not going."

Chapter 7

Diana was the first to emerge from her room, showered and changed into slacks and a shirt that Lillo thought belonged more at the yacht club than at Mac's kitchen table. It made her wrinkled khakis and dirty tee, which she realized for the first time that day she'd never changed out of, look like skid row.

She was such a social moron. She pushed out of her chair. At least she could change into clean khakis and a T-shirt and take some clothes out of her bedroom since it looked like she'd be sleeping on the couch until further notice.

She hesitated, surprised that she hadn't even flinched at the thought. In fact, she was beginning to warm to the idea of a few days of hanging out. It wasn't like she had a job.

"Don't get up," Diana said, scrubbing her short hair into place. "What are you guys drinking?"

"Tea," Jess said.

Diana scowled at them. "And crumpets? Teatime is over—we have almost an hour before Mac expects us. How about a little preprandial champagne to celebrate the 'Flight from Kennebunkport.'"

Jess laughed. Actually laughed. "You sound like one of the old movies we used to watch. Remember, Lillo?"

Lillo nodded as she watched Jess scan the room.

"I don't even see a television. Don't tell me you aren't into the oldies anymore."

Lillo shrugged. "Not so much."

"You don't have a television?"

"Somewhere." She pointed to the window. "This is my TV."

Diana continued to the kitchen. Took the champagne out of the fridge. Looked out to Lillo and screwed up her face. "I don't suppose you have champagne flutes?"

Lillo started to shake her head. Then realized she did. Her heart started pounding. *Just say no. Don't be stupid. Just say no.* "Maybe."

She walked to the hall. Hesitated outside the storage room door. Why was she keeping all that old junk? She wasn't going to use it. Stupid question. She knew exactly why. Maybe this weekend wasn't just about fleeing Kennebunkport, but about "The Unmasking of Lillo Gray." As a movie title, it had a certain ring to it.

She took a breath, grasped the doorknob, slipped through the narrowest possible opening, and shut the door behind her. She knew right where they were. She could name everything and its location without thinking. She grabbed a box of flutes and another of wineglasses.

Her heart was pushing up through her throat. She was afraid she was going to be sick. But she managed to get the door opened and closed without anyone seeing her. When she went back to the sitting room, Diana was still in the kitchen and Jess was on the couch, just as she'd left them, just as if an eternity hadn't passed.

"Here, they probably need rinsing."

Diana took the boxes, and though Lillo was expecting her to make a sarcastic remark about them, she didn't say a word.

"I'll wash. You dry." Diana tossed a dishcloth to Lillo.

Allie came out just as Lillo and Diana were carrying the champagne and glasses to the couch. She took a seat next to Jess and Diana popped the cork. Seconds later they were all raising their glasses in a toast.

"To friends, adventures, and road trips!" Diana exclaimed. They clinked glasses, and as Lillo raised hers to her lips, her cell phone rang.

"It's probably Mac," she said, and put her glass down.

She didn't recognize the number, but she knew who it was. She let it ring while the others grew quiet and watched her.

"It must be your parents."

Jess put down her glass, the energy seeping out of her like water through a sieve. "I'll take it." She reluctantly reached for Lillo's phone.

Lillo pulled it back from her reach. Looked at the others. "I'll handle it." She pressed accept.

"Hello."

"Lillo Gray?"

"Yes."

"Let me speak to Jessica right now."

"Who is this?"

"You know damn well who this is. I know she's with you, so if you don't want trouble, you'll—"

Jess lurched off the couch. Allie pulled her back.

"Mr. Parker. You've obviously been drinking. I have no idea

what you're talking about and I resent being bothered. You told me I wasn't invited to the wedding. You threatened to have me thrown out of the hotel. I realized my presence upset Jess, so I left."

"The hell you did. You took her with you and you can bring her right back. You tell her she has just one hour to get back here and at the rehearsal dinner or there will be hell to pay. I'll bring charges against you for kidnapping."

Lillo ran her tongue over suddenly dry lips. Just like years ago, when he lashed out at Jess with stupid threats. Jess quaking and apologizing, Lillo angry and impotent. But not today. "Mr. Parker. I took time out of my busy life to come to the wedding of a friend I hadn't seen in ten years only to be insulted by you. I left like you ordered me to do. I don't take kindly to these empty threats. Don't call me again."

"Where is Jessica?"

Lillo closed her eyes and turned her back to the room. "I'm afraid I can't tell you that. And I've already wasted more than enough time with you and your family. Don't bother me again." She ended the call. Opened her eyes.

Jess, Diana, and Allie were all staring at her. No one moved. Lillo was afraid if she tried to get back to her chair her legs would betray her.

"He must have talked to the parking attendants," Diana said.

"I'm sorry," Jess said. "I didn't want you to have to lie for me."

"Lie?" Lillo said. "I didn't lie. He told me to leave. I did. I told him I couldn't tell him, and I didn't. And I don't even know anyone named Jessica. Do any of you?"

Diana broke into a wide smile. Handed Lillo her glass and raised hers. "To Lillo. You were fierce, girl."

Lillo made it to her chair and sank into it. "I can't believe I did that."

"Do you think he believed you?" Allie asked.

"No, but it felt good."

"And it may have bought us some beach time," Diana said, and poured more champagne.

Lillo met her eyes over her glass and saw the glimmer of something as Diana topped off her champagne. As if there was an understanding between them. To fight on Jess's behalf? To stand strong against Jess's parents?

She should warn Diana now, before it went further. Lillo was the last person she should depend on.

"But what if he brings charges against you?" Jess asked, her voice tight with anxiety.

Diana snorted. "For giving a friend a ride? It would just make him look like an even bigger ass than he already is. I wouldn't worry. Besides, we couldn't get you back within an hour even if you wanted to go . . . You don't, do you?"

Jess bit her lip.

Lillo felt the all-too-familiar dull pain of disappointment.

Jess shook her head. "Too late. I'm on my own. This time for good."

Allie put her glass down on the table. "I think before we go much further, we should discuss what exactly we're doing here."

"We're on the lam," Diana said.

"No, really. We've descended on Lillo's home. Even though she said it was fine, I don't think you're really comfortable with us being here?" Allie looked the question at Lillo.

Lillo shook her head, shrugged, sent mixed signals. What the hell. She didn't know. At first she hadn't wanted them here. But now that they *were* here, she sort of liked the company. Which was crazy. She had a life. Of sorts.

"Lillo?"

"I think we need to give Jess time to figure out how she wants to handle the situation."

Jess opened her mouth to answer, but Diana plowed on. "You're not going to figure it out when we're all still feeding off adrenaline from last night, and now the phone call." She poured more champagne and began telling a story of an app test gone bad.

It made them all laugh, and after a few more minutes and the second bottle of champagne, they were chatting like they really were on vacation.

Then, in the middle of a story, Diana stood, glanced at her watch, and lifted her glass. "It's six fifteen and all is well," she intoned. "We have officially missed Jess's rehearsal dinner—a fait accompli."

"Hear, hear," Allie said, a little dubiously, and shot a look at Jess.

Jess and Lillo lifted their glasses. "Hear, hear."

They had saved their friend from a wedding she didn't want, stuck it to the Parkers for trying to force her into a loveless marriage, and possibly saved her from a lifetime of unhappiness. But there would be repercussions, Lillo had no doubt about that.

"I wonder what made Jess's father think we could even get there in an hour. Where does he think we are?"

No one seemed to have an answer.

Jess put down her glass. "He'll figure it out. And then there will be hell to pay. Which is okay," she added hurriedly. "I'm up for it. But I do kind of feel bad about all those wedding guests."

"I'm sure they'll have a gay old time even without a bride to toast."

"All three hundred of them," Jess said, suddenly deflating.

"I can't believe you were having three hundred guests," Lillo said incredulously.

"All friends or business associates of her parents," said Diana. "It was more like a trade show than a wedding."

"Diana . . ." Allie admonished.

Diana plowed on. "How many of your friends were actually invited?"

Jess looked around. "Three?"

"That's pitiful," Lillo said. "You have more friends than that."

Allie rummaged in her purse and handed Jess a tissue.

Jess blew her nose. "I do. They weren't invited. A few were, but just because they owned successful businesses or their parents were somebody my parents knew or needed to know. Oh my God, they're so shallow."

Diana flopped back in her chair and stared at the ceiling. "*Now* she figures it out."

Allie gave her a look.

If Jess's predicament wasn't so tragic, Lillo would have enjoyed the trio. Diana and Allie as Dutch uncles to Jess's ambivalence.

"I shouldn't have waited so long. I just—until I saw all of you, I thought I could go through with it."

Diana snapped her head back to eye level. "Thank God you didn't. People make mistakes. God knows I've made mistakes in that field twice, but at least they were my mistakes. You didn't have a say in any of this, did you?"

"I never have, about anything. But I've tried. Remember, Lillo? I used to try."

"You did." But by fourteen, Jess had pretty much given up.

"They'll be so embarrassed. Humiliated."

"Small price to pay for a daughter's happiness," Diana said.

"The worst thing that could ever happen to them as far as they're concerned."

"It will be one of life's little lessons." Diana smiled sweetly but the devil was in her eyes. "Embarrassment fades, and it wouldn't hurt them to dine on crow for a few meals."

Lillo breathed out a laugh she knew was inappropriate, but she couldn't help it. "Talk about *me* being fierce? You're downright scary."

"Thank you. I work at it." Diana crossed her arms and smiled at the other three. "So where do we go from here?"

When no one answered immediately, she went on. "What if we spend a whole week here?"

"Diana!" Allie exclaimed. "Stop strong-arming Lillo. Already a couple of days has turned into a long weekend; now you're talking a whole week."

"Why not?"

"Lillo has her own life, responsibilities; maybe us being here is inconvenient."

"Lillo? Is it inconvenient?"

"Uh, no." What was she saying? Of course it would be inconvenient. What had Diana said in the liquor store? A few days to straighten Jess out.

"Because if you need us out, we can drive to the nearest car rental place tomorrow, but . . ."

They all waited for Diana to continue.

"But?" Lillo finally asked.

"But Jess was right. This is the perfect place to regroup and start again." Diana directed the last part of her statement at Lillo. And Lillo had the oddest sensation that she wasn't just talking about Jess.

She took a sip of champagne and tried to envision waking up to three other women for seven days in a row. Or would one week turn into two? They'd start moving her stuff and making themselves at home. She was surprised at how unimportant that seemed at the moment.

But she did have responsibilities of sorts. Taking care of local gardens, helping Sada out at the community center, minding the lighthouse gift store when Mac was busy, even sometimes mucking out the stables when Ian was away or having a bad spell. She loved and hated that job. Too many memories, too many . . .

And what was wrong with hanging out on the beach drinking champagne with friends for a few days? Not a few. Seven. *Seven whole days*.

"Lillo?" Allie said. "Just say the word and we'll leave."

"No. I'd . . . Please stay."

"You're sure?"

Lillo nodded. She wasn't sure at all.

THE SUN WAS setting behind them as the four women made their slightly tipsy way across the parking lot to Mac's for dinner.

The front of the gift shop was dark, but the aroma of cooking wafted around the corners and a lantern at the end of the garden path beckoned them onward. They had to walk single file, with Lillo leading the way, and the other three duck-waddling behind her so as not to domino into the person in front of them. By the time they reached the back door, they were laughing uncontrollably.

Mac greeted them with a wave of her wooden spoon, but didn't turn from the stove. "Have a seat. Lillo, there's beer and wine in the fridge. Hope the wine passes your inspection, Allie."

"I'm sure it will be fine," Allie said, blushing slightly. "Actually, I think I'd rather have a beer," she told Lillo. "Can I help you?"

"Nah. I'm the official drinks person. Mac will put you to work doing something."

"That's right," Mac said over her shoulder. "Everyone falls into something before they get away." She brandished the spoon again. "I hope you all like shellfish. Seems like these days people have all sorts of allergies and aversions. But don't worry, there's also chicken and vegetables and lots of homemade bread and crackers. Keep these men on their feet."

"Men?" Lillo asked. "How many men are coming?"

"Just Clancy, Doc, and Ian. I'll have a barbecue for the others on Sunday. Give 'em a chance to visit with their hosts. And give us a chance for a nice laid-back, intimate dinner."

Lillo would have laughed if she hadn't been jabbed by a needle of panic. Clancy she could handle even though he always gave her grief for whatever. Ian was having a rough time these days. He would probably just scowl through dinner and excuse himself as soon as the dishes were done. His job.

But Doc. That would be uncomfortable. Well, it was inevitable that this day would come. Except for that disastrous meeting when she'd first returned to Lighthouse Beach a year ago and last night, she had managed mostly to avoid him. At least tonight she would be well insulated by the others.

When Lillo returned with beers and a bottle of chardonnay, Diana was slicing a thick, crusty country loaf of bread; Allie was setting the table; and Jess was attempting to fold napkins with one hand.

Lillo opened a bottle of local brew and took it over to Mac. She lingered long enough to take a deep appreciative breath of the stew. "Smells wonderful."

"Thank you. No fighting tonight."

"You'll get none from me." She quickly kissed Mac's weather-roughened cheek. "I'll keep my mouth stuffed the whole time."

Mac barked out a laugh. "Just see that you do."

Lillo opened two more beers for Allie and herself and put Diana in charge of wine. They all sat down and were recounting the call from Jess's father when the back door opened. Lillo had been anticipating it, but she started anyway.

Doc walked in cradling a bottle of wine in one arm.

He nodded. "Ladies." He added his bottle to the one on the table. "Clancy not back yet?"

Mac, who was ladling stew into deep pottery bowls and handing them to Allie to place on the table, stopped. "Nope. Where's Ian?"

"Couldn't make it." Doc shrugged.

Mac sighed. That was all that was said.

Doc glanced at Lillo but didn't say hello or anything.

He did smile at Jess. "How's the wrist?"

"Okay. Thanks. I think I owe you an apology."

"Not at all." He tried to suppress a grin. Lillo knew it was futile. He burst out laughing. "You could have bowled me over when the three of you walked into the office this morning."

Had he put the emphasis on "three"? He didn't look her way, but Lillo was pretty good at picking up what was unsaid. Especially from Doc Hartley.

They sat down at the table. The bread was passed and silence ensued while they all savored the first bites of the creamy rich stew.

"So, Mac, did they tell you about breaking down on the road last night?" Doc asked.

"Ayuh."

"You'd better take the van over to Olsen's first thing Monday and get a new tire or four. You can't go driving all over creation with that spare. Then I'll have Nando come over and check out the rest of the van when he gets a chance."

Mac saluted and kept eating her stew.

"You were lucky you didn't blow out on the highway," he continued.

"We were," Allie said. "And we can't thank you enough for helping us."

Doc smiled. "My pleasure."

Really. He was so annoying. One minute he comes roaring into town like some hoodlum biker, and the next he's talking like some effete lord from a PBS series.

"I don't think I've seen Lillo in a dress since . . ."

Smug bastard. She looked straight at him. "First Communion?"

"Probably . . . It looked—"

"—better before I started changing the tire."

"Probably that, too." He went back to eating.

"You two have known each other a long time?" Diana asked.

"I lived here for several years when I was a teenager," Doc said. "Lillo grew up here. Stay here for more than a day or two and the whole town will know you."

Lillo couldn't figure out if that was his way of telling Diana to mind her own business, or to let Lillo know he didn't think any more of her than he did of the other three-hundred-plus residents. So she just kept eating.

The stew was delicious, as always. The bowls were cleared, the chicken served. The conversation grew lively with Mac giving her *Reader's Digest* version of the history of the lighthouse and how she had become the keeper and how they had retired her and the lighthouse together. Glasses were refilled. More beers were opened.

But as the evening wore on, Lillo could tell that Mac was becoming more distracted. The pauses in her conversation while she listened . . . for the sound of Clancy's motorcycle?

She and Clancy had been friends since childhood. They fought and laughed and supported each other when the chips were down. Lillo could tell she was worried.

When the phone finally rang, Mac practically jettisoned herself from her chair. She fumbled on the counter for her cell phone, snatched it up.

"Where are you?" she asked without even saying hello.

Conversation stopped and they all looked at Mac. "Uh-huh. Uh-huh. He's sitting right here." She held up the phone. Doc stood, took the phone from her, and walked onto the back porch.

"Is Clancy all right?" Lillo asked.

"Oh yes. He had to take a patient into the hospital in Bristol. Mary Alice Grotsky's boy. Mary Alice . . . well, you know how she is."

Lillo nodded. Mary Alice was like just about everyone in the town. Kept her own counsel and would rather live in pain than go off island to the doctor's.

"Stubborn woman. Clancy says they just got Ely's appendix out in time. Might have ruptured while she was waiting for the docs to get here. He's staying over until Mary Alice's sister can come and stay with them."

Mac looked directly at Lillo. "It could be another day, possibly two."

Lillo looked away. She had good instincts and she wasn't going there. She stood and began to clear the table.

Doc came back inside.

"Looks like you're going to have another busy day at the clinic," Mac said.

"Yeah, halfway through the day I had to have Agnes reschedule the least urgent." He huffed out a sigh. "Until tomorrow."

"Guess you could use some help—just a second pair of hands."

Lillo didn't turn around, just gathered the rest of the dishes.

She heard Doc say, "I could." And Mac saying, "Lillo and Ned here used to help out at the clinic when they were kids."

Lillo turned on the water and dropped a handful of silverware into the dish drain. The clatter didn't drown out the interested murmurs of the others.

"Well, don't you go running off until we've had dessert and I've packed up some food to take to Ian. Guess I better pack it all, since you won't have time for lunch tomorrow."

Allie deposited a stack of plates on the counter. Lillo glanced over her shoulder long enough to glare at Mac.

Ignoring her, Mac went to the fridge and pulled out a covered mixing bowl. "Fresh strawberries, first of the season. With my homemade shortbread and cream. You haven't eaten until you've had Maine strawberries."

Mac insisted on doing the rest of the dishes later and they all sat back down at the table. But the convivial mood seemed a bit strained. Or maybe it was just Lillo. She wanted to get back to her cottage, preferably alone. Why had she ever answered Jess's cry for help?

They all left a few minutes later. Lillo hurried her houseguests, hoping to avoid Doc, who had stayed behind while Mac laded him down with bags of food.

"That was delicious," Diana said. "I can hardly walk, I'm so full. How are you holding up, Jess?"

"Okay. I'll probably have gained ten pounds tomorrow morning."

"Well, you won't know," Lillo said. "'Cause I don't have a scale."

"Brilliant," Diana said. "A no-holds-barred weekend."

They'd almost made it to the path to the cottage when Doc called Lillo's name. She considered ignoring him, but then she would have to explain to the others. She turned and met him halfway.

"I really could use some help tomorrow."

"I'm sorry. I can't."

"I don't think your friends will mind if you leave them for a few hours for a good cause."

"You know I don't do that anymore."

"You could if you'd—"

"Stop it. I know what you're doing. I don't need your pity, or your therapy, or your butting into my life."

"Jeez, I just asked for some help, but forget it. I'm sure I can get Sada or Barbara or even old Mrs. Culhaney to pitch in for an hour or two."

He turned abruptly and strode back across the lot to his bike.

Face burning, Lillo hurried toward the cottage. The others had gone ahead, but she wasn't really surprised to find Diana waiting at the door.

"I guess I don't want to ask what that was about?"

"Please don't," Lillo said, and scooted past her through the cottage door.

Allie and Jess were sitting on the couch deep in conversation when Lillo and Diana came inside. Lillo had been hoping they would all be ready for bed even though it was still early. She was pretty sure they would have questions about why she and Doc were arguing in the parking lot.

She considered walking past them to the bathroom, but she couldn't stay there forever; they would all have to take a turn before they called it a night. Damn Doc for putting her in this position. She'd made it almost two days without having to talk too much about herself. She didn't want to start tonight.

Diana had already sat down. Lillo plopped down in her reading chair and yawned.

It didn't work.

"First of all," Allie said, "are you sure you're okay with us being here? You probably have things you have to do and if Doc Harley needs you to help out—"

"He doesn't. And his name is Hartley."

"I know, but all the kids' drawings call him Doc Harley because of his motorcycle. I think it's so cute."

"Cute," Lillo echoed.

"We couldn't help but notice there was a little tension between the two of you at dinner," Diana finished. "And even though none of us would be rude enough—even though we're dying of curiosity—to ask what it was or why you were arguing in the parking lot, we do want to make sure we're not cramping your style. I mean . . ."

"I have no style," Lillo quipped, but it came out sounding more like the truth than a joke.

"Sure you do. But I meant if you and Doc Harley have a relationship and we're in the way . . ."

"You should have said something," Allie said.

"Me and Ned? Hardly." Ned never gave her a break, but he certainly wasn't interested in her that way. "We have a history but not a relationship."

"Or anyone else? Is having us in your space a hardship?"

Lillo laughed. She could hardly call the occasional appearance of Derrick Quinn, an itinerant fisherman, a relationship.

"Well, is it?"

"It's not a hardship for me. This is the way I live, but you guys—you're used to nicer, bigger things. I'll understand if you'd be more comfortable at a hotel somewhere."

Diana threw up her hands. "I feel like we've already beaten this dead horse."

"Several times," Lillo agreed.

"Then let's put it to a vote. All in favor of us staying, raise your hand." Four hands went up, some faster than others.

"Carried," Diana announced.

"There's only one problem," Allie said.

"What now?"

"I have a flight back to California first thing Monday morning."

"How about asking your in-laws if they'd mind watching little Gino for another few days," Diana said. "And we'll make this a real girls' week away. I'm sure you could use a break from the winery."

"I don't know."

"When was the last time you took time for yourself?"

"I'll see." Allie took out her cell, hesitated. "I should try calling them in case they've heard what happened. They'll be worried." She looked at her cell screen. "Almost ten here, seven o'clock there. They'll be getting Gino to bed. I'll call them tomorrow morning."

"And tell them you're staying a few extra days?"

"I don't know, I'll have to see."

"Good enough. I think I'll make some tea. Anyone?" Diana stood. "Oh, sorry, Lillo. Do you mind if I make some tea?"

"Go for it," Lillo said. "If you guys are going to stick around, you'll have to fend for yourselves. I never quite got a handle on that hostessing thing."

"Not a problem. I run my own corporation. Same thing without the doilies."

Lillo laughed. "I guess we'll have to do a full-fledged grocery run tomorrow." And just like that, Lillo Gray had house-guests.

MAC TURNED FROM the window of the darkened gift shop. She'd dropped everything to spy on Lillo and Doc. It hadn't gone well. She wasn't surprised. Doc was approaching Lillo all wrong. And Lillo? Well, she'd been allowed to wallow in heart-break and self-indulgence for too long. It was time to set a fire under that girl.

She rubbed her eyes, peered out into the darkness. She'd meant to go into Bristol last week, but things had gotten too busy. She didn't relish going into the clinic there. But it was better than having to deal with Clancy or Ned at the local clinic.

She didn't expect good news. Then again she didn't expect bad news. She just didn't want any news. She was getting old, but she sure as hell didn't need to be told to slow down. She hardly did anything as it was.

And there was nothing more she could do tonight. Doc was gone, Lillo was inside her cottage. The lighthouse was a mere shadow in the night. No trespassers, no vandals, no pranksters, but there would be. Further into the season. Kids out of school with nothing to do but get into trouble. She'd be ready for them. But not tonight.

It was still early, but she was tired. Too old to hold watch night after night.

She groped her way across the darkened room, nearly knocked over the postcard stand when she miscalculated the turn into the T-shirt aisle. And definitely too old for skulking around in the dark. She stretched out her hand and reached toward the kitchen's beckoning light.

Chapter 8

It seemed to Mac that it had just been minutes since she'd closed the curtains on the night and yet here she was opening them again. Beyond the kitchen window, the sun was just coming over the rooftops of Lighthouse Beach. It was going to be another bright day. Good. Summer was a time for sunshine, for days warm enough to sit out on the sand, not that she did much of that. Maybe the good weather would bring a few visitors. She hoped it held. There was always plenty of winter for storm clouds.

She went to the pantry and turned on the light. She was stocked. She had everything for Sunday's barbecue and then some. She wasn't sure if Lillo's friends would actually stay or if Lillo would open up to them. Whether they would want to fend for themselves or let Mac feed them a few times while they were here.

She missed those days when stray fishermen, lonely wives, boaters who suddenly needed a port in a storm would stop in for a chat, or to dry in front of the fire, or just sit over a cup of coffee and a hastily prepared meal. No one much came any-more. Not so many fishermen left. Most had moved away, taking their families with them. The lighthouse no longer warned ships of the nearby shoals.

There was barely any traffic in the gift shop and it seemed like no one wanted to climb the stairs of the lighthouse to look at the old Fresnel-type lights that no longer worked.

The world was at their fingertips without ever leaving their computer screens. They could visit any number of lighthouses, have a guided tour, even ask their questions of some unseen face, whether real or robot, at the other end of the chat box.

What was that doing to the new generation? Weren't they lonely? Mac knew she was. And all the Internet in the world hadn't made her feel any different.

She turned on the light above the counter, got out the coffee, and made a full pot. She always did, even though most days she ended up pouring half of it out. She didn't mind. Better to be prepared.

The coffeemaker had just beeped when she heard the knock at the screen door. It wouldn't be Clancy. In the fifty years she'd know him, he'd never knocked even when she was entertaining—*especially* when she was entertaining.

They were best friends. For fifty-some-odd years. They'd married other people, both of whom were now dead. She still worried about him.

"Come in. Coffee's made," she called.

The door opened.

"Ah, up early again?"

"Yes," Jess said. "I didn't want to wake the others. Just tell me if I'm being a nuisance."

"Not at all. I don't get nearly enough company these days. Have a seat."

Mac poured out two large mugs of coffee. Put milk and sugar on the table and sat across from Jess.

"Black is fine."

"I remember you as a healthy girl."

"Fat."

"Strapping. It didn't slow you down. I remember you and Lillo racing down the beach, looking for things swept in by the tide, climbing over the jetty rocks. I could hear you laughing all the way up on the lighthouse widow's walk. I'm not hearing so much laughter now. What have they done to you, girl?"

Jess breathed a cheerless, almost silent laugh. "Girl . . . It's been a long time since I felt like a girl. These days I feel ancient. Ancient and tired and . . . ugh, listen to me. I'm in a gorgeous place with wonderful people, and I just can't seem to relax and enjoy myself."

"Could be because you left a fiancé at the altar, pissed off Mom and Dad, and are on the lam."

This time Jess's laugh almost rang true.

"Well, from where I'm looking, all four of you are in the bloom of youth and you oughta be enjoying it, 'cause all too soon you'll be too damn old to be good for anything."

Jess looked up and wagged her finger at Mac. It made Mac smile; she was usually the one who did the finger-wagging. "You'll never be that old. Everybody depends on you."

"Used to." Mac carried the cake tin over to the table and took off the top. "Made raspberry strudel."

"Oh, Mac, I can't."

"Sure you can. Nobody's making you eat the whole damn thing."

"I'm so hungry all the time, I feel like eating everything in sight. No, actually that isn't true. These days food hardly even tempts me."

"'Cause you've messed up your stomach with all that binge dieting."

"And my metabolism with diet pills and fad diets. And I know that I've done it to myself."

"Well, you did have help."

"I'm a classic case, aren't I? My parents gave or withheld food as reward or punishment. When I figured it out, I ate to piss them off. By the time I went off to college, I was totally whacked out.

"But a therapist on campus really helped me. Diana and Allie were great, supportive friends. I thought I was really normal, then the wedding, and it all started over again. I knew the role so well, I just slipped right back into it. And now I'm back to where I started."

"Nobody is ever back where they started. Use those tools from college to get your life together once and for all. And damn it to hell, stop listening to those parents of yours."

Jess eyed the strudel. Pulled over a plate and cut herself a slice. "That's why I begged Lillo to come to the wedding. I think I knew I had to make a final move and I knew I could never do it alone. That's selfish of me, isn't it?"

"Self-preservation. We're all selfish when it comes to survival."

Though how Jess had lasted this long was astounding. She wasn't out of the woods yet. The way she was deliberately eating that piece of strudel, Mac could almost see the willpower that kept her from shoving the whole thing in her mouth. And if Mac could see it, then so could everyone else.

Poor Jess. Even her name, Jessica, had "Bully me" written on it. And boy, did the kids make fun of her. To one group she was a fatty, to another not fat enough, her parents flaunted their wealth, and she had that prissy name.

The first thing she did after meeting Lillo was to shorten

her name to Jess. But it had taken two weeks before she and Lillo finally settled on something that she could answer to for her whole life. Only to her own family did she remain Jessica Braithwaite Parker.

The real Jess was buried under their expectations, and even when she briefly emerged she was like a supporting character in her own young life. Mac had watched it all unfold. Summer after summer. Watched her blossom as the summer went on, watched it all unravel as she drove away in the back seat of some fancy limo.

And Lillo? She had everything going for her: brains, heart, parents who loved her so much that they were willing to let her fly solo. And one mistake had driven her back here. Her parents had moved away, her reason for being here gone. And yet here she was.

"What if I can't stick it out? I've embroiled my dearest friends in what could become a real bloodbath, figuratively speaking. But it could turn nasty; for them, too."

"In case you've forgotten, that's what friends are for."

Jess slumped back and pushed her cup around in a circle. "Why am I just now getting it?"

"Getting what?"

"Every summer I would come here a total mess, and while I was here I'd start to think I was . . . you know, okay, then I'd go back home and fall into all my old habits and . . . and it wasn't me; I was me here."

"Well, like the sign says, once you visit Lighthouse Beach, life will never be the same."

"But it *was* the same. Summer after summer, I thought I had changed, had gotten stronger. When I was away at school. When I was working in Manhattan. But I couldn't maintain it; in real life, I just couldn't stay me."

"Real life? Honey, *this* is real life. Where a community only has two itinerant doctors who show up every month or so. Half the populace is out of work, and the ones who do work are squeezed for taxes and inflation and the price of bread. They believed promises made to them that no politician ever intended to keep. The kids, when they go to school at all, have to ride a school bus an hour each way, so most of them just stay home until the truant officer comes around. And leave home as soon as the law says they're old enough. And the kids with special needs? They're serviced by a visiting teacher three times a week. During the school year. Shall I go on?"

"You sound bitter."

"Me? Nah. Just pointing out that your idea of real life . . . well, it ain't real."

"Entitled."

"That's a nice way to put it."

"I'm not sure how to exist in this real life."

"Well, then you'd better go back to your anorexic life with a cheating husband and greedy, manipulative parents. No one's stopping you."

"Mac . . ."

"Well, what do you want me to say? You have choices."

"I wish I could stay here. I'm not sure I can make it out there."

"Lighthouse Beach is a sanctuary, not the end of the line."

"But *you* stayed here. Lillo stayed here. All the people who live here stayed."

"For some people it becomes a home. For some an excuse. But get over thinking you stage-managed the four of you ending up in Lighthouse Beach."

"Then who did?"

"Just in the stars, I guess."

"Mac. When did you start believing in astrology?"

"I don't. I believe in celestial navigation."

"We have GPS."

Mac barked out a laugh. The girl still had a spark of life in her. Now, if they could just keep it burning . . . She got up to pour them more coffee.

"Okay, so why did Diana and Allie come? Besides to help me. I mean . . . Allie, after losing her husband, just can't seem to get interested in making a new life. I get that."

"It's hard to lose someone you thought you were going to spend your life with. It takes time."

"Will being in Lighthouse Beach help her?"

"It will."

"How?"

"I haven't got a clue, but it will. It always does."

Jess pushed her hair out of her face. It was looking a lot less coiffed today, and it softened her thin, harsh features. "Okay, how about Diana? Diana is in control of her life. Her company is totally rocking it."

Mac chuckled and pulled the strudel plate closer. Cut them both another slice. "All that means is she's headed for a big fat unexpected detour."

Jess dropped her fork and gave Mac a worried look.

"That doesn't mean it's something bad, but it always happens. Life doesn't like slow and steady. No matter how much you want it to. How much you plan, prepare, persevere. It just has a way of knocking you on your ass. Sometimes for the worse, like Allie's husband dying, and sometimes for the good, like getting you to eat a second piece of strudel . . .

"Even keeping a lighthouse, day after day, year after year, where things were most unlikely to change, I've had my share of bumps in the road, ships in the night, storms, and . . ." She shook her head.

"But you stayed here."

"I found what I needed to find here and it was Lighthouse Beach. Most people need to find something that isn't a place; they find sanctuary here, it provides the safety to look at things in new ways, and then they move on. Some don't even know what's happened to them while they were here.

"But those who do know have a power they didn't have before." Which was a bunch of malarkey, but Mac figured Jess needed all the help she could get.

"And what about Lillo? She doesn't talk about herself. Doesn't really reminisce. She left, but she's back. Is it because what she needs to find is in Lighthouse Beach?"

"That remains to be seen. Now finish up your coffee, I gotta take the van to get a new tire before Doc has a fit."

Jess took their plates and cups to the sink. "Thinking about getting away had become such an obsession; this road trip seemed like an answer to my prayers. I'd like to think it would be good for the others, too. But I'm afraid it's going to turn into something scarier. Not just for me, but for everybody."

"Nothing is too scary if you're with people you can trust. Now skedaddle. I have work to do."

Chapter 9

Diana carried three mugs of coffee out to the deck. "Dee-luxe accommodations." She set the mugs on a wooden table next to a plate of wannabe bagels, cream cheese, and fruit, and looked out at the view. The sun was already warming the air, there was just a tiny breeze, the gulls were wheeling overhead, and the waves created a gentle, rhythmic ripple as the tide withdrew. "Have either of you seen Jess this morning?"

"I heard her get up a couple of hours ago," Lillo said from the chaise she was sitting in. She took a mug and handed it to Allie. Took another for herself. "She probably went over to Mac's for coffee."

"I hope she's okay," Allie said.

"Mac is good for what ails you," Lillo said.

"It *is* rather relaxing," Diana agreed as she perched one hip on the deck railing. She fiddled with her phone. "It would be even more relaxing if I could get a decent signal and get my updates over with. You know you have lousy cell reception here?"

"Yeah, it seems to change with the wind, though everyone

says it doesn't work like that. It does here. You can usually get through by the back door, or if you stand away from the stove in the kitchen; the other rooms suck. Sometimes you can get it out here. Not happening?"

"Not. I got through once, but the call was dropped. Nada since then."

"There's pretty decent reception at the gift shop. It doesn't open until after lunch but Mac would let you in. A couple other places in town have random hot spots if you want to try one of those."

"Dressed like this?" Diana stood long enough to reveal her bikini and gooseflesh.

Lillo shrugged. "It *is* kind of tiny. Do people wear bikinis to spas? I thought it was all big towels and cucumber slices."

"It is, but there's a pool at the hotel. Not that it looks like I'll be getting there. And don't tell me I'm free to go."

"I wasn't going to. Try down on the beach over by the lighthouse jetty. You'll at least be able to hear the caller; they may get waves in the background, but it usually works."

"Needs must . . ." Diana snagged a sprig of grapes and walked down the steps to the sand. She'd been surprised this morning that it actually felt like summer—at least in the sun. She'd never thought of Maine as a place to sunbathe, but it was pretty delightful, not hot and sweaty, but pleasant.

She trekked out to the jetty, munching on grapes and trying to balance in the shifting sand, which was more like rocks than sand. Definitely not the Caribbean honeymoon that Jess had been planning. She popped the last grape in her mouth and made the call while she finished chewing.

The call connected. "Hallelujah!"

"Where the heck are you? Some third-world country?" Her assistant, Maya, was urban through and through.

"I seem to be in the boonies. You have to chase the cell reception. They say it's the wind. Then they tell me not to believe them."

"But where?"

"Someplace in Maine. But as far as you know, I'm still in Kennebunkport."

"That explains it. Did you tell anyone where you were going?"

"Only you. Shit. Why?"

"Because of the continuous calls from the Parkers and from James Beckman all day yesterday . . . they have suddenly stopped. So you can expect incoming any minute now."

"Damn. They probably found Jess's phone. She threw it out of the car so she wouldn't cave. Can you believe it?"

"Good on her. Maybe you can get her to come work for you."

"Working on it. They've already badgered the woman who lives here. It's only a matter of time until they figure out the rest. I'll have to go rogue. I'll call you from the new number. Anything else?"

"No. Go. Enjoy. And if you do see Jimmy boy, kick him where it counts for me."

Diana grinned. She loved her staff. She'd stolen half of them from the company she'd left to start her own app development company. Actually, she hadn't even asked them to bail with her. They'd come of their own accord after she was already gone. No lawsuits for Diana.

"Sounds like a plan on both counts. Talk to you soon." She closed the call. Damn the Parkers and their network of scumbags. She turned back to the deck, stopped, blinked, forgot all about the impending disaster of discovery.

"Hold on, Cinderella," she said. *That can't be. Oh, but it is, a prince on a white horse. Galloping along the shoreline.* Okay, maybe the horse was more gray than white, and the prince was just a man, but pretty buff—at a distance at least.

And for a change she found herself watching the horse. A flood of memories rushed in, stopping her in her trek across the sand. When was the last time she'd been riding? Work, designing and building her company, several disastrous love—she wouldn't call them affairs . . . flings? And two equally disastrous marriages—hadn't left much time for fun.

She still owned two horses. She'd been boarding them at a stable on Long Island and paid her niece to exercise them. Actually, the little darling thought they belonged to her now.

She watched the rider as he slowed the horse to a walk then turned away from the shore and followed a path into the woods and finally disappeared from view.

Diana was jerked back to the present. She trotted back to the deck just as Jess walked through the sliding glass door.

"Update from New York. Your parents have stopped calling the office."

"I'm sorry. What did Maya tell them?"

"That I was in Kennebunkport at a wedding." Diana laughed. She couldn't help it. "But they may be closing in."

"Did I screw up? I didn't call them. I promise."

"Jess, stop blaming yourself. You know how these things work, that's why you unloaded your phone." Diana looked squarely at Jess and lied. "Maya's afraid someone leaked my cell number to James. It was probably my latest whatever, the no-good, two-timing, former whatever he was, Johnnie-Come-Lately Ashton Crawford. I knew I should never have gone out with him, that he'd screw me in more ways than one. And bingo. I'd forgotten that he's friends with the fornicating fiancé. Girls, never go out with a man named Ashton."

"Or James, for that matter," Jess added.

"Or James," Diana agreed. "Or Randall."

"Who is Randall?" asked Lillo. She couldn't help herself.

"Her ex," Jess answered.

"One of my exes, for my sins."

"You were married twice?"

"Yep. But Randall was one of those rebound what-happens-in-Vegas kind of things. Didn't last six months."

"Think you'll try again?" Allie asked.

"Not me. You know what they say. Third time's a charm. And that, my dears, has kept me single."

"Well," Jess said. "If you'd stop dating yourself, you might find someone compatible."

"Thanks but no. The upside of dating someone just as driven, busy, and 'married' to their career as I am is that they don't have time to get in your way."

"That's pitiful," Jess said.

"Says pot to kettle." Diana leaned back against the railing. "If we've finished dissecting my less-than-successful love life, I suggest we—"

"Figure out what we're going to do?" Allie asked. "Jess's parents are probably worried sick."

All three women turned to look at her.

"About their hotel bill and how this will affect their standing at the country club. They're not nice people. Sorry, Jess, but it's the truth."

Jess nodded. "They aren't. Not even to their other children, who turned out more like them."

"Sad but true," Diana said. "It's just a matter of time. Once they've wined and dined the last guests' ruffled feathers, after they fill your voice mail without you calling back, they'll get smart and make sure you're back in Boston. And when that fails they'll start getting suspicious and look for us. They may even find your phone by the side of the road."

"Can they do that?" asked Lillo.

"Sure. 'Find My Phone'? And if that's turned off, they can get someone to find it for them. Like I said, it's just a matter of time, but we can make it more difficult for them, just out of spite. I don't mind a little spite toward the Parkers, do any of you?

"No? Good. But just to save myself the aggravation, and just in case I've been outed, I'm about to jettison this number and set up one of my many dummies. And don't look aghast, Allie. It's nothing illegal; when you work in a highly competitive tech field, you gotta play Whac-A-Mole with some of the best minds in the business." She hesitated. "Or in China and the Soviet Union . . .

"So if we don't want a Parker visit in the next day or so, we need to take protective measures." She looked at the speechless group. "Unless we want to make a run for it?" she asked, only half facetiously.

Jess sank onto the nearest beach chair. "I am so screwed and I've gotten you guys into this mess because I'm such a coward. I should just go back and face them."

Allie reached over and touched her arm. "You're not going back. Not after finally getting away. You deserve to love someone who loves you for yourself."

"You're right. I do and I won't go back, but maybe I should leave. My parents are ruthless. They can hurt you. My father eats small businesses for breakfast and corporations for dinner. He has politicians and bankers under his thumb. And what he doesn't control, the Beckmans do. My father and James's father brokered this marriage, just like they do with everything else. For profit and power. And their wives make sure their social standing is the highest. They're exhausting."

Jess glanced at Lillo. "You remember how they were?"

Lillo nodded.

"They're worse now."

Diana jumped in. "Yeah, yeah, all the things that matter. I'll take them on. Are you with me or agin me?"

"I'm in," Allie said.

Lillo shrugged. *"Mi casa es su casa."*

"Good, now where can I find a prepaid phone or a landline so I can set up a new account."

"The gift shop."

"Great. I'll be right back."

"I think Mac was going to take her van over to get new tires," Jess said.

Lillo got up. "I'll come with you. I've got a key." She shrugged. "I sometimes watch the store when Mac has a tour of the lighthouse."

Diana did a double take. "You work at the gift shop, too?"

"Just help out now and again."

They stopped in the house long enough to pull shorts over their suits and for Lillo to get the key, then headed across the parking lot.

"Have you always been a gardener—slash—gift shop clerk—slash—clinic helper?"

"I do other stuff, too."

"I wouldn't be surprised. Hey, one of those jobs wouldn't be helping out at a local stable, would it?"

Lillo looked sideways at her.

"What? Not into shoveling shit?"

Lillo shrugged. "Are you into it?"

"I've shoveled my share. Haven't in a while, but I still own two horses. I wouldn't mind riding a bit while I'm here. I saw a guy riding on the edge of the woods when I was down by the jetty. And I might add, a fine figure on a horse he was."

"Aha . . . That was probably Ian, the local vet."

"Ian, the man who didn't come to dinner?"

"The very one. Where he lives used to be a stable, among other things. Now it's primarily a veterinary office. He keeps a few horses."

"Does he rent them out?"

"Um . . . I'm not sure. I believe he does on occasion. I know he gives lessons."

"Great, if he won't rent me a horse, I'll take a lesson. I don't suppose you have a spare pair of jeans lying around?"

"Not any that would be long enough for you. But the consignment shop probably does . . . if you don't mind wearing secondhand clothes."

"If they're clean. But first things first. Time to make the Parkers' lives more difficult. Then I'm going to see a man about a horse."

Lillo let them into the gift shop, where Diana wrote an IOU for the prepaid. She'd wanted to pay but didn't have the correct change and Lillo didn't want to bother with opening the cash register.

When they were back in the parking lot, Lillo pointed the way to the vet's house and office.

"You're sure you don't want to come put in a good word for me?"

"No. I think he'll be more amenable if you went alone." Lillo grasped Diana's arm. "He's perfectly safe, just a little quiet."

Diana thought that was a pretty odd thing to say, but the man was a vet, so people must go to his office all the time, and if he gave riding lessons . . . What wasn't Lillo telling her?

"Go down the road there until you see the sign for the vet. The house is about four hundred feet up the drive. I have a bike in the shed but the terrain is a little rough once you get off the paved road."

"Thanks, but I haven't honed my bike-riding skills since middle school. I'll walk." Diana started out across the pavement. At first, the walk was pleasant. The road was narrow but she didn't meet any traffic. No exhaust fumes and the only sounds were the waves off to her left and the birdcalls in the woods. The best of both natural worlds. A double nature whammy for her week off, then back to the city, where she belonged. But for now . . . she breathed in the fresh air.

She almost passed the sign that said VET. Black hand-painted letters on a weathered wooden board. No "Lighthouse Beach Animal Clinic" or "Paws for Your Pets," or any other marketable branding, just VET. And you'd have to be looking for the place to find it; someone should cut down the bush that was half-hiding it from view. And the sign itself seemed parsimonious at best. On the other hand, maybe everyone who needed a vet knew where it was.

She sighed and started up the drive. She should have worn better shoes . . . well, more durable shoes than her Jack Rogers sandals. But she hadn't thought she'd be anywhere but the yacht-club bar and the spa this week. Twice she had to stop to shake pebbles out of her sandal, and by the time she came to the end of the drive, her toes and ankles were covered in dust, which was odd since she had arrived two days ago in torrential rain.

She stepped into the clearing and stared up at the two-story wood-frame house. A little the worse for wear, with a wraparound porch that seemed to be used only for storing cardboard boxes and tarp-covered mystery items. A shame, because it was charming in a Maine country way.

There was no welcome sign, so she guessed the veterinary office was in one of the outbuildings set back from the house. She followed the clearing around the side of the house, past a woodpile higher than her head, several oil drums, and a chicken coop that looked deserted.

A stable barn was another two hundred feet farther on. A long annexed one-story building extended off to one side. It had a pedestrian door, so Diana walked up to it and turned the handle. It opened into a small room with seating along the perimeter and a desk along the back wall next to another door. The whole place looked deserted, but spotlessly clean. Not a magazine, not a brochure, not even a little bell to ring. Maybe the staff was at lunch.

She guessed the examining rooms were behind the door, but she wasn't sure she should knock. Then again, how would they know she was here if she didn't?

She knocked.

No one opened the door. She decided to look around outside. She might spot someone through the window.

Maybe he didn't work on Saturdays. But wouldn't that be his busiest day? Maybe he was still out riding. She'd wait awhile. And explore a little. She walked along the side of the building but didn't see a sign of life, though she did hear some animal sounds coming from inside.

The door was ajar, so she stuck her head in. It wasn't the stable proper but another large brightly lit room filled with cages and pens and various animals. The noise, she realized, had been coming from a pig and several piglets. There was something that might be a fox running up and down a dog run, and a cage with several perches, occupied by two bandaged really big birds. Vultures? Surely not. An eagle or a raptor. Whatever they were, they were big.

Not a vet in sight.

But she could hear someone on the other side of the wall. She slid the door open.

"Hello?" she called, sending off a chorus of animal responses that had her running into the next room in sheer fight-or-flight reaction.

It was a horse barn with stalls lining the right side along a wide center aisle. Five of the original eight or nine stalls had been refurbished, with new frame-and-brace stable doors, hinged with shiny hardware. The ones farthest away were older, duller. Several more stalls and tack, feed, and utility rooms ran along the other side of the aisle.

A work in progress. Or better days on their way down. It was hard to tell. She was intrigued. Her horses were well cared for and pampered; boarded in pristine stables with state-of-the-art training facilities. A veritable equine country club.

But there was something about this barn that spoke to her, brought back her first days in the saddle—English riding saddle, jodhpurs, helmet. All the students attentive, well groomed, like their steeds, and eager to learn. Diana's favorite moment was before all that began. When she would run out to the pasture, climb up on the old pump, and throw herself across Hopalong's back and ride him back to the stable to be saddled and reined and put through his and her paces.

She passed down the center aisle, staying close to the stalls. Peered in the first one: fresh hay, no occupant. Nor in the second stall. She walked along, listening for a sound of human activity. Hay dust tickled her nose. Shafts of light fell diagonally from high windows, spotlighting the motes of dust that seemed to hover in the air, and that made the rest of the interior all the more dark and mysterious. She heard the scrape of metal somewhere in the barn.

A whinny came from the next stall, followed by a chestnut muzzle with a star down the front.

"Hello, beauty." Diana ran her hand down the horse's muzzle. He lifted his nose, rubbed it against her open palm.

Another nose appeared in the adjacent stall. This one a bay sprinkled with gray hairs. The horse looked curiously at her

then lowered his head and returned to his old-age rumina-
tions.

But two stalls down, the gray she'd seen along the crest of
the beach was waiting for her. Head lifted, expecting attention.
She walked on without looking his way. And was rewarded with
an energetic push with his nose. It was strong enough to make
her stagger forward.

She turned back to the culprit. "You're a rogue, aren't you?"
She had reached forward to give him a healthy pat when a man
strode down the aisle toward her.

"Can I help you?"

Diana turned slowly. He didn't sound like he wanted to help
her, but she would give him the benefit of the doubt.

He looked like he wanted to kill her. But God, was he handsome. Except for the scar down his cheek. His eyes were dark,
deep; sunken as if he'd been pulling all-nighters. But what the
hey. The rest of him wasn't shabby. And besides, she just wanted
a horse.

He stood facing her, intensity incarnate. Not someone to
meet alone in a dark alley, but in a stable full of calm, well-
cared-for horses? It worked for her.

"Actually, I came to see if you rented out horses."

His eyes narrowed, dark eyebrows dipped toward the center
of his nose. "No."

"No?"

"No. I don't."

"For an hour or two?"

He did a slow pan from her face to her Jack Rogers sandals.
Shook his head.

This was more than crusty old New Englander. Besides, he
wasn't old, she didn't think; the phrase "old before his time"

came to mind. Probably forty? Maybe not even. It was hard to tell behind that scowl.

"Hmm, Lillo said you gave lessons."

"I do."

"Then I'll take a lesson."

"Not in those clothes."

Diana sighed. "Obviously not."

His eyes narrowed even farther, until they were almost closed, and Diana wondered if maybe he was in pain. His hand reached out, not toward her but toward the gray, who stretched his neck to meet him, drawing the hand and the man closer until he leaned his forehead against the horse's throat.

It was a moment so intimate that Diana was startled off her game and could only watch, voyeur to a silent communication that lasted only for a timeless moment before they broke apart and the man said:

"I don't think so."

"How about this? I'll help you exercise your stable and I'll pay you to let me do it."

"There are other stables better equipped on the highway."

"But I'm staying in Lighthouse Beach."

"Where?"

Not much on social skills.

"At—"

"Lillo's," he finished for her.

"How did you know?"

He shrugged. "If you come back tomorrow morning in riding clothes, I'll let you exercise one of the horses."

She nodded, stepped away.

"If you pass muster."

She saluted.

"You'll have to do your own saddling and bridling."

"No problem."

"And muck out the stall."

"Looking forward to it. How about eleven?"

"I have rounds."

"Okay. Eleven thirty." She did a military toe turn and marched out of the barn.

"If I don't have any new patients," he called after her.

"Aye, aye, *capitaine.*"

"Fifty bucks."

She toodled her fingers at him and slipped out the door.

The walk back to the cottage was faster than the walk up, and Diana wasn't quite sure if it was because she wanted to get away from Ian Lachlan or because she was anxious to buy jeans and come back.

LILLO, ALLIE, AND Jess were just coming out of the cottage door when Lillo saw Diana walking down the road from Ian's. She waved her over. "We left you a note. We're going into town."

"Good. I need riding clothes." Diana added herself to the group. "I just had the most unusual encounter." She recounted it to the others as they walked toward the two-block shopping district.

"Is that what he said? Riding clothes?" Lillo asked.

"First he said, 'Not in those clothes' . . . well, duh, and then he said 'in riding clothes.'"

"I doubt if he meant jodhpurs and velvet hunting jacket. And he has helmets there. He said he'd take you riding?"

"Well, after much negotiation, we cut a deal. He said I could exercise the horses with him and muck out the stable, if I paid him."

"Weird." Lillo wondered if this was an attempt on Ian's part to be sociable—unlikely. Humorous? Even more unlikely. Or to be nice to one of Lillo's friends? That seemed just as unlikely.

"Another crusty New Englander?" Allie asked.

"Yeah, just like the doc, only this one was even more amazing looking than the crusty young physician. What? You only allow good-looking men in Lighthouse Beach?"

"I think you just met all two of them," Lillo said. "Though actually we have some decent-looking guys, the ones who still have their teeth anyway."

Allie's mouth opened.

"Just kidding. You'll get to meet the rest of the locals tomorrow night when Mac has her 'gang bangah.'"

Allie's mouth opened a little wider.

"It's Mac's little joke, because she holds a welcoming barbecue whenever the bikers come to town for the bikers and their host families."

"So what is their deal, really?" asked Diana. "I don't know many people who can take off months at a time and still hold down a job."

"It changes. Whoever can get away and wants to go on a road trip. The only two steadies are Doc Hartley and Doc Clancy. Doc Clancy was Ned's—Doc Hartley's—mentor."

"His name is Ned? That's so old-fashioned," Jess said.

"Don't you remember him?" Lillo asked. "He used to help Doc Melville out at the clinic."

Jess shook her head. "I just remember that beanpole—oh my God, that's him?"

Lillo laughed. "Yep."

"But doesn't he have a practice somewhere?"

"He's a staff surgeon in Portland. But he always takes the summer to travel up and down the coast with his band of merry men—and sometimes women."

Diana raised a skeptical eyebrow. "He can hardly make a living when everything is free."

"That's why he's a staff surgeon. He works on a specific schedule and blocks out times for his travels. The hospital supports the project. Saves them from a lot of last-minute emergency surgeries if Ned can get to them before it's an actual emergency."

"Interesting people you have here. What's Ian-who-didn't-come-to-dinner-and-is-a-vet's story?"

Lillo looked away. She and Ian were two broken souls and she certainly wouldn't reveal either of their stories to the others. She shrugged. "You'll have to ask him. I know he met Doc in college and years later he came to town and bought my parents' house and settled down."

"That was your house? The stables and the outbuildings?"

"Yep. I grew up there."

"Huh. Wife? Kids?"

"What?" Lillo shook her head. "No, but, Diana, he doesn't really . . ."

"Like women? Such a waste."

"No, or actually, I don't know. The subject never came up. It's just that he isn't very sociable. And he can be moody."

"That sounds ominous," Jess said. "Moody as in dangerous?"

"Oh no, at least I've never even seen him lose his temper. But he does get on with animals better than with people."

"I'll keep that in mind. Now, where is Carroll's Consignment Store?"

They passed a gift shop, a drugstore, an empty boarded-up store, then the grocery and liquor store they'd visited yesterday.

"Cute town," Diana said. "And quaint, but deader than a doornail. What you need is a good publicist and several coats of paint, though maybe you're not interested in tourists."

"We have to be," Lillo said. "Fishing has dried up, so to

speak. But there's nothing really to see but the old lighthouse, just like hundreds of other abandoned lighthouses along the eastern coast."

They came to the end of the block and Lillo stopped to look both ways even though there wasn't a car or truck in sight. Two doors later they came to Carroll's Consignment.

Diana stopped them at the door.

"You're having second thoughts?" Lillo asked.

"It's a used-clothing store," Diana said.

"That's what 'consignment' means."

"I know. I just wasn't picturing it."

"Do you need riding clothes or not, because we're not driving over an hour to the nearest mall."

Diana sighed. "All right, but if it's gross, we'll just thank Ms. Carroll and get the hell out." After a look at the others, she grasped the knob. "All right, troops, we're going in."

Chapter 10

Ned kept a supportive arm around Francine Hallerin as he helped her into the back of the ambulance that was going to carry her husband to the nearest hospital.

"We got to him in time," he reassured her. "You were right to insist on bringing him here when you did." He gave her a squeeze. "Agnes called your son at work and told him to meet you at the hospital."

She waved at him, unable to speak, her face twisted in fear beneath her summer hat as the ambulance doors closed behind her.

They'd been on their way to the Presbyterian pancake breakfast when her husband suddenly felt short of breath. Instinct had her turn away from church and breakfast and into the clinic's parking area. She'd saved his life . . . so far anyway.

The siren squealed to life and Ned turned to go back into the clinic. He was met by a crowd of patients.

"He gonna be all right, Doc?"

"Sure hope so." Ned didn't know. But at least the ambulance

had equipment he didn't. He'd kept Zeke Hallerin alive until they'd arrived. The EMTs would have to do the rest until they reached the hospital.

"We don't know what we'd do without you, Doc."

"Hope you never get tired of us."

Several people patted him on the back as he walked past them before they followed him back inside to wait their own turns with the doctor.

"You just take your time, Doc. Have a cup of coffee. We'll wait."

"Thanks, Sam. I could use a cup." Sometimes he wished he could just turn over the "Closed" sign and spend a Saturday watching whatever sport was on television and drinking beer all day. But he never did. When he wasn't working at the hospital, he was helping out in a clinic or doing what he loved doing, riding his bike to the places that really needed him. God knew he wasn't making any money at it. He wouldn't retire with a pension, or amassed real estate holdings, or even a fat IRA.

Agnes already had a cup ready for him when he passed through the waiting room and into the back.

"Thanks. You'd better call Clancy at the hospital and tell him we've another patient coming in by ambulance. He'll want to check on them."

"And stay with Francine until Zeke's out of the woods. Don't you worry about them, I'll get on it. You just take a minute, then do what you been doing at the pace you can. That crowd isn't going anywhere."

No, it would just keep growing. Some of his patients just waited until he and Clancy got to town to take care of their health problems, out of laziness or because they were too busy to consult another doctor. But there were others who couldn't or wouldn't go to a mainland doctor for anything.

He knew he was reaching people who wouldn't normally be reached by the standard medical community. Like Mr. Hallerin. He would never have lived long enough to get to the hospital.

Being able to do this was pretty special and he loved what he did with the people he rode with. But with Clancy staying an hour away at the hospital, Ned wished for one more doctor and a couple less plumbers or mechanics.

He took his coffee back to the kitchen, now mostly a storage room, and sat at the one clear space at the table. The coffee was nice and strong. Agnes, angel that she was, made good coffee, was an excellent office manager, and had a better bedside manner than most nurses.

A nurse. Maybe he could find some biker nurse who would be interested in doing a couple of summer tours with them. A nurse practitioner would be even better.

Ned laughed at himself. Might as well ask for a mobile surgery. Not on his salary, plus then he'd be stuck driving an RV and his bike would sit idle. He didn't think of himself as a selfish man, but his bike was where he drew the line.

That's how a good symbiotic relationship worked. Mutual needs met. His expertise helped people and kept his bike tuned. And his bike kept him sane enough to help others.

He laughed again. Stopped. His amusement cut off like an oxygen feed yanked away. He had nothing to complain about.

LILLO WAS A little embarrassed about taking her friends into the consignment shop, especially when she'd spied the dress she'd been planning to wear to the wedding hanging in the window. Of course, the others had never seen it. So they didn't have to know.

"That dress in the window was kind of cute," Allie said as they all stood just inside the door.

"This might be fun," Jess said.

Lillo made some noncommittal noise and prayed that Barbara wouldn't let slip that Lillo had borrowed the dress for the wedding. Barbara did things like that, and you never knew if it was just her being enthusiastic or a subtle passive-aggressive dig she just couldn't resist.

"Well, come on," Jess said. "We all need some clothes to wear while we're here."

Jess and Allie went inside. Lillo followed Diana, who stopped just inside the doorway to look around.

"Are you sure the clothes are safe?" Diana asked, looking around at the tables stacked with folded tees and the shelves of jeans, the racks of dresses, pants, jackets, blouses, and the occasional poncho.

"What do you mean?" Lillo never bought clothes. And she rarely went into the consignment shop. She'd just feel weird walking through town wondering if someone she passed was thinking, *That outfit looked so much better on me.* Or *Isn't that [insert name's] old coat? I thought she gave it to Goodwill.* Or some other embarrassing comment.

"You know . . ." Diana lowered her voice. "Fumigated?"

"Oh, you mean are they clean? Of course. Barbara always has things washed or cleaned before she puts them out for sale. And she only takes clothes in good condition. And some of the clothes are pretty nice. Maybe not designer fashion, which we don't have too much call for in Lighthouse Beach. But certainly respectable labels. Of course, there's a lot of junk and just funky bad taste," she added hastily, and waved to Barbara, who was hurrying toward them from the back of the store.

Barb Carroll was in her late forties, fairly voluptuous, and wore her clothes, according to Mac, "like she was shrink-wrapped into them." Today she was wearing a navy blue knit skirt with a magenta cowl-neck tee and heels high enough to augment her five-foot-two frame.

"Lillo, you've brought your friends from the wedding," she said, making it sound as if she were a hostess instead of a retailer.

The other three smiled; Lillo realized they were all expecting her to say or do something. "Uh, yeah—Jess, Allie, and Diana. Diana needs something she can ride in."

"Ah." Barbara's head swiveled from one to the other, then settled on Diana.

"I need jeans," Diana said, eyeing first Barb and then the stacks of folded denim suspiciously. "Size twenty-eight to thirty."

"Over here. Would that be a four or six or eight?"

Diana rolled her eyes at Lillo and followed Barbara over to the shelves of jeans.

Allie had already discovered the children's section and was rummaging through stacks of children's T-shirts. Jess wandered off in the opposite direction. Lillo just stood there, amazed. Not one under-the-breath comment. Not one whispered "Let's get out of here." Diana might be determined to get jeans, but Allie and Jess were happily searching through the crammed display tables and racks.

Lillo wasn't a shopper at the best of times. She had a roomful of old clothes that she should probably donate. She knew a portion of the consignment-shop sales went to the community center. She turned to the nearest table. Women's shorts and tops. A sign that read HOT SUMMER BEACHWEAR surrounded by hand-drawn pictures of beach balls and flip-flops.

Barbara, carrying several pairs of jeans over her arm, took Diana to the back of the store, where a row of three changing booths was curtained by colorful sailcloth panels.

As soon as she got Diana and the jeans settled into one of the cubicles, she came directly up to Lillo. "Your friends are so . . . so . . ."

"Not like me?" Lillo finished.

"Oh, you." Barbara gave her a playful jab in the ribs. At least Lillo thought it was playful. With Barb, you couldn't always tell. "You would have rocked that dress at the wedding; though if I had known how rich they were, I would have loaned you something from my personal closet. The blonde—Jess, is it? That has to be a—" She named some designer Lillo had never heard of.

Jess turned around at the sound of her name.

"Find something you like?" Barbara asked, not even having the grace to be embarrassed. She hurried over.

Lillo wandered over to the plate-glass window and looked out at the street. She was standing there when an ambulance drove past, siren blasting. You didn't see many ambulances in Lighthouse Beach. There was a police station and EMT about a half hour away. Must be something serious. They were probably coming from the clinic.

And Clancy was still at the hospital with Mrs. Grotsky and her son. An emergency would certainly set Doc back in his schedule of patients. Was she being an ass for not offering to help out with nonmedical stuff? She didn't want to have anything to do with medicine ever again. But did that mean she couldn't be a conduit for supplies, a gofer? She did that as a teenager with no experience. But at the mere thought of walking into the clinic, she broke out in a sweat. Besides, Ned had said he could get someone else.

They could make do without her.

"Well," Diana said from the back of the store. "What do you think?" She twirled around to show off faded jeans, with one distressed knee, which—Lillo couldn't tell—was either a fashion statement or the result of long wear. She wore a plaid shirt, sleeves rolled up to the elbow, and opened down the front to show the silk tee she'd worn into the store.

Jess laughed. "All you need is a ten-gallon hat and a straw to stick between your teeth."

"And boots," Allie added. "Pointy toes and tooled leather."

Diana made a face and turned to Lillo. "Will these pass as appropriate 'riding clothes'?"

"They're fine, but you may need a belt."

Diana yanked the jeans up. "I know. The problem is to get them big enough so you don't lose circulation in your legs while clutching a saddle but small enough to make an impression and not have them slide down your butt."

"Or when you bend over. Ugh," Allie added.

"Bend from the knees, my dear," Diana said haughtily, "and they'll never mistake you for a plumber." Hoisting her jeans up, she began perusing the belt display.

"I'll just look for a smaller size," Barbara said.

They left the store a half hour later, much poorer than when they went in and Barb very happy. Jess and Allie had bought Lighthouse Beach shorts and tees, long pants, and sweatshirts. Diana was fully outfitted in several pairs of jeans, and tees and windbreakers, and directions to Seaside General Store.

At the general store they loaded up on sneakers and socks for Diana, sunscreen, bug spray, sun hats, and beach flip-flops, which Lillo could have told them would be totally useless on her coarse sand beach, but they were having too much fun for her to bring them down to earth. Let them enjoy this time while they had it. Lillo had no doubt that the Parkers wouldn't let Jess go without a fight.

THEY WERE LOADED down with parcels when they decided to call it a day.

"Not a cab in sight," Diana moaned, but only halfheartedly, Lillo thought. Lillo hadn't bought a thing. Of course, she lived here, so she had access to all her possessions. Still, she wished for a few moments that, just for fun, she'd had ready cash to spend.

Even when they had insisted on buying her a wide-brimmed straw hat, she put it back on the shelf. What was wrong with her that she couldn't let her friends buy her a present? To show their appreciation of her generosity, which she didn't feel. *Generosity?* She would have sent them on their way if Diana and Mac hadn't joined forces against her.

She was glad they decided to stay . . . now. She wished . . . well, it didn't matter what she wished.

"How good is the pizza?"

"What?" Lillo asked, jolted back to the present.

Diana pointed to the sign written across the window of SAL's BEST PIZZA IN LIGHTHOUSE BEACH.

"It's the best pizza place in town," Lillo said seriously.

"But? I'm sensing a 'but' here."

"It's the only pizza place in town ever since Sam's Pizza closed. For a while we had dueling Toscani brothers' pizzerias, but then Sam moved to Portland and Sal became the undisputed champ. But to answer your question, it's pretty good."

"Well, pretty good is good enough for me. I'm starving."

"Should we call Mac and invite her to join us?" Allie suggested as they wrestled their packages through the door.

"She's not a pizza lover," Lillo said as she followed them inside, and bumped into Allie, who had stopped suddenly. "Keep moving up front."

"This looks just like an Italian pizza parlor," Diana said.

"Probably because it's called Toscani's?" Lillo nudged her forward.

Diana made a face at her over her shoulder. "Doesn't mean they know the difference between fusilli and fettuccini. His name could really be Sal Yankowicz."

"O ye of little faith." Lillo slipped through the group and led the way to one of the red upholstered booths.

"Yo, Lee-loh," Howie King hollered from the round booth in the corner where he was sitting with four other members of the biker and Mr. Fixit gang.

"How-wee," she intoned back, and went over to say hi. Howie was a good six foot three, with a wisp of hair in the center of a bald pate, big ears, and huge hands that could solve the most delicate wiring problem.

"How ya been?"

"Good. You?"

"Good."

She said hi to the other guys: Roy, the carpenter of the group; Assam, the painter-spackler, small-repairs guy.

"And this is Nando. CPA, financial adviser, and car mechanic extraordinaire. His first trip with us."

They smiled and nodded to each other.

"And Jerry, your plumbing specialist."

Over some mild joking they said hello.

"I see you brought some friends," Howie said, looking over Lillo's shoulder at Diana, Jess, and Allie.

"They're visiting from out of town."

Howie lowered his voice. "Didn't think they were from around here." He winked.

Lillo called the women over. Introductions and small talk ensued, and with the promise to meet again at Mac's barbecue, the four women retreated to their own table.

"Does everyone know everyone in town?" Diana asked once they were seated.

"Pretty much. And everyone's business, in case you're wondering."

"So-o-o-o, they know about . . ." Diana gestured around the table.

"My guess is yes. Not that Mac or Doc would gossip . . . much, but people are pretty good at piecing things together. On occasion, speculation does get out of hand."

Jess groaned, but Lillo noticed it didn't sound nearly as heartfelt as the ones the day before.

"They may gossip among themselves, but they are extremely loyal to each other, and that includes friends of friends—if you're worried about gossip."

"Huh," Diana said. "Does that mean no one is on the phone in order to win big with the Parkers for giving out the location of their daughter?"

Lillo shook her head. "Very unlikely." The townspeople fought and bickered and held grudges for a while, but they never let each other down. Lillo had grown up thinking this was the way all towns were. She'd been wrong. Really wrong.

They ordered salads and Sal's Special Pizza without the anchovies by unanimous consent. Lillo hadn't been to Sal's in ages, and when the salads came, she noticed Sal had upgraded from iceberg to iceberg with some field greens mixed in. Keeping up with the times, she guessed. She'd always liked iceberg herself.

But the pizza was as good as she remembered it, and after a "Told you so," she settled into enjoying her slice.

The bikers left with waves and promised to see them at the barbecue. The girls just waved and made affirmative noises through mouthfuls of Sal's special pie.

"Okay, that was good," Diana said when they were back on the street. "Would have been even better—"

"With a good Chianti," Allie said. "We may have to go back before I—oh, rats. I have to go back on Monday."

"Really?" Diana said as they began walking back toward the cottage. "Can't you stay a couple of more days at least? If it's the money—"

"It isn't the money, and Maria, my mother-in-law, said it would be fine. Actually, she told me to stay as long as I like. I should have some fun. Gino is doing fine."

"Well, there you go," Diana said.

Lillo thought she was being gratuitously obtuse, because even she could see that Allie was worried about something.

Or was Lillo the one being obtuse, expecting ulterior motives from everyone?

The women grew silent, replete with food and concentrating on holding their packages as the wind grew stronger and they walked downhill to the cottage.

"Getting a bit nippy," Diana said.

"Definitely sweater weather," Jess agreed. "And it was so warm earlier. I remember that it would do this; we'd be swimming in the sun in the afternoon, and back to long pants and sweatshirts at night."

"Yep," Lillo said. "And there's a wind tonight. At least the cottage is sheltered by the two jetties. Keeps the wind down to a bluster . . . most of the time. It can get intense out on the water and up on the bluffs."

Everyone dumped their packages, changed into warmer clothes, and met back in the kitchen.

"Since we drank seltzer—Sal should really get a liquor license—I vote for a full-bodied Cabernet in front of the picture window." Diana waggled her eyebrows at Allie, who had seemed quiet since returning home.

Allie just smiled back and went to pick out the bottle of wine.

They gathered at the picture window, Jess and Diana on the couch, Lillo in her reading chair, and Allie in the wingback. And it struck Lillo that they had already claimed their space, settled in like maybe they belonged there.

She sighed and looked out at the night. The sky behind the lighthouse was already growing dark as the sun set. The lighthouse stood tall and dark and empty. Lillo could remember when it was still an active lighthouse. In the winter she could see it through the trees from her bedroom window. Far enough away not to keep her awake at night, but close enough to be comforting. A beacon that said home.

"Ah," Diana said. "I think this might be better than the spa."

That made them all laugh until Diana said, "Look."

They all looked out the window.

"What? Shooting star?" asked Jess. "I don't see anything."

"There. Up in the tower."

Lillo saw it, too. A flicker of light high up in the lantern room. "What the—"

"There it is again," Diana said, pointing, though by now they all knew where to look.

"It's probably Mac. She sometimes does the rounds, especially in summer. Though she doesn't usually go all the way up to the lantern room. A lot of nights she sleeps out there. If that's her, she'll be there all night; the tide's coming in."

The tide was already washing over the jetty walkway that led to the lighthouse.

"Why didn't they just build the jetty higher?" Diana asked. "It doesn't seem like good planning."

"Originally the only way to get to the lighthouse was by boat. The jetty was an afterthought. And I don't think they planned on the water level rising as much as it has since they built it. In those days, most lighthouse keepers kept rowboats.

Mac still has one, but she's getting a little old to be rowing in the ocean at night. At least Clancy put a stop to that a few years back."

"There's no electricity?" Jess asked. "Mac really stays there with only a flashlight?" She shuddered.

"She has a lantern."

"If that's Mac in the tower," Diana said, "who is *that*?"

They all turned to look at the jetty, where a bobbing light was working its way slowly toward the lighthouse.

"That's Mac," Lillo said, and jumped from her chair. "Those damn boys must be in the tower again. She's going after them. She'll never make it across, the rocks are wet. The crazy old—" She didn't finish her sentence but grabbed a torch from the closet and ran to the front door. It was the fastest way to the jetty. She was vaguely aware of the others running behind her.

"Mac!" she yelled. "Stop."

Mac was a mere silhouette by now; she seemed to hesitate, then suddenly the flashlight went out.

IAN HANDED Doc a beer and sat down at the table. "I met one of Lillo's guests this morning."

"Which one?"

"Didn't get her name. Tall, dark hair. Has an attitude."

"Ah, the CEO."

Ian took a long draft of his beer. "Figures."

"And how did you meet the lovely Diana?"

"Her name is Diana? We didn't get to introductions."

Doc smiled around the neck of the bottle. "Why am I not surprised?"

"A misnomer, if you ask me."

"A goddess maybe. She's pretty decent to look at," said Ned. "But not of the hunt."

"Not a goddess, and I bet the only hunting she's ever done is for heads."

Doc laughed. "A fortuitous meeting. She seems to have brought out the best in you."

"Funny," Ian said, scowling. "She wants to ride."

"And I thought she'd come for your handsome face and winning personality."

"I told her it would cost fifty bucks for each half hour and she'd have to muck out the stables."

"And she said?"

"The bitch of it is, she didn't blink. She said she'd see me tomorrow at eleven thirty . . . well, that was the gist anyway. She won't show up."

"I wouldn't be so sure," Doc said. "Better wear a clean shirt."

Chapter 11

Lillo's heart was pounding harder than her feet on the pavement. Mac had no business going out in the dark during a rising tide. None of them did. She sucked in a breath and pushed herself harder.

"Wouldn't it be faster across the beach?" Diana yelled.

Lillo couldn't even answer. The gravelly sand would slow them down though the distance was shorter.

She reached the gate and scooted around it. Stopped long enough to shine her flashlight over the rocks. Caught Mac in its beam. She was bent nearly double trying to keep her balance against the gusts of wind and the slippery surface of the paved path to the lighthouse. "Mac. Come back!"

Mac raised her hand but kept going.

"Mac, stop!"

Diana slipped past the gate. "What can we do?"

"Stay here. Be ready to call for help if we need it. Hopefully we won't."

"I have my phone. Be careful."

Lillo stepped onto the jetty. The waves washed over her feet. Damn. If she didn't hurry, both she and Mac would be spending the night at the lighthouse. She put her shoulder into the wind, and keeping the flashlight beam alternating between the path before her and Mac's progress, she pushed ahead.

Mac was moving slowly and Lillo caught up to her halfway across. She grabbed her arm. "What the hell are you doing?"

"It's those damn boys."

As she said it, they heard a motor catch and the sound of an engine puttered above the sound of the waves. Lillo gritted her teeth. "They're gone, the little shits. Come on, let's go back."

"I should check—" Mac had to yell to be heard.

The water was rising fast, as it always did. A few more minutes and they'd have to swim for shore.

"It'll wait until tomorrow." Lillo pulled at Mac, but she resisted and they both almost went down.

"Can we please go back? My shoes are getting ruined."

Mac nodded.

Lillo held on to her and they slid and stumbled their way back to dry land. By the time they reached the others, water had covered the jetty.

Jess and Allie each took one of Mac's arms and led her toward the gift shop.

Lillo and Diana were left looking at each other.

"Does she do that often?"

"Mainly in summer. Season for camping, hiking, and vandalizing."

They started toward the gift shop, Lillo's shoes squishing with each step.

"Is that why you stay?" Diana asked.

"No. Clancy is here off and on during the winter. And like I said, they're mainly kids from town who are out of school with nothing to do and think it's cool to climb the lighthouse at night."

"What about a lock?"

"It *is* locked. They just break the windows. And climb up. They always find a way. Once someone stole the key. We had the locks changed. And they still got in."

"They come by boat?"

"Yeah, or they slip through the gate like we did tonight. There needs to be a better barrier but there's hardly enough money to keep the lighthouse from being razed. No one wants that. Plus, it was Mac's life. Still is."

They reached Mac's back door to find light flooding in from the kitchen and an argument in progress. When they stepped into the kitchen, Mac turned on Lillo. "And don't you start."

Lillo threw open her hands in a helpless gesture.

Mac exhaled. "Jess and Allie are already on my case."

"Well, it's dangerous to go out alone at night, regardless of whether the tide is in or out," Allie said, giving Mac a stern look.

"As well as stupid," Lillo added.

Mac glared at her. "With all the excitement, it just crept up on me."

"What did?" Lillo asked.

"The summer. And damn them if they aren't starting early this year. Is school out already?"

Lillo nodded. "Looks like it."

"I'll just have to sleep out there until summer is over."

"There's no electricity, no running water. What are you going to do, hang your butt over the windowsill when you have to pee?"

"Lillo!" Jess said.

"You gonna pay the insurance if somebody gets hurt?" Mac

countered. "If we can even keep the insurance. They'll deny us coverage and they'll close us down completely."

"You need a better security system." Lillo had been party to this argument time and time again. Sometimes Clancy joined in, sometimes it was Ned. Mac was determined to keep the lighthouse. The town was determined to keep it. It was a landmark, but there wasn't a penny in the coffers to keep it up.

They should have sold it to that New York billionaire when they had the chance. It was a whim on his part and evidently the whim had passed. They hadn't had another offer.

"Well, they won't come back tonight," Lillo said. "Tomorrow we'll make a plan. But no going back out there tonight."

Mac looked everywhere but at Lillo.

"Promise me."

"Oh, all right. Now you four go on and let me get back to what I was doing before those damn kids interrupted me."

"What was that?"

"Looking for the cocoa."

"I saw it when we were here the other day," Allie said. "In the cabinet by the fridge."

Mac went over to the cabinet. Opened the door, peered inside.

"There," Allie said. "There. Next to the tea bags."

Mac reached up and fumbled for the canister of cocoa.

"Let me." Allie reached over and pulled it from the shelf.

"Thank you, dear. Think I must be getting shorter in my old age. Now I'm gonna have myself some cocoa and go to bed."

The four women filed out the door.

"Want us to turn off the porch light?" Lillo called.

"I'll get it. You gals go have some fun."

Fun was the last thing on Lillo's mind when they reached her cottage. The lights were on, the wineglasses were still half full, and she was thinking about what Diana had said about her staying because of Mac.

They returned to their same places as if they'd been sitting in the same spots for years instead of a couple of days.

"Whew," Allie said. "Does she do that often?"

"No, she usually scares them away before they get that far. She used to fire a shotgun in the air. But Clancy put an end to that." Lillo chuckled. "She's a pip. She's stubborn and speaks her mind, and doesn't mind telling you what you need or to mind your own business, but she's what they call salt of the earth, you know?"

"Beginning to," Diana said. "Well, I'm off to bed. All this fresh ocean air, heavy food, plus I want to be my best for my riding lesson tomorrow." She sashayed down the hall.

The other two soon followed. Lillo washed the wineglasses and spent a long time looking out the window at the sea. It was frightening sometimes, the sea at night. Like it could swallow you whole if you blinked for a second. Mostly it made her feel safe. But she was feeling not so safe tonight. Something in her was shifting, like the sand when she climbed a sand dune, but inside her. Not a smooth transition, but in awkward hiccups.

Was it because Mac could have literally been swept out of her life? Or because she'd let these three women into her house and unintentionally into her life? What would happen when they left? Would life go back to what it had been before they came? What if she lost Mac?

Stupid, she thought. *Big deal. You have houseguests. People do it all the time. And Mac isn't going anywhere for a long time.*

WHEN DIANA MADE her appearance at breakfast the next morning, she was dressed for riding. She found the other three in the kitchen making coffee and talking and laughing like they were at a coffee klatch. They stopped when they saw her.

"Well, la-di-da," Jess said.

"What? You never saw me in jeans before?"

"Not like those," Jess quipped.

"You mean baggy jeans and a denim shirt?" Her consignment-store jeans sagged in the butt and had to be belted at the waist. Though she had also bought another pair that fit pretty well considering someone else had already stretched them out. She was saving those for the barbecue.

She twirled, stretching her arms out like Wonder Woman. "Do you think I'm dressed appropriately for the stables?"

Lillo just stared at her. "Yeah. That works."

"Could you pour me some coffee from that carafe you're holding? I need a little jolt before I 'howdy, partner' my way over to the stables." Diana held out her mug. "Do you think he has English saddles?"

Lillo made a face. "I wouldn't count on it."

At eleven fifteen Diana began her walk up the road to the vet's. Ian Lachlan. Lillo had told her his name, but that was about it. She was a little nervous. She wanted to ride; seeing him mounted yesterday had brought back fond memories of riding. She'd have to make more of an effort to visit her own horses. How had she managed to just ignore them for the last few years?

Two words. "Start-up company." Or was that three words?

Either way, it was up and running. Surely she could loosen the reins—she smiled at herself for the apropos expression—and let someone else run some of the day-to-day operations. It would give her more time to design, which is what she really liked to do.

But today she was going to enjoy an hour out in the sunshine on the back of a horse. Hopefully not one of the old hacks she'd seen at the stables, but one with a little get-up-and-go.

She arrived at the vet's office as the door opened and a man stepped out. Ian came right behind him. He was wearing a white coat and carried an animal, a lamb or a goat maybe, in his arms, like those shepherds you saw on Christmas cards. The man ran ahead to lower the gate of a banged-up pickup truck. He unlatched the door of a mesh crate in the truck bed and the two men maneuvered the animal into it.

They said a few words, shook hands, and the man drove away.

Ian turned and walked past her without a word. She followed him into the reception room. Into the examination area, where he dumped his coat into a basket and stepped over to a large sink, ran the water until steam rose, then scrubbed his hands and arms up to the elbows while Diana watched and tried not to imagine where those hands had been this morning.

She followed him into the barn. He didn't even look back, probably hoping she would disappear if he refused to acknowledge her. Well, he'd soon learn.

Instead of opening one of the stalls and leading the horse out for her to ride, he merely tossed her a pitchfork that was leaning against the wood.

"You can start with this one. Shouldn't take more than a half hour." He walked away.

Diana started laughing. God, she was having a good time.

She saw him hesitate, then continue walking.

"Hey, don't you know never to turn your back on a woman with a pitchfork?"

He stopped completely for a second and then walked out of the barn.

"See you in thirty," she called after him, and carried the pitchfork into the first stall.

She was sitting on a bale of hay when he returned a half hour later. He looked at her, checked the first stall. Moved to the second.

"Won't find a piece of shit anywhere," she said, thinking, *You're the only one left*. But she didn't mean it. She didn't get him, but she was definitely entertained by him. The few short sentences he'd spoken in their two brief meetings told her he was no dummy. So what was his story?

"I only have trail saddles," he said without responding to her statement.

"That's fine." She stifled the urge to say, *Real riders ride English*.

She braced herself, expecting him to toss the saddle at her— not that anything would have kept her on her feet under the weight of all that leather. But he hoisted it over the half wall of the stall and went in to lead out a bay who looked like she'd been treated well, except for some scarring along her side.

Diana moved closer; the horse stepped back until she reached out her hand and stroked her flank. "What happened to her?"

"Barn fire. Not this one," was all he said, and led the horse out to be bridled and saddled.

"What's her name?"

"Princess." He said it with no intonation at all. But when Diana smiled at him, she saw one side of his mouth quiver as if he were fighting the absurdity of the sound of "Princess" on his fairly inviting lips.

Too bad he was such a grouch.

Diana stood at Princess's nose while Ian saddled her, then waited until Ian opened the stall to the gray she'd seen him ride yesterday.

He slipped a bit into the gray's mouth, then lifted his chin toward a back door.

"Aren't you going to saddle him?"

"Not today."

"Is his name Prince?" she asked, mainly just to be provoking.

"Loki."

"Loki as in the Norse god or as in an equidistant location between several points?"

He didn't bother to answer.

She just smiled complacently and led Princess out of the stable.

It was sort of like Dorothy opening the door to the land of Oz. From the insular lighting of the horse barn into the bright sunlight of an open field that stretched to the horizon on one side and was bordered by woods on the other. Outcroppings of dark granite heaved from the earth in a number of places. Closer to the barn a large paddock was freshly repaired.

Ian lifted the latch and motioned her in. Evidently she was going to have to prove her prowess before he let her out in the wild. If he tried to walk her in a circle for the next half hour, she'd show him how a horse named Princess and her Manhattan rider could take a fence even in a western saddle.

She led Princess inside.

"I suppose you need—"

Diana shoved her new sneaker into the stirrup and hoisted her butt into the saddle. She'd probably be crippled the next day, but she'd be damned if she was going to let this good-looking rube belittle her every time he opened his mouth.

She'd been on enough vacations to have learned about riding western. Princess danced a little, but Ian didn't move to calm her, and it only took Diana a few seconds to have her walking around the perimeter of the paddock. She turned her and came back the opposite way, in increasingly small circles.

When she'd completed her smallest circle, she looked down at him. "Does she know her Airs Above the Ground?"

He smiled. Diana almost slipped from the saddle.

No wonder he was so taciturn. If he even hinted at being

charming, he would be overrun with every fawning local lady from miles around. Though she didn't for a minute think that was what made him so distant and . . . solitary.

And she wasn't sure she really wanted to delve deep enough to find out.

She rode Princess out of the paddock. Watched as Ian threw himself effortlessly onto Loki's bare back. This was just getting better and better. They walked the horses side by side for a while as they headed toward open land. He stopped when they reached an opening in a fence that might mark his property line.

"Princess is good-tempered, she won't bolt with you or throw you if you're gentle with her. But don't go too near the ledge. She'll shy, and you both would go over. So if I tell you to stop or come back, you will do so. Immediately."

She nodded. She had no doubt his concern was more for the horse than the rider.

He nudged Loki through the gate; Princess let him take the lead and they rode single file along a narrow path through the rocks and grasses interspersed with moss and greenery that she had no name for. She wondered if Ian knew but she didn't ask. She was enjoying the feel of the horse beneath her and the freedom.

He nudged Loki again and the horse broke into a faster but comfortable gait, which Princess mimicked without Diana having to direct her. The horses were moving in tandem, probably used to these trails and all sorts of riders. They were both well trained and not on their last legs.

The sun beat down on their heads and backs, and a breeze kicked up now and then only to swirl away. Diana lost her sense of time and thoughts of work or even what her friends were doing or when they expected her to return.

Occasionally Ian glanced back, but his gaze didn't linger. Evidently she was passing inspection.

They followed the trail along the edge of the bluffs, where she'd seen Ian riding yesterday as he headed toward the wood closer to the stable. Below them the ocean sparkled far off to the horizon and the waves rolled in, cascading white foam on the shore.

They turned away from the bluff and entered a copse of trees where the air became cooler and damp. Ian urged Loki forward; both horses broke into a canter and were soon on the other side and back in the sunshine. They were headed back to the horse barn.

All too soon the ride was over and Diana reluctantly dismounted and led Princess back into the stable barn. It had been glorious and all too short, though she had no doubt she'd be feeling it the next morning.

Ian showed her the tack room. She knew just what to get for grooming a horse post-ride. They had walked most of the time, so Princess wouldn't need a serious hosing. She took the equipment and went to work. She was checking Princess's forelegs when she realized Ian was standing behind her, watching.

Her first instinct was to be creeped out, but she realized he was just overseeing her technique.

"Ever diligent?" she asked.

He shrugged and walked away.

Diana went back to her task. Princess stood perfectly still. She seemed to be enjoying the attention. Diana stood and tossed the comb back into the pail. "There you go, Princess girl. I'll see if I can rustle up a carrot or apple for you."

She went in search of Ian, whose head she could see over Loki's stall door. She was about to ask him where he kept the treats when she realized he wasn't grooming Loki but had stretched his arms along his side, his cheek pressed to Loki's coat.

Horse whisperer? Figures. A man who could commune with animals but obviously not people. She wouldn't interrupt him. She'd just look for a fridge or apple bin.

He found her rummaging around in the feed room. "Just looking for a carrot or something."

"Hungry?"

"For Princess. I might point out she's much too elegant for her name."

He shrugged, picked up a carryall and reached inside, came out with two carrots, and handed her one.

"I keep them in the house. Too many marauders."

"Two-legged or four-legged?"

"Both."

She said good-bye to Princess, who was enjoying her carrot and nuzzled Diana's neck in gratitude. Diana gave her a good pat. "See you tomorrow, fingers crossed."

Five minutes later she was walking back down the road. Her legs were definitely going to feel the unhabitual exercise, but she'd managed to convince Ian to let her come to the stables the next day. She didn't think the others would mind, it was only a couple of hours. And it did more good to her spirit than all the spas in Massachusetts could have done.

Now if she could just get a handle on the horse-whispering vet.

Chapter 12

"I wonder how Diana is enjoying her ride?" Jess said as she dropped another peeled potato into the vat of cold water.

Allie looked up from her own half-peeled potato. "She's been gone for almost two hours, so she must be having an okay time. What do you think, Lillo?"

"Either that or she and Ian are having a staring contest and we might not see them for days." Lillo dumped another bag of potatoes on the kitchen table.

"She can hand it out." Allie laughed. "We had some great times back in college, didn't we?"

"We did and we are." Jess dug an eye out of her potato with undue force.

For people having such a good time, there were a lot of sub-surface emotions going around. Lillo understood Jess's jumpi-ness, but there was something unsettled about Allie, too. Maybe she just missed her kid. And would be happier at home. But she kept saying that her mother-in-law was encouraging her to stay longer and have a good time. At least that's what she said after every one of her many, many calls. Maybe she was feeling guilty for imposing her son on his grandparents for a whole week, but that was crazy. Didn't grandparents dote on their grandchildren?

Regardless, it was none of Lillo's business. She was on overload already. In a good way; she was having fun, but it took so much energy.

Energy. She'd never lacked energy. Before. She'd been indefatigable when she worked at the camp, which she didn't enjoy, and then in medical school, which she did. And at the hospital. Until the end. And since then? What had she done? Slowly let herself fade away. She was gradually disappearing, and one day she would be gone, no shadow or trail or significant achievement left behind.

The pain was sharp. But not from the realization; from her finger. It was bleeding. "Ouch." She dropped the knife she was holding and yanked her hand away from the table. It wouldn't do to contaminate the potato boil.

"You've cut yourself," Allie said unnecessarily.

It was pretty obvious. Blood was dripping on the kitchen floor.

"Stupid. I wasn't paying attention. Mac, hand me a paper towel."

Mac stripped off several pieces and handed them to Lillo, who wrapped her hand up and went into the bathroom to get a better look. She was pretty sure the cut was superficial. Served her right for letting her mind wander while she had a blade in her hand. The last thing on earth she wanted was to make a trip to the clinic.

She held her hand under the water until the blood turned pink, then took a closer look. A slice across the pad of her forefinger, not terribly deep, a third of an inch long. She was up on her tetanus shots, so all was good. A little Bacitracin and a couple of Steri-Strips and she'd be good to go.

Fortunately, Mac's medicine cabinet was stocked and the operation was over in three minutes. She put a Band-Aid over the Steri-Strips, pulled a couple of latex gloves out of the cardboard container Mac kept in the linen closet—better safe than sorry—and headed back to the kitchen.

"Done and done," she announced before anyone could ask about the cut, then realized Diana had joined them while she was in the bathroom.

"I missed all the excitement?" Diana asked.

"Just one of my many attempts at juggling kitchen items," Lillo returned. "I see you survived your ride."

"It was glorious. I'm going again tomorrow if that's all right with everyone. I'd forgotten how much I love riding."

"And Ian showed you the trails?" Mac asked.

"Yes. He's got a beautiful gray."

"Loki," Mac said. "Please say he didn't make you ride Clara."

"Clara? No. Is she the old bay?"

"Ayuh. And slow and slower. He usually saves her for the kids."

"Kids?"

"Yeah, he gives the local ones rides. Teaches some lessons."

Diana sighed. "Well, I hope he's as friendly with kids as he is with animals. His adult skills are minimal at best."

"Keeps to himself," Mac agreed.

"Is he as good-looking up close as he was yesterday?" Jess asked.

"Well, mostly I was looking at him from behind. But he knows how to handle a horse."

"I wonder if he'll show up tonight?" Jess said. "I wouldn't mind getting a look."

"Don't hold your breath," Lillo said. "And you're on a hands-off-until-you-get-over-the-last-one diet. Now, what should I do that doesn't involve sharp edges?"

Jess made a face at her. "Mac, do you think these are enough potatoes?"

Mac came over to the table and peered into the pot. "Maybe a few more. With the boys and their host families plus you four, there should be a good thirty people and a few kids. Better do another bag."

Jess groaned.

Allie went out to the porch for one more bag.

While they were in the kitchen they heard a truck pull up to the parking lot.

"That'll be Sonny Dumas with the grills." Mac wiped her hands on her apron and went through the gift shop to greet him.

"These grills are huge," Lillo said. "You gotta see them." They all fell in behind her and followed Mac to the front window to see. Sonny's truck was backed up to the near edge of the parking lot, and Sonny, a big, muscular guy, and his two equally-if-not-bigger, muscular teenage sons were unloading two barrel grills to the pavement.

"Wow," said Diana. "Not your everyday hibachi."

Mac tapped on the glass, Sonny gave her a thumbs-up. She turned around to go back to the kitchen. Her shoulder caught the edge of the historic-sights-of-Maine display, sending several pamphlets to the floor.

"Damn, I keep meaning to move those things, I must pick them up ten times a day."

Lillo bent down to pick them up. When she stood, Mac was rounding the corner to the kitchen and Allie was looking after her.

"What?"

"Huh, nothing." Allie glanced at Diana and the two of them herded Jess, who had stopped to look at a local jewelry display, back into the kitchen.

Lillo got back in time to hear Jess say to Mac, "Why isn't the gift shop open?"

"Nobody comes to it much. I open it when they do."

Jess shook her head and took the drying cloth Mac handed her.

At four, they all carried what seemed like a ton of brisket and ribs out to Sonny and continued on their way to change into long pants and sweatshirts for the evening to come.

As soon as Lillo changed into jeans and tee and hoodie, she went to the kitchen to forage for something to take over to the barbecue. The others came out from their respective rooms a few minutes later.

Allie was wearing a T-shirt and pair of khakis that she'd brought with her covered by a plaid button-up shirt she'd found at Barbara Carroll's shop. Jess had borrowed a pair of Lillo's overalls, with the cuffs rolled up over a Tweety Bird sweatshirt that she'd bought yesterday. Diana was wearing a pair of jeans that fit marginally better than her riding jeans and a denim jean jacket over a long-sleeved striped T-shirt. Sort of a sailor-cowboy look. And Lillo could tell she was having a blast.

They were contemplating a prebarbecue cocktail when the sound of cars in the parking lot had them running out to help the newcomers. The Emersons climbed out of their old Chevy. Jed balanced a chocolate cake on the palm of one large cal-loused hand. Two apple pies were stacked on the other.

Lillo rushed to take the pies from him.

"Lord, if it ain't Lillo Gray. Haven't seen you in forever. Don't get in to see Mac as much as we'd like. Gretchen's got the arthritis. It's the damp weather, you know. Gretchen, get on over here and say hello." His wife made her way around the car, leaning heavily on her cane.

"Perfect timing, Lillo. I didn't know how Jed was gonna get those things in the house without dropping them all. We ran into Howie and Roy in town. They're coming later. They wanted to finish up some work on the Baileys' new addition. What a godsend, those two. And I hear the two new boys have been helping out at Nimbly's farm. Smart thinking of the two docs to get us some farm experts. They never let us down."

Gretchen Emerson chattered all the way to the picnic tables, where Mac met her and invited her into the house to sit while she finished up in the kitchen. Lillo followed them inside and deposited the pies on the counter.

"I'd better go retrieve the cake from your husband. I think he stopped to talk to Junior Nomes. They were just driving up when we were coming inside."

Sure enough, the Nomeses had arrived. Jed, still holding his chocolate cake, stopped to speak with Ike while Hilda wrestled two huge casseroles out of the back seat. She handed them to Ike. "Where are the boys? Boys!" she called. "No getting near the jetty," she yelled as all three of her children raced for the shore.

Lillo retrieved the cake and she and Hilda with her casseroles left the men to pull out the cooler and help carry three long picnic tables from the gift-shop shed.

When she came back from the house they had placed them in a row along the grassy verge in front of the jetty and beach. The big chest cooler was set up a little ways away and was being filled with bags of ice from Junior's car trunk.

More families arrived. The fire was going and the coals were just getting ready to cook when the first motorcycles roared into the parking lot and parked on the edge of the lot away from the cars. Howie, Nando, and Assam strode toward the group carrying six-packs and bags of potato chips. The tables filled up with food, the cooler with beer and wine and soda; hamburgers and hot dogs were piled up next to the grill, ready to go.

Others arrived, parking the cars and trucks at the far end

of the parking lot to make room for the festivities. Everyone brought a six-pack of beer or soda or a bottle of wine to add to the cooler.

Lillo stood back, just soaking it all in. These were people she had known for years, but didn't see too much of, mainly because she didn't leave home much. She'd missed last year's barbecue and picnic and maybe the one the year before. Before that, she'd been away at school.

Even after she'd returned to Lighthouse Beach, she had avoided most of the residents. Tonight everyone seemed glad to see her. And though she knew they all knew of her epic crash and burn no one looked askance.

So she pushed her own disappointment in herself aside and went to help with preparations.

Barbara Carroll arrived a few minutes later with the two new guys who were staying in her garage apartment between renters. She saw Lillo and hurried over. She was wearing tight denim leggings, a boatneck sweater, and large dangling earrings, and was far better dressed than the New York contingent.

"Doc isn't here yet?"

"Haven't seen him. Maybe he's coming over later with Ian."

"Oh, Ian, he never goes anywhere. A waste of handsome male if you ask me."

Lillo smiled. Ian lived by his own rhythms. You never knew if he would show or not. Everyone always made enough food for him, and if he didn't come, they sent it home with someone to take to him.

They all knew it wasn't rudeness. It was just Ian. And they accepted him as they accepted Lillo and all the other people with stories who lived here.

"Oh, there's Hilda Nomes. I've been trying to talk to her for ages." Barbara hurried away.

Lillo made herself a plate of food and looked for her friends. Mac was sitting with a group of men, probably talking about fishing, though she hardly ever fished. Nearby, Diana was talking animatedly to several teenage boys, probably about apps since they all had out their cell phones. She couldn't find Jess but assumed she was having a good time. She did see Allie sitting at the end of one of the picnic tables talking to Nando, the CPA mechanic.

She saw her friend Sada sitting at a table with some other women and went to join them. Sada moved over to make room for her.

"We were just talking about Mary Alice Grotsky's boy. Is Doc Clancy still at the hospital with her?"

"I believe so. And I saw an ambulance in town yesterday."

"That was Zeke Hallerin." Gretchen Emerson slid a bowl of coleslaw toward her. "Had chest pains on his way to the pancake breakfast. Francine brought him into the clinic. Doc Hartley saved his life."

Lillo nodded; the bite of baked beans she'd just taken turned to sawdust.

"He's a godsend," Gretchen declared.

"He is," Lillo agreed.

"Think you'll ever get back to practicing medicine? We're all hoping we'd have two doctors settle down in town."

Lillo moved her head, shrugged her shoulders, and stuck a rib in front of her mouth. The conversation switched to the new pastor at Bethel Church and who was making what for the Fourth of July town picnic.

Lillo finished eating. Excused herself to help in the kitchen, and tossed her plate in the trash as she headed for the gift shop.

She passed Ned on his way out. "Oh. I didn't know you were here."

"Just got here and went in to drop off some wine for Mac."
He lowered his voice. "Not for public consumption."

"Hope you hid it well."

"In the normal place. Mac said you cut your finger."

"Well, you know me in the kitchen."

"Want me to take a look at it?"

She held up her finger, noticed a smear of barbecue sauce,
and put it down again. "Thanks, but I can put a Band-Aid on
a finger."

I know you can, I didn't mean to—"

She turned away. "Good heavens, Ian is here."

"Yep. And he's talking to your friend the CEO."

"Diana. She went horseback riding over there today."

"Well, don't let Mac see them; she's been trying to get him a
girlfriend since I can remember."

"I know."

Doc laughed. "Yeah, the only difference is you didn't chase
after him, like everybody else."

"Two hopeless cases, Ian and me."

"Oh, I don't know."

"Ned, don't."

"Listen. I just want to say that the other night after dinner,
I didn't stop to think that you had guests when I asked you to
help out at the clinic. One-track mind. Are you all having a
good time?"

"Pretty much. How is it going without Clancy?"

"It's going. He won't be back until the end of the week, so I'll
just make do."

She looked at him; in the twilight, he definitely looked
tired, like he wasn't getting enough sleep. What was wrong
with her? Why couldn't she just go and stock cabinets, empty
trash cans, and stuff like that? He'd asked for her help and she'd

panicked. He was working to help the community and she was being selfish. Surely she could help out a little without getting sucked back into the whole sordid world she'd left.

"Listen, Ned—"

"Oh, there you are." Barbara hurried toward them. "I've been looking everywhere, Ned Hartley. I was beginning to think you weren't going to show."

"Well, I'm here and you found me. What can I do for you?"

Lillo started to leave but Ned shifted slightly, blocking her way.

Barbara slapped playfully at his arm. "It's what I can do for you. I found someone to watch the shop tomorrow, so I can help you out at the clinic."

"Oh, that's great, Barb," but he was looking at Lillo.

"Well, I'll leave you guys to schedule the day." This time Lillo slipped past Barbara and made her way into the crowd.

The families with young children began making preparations to leave. Others settled in for the evening. The men were ensconced in lawn chairs and on benches drinking beer and exchanging stories. The women would eventually migrate into the kitchen, but for now, they were sitting at the picnic tables picking at the last pieces of cake and exchanging the latest recipes and gossip.

The sound of another vehicle didn't cause much interest until a black SUV screeched to a halt at the edge of the group. Three men jumped out. They were wearing black suits and dark glasses, though the sun was well below the point where they needed them.

"What the hell?" Howie King stood to face them.

"Damn. It's the Secret Service. What you been up to, Mac?" Several men laughed, but as the three newcomers descended on the crowd, they stood, too.

Sonny and his sons moved to block their way. "Sorry, fellas, this is a private party," Sonny said, and crossed his arms.

"We're looking for a missing person."

Sonny rocked back on his heels. "I think we're all accounted for." He looked back over one shoulder, then the other. "Anybody here missing?"

"Not me."

"Not me either."

"I think we all know where we are."

"Nope, didn't lose a soul."

"Shit," Diana said, coming up beside Lillo. "I got a bad feeling."

"Me too."

"Are you FBI?" someone said.

One of the men reached inside his jacket pocket and pulled out a photo. "We're a private security firm. Has anyone seen this woman?"

Jess appeared at Diana's side. Allie was right behind her.

Slowly one person after another turned to zero in on Jess.

"Miss Parker, your father sent us to bring you home."

Jess lifted her chin. Lillo held her breath. Diana and Allie practically vibrated with suppressed energy.

"They look just like the Blues Brothers," Diana said in her snarkiest voice.

The crowd tittered, some laughed outright.

"She done something illegal?" It was Howie King.

"We have evidence that she's been kidnapped and her father hired us to find her and bring her home."

"Hell, that's the dumbest thing I've ever heard." Sonny shook his head. "Does she look kidnapped to you?"

Now everyone turned to look at the four women.

"Not our call, we're to transport her back to Boston."

"Well, we need to see the ransom money first," Howie said.

"God bless Howie and Sonny and sons," Lillo said.

"This has gotten totally out of hand. I'm sorry." Jess took a step forward.

"Jess, don't—" Lillo began.

Mac sidled up to them; she had somehow managed to get her shotgun from the house.

"Don't even think it," Lillo said under her breath.

"Ain't loaded, but they don't know that."

Jess smiled at Mac. "Thanks, Mac. I've got this." She squeezed Mac's arm and went to meet the posse.

"Don't let her cave, not now," Lillo prayed.

"I think he's being totally ridiculous," Allie said. "We have to do something."

Diana growled like an angry dog. "Damn George Parker. That asshat thinks he's super-don, and he's not even connected—that I know of."

Jess walked stolidly forward. The crowd parted for her, but she stopped several yards from the security men. "You've wasted your time. I'm not missing. I haven't broken any law. I wasn't kidnapped. I'm thirty-two years old. I'm not going back."

Lillo gave a mental fist pump.

Diana and Allie hugged each other.

"Your parents are very worried about you, Miss Parker. They know you were brought here under the influence of these sad women, and they're willing to forget everything if you'll just come back with us."

"Sad women?" Diana exclaimed. "Give me that shotgun, Mac."

"No," Jess said, her voice sounding surprisingly calm. "These are my friends, and I came with them of my own free will. Neither you nor my father can make it into anything else. And these fine people surrounding us are my witnesses. I'll take you all to court if necessary."

"Holy shit," Diana said. "I never thought I'd ever. You hang in there, girl."

"Be reasonable, Miss Parker. You can't leave things like this. We must really insist you accompany us."

The three security men stepped forward.

"What? Are they going to carry her out bodily? We'll see about that." Diana headed to Jess's side, but before she got there, Doc and the whole biker brigade stepped in front of Jess, forming a wall and blocking their way.

"You heard the lady," Doc said. "Either show us a warrant or leave town. Now."

"You don't understand. We have orders to—"

Another biker stepped forward. "If you take her against her will, you will be the ones facing kidnapping charges."

"Which one is that?" Diana said.

"Nando," Jess said. "He's a CPA and mechanic. And right now my hero."

The three private security goons looked at each other and back at the crowd that had filled in behind the bikers. They consulted with each other for a brief moment.

"I think we'd better call for instructions." The main security guy whipped out his cell phone.

"Good luck with that one," Lillo said. "He's standing in a dead zone."

The other two had pulled out their cells as well and were trying to find a signal.

The crowd had subtly shifted, covering the one good reception area in the lot.

The three goons milled around holding their cells in the air, to no avail.

"I think I saw a movie like this once," Allie said.

"I think I saw that one, too," Diana said. "Now, if they would just go away."

At a motion from the one who seemed to be in charge, they pocketed their phones and got back in the SUV.

They screeched away, throwing out sprays of sand that always washed onto the parking lot.

The crowd congratulated Jess, the bikers, themselves, and went back to partying.

Jess stood where they'd left her. Lillo, Diana, and Allie surrounded her.

"I can't believe that everyone stuck up for me like that."

"It's Lighthouse Beach. It's what we do," Lillo said, and realized it was true.

"And you did it yourself," Allie said. "Jess, you were fierce."

Jess looked bewildered, then smiled. "I think a girlie drink would be in order. Before my knees give out."

They all turned back to the tables, but Diana was looking through the crowd.

"What?" Lillo asked.

"Do you see Ian?"

Lillo looked, shook her head. "He's bound to be somewhere." But maybe not. This was just the kind of situation to set him off. But that wasn't Lillo's story to tell. "Come on; let's get a drink and some more food. I'm suddenly famished."

It was late when Ned parked his bike back at Ian's. The house was dark except for the porch light they'd left on when they left for the barbecue. It didn't matter, he knew where to find him.

He walked past the house and around back to the horse barn. Went inside. It was dark here, too, but Ned turned on one bank of lights and walked down the center aisle to Loki's stall.

They were there, both of them, standing together, horse and rider, so close as to be almost one.

Neither acknowledged Ned as he stepped into the stall; they might both have been sleeping on their feet, but it was something deeper than that.

"Some barbecue," Ned said softly.

Ian straightened away from Loki, who shook his head at the bother.

Ned waited for Ian to move toward the stall door, and when finally he did, Ned fell into step with him. They closed up the barn and headed for the house as if nothing had happened. And Ned figured that for Ian, nothing had, and that was a good thing.

So they walked toward the house. Silent.

"She probably thinks I'm a coward."

Ian's voice was such a surprise that Ned started. "No one who knows you would think that."

"It doesn't matter."

They reached the porch steps.

"Wait, who are you talking about?"

"Nobody."

Doc studied his friend's profile in the moonlight. Nothing looked different, but something had changed. "Oh my God. It's the CEO, isn't it?"

Ian shook his head and climbed the steps.

"It is," Doc said, amazed and a little uneasy. "Well, well, well . . ." But he was thinking, *Holy shit, not the CEO.*

Chapter 13

It had been really late by the time everyone left the barbecue. Lillo and company had stayed even later, cleaning up, toasting Jess for standing up to her father's goons, and reliving every moment of the confrontation, and Lillo was bleary-eyed when someone shook her awake the next morning.

"Whaaa?"

Jess's face loomed over her.

Lillo bolted upright. "What?"

"I just thought of something."

"Something that requires coffee?"

Jess nodded.

Lillo threw off the comforter and struggled up from the couch. "Okay, hit me with it," she said as she padded to the kitchen.

"I need to do some banking. Do you know where I can get to a private computer with Internet access?"

Lillo scrubbed her face. "I have money, if that's what you need. You can pay me back."

"No. I just realized that my father has access to at least two of my bank accounts. I wouldn't put it past him to clean me out."

"He wouldn't dare." Lillo got down the coffee canister and opened it.

Jess gave her a look.

"Okay, I guess he would."

"I need to change my passwords and move some assets around so he can't get to them. I'd use my phone but I threw it out. And since he now knows for certain I didn't go home and I don't intend to, I really need to hurry."

"Okay, let me think."

Jess took the coffee from her and measured it into a filter, filled the coffeemaker with water, and turned it on while Lillo thought.

"What time is it?"

"After ten. We overslept."

"Then let's see, Barb probably has one, but she'd be at work by now."

"You don't have a computer?"

Lillo glanced toward the unused bedroom. "Somewhere in there. But the battery's bound to be dead, and who knows where the power cord is. I know. Sada."

"What?"

"Who. My friend Sada runs the community center. They have a computer there. I know a lot of people use it because it has Internet access. I'm sure she'll let us use it. I'll call her." Lillo went to find her cell phone.

When she came back she ran into Allie and Diana shuffling into the kitchen, still in their nightwear, such as it was.

"Why are we all up and clanging around in the kitchen?" Diana asked on a yawn.

"Semi-emergency," Jess said.

"What's wrong?" Allie asked, her voice suddenly awake and strident.

"Everything is fine, but it occurred to me that my finances aren't. I'm afraid some of my assets may be compromised."

Diana screwed up her face. "Is this a joke? What assets are you talking about?"

"Don't be dense. My bank accounts, mutual funds, those kinds of assets."

"Oh shit. He doesn't have your passwords."

"He does to a couple; it was supposed to be so that there was always a second signer in case of an emergency. Of course, I know that it was really so his heavy hand could control me as well as my ability to be independent. If he sent goons to drag me back, he wouldn't think twice about ruining me financially. He's probably got hackers on it as we speak."

"Surely he wouldn't do that," Allie said. "He's your father."

"He would," Diana and Jess said simultaneously.

"Is he really that bad? I mean, I've met him and seen him in action, but nobody—"

"Allie, there are some nasty characters in this world and my father is one of them."

Allie gave her a quick hug. "I'm sorry."

Jess hugged her back. "I've lived with it for a long time. I've finally—with a little help from my friends—started fighting back."

"Then grab two travel mugs out of the cabinet and let's hit the road," Lillo said. "Sada's warming her up for us."

"Warming her up?" Diana asked. "What kind of computer are we talking about?"

"Dial-up, but it won't boot Jess off midtransaction."

"Oh, just shoot me now," Diana said, and reached in the cupboard for coffee mugs. "Do you need me to go with you?"

"No, but thanks," Jess said. "You get your riding fix and all will be right with the world."

"We can but hope," Diana said.

"Then I'll go see if Mac needs any more help cleaning up from last night," Allie said. "I thought maybe she'd let me tag along on the next lighthouse tour."

"I'm sure she'd be happy to give you a private tour," Lillo said. "As you've probably noticed, there haven't been too many visitors to the lighthouse."

"Except renegade boys and other vandals," Jess said. "Somebody should do something."

"Yeah, but not today," Diana said. "Now get going."

Ten minutes later, Lillo and Jess were driving the van to the Lighthouse Beach Community and Recreation Center.

"I can't believe I didn't think of this sooner," Jess said as Lillo turned onto Main Street.

"I can't believe you're over thirty and your parents still have the passwords to your bank accounts."

"I know it sounds weird. But my family isn't like other families . . . or normal families anyway. They are like financial amoebas. It's all done for the security of the whatever. Like having power of attorney—which I probably should change, too, come to think of it."

"Oh, Jess. What about your brothers and sister? Have the sibs totally bought into building the Parker empire?"

"They've drunk the Kool-Aid. My father has us so tied up in red tape that it would be hard to extricate myself from it if I hadn't already made contingency plans. None of them, including my mother, can believe I don't want to be a part of the 'empire'; therefore I must be a fat, ugly loser and they'll do whatever they can to fix me so I can be like them. Oh my God, I hate them. And they're my family."

Lillo glanced over at her friend. She'd spent many summers watching Jess desperately trying to find herself with everything stacked against her. Lillo had never really understood until this week. It was insidious. Not just overly involved, we-know-best helicopter parents, but really mean-spirited greedy people.

"That sounds horrible, doesn't it? I don't expect anyone to understand. I've never even admitted it to myself until now. You had great parents. I know they were probably pains in your butt sometimes, but they loved you and really wanted what was best for you, really what was best for *you*.

"My parents don't love me, they just pay lip service to wanting what's best for me. They love my siblings; *they* all are financial successes—cold fish, but successful. The swans to my ugly duckling. I don't have anything to do with them. And it doesn't matter. But my parents . . ." She shrugged. "I just wanted their love."

She blinked, furiously trying not to cry, but Lillo felt like crying herself—for Jess, whose parents were mega-cretins who could never appreciate their compassionate, smart daughter, people who were not capable of real love. And for herself, whose parents were great, did love her, had sacrificed to help her achieve what she wanted, and never once blamed her for being the failure she was.

Lillo turned onto Shandy Way, not because it was the only street that led to the community center, but because she wanted to drive by the clinic. And that was a first. She usually avoided it like the plague, but today she wanted to drive by. As a punishment maybe? She didn't know, she just needed to drive by the place. But halfway down the block she decided she'd been wrong and vowed not to turn and look as she drove by.

It didn't do the least bit of good. She couldn't help herself . . . she turned, looked, and almost drove into the other lane.

"What happened, Lillo?" Jess's voice came from far away.

"Just trying to avoid a pothole," she said automatically.

"I mean with medical school. You wanted to be a doctor, you made all those plans."

"It didn't work out."

"It's not my business, but was it the money? Because if it was . . ."

"No, it wasn't the money. I just changed my mind. We're almost there, see." She pointed ahead to a white clapboard building and a large parking lot.

"The church?" Jess asked.

"It used to be a church. Not anymore. Now the sanctuary is a gymnasium and activity room, the Sunday school classrooms are meeting rooms, and the rectory next door is the food bank and other stuff."

She pulled the van into the parking lot and stopped by a side door. They entered a small hallway and turned right into the old sanctuary, where tables were set up and Sada Jensen was giving instructions to a group of quilters. Sada was tiny and effervescent and one of the few young people who hadn't left for a larger city, a better income, and a rosier future.

"Hey, Lillo, and you must be Jess. I've got the computer all ready for you, connection and everything." She looked at Jess's wrist. "Are you going to be okay to type?"

"I think so, thanks."

Sada led them down the hall to what must have once been the choir room but now served multiple purposes, from office to storage room to lost and found.

"Take all the time you need."

Jess just stared at the old desktop computer.

Sada leaned in close. "Works just like your laptop, only slower."

"Ah, thanks." Jess sat down at the desk.

Lillo and Sada walked back into the hall. "I've been meaning to come over," Lillo began.

"I know, you've had houseguests."

"About your dress. I had to change a tire in the rain; I'm afraid it might be ruined. I'll get you a new one."

"I heard that, too."

"From Doc, I suppose."

"No, actually, I haven't even seen him. With Clancy at the hospital, he's pretty swamped."

"Don't look at me like that," Lillo said.

"Why not? You could help him, if you weren't so stubborn."

They'd reached Sada's office and sat down on the lumpy love seat that she reserved for guests.

"Actually, I almost broke down and volunteered last night, but Barbara Carroll beat me to it."

"Oh mercy, that Barb. Every time Doc comes to town, she's all over him like flypaper. The man's a saint for even being civil to her."

"Okay, you've totally guilted me. I'll go see if he needs help tomorrow. Maybe."

Sada grasped her hand. "You can do it. Now, could you help me carry these boxes down to the basement? Lynn Ann's out with the flu. Whoever heard of having the flu in the summer?"

They carried boxes down the stairs to another large room, once the church's hospitality room. They were just finishing up when they heard a commotion above them.

"Kids are here." Sada hurried upstairs. Lillo followed and ran into Jess coming out of the office.

"Get everything done okay?" Lillo asked.

"Yes, I should be safe for now."

They walked down the hall to find Sada surrounded by kids.

"Are we going horseback riding today? Are we?"

"Yes, once you've calmed down and had some lunch."

"Can Joey go? He got in a fight."

"Weren't my fault. That Tommy Clayton started it, him and his gang."

"Joey," Sada said. "All of you. How many times have I said to stay away from those boys?"

"Aw, Sada, some of them are okay."

"Being in a gang is not okay."

"I know, but you can't tell which ones are which, can you?"

"So can he go? Sada?"

Sada pursed her lips. "This time, but no more fighting. And stay away from Tommy Clayton. Now go sit down and one of the ladies will bring you something to eat."

"I recognize those boys," Jess said when Sada joined them. "And he's telling the truth. We were downtown after I got this fixed." She held up her bandaged wrist. "Joey and another couple of boys were walking down the street. I recognized the little one."

"Joey's little brother, Bobby. Severe learning disabilities and trauma. A sad story. He gets picked on a lot."

"Well, they were picking on him, and Joey came to his rescue, and forgive me if I'm out of line, but I say good for him."

Lillo stared at Jess in astonishment.

"Sorry, but it makes me mad to see that happen. I've been bullied all my life and it isn't right."

"It makes us all mad. But those boys have got too much time and not enough attention. Not much to do around here except get into trouble. And all this nonsense about gangs. Tommy Clayton is eleven, he and some of the others need a good what-for, but most of them just go along because it makes them feel like they belong. You know. Same old story. Parents mostly have to go to the mainland to work, leave early, get home late.

Work two jobs. Kids leave as soon as they're old enough to find a better life. The little ones just sit around waiting until they can leave, too.

"Whew, sorry for the rant. Guess I just got set off this morning."

"Sorry if I set you off."

"No, it's good to know we have sympathetic friends. Wish I had more to work with than pickup basketball games and free lunches. Well, I better go make sure they're eating their sandwiches and not throwing them at each other. Glad you came in. And, Lillo. You know what they say. Just do it."

"Right, and thanks." Lillo and Jess returned to the van.

"What was Sada talking about, 'Just do it'?"

"Nothing important. But thanks for showing an interest in the kids."

"Why wouldn't I?"

Lillo shrugged and put the van in gear. "Most people wouldn't, but I think it's pretty cool that now you've stopped letting your parents bully you, you're ready to go to bat for kids you don't even know."

"Well, someone should. Don't they have classes in school these days about how to deal with bullying?"

Lillo snorted. "They've got classes for everything . . . doesn't mean people practice it on the outside."

"Well, they should," Jess said. "They just should."

DIANA SET OFF for the stables not knowing exactly what to expect. A situation that she didn't experience often. She liked to know the score before going in, to have contingency plans in place. But dealing with Ian Lachlan was like sticking a straight line in a non-Euclidean universe. He had his own rules. Or maybe he had no rules.

She was without a clue. They'd actually talked a bit last night at the picnic. He'd seemed to have forgotten that they'd barely shared a word that morning. And he'd resented her presence from the get-go.

They could have been old acquaintances exchanging small talk at a party. Then the Parkers' goons showed up and Ian disappeared. For a wild second she thought maybe he was hiding out from the law. But for what? And why would a whole town protect a felon?

There was definitely something odd about the man. She had no idea what reception she would receive today or if he would even allow her in the barn.

She'd gotten herself so frazzled by the time she left the cottage—something totally not her—that she'd asked Allie if she wanted to come with her.

But Allie had decided to visit Mac instead. Maybe her sense of self-preservation was better than Diana's own.

This is nuts, Diana thought as she strode up the dirt road to Ian's office and stables.

She slowed when she reached the clearing in front of the house where he lived. At least she guessed he lived there; she'd just assumed he did. Not a good habit when dealing with an anomaly like Ian.

She took a fortifying breath and marched around to the horse barn. The door was open, so she stepped inside.

He was there. She could see his dark hair over the top of Clara's stall. He was talking to the old horse as he might talk to his mother. She decided not to confront him but to act like she belonged there. Most of the stalls were empty; he must have let the other horses out into the paddock in order to clean the stalls. Looked like he was running late today, too.

She went to the tack room, took a manure fork and shovel

out to a wheelbarrow, and rolled it to an empty stall at the far
end of the row. *If my friends could see me now,* she hummed,
smiling at the ridiculousness of it all. She could be sitting back
on the deck with another cup of coffee, looking out to the sea,
and doing . . . nothing. But instead . . . She actually was enjoying herself.

She thought for sure Ian would hear her and come to either
say hello or tell her to hit the road. But he didn't and she began
to feel like a teenager who hung out in a high school hallway on
the outside chance that a popular boy would see her and say hi.

That made her laugh out loud.

"Enjoying yourself?"

She turned around and the sight of Ian's scowling face made
her— *Oh, get a grip.* "Actually, I am," she said, taking the time
to settle her embarrassing reaction to him.

He grunted something noncommittal and strode off down
the aisle.

Diana moved to the next stall, angry at herself for being attracted to an incorrigible backwoods loner. This was so not her.

She attacked the stall with a vengeance. She'd completed
four before Ian appeared again, this time leading Princess and
Loki. Princess came right up to her and nudged her with her
nose. Diana laughed. "I know you're only after my carrots. And
the cupboard is bare."

She caught a glimpse of Ian looking like thunder and confu-
sion and she had the strongest urge to kiss that scowl off his
face. But her sense of self-preservation made her walk past him
to get Princess's saddle. She knew how to handle men. But not
this one. Even if he did hit all her hot spots.

They took the same route as the day before over the grassy
slopes; only today, instead of turning into the trees, he continued straight, Diana following, down a path that ended at a wide

sandy beach that stretched around a point of land and continued who knew how far.

Ian gave Loki his head and they galloped to the water's edge. Princess followed but more sedately, sliding from one gait into another without effort. The horses loved the water and Ian let them take a few minutes to gambol before he reined Loki in and continued down the beach.

The wind was sharp here, challenging the sun to warm them, and Diana was ready when Ian turned Loki up an unseen path back to the bluffs. This path was steeper, and she had to pay attention. Ian didn't turn around to see if she was okay. But she felt like he was reading her progress through some kind of human osmosis.

When they crested the hill, Diana half expected to see an alien spaceship waiting for them.

Crazy! She'd obviously had too much vacation—or too much hard cider the night before. All too soon they were back in the barn. They unsaddled the horses and took them outside to wash off the salt water. It was a messy job because Princess and Loki had decided to have some fun. Both riders and horses got pretty wet and Diana found herself smiling and wondering how she could prolong the day.

Her thoughts along that route ended abruptly with the sound of a car door slamming and the rowdy high-pitched voices of . . . children.

She turned to Ian. "Oh no, I don't do kids."

He looked deadpan. "You want to come back?"

"That's not fair," she said as he started walking toward the car. "I really don't know anything about kids."

In what she was coming to recognize as typical Ian fashion, he ignored her.

The kids saw him and broke away from their keeper and

raced to jump up around him, pulling him one way, then the other, and talking all at once. And Mr. Taciturn stood there perfectly content to let them carry on.

Amazing. Diana exchanged looks with the woman, who shrugged. "I'll be back in an hour," she called to Ian, and got into the station wagon and drove away.

"Okay, line up," Ian said, and suddenly the clamor ceased and they fell into line.

He walked down the line until he got to one kid who had a serious black eye.

"What happened?"

"Sada said I could come."

"Good, but what happened?"

"Got in a fight."

"Tommy Clayton called Bobby a moron," another boy volunteered. "And Joey popped him one. Then they all jumped him."

They all turned to look at Joey. A smaller kid was standing in front of him, and Joey put an arm across the kid's chest and pulled him close.

The little one must be Bobby, thought Diana.

"Just 'cause Bobby said he wanted to climb up to the lighthouse."

"Come on, guys, you know the lighthouse is dangerous; plus, it's private property."

"We know, Mr. Ian, but Tommy said."

"Said what?"

God, the man had the patience of Abraham . . . or was it Job?

"Tommy was bragging about how he'd stolen two cans of his dad's beer and how he was gonna climb up the lighthouse to drink it. And Bobby said he wanted to climb up, too, and Tommy said he couldn't because he was a moron."

"Bobby's not a moron," Joey said.

These must be the kids Jess was telling them about the day they went to the liquor store. They looked a little young to be involved with gangs.

Bobby cowered back against his brother and Joey held him even tighter. "He's not a moron, Mr. Ian. Is he?"

"B-B-Bobby's a moron," said another boy, whose head bobbed on his neck, making it appear he was searching the rafters.

Diana realized that several of the boys had physical or possibly mental disabilities. And there were seven of them.

"Is he, Mr. Ian?"

Ian knelt down beside Bobby. "Nope, he's my buddy." He scooped the little guy up as gently as he'd carried the lamb/goat the other day at his office and swung him to his shoulder.

"Am I your buddy, Mr. Ian?" asked another of the boys. Then they were all asking.

"Am I your buddy?"

"Am I?"

"Me too?"

"Yep. You're all my buddies."

Diana swallowed a hideous lump in her throat. She didn't do compassion. She should quietly go away. And leave Ian with seven needy children?

Ian Lachlan was one big surprise after another. He was the last person Diana would imagine being a buddy to children. The man never talked.

"Who we going to ride today, Mr. Ian?"

"Pete, let's ride Pete."

"You won't let go, will you, Mr. Ian?"

"No, Sam, I won't let go."

"Promise?"

"I won't let go."

Then they were gone. Headed to the paddock, Diana guessed. Now was her chance to slip away. She wouldn't know what to do with the kids, but Ian certainly did. She might drop one of them getting them into the saddle, or get one trampled while she wasn't looking. They probably had germs and bugs and she didn't know anything about kids, especially kids with special needs. What if they fell? Started crying? Got scared?

Mucking out the stalls was one thing. Babysitting? Nope, not happening. She finished putting her tack away, then with every intention of going back to the cottage for a hot bath and a cold drink, Diana Walters, CEO and app designer, urbanite entrepreneur, single childless woman—who intended to stay that way—walked out of the barn and turned right into the paddock.

Chapter 14

Mac settled back in her Adirondack chair. She'd turned it so she could see the lighthouse as well as anyone coming toward the gift shop—not that she expected any tourists today. People just didn't come like they used to. Even though it was a sunny day, a perfect day for going to the beach and climbing up to the tower to look over the vast ocean. Maybe even see whales or dolphins. But people were busy, their vacations were just strict itineraries of activities.

And it was supposed to rain midweek. Bad for business but at least it would keep the kids from trespassing.

She closed her eyes; the sun was good, it warmed her old bones, made things bright. She'd loaned the van to Lillo and Jess this morning. Watched Diana on her way to the stables. Second day in a row. Diana was also talking to Ian at the barbecue the night before. She was a go-getter, but someone should warn her not to play with Ian. It wouldn't be fair. To either of them.

Though stranger things had happened, she guessed. Maybe

Diana was the one who could unlock that man's heart. *And un-lock what else, old woman?*

No, it was best to stay out of it. She wished Clancy would get back. He always knew what was what.

She opened one eye to look over at the cottage. Allie must still be inside. Now, *she* was an interesting one. Easy not to no-tice. Kind. Helpful. Even-tempered.

And not happy. She must be missing her child and her hus-band who had been taken from her all too soon. Enough to make anyone depressed, but Mac thought it was more. And it was too bad that in the excitement of Jess's escape, and Diana's energy, and Lillo's doggedness not to look at her own life, Allie was bound to get lost in the shuffle. If Mac didn't do something.

The girl was supposed to have left today. Her flight was from Boston. Getting there would be a logistical nightmare. Maine was a wonderful place; it just wasn't that easy to get to, and once you were there, not so easy to get out of.

It would take extra flights or a bus to get her to the airport, and time was passing. Maybe that's what Allie was doing now. Packing. Mac would hate to see her go, but on the other hand, it might be better if she did.

Mac pushed to her feet. Sitting in the sun was all good except that it turned your skin to leather. But she was way past caring.

With a last look down the road, she walked round to the back door. Paused at the porch steps. Three little steps she'd been climbing for decades. Last week she'd misjudged the second one and landed on both knees on the porch floor. She'd never given those steps a thought; now she had to pay attention.

It was a bitch. She'd make some homemade lemonade. The girls were sure to stop by before the day was done.

Mac was just getting the lemons out of the bin when she heard her van pull up and stop. She knew it was her van by the sound. She peeked out the window anyway. Lillo and Jess were going down to Lillo's cottage.

She turned on the overhead light and got a knife out of the knife drawer. She sliced and squeezed and sugared and was just putting a large pitcher of fresh juice in the fridge when there was a knock on the door.

"Come on in," Mac called. "Door's open."

Jess and Allie. "Lillo had to go help a Mrs. Oreton with her tomato plants."

"Ayuh. Figures. Poor thing. Her arthritis is so bad she can't get the stakes in properly. Still tries, though." Mac chuckled. *Just like the rest of us old folks,* she thought. Only she wasn't that old. At least not to her way of thinking.

"And Diana isn't back from the stables yet, so we thought we'd come see what you're doing. You look busy."

Busy. Ha, Mac hadn't been busy in years. "Just making lemonade. And never too busy for company."

They came in and sat at the kitchen table like Lillo had been doing for years, and Lillo and Jess back when they were kids. Mac had thought her table would be empty from now on. This might just be a respite along the road to being alone, but she welcomed it.

Mac wondered if she should bring up the events of the night before. Jess seemed in decent spirits, so maybe mentioning it would be tempting fate. She was holding up pretty well. In fact, there seemed to be an aura of relief around her.

"I wanted to get a better look at that jewelry in the gift shop when it's convenient," Jess said. "And then we thought maybe today or tomorrow you could give us a tour of the lighthouse."

"Or we could just tag along when you have your next tour," said Allie. "I wanted to see it before I left."

"Aren't you supposed to fly home today?"

"I was."

"Her mother-in-law talked her into staying the whole week. Isn't that great?" Jess winced. "Great for us, anyway. Would you rather go home? You miss little Gino, I get it," she said. "I hope I have the opportunity to feel the same way . . . someday."

Mac had had that opportunity, but only for a few short weeks. It seemed like another lifetime ago. But in that short time, she had felt what Allie must be feeling now.

"You will, Jess." Allie looked down and blinked back tears. "But it isn't just that."

Oh dear, thought Mac.

Jess put her arm lightly across Allie's shoulder. "What is it? You can tell me and Mac."

Allie shook her head.

Jess shook her gently. "Al, what's wrong? You've always been there for me; let me help."

"You can't. It's nothing, really."

"It must be something," Mac said, "or you wouldn't be here trying to convince us it's nothing."

"We'll get you to Boston and you can fly out today if you want," Jess said. "We'll get a rental car and drive you down to the city if we have to."

"It's not what I want. But it should be." Allie sniffed.

Tears were already brimming in Jess's eyes.

This was in danger of becoming a sob fest. Those never actually solved any problems, just made eveyone feel better and put off dealing with what they needed to deal with.

"I'll fix some lemonade and you can tell us all about it." Mac hurried to the fridge, got some ice out, and put it in three glasses.

There was more going on with Allie than just being homesick for her child—or maybe she was realizing just how lonely she was without her husband. It hadn't escaped Mac's notice last night that Allie and Nando had hit it off. And he'd stood up to the Goon Squad. Ayuh. There was more than homesickness brewing inside the sweet, even-tempered Allie.

Mac handed out lemonade and sat down across from the girls. "Now."

Allie looked at her lemonade. Picked up the glass, put it down again. She obviously needed a little push.

Mac didn't hesitate to give her one. "Are you feeling guilty for staying away longer than you planned?"

Allie shrugged. "A little."

"But you said that Gino was fine there and your mother-in-law said you should stay and have fun," Jess said. "You shouldn't feel bad about that."

"I don't. I miss my little boy, but he loves staying with his grandparents. We live in the same house with them. So nothing has really changed, except that I'm not there. When Gino was still alive, we used to leave him with the family a lot, we traveled for the business and just to get away for relaxation, but since Gino . . . died . . . it's not the same."

"So what's the problem here?" Mac asked. "Do you think that because their son died, your in-laws are anxious for you to get back?"

Allie looked up, her face stricken. "That's just it. I think they'd be happy if I stayed away."

"They just want you to have a good time," Jess said.

"No, I mean stay away forever."

Allie's statement fell between them like a rock to the sand.

Jess pulled Allie into a hug. "Al, I'm so sorry. I've been so caught up in my own worries I didn't even think to ask."

"So ask now," Mac urged.

"Allie?"

"I was so happy. Gino and me and little Gino. We were mod-

ernizing the vineyard and winery. Everything was still done on
paper when we got there. Ordering and inventory was a nightmare. Papa Lusano was all for it, but some of the others, the
uncles, they were old and set in their ways. They came around
eventually, but ever since Gino was killed . . . I don't know, I
feel like a stranger in a strange land.

"They're family and yet, not really my family. And little
Gino is one of them. The vineyard is his heritage. But it isn't
mine. At least Gino and I planned to move into our own house,
but when he died, that idea sort of died with him. The Lusanos
are wonderful people, loving and supportive, but I want my
own home, where Gino can have a swing set and a dog that's
just his, and I can have my own curtains, my own teacups, my
own . . . life."

"Have you told them how you feel?"

Allie shook her head. "I can't. They've opened their home to
me because of their grandson and the memory of their son. And
I love and respect them for that. Gino is their grandson, but he's
my son. They would never part with him. And neither will I."

"Good Lord," Mac exclaimed. "Sorry, but what you need to
do is sit down and talk to Mama Lusano."

"I've tried. And she's so understanding. She's the one who encouraged me to come to the wedding. To stay and have a good
time. She even said I should start having a real life again. But I
know it's because they're happy having Gino to themselves. Not
consciously, but they wouldn't miss me, not much anyway. They
could go back to the old ways with their new grandson.

"I'll never leave him. So I'll have to learn to be happy there.
I *am* happy there. It's just . . . I don't know. It will never be any
different."

"And you'll never find love again," Mac said.

Both girls stared at her.

"You make it sound so melodramatic."

"Well, hell. Love requires overpowering emotions, commitment . . ."

"I can't. I've had that conversation with myself a thousand times. Just to have someone's arms around me that isn't my father-in-law or uncle or cousin by marriage—or child. To fall into— Oh God, what am I saying? I should just go home." She stood abruptly.

"You should go on a tour of the lighthouse." Mac pushed her chair back. "Come on, that's enough philosophy for one day."

LILLO TOSSED THE roll of gardening twine back into her carryall and surveyed her handiwork. Two perfect rows of staked tomato plants. A job well done. Very neat work. Mrs. Oreton had been so grateful. Gave her a bag of freshly baked cookies. Oatmeal chocolate chip, Lillo's favorite.

So why didn't she feel more satisfied?

She picked up her carryall and headed for home.

It was a warm sunny day, Mrs. Oreton's door thermometer had read eighty-four, practically a heat wave. Lillo wondered what Jess and Allie were doing. If Ian had welcomed Diana's second visit or had sent her packing.

She cut diagonally across the street, nodding and waving to people who were out enjoying the weather. Several blocks later she turned onto Main Street, which looked bustling by comparison to most days. The sidewalks were actually semicrowded.

Which was probably the reason she didn't see Doc Hartley until he was practically in front of her. She skittered to the side to miss a collision, but he'd had the same idea and they did a little dance step before finally giving up and standing still.

Lillo laughed; nervously, she thought. Took a breath. "Don't tell me you escaped the clinic for a minute."

He held up a brown paper bag. "Lunch." He blew out air. "Had to take a break."

"Clancy still not back?"

"Nope. Which is bad enough, but—" He shook his head.

"But what?"

"What's in the bag?" He nodded to the carryall that hung over her shoulder.

"Gardening tools. I was restaking Mrs. Oreton's tomatoes."

"Ah," he said.

"But what?" she prodded.

He looked around, leaned toward her. "Barb came in to help this morning and she's driving me nuts."

Lillo laughed outright at that. He did rather have the look of a trapped animal.

"So you escaped and left Agnes to cope?"

"Left Agnes to tell her thank you very much, but we wouldn't be needing her this afternoon."

"Oh, Ned. She'll be so hurt."

"That's why I left Agnes to deal with it. Barb will think it's jealousy on Agnes's part, and I won't get the blame and Barb won't feel rejected."

"Sneaky."

"I took a whole hour off, I've got about forty-five minutes left. You want to share my egg-salad sandwich?"

"Thanks, but . . ."

"No buts. Just say thank you, you're starving, and couldn't think of anyone you'd rather have lunch with."

What was the harm? And she used to enjoy his company.

"A cloud just passed over your head. Is it me?" Ned asked.

"No, of course not, I'd love to share your lunch. And I *am* starving."

Without speaking, they crossed the street and walked down

the hill toward the boat landing, continued on until they came
to a little sandy beach tucked in between a rock embankment
and a grassy verge.

Lillo wondered if she was making a mistake, if Ned would
start badgering her about coming back to the clinic—or to medicine. But something had been happening to her in the last few
days. In the days since Jess, Allie, and Diana had come to stay.

She'd forgotten what it was like to have friends near her own
age. She'd forgotten how to have fun, to appreciate silly things.

Ned took her elbow and guided her over the rocks to a flat
place that overlooked the sea. She didn't need help, she knew
where they were going. But Ned was like that, ever the gentle-
man; he'd been that way as a teenager, even to her, who was
light-years younger than he at that age. Now there wasn't so
much difference . . . Except he was following his dream, and
she wasn't.

They sat and Ned reached inside the bag and took out a wad
of napkins. "The guys at the deli must think I'm a slob." He
made a face. "Well, maybe I am a little."

Next came the sandwich wrapped in wax paper. "So you
enjoy gardening as a way of life?" he asked, unwrapping the
sandwich with surgeonlike precision.

She knew it had been too good to last. "I don't kill flowers."

"Lillo . . ."

"Is that why you brought me down here. To lecture me?"

"I invited you to have lunch. Why do you think everyone has
an ulterior motive?"

"Most people do."

"Well, I don't." He handed her half of the sandwich. "Though
now that you mention it, there *is* something I want to ask you
about."

She stiffened.

"Not about you. About your friend the CEO."

"Diana?"

"About her and Ian."

She'd been about to take a bite of her sandwich but she put it down. "He's letting her ride in exchange for mucking out the stables. I know it's a weird arrangement, but she wanted to ride and that's what he demanded." She saw his skepticism. "Diana is a successful businesswoman and she's willing to negotiate for what she wants.

"We had to buy her clothes to ride in. You should have seen her reaction to Barb's store. But she went in like a trouper and ended up buying a bunch of stuff."

"Ian said she was coming back today."

This time the sandwich almost made it to her mouth. "So?"

"She's spending a lot of time at Ian's."

"She's been there twice, three times if you count her going to see if he would rent her a horse. She's only here for a week, so she doesn't have time to waste." She finally got the sandwich to her mouth and took a big bite. It was delicious.

"I just think it's odd that he keeps letting her come back."

Her mouth was full, so she raised her eyebrows in question.

"I don't know, but the mere fact that he's letting her return day after day is . . . unusual. And he . . . Well, you know he has coping problems; he's not like other guys that you have fun with for a few days and then leave without a backward glance."

Lillo forced herself to swallow. "Crap. Are you serious? She's just riding. She has her own horses that she never sees and she went riding on a whim."

"And she went back today?"

Lillo shrugged. "Yeah, but it's perfectly harmless. I think. She did say he was attractive or something like that. Well, that's no secret. He's really good-looking, and buff in a skinny way."

Doc gave her a curious look.

"That's a perfectly normal reaction. It happens all the time: you see a guy and make an evaluation."

Ned burst out laughing.

"You know what I mean. It doesn't mean she—they—they're not . . . are they?"

"I don't know how far it's gone, he hasn't said anything, but he's different."

"Different in a good way?"

"I don't know. I just know that the way he's acting isn't like Ian, and I don't want him pushed back further into his private hell if she leads him on then disappears."

"I think you're overreacting. It's only been two days."

"When it happens, it happens. It doesn't take long."

No, it didn't, Lillo thought. Not too long ago she'd thought it had happened to her. And what about Jess? And Diana had been married twice. None of them had good track records. "I know I'm the last person to ask someone about their life. But do you want me to talk to her?"

Ned shook his head. "I'm probably being overly cautious, but I'd hate for him to have a major setback because he misread her intentions."

"He's a grown man. He can make his own decisions."

"Sure, but when he came here a few years back—you were gone then. He was a total recluse. These days he's the life of the party in comparison. But he still has dark times and probably always will. Consistency is important."

"You can't protect him."

"Of course not, and maybe I shouldn't butt in, but we go back a long ways."

"And you care. I'll see what I can do. Now can I eat my sandwich?"

"Yes."

"Did you get chips?"

MAC UNLOCKED THE gate to the jetty and waited for Allie and Jess to walk through before locking it again. When she had a big tour she sometimes left it open for stragglers, but with the walkway over the jetty beginning to disintegrate, she wasn't keen on having individuals striking off on their own.

The girls seemed eager to see inside. She appreciated their enthusiasm and didn't want to spoil it by reminding them to be careful on the jetty. So she just bent her head to watch her own steps, which slowed her down considerably; they were waiting by the door when she reached them.

The locks had been changed many times over the years, but Mac always kept the old keys on the original key ring, an iron ring almost five inches in diameter and heavy as hell, but possibly original to the lighthouse. And whether true or not, it lent a historical mood to the visitors.

The inside of the lighthouse was several degrees colder than outside and a bit damp. The thick stone-and-plaster walls could withstand all sorts of weather, but like old bones, once the cold seeped in, it was hard to get it warm again.

Above their heads equally spaced windows allowed in enough light to see comfortably.

"Wow," Allie said, turning slowly around.

Mac wasn't sure if she was awestruck by the magic of the space or shocked by the fact that it was a rapidly deteriorating ruin. What was left in the oil room was rusted almost beyond recognition. The storeroom next to it was a little better only because Mac had cleared it out to make room for a narrow cot, a small table, and a straight-backed chair for the nights she sometimes stayed here. Only the circular iron staircase looked anything like a working lighthouse. No wonder people weren't interested in seeing it.

Two old has-beens, Mac thought. Broken-down homages to a past no one remembered.

"Oh, Mac," Jess said, "I remember you bringing us here and we'd watch the sailboats from the very top."

"The watch room," Mac said.

"And if the weather was nice and not too windy, you let us go out to the widow's walk, and we'd inch our way around until we could see the whole panorama, and we used to point to where we thought England and China and the North Pole would be."

Mac smiled. "Until you turned twelve and then you spent the whole time trying to decide where Leo Denton lived."

"Leo . . ." Jess smiled and sighed. "I remember him. He was such a gorgeous boy. Everybody was in love with him. He worked with his father and sometimes waved to us from his boat."

Mac laughed. "Ah, youth. Did you ever even get close enough to him to actually see what he looked like?"

"We did. Sometimes Lillo and I would sneak down to the docks and watch the fishermen come in. Leo was always nice to me. Most boys weren't. But one day, one of the rare days my parents came to visit—checking up on my weight-loss status really—we saw him downtown, and he came up and introduced himself to my parents.

"I thought that was the neatest thing ever. But Mother pulled me back and said—I'll never forget what she said. 'Good God, Jessica. Is this the kind of riffraff you consort with at camp? The boy reeks of fish.' And she pulled me away. Leo just stood there as she dragged me away. I was so humiliated, I never went down to the docks again."

Jess sniffed. "I'm sure he did smell like fish, but I didn't care."

Allie laid a hand on her back.

Mac felt a deep rush of anger. That someone blessed with a child should be so hateful . . .

"Whatever happened to him?" Jess asked. "Is he still around?"

"No. He and his dad hung on as long as they could, but when his father was forced to retire—his back just couldn't take it anymore—Leo sold out and moved to the mainland somewhere. I heard he got married, but I don't know what he does for a living . . . not fishing."

"Everyone leaves, don't they?"

"Not everyone; the ones who stay usually have to work a half hour or more away."

"People in a lot of places commute much longer every day."

"I know, but there isn't much to keep young people here."

"Can we climb up?" Jess asked tentatively, and Mac knew she was thinking Mac was too old to climb the three flights of stairs. Well, she wasn't. Actually, she might be, but that had never stopped her before and it wouldn't stop her now.

"We'll all go if Allie's game."

Allie frowned at her. "Are you sure—"

"Oh, come on, Al," Jess said. "It's safe, isn't it, Mac? And if you get tired you can rest on the landings."

"Me tired?" said Allie. "We'll see who's huffing and puffing when we get to the top."

Mac let them run ahead. She knew who would be out of breath.

"Just hold on to the rail," Mac warned them. "The stairs are sturdy." At least they were the last time she checked. "But no telling what those boys did the other night, there might be bottles and trash everywhere. Just watch your step."

They started the ascent, Mac bringing up the rear. It seemed to her that for such a bright day, the lighthouse seemed dark.

She had to concentrate on not missing each tread. That's the problem with circular staircases, she thought, not big enough for your whole foot. She'd never thought about that in all her years as keeper. But she was thinking about it now.

The girls were ahead of her now. She could hear their steps ringing on the iron stairs above her. She trudged on; each time she thought she'd just give in and wait below, the light would pour down on her from the windows of the next landing and keep her moving.

When Mac finally reached the watch room, which she had arranged in some semblance of the storeroom, workroom, and observation post that it had once been, Jess and Allie were peering out the windows, as happy as a couple of children.

If grown women could enjoy themselves here . . . unfortunately, they weren't the only ones who enjoyed themselves. Several candy wrappers and soda cans were strewn across the floor as well as cigarette butts.

Mac bent over to pick them up. Allie and Jess were quick to help.

"Maybe you should have a spruce-up-the-lighthouse day and get the kids to clean up after themselves," Jess said.

"I'd like to see it," Mac said.

They shoved all the garbage and the soda cans into the plastic bag Mac always kept in her pocket for just this purpose.

Jess brushed her hands off on her new consignment-store shorts. "Is the old lamp in the . . . let me think . . . the lantern room?"

She remembered, Mac thought, gratified. "It is."

"Can we go up?"

"Ayuh."

The last climb was the easiest since Mac knew what was waiting for them. They came out into brilliant sunshine. So dazzling that Mac had to close her eyes for a few seconds then carefully open them again.

"You can see forever," Allie said. She sighed. "I sometimes feel that way standing on a hill in the vineyard. Rows of grapevines as far as you can see."

Her statement didn't seem to require an answer, so the three of them stood looking out the window, tacitly moving in a circle to take in the whole view. Until Jess stopped.

"Look at that sailboat out there. See?"

They all looked.

"And out there. What is that?"

Mac had no idea.

"Maybe a cruise ship or a barge?" Allie guessed. "I guess GPS or whatever they have keeps them on a steady course. It's kind of sad. To think of all those sailors, all those ships, and the fishing boats that depended on this lighthouse to lead them home . . ." She sighed. "And now here it sits, unlit and forgotten. It just doesn't seem right."

"No, it don't," Mac agreed.

"Oh, I don't know about that. I think maybe—" Jess's voice cracked. "Maybe it's led me home."

Chapter 15

Lillo was just going into the cottage when she saw Diana striding down the road. She looked tired, and dirty, and about as disheveled as Lillo had ever seen her. Make that the *most* disheveled she'd ever seen her.

"Don't ask," Diana said as she walked past her and down the path to the door.

It obviously wasn't a good time to discuss her intentions toward Ian. Lillo bit back a smile. The whole idea sounded ridiculous.

Lillo caught up to her at the door. Diana looked even dirtier up close.

"Really. Don't ask."

They went inside.

"I'm out here," Jess called from the deck. "I've started happy hour early. Bring a glass and come out. It's glorious!"

Diana and Lillo exchanged looks.

"That was the quickest rebound in history," Lillo said.

"Or else she's at the happy stage of drunk."

"Might as well join her," Lillo said, and took two glasses from the dish drainer.

"I think I'll shower first."

"Oh no you don't. I'll bet you money that Jess has never seen you like this."

Diana shook with rueful laughter. "No one has." She rubbed her hand across her face.

"No, don't get rid of the smudge. That makes the whole look."

"What smudge? Do I have a smudge?" Diana followed her out to the deck.

Jess was stretched out on a chaise, an open notebook in her lap, a glass of wine on a table next to her chair.

She waved a pencil at them. "Wine is in the ice bucket. Didn't think you had an ice bucket, so I used a real bucket I found under the sink. I washed it out."

"Good move." Actually, Lillo did have an ice bucket. She'd never used it. Had never taken it out of the box. She never would. Though . . .

"OMG, Di," cried Jess. "What happened to you?"

Diana took a glass from Lillo and poured herself wine. "I just spent an hour tethered to a horse named Pete and riding kids around in a circle. It was so weird. Not to mention dirty. And sticky. And . . ." She shuddered.

"No way. You don't even like kids."

"I know. He trapped me. I told him that I didn't know shit about children, and he just acted like I had said, 'Oh, goody,' and handed me one end of the rope." She plopped down in a chair. "It was exhausting and—did I mention?—dirty.

"Then he sticks me with these kids all wanting a ride, until they found out I was going to be overseeing them, then they all balked and wouldn't get on the horse unless he was there." She took a sip of wine, then another.

"So he squats down to their level and talks to them. For a long time, and they keep looking over at me, then finally when I'm thinking I'll just wander on down the road now, he stands up and says, 'It's okay,' and takes two of them away.

"I swear, a man who hasn't said twenty words to me in three days is suddenly Chatty Cathy with a bunch of munchkins.

"So while he's spending the hour with two brothers, I'm walking in a circle while one kid rides Pete and the other four stare at me from the fence." She leaned back and closed her eyes. "I may never be the same."

"I wonder if they were the kids we saw this morning," Jess said.

"Beats me," Diana said, her eyes still closed. "All I know is that while I was hauling kids on and off Pete's back while giving them a few pointers about riding, he spent the whole hour hugging Clara, this old gray, with Joey and Bobby, the two brothers. The little one is somewhere on the spectrum for something, I think.

"I was trying to watch to see what he was up to, but I was petrified one of the little buggers would fall off and I'd get sued for everything I'm worth."

She settled into silence. Lillo poured herself a glass of wine. It wasn't like she had to drive, or work, or do anything but sit and relax. She sat down.

"Then . . ." Diana continued, getting her second wind—she'd seemed to have forgotten about her shower. "When the kids get picked up, I start leading Pete out of the paddock. Ian comes up and says, 'Never mind, I'll do it.'"

"And I said, 'I don't mind' and 'Are you going to tell me who those kids were?'"

"He just looked at me, said 'Just kids,' moved me physically out of the way, and led Pete into the barn.

"So of course I follow him and ask him what the hell is wrong. He says, 'Nothing.' Before I could react, he says, 'Just go away.' Then he storms off and leaves me standing there. Do you think I just got fired?"

"Do you want to go back after that?" Lillo asked.

"Of course. I deal with ruder people than Ian Lachlan every day."

Jess sat up. "Maybe you shouldn't."

Exactly what Ned had said, thought Lillo.

"What? You think I'll go down without a fight? I'm just getting warmed up."

"I don't know. He sounds strange."

"He *is* strange. I like him, I'm even attracted to him, but he has some serious quirks in his personality."

Jess guffawed. "You're attracted to all men."

"I am not. Though I admit I do rather like them." She sipped her wine. "And I have to admit, this one is different."

"Oh Lord," Jess said.

"No, I mean it. What's his story, Lillo? I thought he was a vet."

"He is."

"And what else?"

"Please don't say 'psychopath,'" Jess said.

Lillo shook her head. Though she wasn't sure, actually. Everyone kind of knew his story. No one talked about it. They trusted him with their livestock and their pets . . . and their children.

"He's great with the kids," she said. "As you saw today."

"A man of many talents?"

"Well, yes, but . . . there are times when he—" *When he what, Lillo?* Can't stand being around people, can't bear to look at them, be with them? Can't even stand to be inside his own skin? Is that what he felt? She couldn't even begin to imagine.

"When he what? What were you going to say, Lillo?"

"I don't know. He's great with kids, not always so great with adults. Something you might want to remember."

"Are you warning me off? You and he don't . . . aren't . . ."

"Aren't what?"

"Lovers?"

"What? Good God, no." The two most screwed-up people in town? It was laughable.

"That's not much of an endorsement."

"Nothing to do with him. We're friends. He's a nice guy. He just, like you said, has a few quirks."

"But he's not dangerous or anything?" Jess asked.

"Only for my peace of mind," Diana said.

And Lillo let it go at that.

"And speaking of quirks, what was he doing with those kids, Joey and Bobby? I think they're brothers."

Lillo said, "Joey and Bobby are special cases. He works with them a couple of times a week."

Diana frowned. "Is he trained as a therapist as well as a vet?"

"I know he's studied a lot of stuff; they have to post their credentials where they can be seen."

"I didn't notice."

"Well, one of them is in EAL."

"Which is?"

"I'm embarrassed to say I'm not really sure." Lillo had been so consumed with her own issues she'd not paid much attention to Ian's. Mac had told her a little, but the people of Lighthouse Beach didn't share everything. A little gossip. A story told once and locked away. If you had something to hide, Lighthouse Beach was the safest place you could be.

"You mean he's like a horse whisperer?" Jess asked, her pencil poised over her notebook.

"I'm not sure about that either. Not even sure what a horse whisperer does."

"Oh, come on," Jess said. "Don't tell me you don't remember the movie?"

Lillo shook her head. She didn't even know there was a movie.

"Really?" Jess said, dropping her pencil into the crease of her notebook. "We watched it about a dozen times. What happened to all your tapes? You had shelves of them. You transfer them to DVD?"

Lillo shrugged. "When my parents sold the house, they got rid of a lot of stuff."

"I don't believe you'd let them throw those out. Some of those were classics."

"Yeah, I know." And they—along with the rest of her life—were buried beneath piles of stuff in the extra bedroom.

"Hey, where's Allie?" Diana asked.

"Well," Jess said, sitting all the way up and putting her feet on the floor. "We went over to Mac's. I didn't know, but Allie's worried that her in-laws would be glad if she left little Gino with them for good."

"No," Lillo said. "Maybe we should encourage her to go back instead of staying to the end of the week."

Jess smiled slowly and shook her head. "Guess where she is now? Talking to the sexy Nando."

Diana opened her eyes at that.

"Mac gave us a tour of the lighthouse. Wow, I had forgotten how cool it was. It's in bad shape now, but with a little TLC—"

"What about Nando and Allie?" Diana asked.

"Oh, well, we were coming out of the lighthouse. Nando had come over to tune up the van. We said hi, Allie and Nando kept talking, and Mac hustled me away. That Mac. I think she has a plan for those two."

Lillo thought Mac should mind her own business. If Allie was worried about her future, she didn't need distractions of that kind.

"Well, good for her," Diana said.

"That's what I say." Jess picked up her pencil.

"Jess, what are you doing? Have you suddenly taken up sketching?"

"I wish, but I can barely draw using a graphics program. But . . ." She turned the notebook for the others to see. Odd shapes and lists and arrows pointing everywhere. "I do have some ideas on how to turn the lighthouse into a profitable venture."

They heard the front door open and close. Footsteps running through the house.

Allie catapulted through the doorway and collapsed onto the nearest deck chair. "I'm in big trouble."

"Would this have anything to do with Nando of the luscious lips?" Diana asked.

"What do you know about his lips?" Jess asked.

"I pay attention," Diana said, and poured Allie a glass of wine.

Allie's eyes widened. "What happened to you?"

"Children, horses, and a stableful of hay." Diana handed her a glass. "But enough about me. Why are you in trouble?"

Allie pulled her chair closer to the other three. They all leaned forward as if they were about to hear a deep secret.

"I don't know. I just— Mac sent me over to ask Nando if he wanted some lemonade and we started talking and he—Nando— offered to take me for a ride on his bike tomorrow because I told him I'd never ridden on one."

"Well, absolutely you should go," said Diana. "Is that the trouble? You don't have anything to wear for a cycle excursion. Now, *that's* trouble, but I'm sure the consignment shop can fit you out."

"Stop it," Jess said. "She's upset."

Lillo had noticed it, too. Allie looked extremely pale except for two fiery marks across her cheeks.

"Okay, girl, spill it."

Allie took a healthy sip of wine. Shivered.

"Uh-oh, we may need more wine." Diana reached for the bottle.

"It's just that while we were talking . . . I mean I hardly know him . . . but it was just . . ." She ran a tongue over her bottom lip. "Well, kinda hot."

"That's great," Diana said. "You're back in the land of the living."

"I mean really hot."

"How far did you go?" Diana asked in her deepest voice.

"We didn't go anywhere, except I think he was . . . you know . . . and I certainly was." She leaned back in the chair so hard it wobbled. "Thank God there are only a few more days before I leave."

"Ha. Time enough to do a quick exploratory affair."

"I—no. I can't. I won't."

"Come on, Allie. You deserve a little fun. And that's all it has to be. A little fun. Gino wouldn't begrudge you that."

Allie shook her head and her eyes filled.

Diana put down her glass and took Allie's hand. "Allie, it's been almost four years since Gino died. He wouldn't want you to curl up and never find love again."

Allie pulled her hand away. And covered her face with both hands. "We were supposed to be together forever."

Lillo bit her lip and looked out to the waves to calm herself. Forever could sometimes be much shorter than you thought.

"Okay. If you feel like you have to leave, I'll rent a car and drive you to the airport." Diana looked at Lillo.

"There's a rental place on the mainland," Lillo said. "We can borrow Mac's van to pick it up."

Diana reached for her glass. "So, it's all good. Whatever you want to do."

"I want my husband back."

Jess, Diana, and Lillo exchanged looks and said nothing.

After a few moments Allie shook herself and looked up. "Are those crackers on that plate?"

Jess passed her the plate.

"Did Jess tell you about visiting the lighthouse? It was so interesting, wasn't it, Jess?"

Jess nodded.

"That's it?" Diana asked. "Soooo?"

"Mac said to come over at seven and bring our appetites."

"Talk about changing the subject."

"I . . ." Allie swallowed convulsively. "Just this once. I want to stay."

Diana let out a slow breath. "It's this town. It's like one of those places that just shows up when needed—like a latter-day Brigadoon appears out of the mist when someone needs help. Is that what the sign means, Lillo? Life will never be the same after you visit Lighthouse Beach?"

"It's just a sign," Lillo said. "You know, marketing."

"I wonder."

Jess sat up. "Di, this is so not you. Are you going all woo-woo on us?"

"No. But I know a tightly run corporation when I see it. You protect each other. You protect strangers. Look how they stood up for you the other night. How no one seems to pay anything to the clinic. How Doc Clancy drops everything and spends days at a hospital with his patient's mother just to be supportive. Is everyone in town like that?"

They looked at Lillo. She shrugged. "I can't answer for everybody."

"It's like we were drawn here."

"Ridiculous."

"Jess needed help. She wanted to come here. Because . . . I'm not sure why, but she knew where to go."

"Oh, come on, Diana, it's because she remembered good days here as a kid. Plus, I had the car."

"What about me and Allie? Are we here because we need help, too?"

"Allie came because she's Jess's friend. You're here because you invited yourself."

Jess crowed. "Well, she's got you there."

Diana looked over to Lillo. Lillo held up her glass to Diana.

Diana returned the air toast, drained her glass, and stood. "And why are you here, Lillo?" She put her empty glass on the table. "I think I'll just go wash off my 'trail dirt' before dinner."

Allie and Jess were left looking at Lillo.

"Why did you come back, Lillo?" Jess asked.

"Because it's my home." And because she felt safe here. At least until this week.

What was happening here? Until this week, she would have said she was happy staking tomatoes, and tying up peonies, pulling weeds, and deadheading spent blooms. Now it just didn't seem like enough.

Even Ian, as damaged as he was, helped others, accepted the kids, though it must be nearly impossible for him. And here she was, staking tomatoes and feeling like her life was over, when she should have been giving, too.

Maybe Diana was right about the sign. She'd lived here for most of her nearly thirty years and had never given it a second thought; until now.

Chapter 16

Diana, Allie, and Jess were still sleeping when Lillo, dressed in clean slacks and a T-shirt, quietly slipped out of the cottage the next morning. Now she was standing across the street from the clinic wondering if she would actually go inside, and if she did, whether she would be making a big mistake.

But Doc and Ian hadn't come to dinner last night. And if Doc was too tired to eat Mac's cooking, then he needed help. She'd actually been disappointed not to see him. And she knew Diana was disappointed that Ian hadn't come, but all she said when Mac remarked on it was, "He keeps my wits sharpened."

Lillo knew Diana was intrigued by Ian, but she wasn't sure if it was because he was an enigma to be cracked or because she really cared about him. Lillo had to admit she had a wild urge to see the immovable meet the unstoppable. She'd put her money on Diana and her hope on her doing Ian a world of good.

If not . . . well, she didn't want to contemplate that endgame. She really didn't want to contemplate her own situation either.

Situation? She was up to her chin in quicksand, and if she didn't haul herself out soon, she would disappear forever. Would that be a bad thing?

"Yes." *Get your shit together. Now.*

Lillo stepped off the curb, crossed the street. She didn't go in the front door, even though she knew Agnes would already be there, and coffee would be freshly made; though at the moment she had so much adrenaline coursing through her body the last thing she needed was caffeine.

She walked around the side of the clinic. Slowed down as she neared the back door. She just needed another second or two to pull herself together. Such a simple thing: turn the doorknob, step inside, tell Agnes she was only here to unpack supplies and restock shelves and cabinets.

The whole hello thing would take thirty seconds max. Then she'd pour herself a cup of coffee and the world would stop tilting. She'd organize and reorganize, say good-bye, and leave before Ned could say thank you or smile at her like she'd done a good thing.

All the good things in the world couldn't make up for the one thing she couldn't undo. She sat down on the stoop. She just needed another second to regroup.

And that's where Ned found her when he rode into the driveway and came to a stop.

Lillo shot to her feet. She'd meant to be hard at work before he arrived so she could just keep doing things and he couldn't make a big deal about her being there. Agnes would have already given her instructions, because that's the way it had been since Lillo had volunteered there as a young girl. And she and Ned wouldn't have to talk about stuff.

She'd move supplies around and clean up between patients. A glorified janitor. Her penance. It was about time.

Ned walked up the steps toward her, taking off his helmet. "Isn't Agnes in?" he asked nonchalantly, no shock at seeing her, no questioning look. Not even a smug smile. He walked past her to the door.

"I don't know. I haven't gone in yet."

"Door's open. She must be here." He held it open for her.

Lillo went inside. And it was done.

Agnes was surprised—and happy. She jumped up from her desk, scattering files, and gave Lillo a hug. "It's been a long time since we've seen you at the clinic. Welcome back."

"I'm not—I just—I'm just here to restock shelves and things like that, so you and Doc can catch up on the patient list."

"That's great. Let's grab a quick cup of coffee and I'll show you what's what. We've moved some things around since you were here last."

Lillo followed her to the kitchen. It looked just like it always did, except for more boxes of supplies, more file cabinets, and less space at the table.

She and Agnes stood in the little patch of free floor space, sipping their coffee and trying not to feel awkward—at least Lillo was trying.

Finally, Agnes looked up from her cup. "Thank you so much for coming in. With Doc Clancy not here, Doc has had his hands full and more. I stocked the cabinet in his exam room before I left last night, but he'll be needing things moved back and forth before the morning's out."

Lillo started to say she'd just planned to stay for the morning, because she had out-of-town guests, but the explanation refused to come out. And when they'd rinsed out their cups and Agnes handed her a stack of boxes, Lillo followed her down the hall to Ned's office and examination room.

"I'll give you ten minutes to get organized, then I'll call in the first patient," Agnes said over her head, and left her standing in the doorway.

MAC LEANED IN a little closer to the window and squinted to see who was standing in the parking lot. It was another bright sunny day. Good for the girls' vacation, but it made everyone look like black silhouettes to her. She thought it must be Allie or Jess. Because Lillo had left a good hour ago. It was probably Allie looking for a signal for her phone. Mac didn't know why she just didn't come in and use the landline. It wouldn't break the bank any more than anything else.

And if she wanted her privacy for calling her in-laws, talking to her child, making new plane reservations, she could shut the door. Mac liked the girl, enjoyed having her here, and she was pleased as punch yesterday when her lemonade ploy worked and Allie actually stayed and talked to Nando. She thought they must have hit it off. She'd heard their laughter through the open window.

That was a good sign. And she was taking all the good signs she could find these days. She'd spent a good part of last night watching the lighthouse for marauders. There had been a hefty cloud cover and it was dark as pitch. Several times she thought she saw shadows moving, but it was only the wind and clouds. At least that's what she hoped. She went out as soon as the tide was out this morning to double-check. Everything looked untouched.

And old. Old like her. Older and in worse shape. She hadn't realized it until she tried seeing it through Jess's and Allie's eyes. If it didn't get some much-needed refurbishing, the lighthouse would soon be beyond repair. Soon both of them would be beyond repair.

Her whole adult life had been spent there. Her version of a

family home. The gift shop had been the actual keeper's house, but she had always felt more at home in the lighthouse. "Like Rapunzel's tower," Lillo had once said. But that had been a long, long time ago, when Lillo was a little girl, and Mac doubted if she even remembered saying it.

The lighthouse had been automated decades ago. It had stayed active for a while after that, with Mac mainly responsible for technical maintenance. Then it was shut down completely.

The town bought it for a song and gifted Mac the keeper's house for as long as she lived. Which was very generous, but what would happen to it when she was gone? Torn down or left to fall down; either way the lighthouse would cease to exist. Because unless there was a sudden surge in real estate or tourism, which seemed unlikely, the two-member historical society would never be able to raise the funds to sustain it.

But by then, hopefully, Mac would be beyond caring. Did you wonder about things when you were dead? Mac doubted it. She didn't believe in an afterlife.

And you shouldn't be wasting your earthly life thinking about it, old woman.

Allie—Mac could see it was Allie now—was walking toward the gift shop. She put on a fresh pot of coffee.

A minute later the back door opened and shut.

"Mac?"

"Come on in. I just put on coffee."

Allie stepped into the kitchen and Mac mentally patted herself on the back for her perspicacity. The girl was dressed for success. An outfit she'd surely brought with her. Because of Nando? Mac hoped so, not that she thought anything lasting would come of it, but that girl needed to awaken to life again.

"I need to ask a favor," Allie said.

Uh-oh, thought Mac. She sounded serious. This was not the time for her to be serious. Had she scared herself?

Allie's gaze flitted away then back to Mac's face.

"Ask away," Mac said with more enthusiasm than she was suddenly feeling.

"First I have a question."

Mac nodded. What was with the girl?

"How long have you been losing your eyesight?"

NED SPENT THE morning trying not to pay attention to Lillo quietly restocking shelves and cleaning and resetting the examination room. She was a natural, waiting for him to walk out with a patient before slipping into the room and slipping out again as he showed the next patient in. Sometimes she wasn't fast enough and a patient stopped to ask how she was.

She was attentive and kind but managed to slip away quickly. Ned tried to convince himself that she was just being efficient, but he was pretty sure that she just didn't want to be seen.

All morning he'd been treading carefully, careful not to fall into the easy camaraderie they used to have when she was off from med school and he came in for his brief stint as visiting doctor, careful not to be caught watching her. Trying to look steadily expressionless when it was necessary to talk to her or ask her to get something he needed.

It was humiliating for both of them. Both denying the gift she had. Pretending like things hadn't derailed for her in a tragic way. Knowing he could never convince her to get back to what she did best. That the world needed her. But it wasn't his place. Not anymore.

It was around lunchtime when he happened to overhear Lillo tell Agnes she was going to leave. She offered to pick up sandwiches and bring them back before she called it a day. Was she going to sneak away without at least asking if he still needed her? Not that she owed the clinic anything. But the two of them had fallen into such a comfortable, efficient, stressless rhythm that he knew he would miss her the moment she was gone.

Fortunately—for him at least—Dora Wilson brought her daughter Callie in with a gash on her leg. While her mother held her and tried to soothe her, he and Lillo quickly cleaned the wound and stitched her up.

He was unnerved at how easily Lillo had slipped back into her role of physician, and dreaded the moment when she realized what she'd done. He knew there would be repercussions; he just hoped that when the dust cleared, they would all be on the right side of the outcome.

They were cleaning up after Callie when Ned heard a motorcycle turn into the backyard of the clinic and come to a stop.

Lillo heard it, too; she stopped to listen and Ned could see the reality beginning to sink in. She hurriedly pulled off the used paper table cover, wadded it up, gathered up the used gauze and swabs, dropped the instruments into the metal tray, and carried them all toward the door.

She was moving at warp speed as panic took over. He could see it happening and there was not one damn thing he could do about it.

Ned wanted to run and stand in front of the door, barring her way out. Convince her she was screwing up her life for all the wrong reasons. But he didn't have a chance.

And as it turned out, he didn't need to.

She opened the door and walked right into Clancy Farrow.

They both stopped cold, one of those suspended moments

where the only reaction you could have—when reaction came—
was surrender.

Clancy broke first. "Lillo, great to have you back." A quick
glance over her head to Ned. "Sorry I left you two in the lurch
for so long. If the people in this town would only go to the
doctor before it became an emergency, everyone would be a lot
better off."

Lillo smiled and slipped past him, leaving Ned and Clancy
looking at each other.

Clancy raised his eyebrows and shut the door. "How did you
manage that?"

Ned shrugged. "I didn't. She was sitting on the stoop when
I got here this morning. I didn't ask, just acted like it was perfectly normal." He exhaled. "I've been walking on eggshells all
day hoping I wouldn't scare her away."

"I think *I* might have—scared her away."

"We'll see. Maybe she'll remember how good she was at this
doctoring business and won't be able to stay away."

"Perhaps."

"But you don't hold out much hope. Neither do I."

Clancy tossed his helmet on the coatrack and shrugged out
of his jacket.

Ned slouched down in his desk chair and watched his mentor and old friend. A little more portly, a little less hair, but still
as vibrant as the day they'd met. "You wouldn't believe how
smoothly everything went this morning, and all she was doing
was replacing supplies and making patients feel more relaxed.
Then Callie Wilson came in with a pretty deep leg wound; it
required a couple layers of stitches and she didn't miss a beat."

"Stitches are pretty standard stuff," Clancy reminded him.

"I know, but it's a start."

"True. Anything else happen while I was gone?"

Ned burst out laughing. "What didn't happen?"

DIANA LOOKED UP at Ian's house. She'd gone straight to the stables when she'd arrived. He wasn't there. He wasn't with patients or in his office. Loki was in his stall, so this was the last place she knew to look.

She didn't know whether he was purposely avoiding her or if he'd been called out on an emergency. He might be skulking around on the second floor of his house watching her through dingy windows, hoping she'd go away.

Then why not just tell her? She winced. Actually, he had. Several times.

She climbed up the porch steps. She'd just knock. What if he'd fallen and couldn't get up or had the flu and was hallucinating?

She knocked, waited, tried the knob. The door wasn't locked; she opened it. Called out. Got no answer. Peered into the shadows.

She didn't go in but she did look around. The front room was large—barely furnished. "Spartan" would be a nice way of putting it. She could see a fairly modern kitchen off to the right, with a big butcher-block table in the center.

She was dying to get a closer look but she didn't dare. He was prickly enough as it was. So she backed out of the door and returned to the barn and started working.

She let the horses out to the pasture while she cleaned the stalls. Put down fresh bedding. Filled the feed bin. Picked out the rotting apples from the treat box.

Time passed and still he didn't return.

She should probably just bring the animals in and leave. She couldn't believe the flood of disappointment she felt. Totally over the top and out of proportion; she barely knew the man. Except for the night of the barbecue, they'd hardly spoken.

She brought in the two ponies first. They were sweet animals and perfectly child-size. She went back for the others, dragging her feet like a child. Clara and Pete came dutifully back to the barn and began to munch on fresh hay.

When she went back out for Princess, the mare nudged her shoulder. But when Diana reached for her bridle, she danced away, shook her head, and stood her ground. She wanted to play. Diana wasn't in the mood.

"Come on. He's obviously not coming back in time for a ride and I wouldn't dare take you out without him. He'd have my head. So come here. Come on."

Loki came up to see what was going on, then walked over to the fence. Diana could swear he was looking for Ian.

And suddenly there he was, walking toward them from around the side of the barn. "You have better ears than I do, boy," Diana said, and waited for Ian to reach them.

Wherever he'd been, he was squeaky clean, freshly showered, his hair was still wet, clothes newly laundered. He glanced at her but went directly to Loki. Loki lowered his head until man and horse were forehead to forehead.

Diana had seen this ritual before, some kind of human–equine communication that shut out the rest of the world. Princess stood by patiently then eased over to get her share of attention. Ian reached up to caress her neck. Diana was so tempted to join them, but she wouldn't grovel.

And truth be told, it was such a fragile, peaceful moment that she was afraid to break it.

The very thought made her want to laugh. Ms. Sensitivity she was not. The whole idea was ridiculous. But for better or worse, being here, doing this was so much more entertaining—more inviting—than a week at the spa. The only thing that would make it better would be if she could actually crack the enigma that was Ian Lachlan.

She turned and leaned back against the fence, and waited for him to finish his communion with the horses. She tried picturing herself in shitkickers and a cowboy hat, a piece of hay in the side of her mouth. *Just kick back and relax, at home in the paddock. Horses are my middle name.*

When he finally straightened up, she pushed away from the fence, the hat, the boots, the straw dissolving in an instant. "We were beginning to miss you," she said laconically. She was trying so hard she was surprised her words didn't come out with a Texas accent.

"I was out on a call. Several."

"Everything okay?"

"Fairly serious case of bovine mastitis. Colic at the alpaca farm and a nasty, difficult foaling."

His tone brought her back to herself. "Mother and baby okay?"

"So far. A case of wait and see."

"Frustrating."

He looked at her. Looked away.

She had no idea what that reaction was about.

"Guess you want to skip riding today?"

A twitch more than a shrug. Maybe he just didn't want to ride with her.

Suddenly this didn't feel like a game anymore.

"Guess I'll see you tomorrow, then." She started to move away.

"No."

"No, you won't see me tomorrow?" Was he ditching her? Because of a bad foaling? Or because she had worked with his animals while he was gone?

"No. We'll ride today. If you want."

They rode, like always, one after the other, Ian leading without talking, never looking back. And Diana wondered if maybe he wasn't consciously ignoring her, if maybe he'd just forgotten she was there.

Today he took a trail through the woods; they climbed up and up; the trail narrowed until the brush was touching their legs.

And Diana, much to her dismay, remembered Lillo's words. "He isn't dangerous." Why had she said that? And why was she thinking that now, when she was alone in the woods with a man she didn't know and whom she couldn't begin to fathom.

Good sense told her to turn around and go back to the barn. But curiosity and a sense of inevitability kept her going.

Abruptly, the woods ended and the trail opened onto a wide rocky bluff. The sea stretched out below them in dazzling blues. The wind was strong and it whipped Diana's hair across her face. She shivered. Ian slid off Loki's back and walked him over to a dead tree that lay half hidden by undergrowth. He tethered him and then reached back for Diana's reins. She climbed down and handed them to him. He tethered Princess next to Loki, stayed a minute to stroke and reassure the horses. Then he walked back to Diana.

She stood waiting, her heart racing, caught somewhere between anticipation and fear.

He took her arm; she stiffened, but it was a gentle touch, like he used with the horses, and Diana, like Loki and Princess, calmed, and let him lead her to the edge.

He climbed down the rocky outcropping and reached back to help her down to where the path widened into a flat semicircular platform. There the ocean spread before them, behind them, the bluff's wall protecting their backs from the piercing wind. And running along the wall was a bench of rock so perfect for sitting that Diana thought nature might have deliberately carved it as a scenic lookout.

Ian sat down. Diana sat beside him. They both stared out at the water. The wind blustered around them. Below them, the waves crashed on the rocky shore. But in the small sanctuary of the bluff, the silence was complete.

She could feel Ian calm as the intense energy that seemed to be his normal state left him. The change was almost tangible as the man next to her surrendered . . . to what? Nature? Being with her? She flushed at her own egotism. More likely this was Ian Lachlan's Batcave.

At least he'd deigned to share it with her. Or was she misreading him completely? Maybe it was time to find out.

"When did you get interested in kids?" Diana risked a sideways glance at him. And realized everything about her dealings with Ian included some amount of risk.

"Why?"

She'd given up thinking he was going to answer or even look at her, and the sound of his voice made her jump. "You just don't strike me as the kind of guy who would be."

"Be what?" He was still looking straight ahead.

"I don't know." *Patient? Gentle? Understanding?* All those words came to mind, and Diana realized he was all those things, just taciturn. But the horses didn't mind, and the kids adored him, though, come to think of it, he wasn't taciturn with them. She'd actually heard him laughing with Joey and Bobby the day before.

He didn't laugh with her. He barely talked to her. But he was talking now.

"Are you trained in child psychology? I mean I know you're a vet, but . . ."

"They come to ride horses."

She gave him her bullcrap look. "Joey and Bobby didn't ride that much, mainly they just hugged Clara and led her around and things."

"EAL, Equine Assisted Learning. I passed the course, if you're worried about my credentials."

Diana turned to face him. "Why do you take the worst possible meaning out of everything I say? I was just curious. People are curious beings, in case you've forgotten."

"I haven't."

"Haven't forgotten how to be curious?"

"Haven't forgotten what curiosity can do."

LILLO DIDN'T GO home right away. She wandered away from town, toward the water. She just didn't want to run into anyone who had seen her have lunch with Ned, or had seen her go into the clinic. Who would make assumptions, would ask her questions.

Hell, what was she thinking, everyone would know she'd been there. How many patients had they seen?

She stopped dead. *Patients?* How dare she. Ned was the doctor, not her. Not now. She never would be. Couldn't be. But no sooner had she stepped into the clinic than it all seemed so natural, so right. She'd welcomed the unique odor of old house and antiseptic.

It had been a mistake. Well meaning, but a mistake all the same. Still, she could kick herself for running out like that. She should have shown a little discipline and made a dignified exit. They were probably all talking about her—Agnes, Clancy, and Ned—thinking she was a basket case, and they'd be right.

She should never have gone. She wouldn't return. Doc Clancy was back, they wouldn't need her. Of course, an extra pair of hands was always welcome in a free clinic. But not hers.

She climbed down the grassy verge to where she could see the lighthouse and the keeper's cottage. That was where she belonged. A quiet life in a quiet town. No questions asked. She saw Mac and Allie come out of the house, get into the van, and drive away.

Wondered where they were going in the middle of the day. Had Allie not gone on her motorcycle ride with Nando? Were they driving to the mall to buy her some motorcycle riding clothes? Or had she chickened out and canceled, and Mac was driving her to the bus station so she could catch a flight home?

Tears stung Lillo's eyes, surprising her. At first she thought maybe she'd gotten some fleck of pollen or dust in them. She didn't cry. Lillo Gray had stopped crying a year ago. She wouldn't start again.

Chapter 17

"Wasn't that Lillo we just passed?" Allie asked as she maneuvered the van down the two-lane road.

"You're asking me?"

"Oh, don't be such a grump, Mac. Maybe you just need glasses. If the place we're going is like other eyeglass places, they get your prescription and have a pair ready by this afternoon." She reached over and patted Mac's thigh.

The gesture just made Mac feel like an old lady. "Or maybe I have a brain tumor."

Allie glanced over at her. "Maybe, but at least going to the optometrist today can put us on the right path."

"My path to doom. You'll all leave and I'll be kicked out of my house to die a lonely death on the streets of Lighthouse Beach."

"You're just being difficult, right? You're not really afraid, are you?"

You're damn straight I'm afraid, Mac wanted to tell her. *I've been hanging on by my fingernails for years now.* One little slip and . . . where would she be? Who ever heard of a lighthouse keeper who couldn't see?

Not that it mattered. The lighthouse was as dead as she was blind. Two old gaffers past their prime.

"Me? Nah. Just damn inconvenient."

"And what major plans did you have today that you're having to give up?"

Nothing under the sun, thought Mac. It was just pitiful. "Take the right fork up ahead." She had half a mind to take them all the way up the coast instead of into the town and the optometrist's office.

Allie turned on the blinker.

"I mean the left fork."

Allie changed the blinker. "Are you trying to pull a fast one?"

The girl was no dummy. "No. Just confused for a minute. You know how us old folks get."

"Oh, stop it. Is that what you're afraid of? People will think you're losing it? Lots of people wear glasses. You should get out more."

"Says the girl who's afraid to take a ride on a man's motorcycle."

"I'm not afraid of riding a motorcycle."

"Nope. Just afraid of the man."

Allie stared straight ahead and Mac knew she'd hit the mark. Well hell, you didn't need 20/20 vision to see what was going on with that girl.

"You're a pretty wily one, aren't you, Allie?"

Allie glanced over at her then back to the road. "I don't understand."

"You show up in Lighthouse Beach in the middle of the night, just one of the girls, saving a friend from certain disaster, supportive, quiet, and totally self-effacing. That's a gentle word for 'afraid to show your insides to the world.'"

"That's not true."

Allie's voice caught. Mac chuckled. The girl was a terrible liar, poor thing. "Tell me. What do you do at that vineyard of yours?"

"It's not mine. It belongs to the family."

"Then what do you do at the family's vineyard? Turn left up here at the stop sign."

Allie slowed, stopped, and made the turn.

"Well?"

"I . . . since Gino's death, I've sort of taken over running the business. They were really floundering and not using what resources they had. I computerized everything, hired marketers and publicists. I keep everything organized and running smoothly while growing the business."

"Sounds like they really depend on you."

For a second Allie didn't answer. "I think they'd be happy to go back to the old ways."

Mac could certainly relate to that.

"And I have my son. He's really the joy of my life."

"Keeps you pretty busy."

"He does."

"But still doesn't fill the hole left by your husband's death."

Mac didn't have to see her reaction. That startled whimper, quickly cut off, told her everything she suspected.

"If you need to pull over, do it. I don't want to die because you can't see the road."

"I don't need to. That was mean."

"No, it wasn't. It's the truth, isn't it? You're not the first person to lose someone you love. You grieve and one day you move on. It doesn't happen in a day, but you know what I mean. You can try to stay busy, you can try to stop living, you can try to bury yourself, but sooner or later life wins out." Mac sighed. "Don't wait until you're too old to care."

Allie's head swerved toward Mac—and so did the van.

"Eyes on the road."

Allie straightened the wheel and hunkered down.

"It's a gift to have that kind of love, even if you couldn't keep it. It doesn't mean you can't try again. Or just have a little fun along the way. Like a ride on the back of Nando's motorcycle."

Mac looked over at Allie, who was studiously ignoring her. She was like a crocus in spring just waiting for the thaw, waiting to come out and bloom.

And Nando might just be the heat she needed. Mac chuckled. She couldn't help it. She hadn't thought about those things in years.

"What?"

"Nothin' . . . much." Mac would love to see it: Allie learning to love again. Wouldn't that be something. *Stupid old woman, you better hope you can keep seeing anything at all.*

NED AND CLANCY finished up at six. Clancy was in a hurry to get to the keeper's house and relax. He'd been doing double duty as physician and caregiver, had driven to the clinic and worked a full day.

Ned was tired, but he was antsy, too. He wondered what Lillo was doing. Whether she was feeling good about the morning or castigating herself for even giving it a try. With Lillo, he could pretty much guess it was the second.

He'd never known a woman so intent on ignoring her own best interests.

"You going after her?" Clancy asked, shrugging into his jacket.

Ned started. Leave it to Clancy to always know what he was

thinking. "No. I'm afraid of making things worse instead of better."

"Smart choice. If I see her, I'll thank her and tell her I hope we'll see her tomorrow."

Ned started to tell him not to.

"You just have to learn how to handle these skittish ones," Clancy continued.

"That sounds very chauvinistic."

"Only in your mind. I was talking about patients, male or female, adult or child, human or animal. The skittish ones need a soft approach."

"She needs a good shake."

Clancy snorted. "I believe you already tried that approach."

"With dire consequences. I remember." How could Ned forget. He'd been so furious when she showed up in Lighthouse Beach a year ago. Her car packed to the roof with her belongings. She moved into the cottage and didn't come out for six days.

He'd heard what had happened. He doubted if there was anyone in the medical community who hadn't. But he hadn't expected her to just turn tail and run home.

She might have stayed there for the whole few weeks Ned had been in town if he hadn't forced his way in. Well, "forced" wasn't exactly the word he would use: the sliding glass door had been unlocked.

He'd meant to help, but she looked so destroyed that he got angry all over again, not at her, not really, but about the whole thing. And angry at her, too. For letting what happened make her give up everything she'd worked for and was good at. He'd said some things meant to shock her into coming back to them, but it had only driven her away and gained him a black eye in the bargain.

They hadn't seen much of each other since then. The last time he'd been in town she'd left; whether it was coincidental or on purpose, he'd never asked.

They'd gotten off to a bumpy start this trip. But it was like everything was bringing them together. And she'd showed up today. Maybe it was the beginning of her getting back to work. He mentally crossed his fingers. He didn't know why it mattered to him. People quit medical school, residencies, practices all the time. It all got to be too much, too hard, or just too life-consuming. But he remembered her fire and her determination and her sacrifices. And her parents' sacrifices.

"Don't sweat it," Clancy said, lifting his helmet off the peg. He paused at the door. "She'll either come back to medicine or she won't. It's her decision to make, not mine, yours, or anybody else's."

"She's got cataracts," Allie announced as soon as they had all been introduced to Clancy and sat down to dinner.

Lillo watched Mac ignore them all as she lifted a pot roast onto a platter. No one said anything. She carried the platter over to the table and dropped it on the table in front of Clancy. Gravy sloshed over the sides.

Clancy lifted one side of his mouth. "I'm guessing that spill is your temper and not 'cause you're blind as a bat."

Mac turned on him. "That's just why I didn't want her to say anything."

"Well, at least it isn't a brain tumor. I'm starving." He picked up the carving knife and attacked the roast with gusto.

"That's great news," Jess said. "Isn't it just an in-and-out procedure?"

"Portland has a good outpatient center," Clancy said. "Stay

there overnight, get your post-op evaluation the next day, and you're back here for lunch."

"And who'll watch the lighthouse?"

"Lighthouse can watch itself for a night or two."

"Are you going to pay the insurance when some damn tourist or kid trespasses and gets hurt and sues the crap out of the town?"

"Oh, hang the lighthouse. Or get old Harry Packard. He can watch it and be glad of the work."

Mac handed a bowl of potatoes to Jess to pass. "Harry Packard's a drunk."

"I'll be here to watch Harry," Lillo said, taking the bowl from Jess and helping herself.

Clancy rolled his eyes at her. She knew how he felt about her "decision," as he and Ned insisted on calling her move back to Lighthouse Beach. It hadn't been her decision. Her misfortune, her bad luck, her stupidity had been the factors that decided her fate.

Lillo put down the bowl. "Why didn't you tell me you were having trouble seeing? We could have taken care of this weeks, months ago." She glared at Mac, angry that she didn't trust Lillo with her problems, and even more, she was hurt that Mac couldn't.

"You have your own life to deal with."

"No, I don't. I mean—" Lillo swallowed the sudden tightening in her throat. Would she never be trusted again? Hell, would she ever stop making everything about her? Mac was suffering.

"I don't have anybody to drive me," Mac groused.

"I can drive you," Lillo said.

"Hell, I'll drive you," said Clancy, "providing that old bucket of yours still runs."

"You won't be here."

"Why not? I can be here, I'm retired—basically."

"That's just why I didn't want Allie to announce this to the world."

"Oh, shut up, woman. Nobody's feeling sorry for you. You're too damn ornery to feel sorry for. If a friend wants to help you, let 'em."

"Hear, hear," said Diana.

"Absolutely," Jess added.

"Fine, if just to shut you up."

"Whew," Allie said under her breath.

"You did good," Lillo told her, just as quietly.

"Glad that's settled," Clancy said. "Diana, keep moving that bowl of mash around. I'm starving."

"You know," Ned said, "we could be at Mac's right now, eating whatever she cooked, and it would be better than this." He lifted a spoonful of the thin goulash and dribbled it back into his bowl.

"Why don't you go on, then?" Ian said.

"Because believe it or not, I'd like to spend time with my old friend."

"Or are you just afraid to sit down at the table with Lillo and have her bite your head off?"

"She came in to help today," Ned said, pushing the goulash away and going to the fridge to look inside. "Totally empty. How do you survive?"

"Usually I go to the grocery. But I've been busy this week."

"How are the foal and mother doing?"

"Nimbly called. They're both on their feet and eating."

"Which is more than I can say for us. You didn't make this, did you?"

"No. Mrs. Kravitz did and it was good the first couple of times, but then I had to add water to it."

"The mind boggles. How is the new CEO?"

"What CE— Oh." Ian gave him a dark look and pushed his bowl away.

"I'm calling Sal and asking him to deliver some pasta and salad." Ned pushed his chair back from the table. "But you're not off the hook about the CEO." He went into the hall to phone Sal, then came back to the kitchen. "Twenty minutes. Want another beer while we wait?"

"Sure."

Ned opened two more beers, set one down in front of Ian, moved the bowls of diluted goulash to the sink, and sat down.

"Okay, what's going on?" Ned asked.

"Nothing."

"She's been here nearly every day since they arrived . . . I'd say that's something."

"She won't stay away."

"Do you want her to?"

Ian studied his beer bottle. Turned it around so the other side was facing him. "No."

"So you guys get along?"

"Not really. We just ride."

"You know you're getting harder to talk to every time I visit. You need to get out and practice, man, before you become some rusty old recluse with a long beard and crossed eyes who only converses with horses."

"That's pretty much me already, except for the beard and the crossed eyes."

"Do you think that's healthy? Why don't you go into Portland and do some group? It helps. You know it does."

"I know. I'm just busy."

"Bullshit, but I know better than to argue. So tell me about the CEO."

"Her name is Diana."

Ned took a swig of beer to hide his grin. He'd learned over the past few years that if you wanted to get information from Ian, you had to wait for it.

"So Diana, what about her?"

Ian pushed his fingers through his hair, a gesture that surprised Ned. "Hell, I don't know how to talk to her. Hell, talk to anybody, but especially to her.

"And I took her to the bluff and she said I didn't seem like the kind of guy who liked kids."

"What would she know? Those types are married to their career."

"I thought she was questioning my expertise."

"Was she?"

"No, she said I always did something, I forget what exactly. That I always took what she said in the worst way or something like that."

"And you did."

"Pretty much."

Ned looked across the table. He'd known Ian for almost twenty years. He'd been full of fire and optimism with a belief in his ability to make the world a better place. Ned didn't understand people like him. The Doctors Without Borders types who selflessly gave their time and expertise to people who as soon as they were healed from one thing were just as likely to succumb to something else—poverty, disease, or war.

Ian had learned that the hard way. And he'd reacted like any normal man would . . . and he had never forgiven himself for it. Ned saved lives, but he never put his own life on the line to do it. He didn't think he had the temperament or even the guts to put his life on the line once, much less day after day, month after month, year after year.

"Go for it," he said. It was a stupid idea . . . a CEO and a traumatized veterinarian. But could it do either of them any real harm?

"I'm not sure I remember how. Or even if . . . nah. They'll be gone and things will go back to normal."

"Hell, Ian." Ned pushed his chair back and stood. Walked across the narrow space in the kitchen not taken up by the table. "You and Lillo, two of the most talented people I know, are sitting here, wasting away, because of shit that was totally out of your control."

"The difference being," Ian said as calmly as Ned was frustrated, "for Lillo, things *were* out of her control. For me, *I* was the one out of control. There's a difference."

Ned collapsed back onto his chair. "I get that. I just don't get why she's still so fucked up."

"Count your blessings."

Neither of them spoke for a while, just drank their beer, thinking their own thoughts. Ned had never been so glad to see a delivery guy in his life. He never knew how far to push Ian. He'd certainly pushed Lillo too far last year. Had he done more harm than good? Had he pushed her further into her isolation? He didn't want to do that to Ian.

He loved them both dearly, and he just couldn't figure out how to help either of them.

THE RAIN CAME overnight like the reports said it would. It was a doozy. Rattling the windows of the cottage, the wind howling around the corners like something from a ghost story. The lights must have gone out sometime during the night because when Lillo dragged herself out of bed at eight o'clock, according to her phone, the kitchen clock said five thirty.

She made coffee and looked out the kitchen window. The rain was still coming down, hitting the puddles of the parking lot at an angle and setting off sprays of water. A day for curling up with a good book. Except that she had guests, didn't have a good book at hand, and had meant to make herself go back to the clinic this morning.

Who said the road to hell was paved with good intentions? Well, if she was going to the clinic, she might as well get started. She was sick to death of having her life on hold. Self-imposed though it was.

For the last few months she'd actually thought she was getting her life back on track, learning to live with her failures and her hideous mistake. She didn't dwell on it 24/7 like she had done during the first few months back in Lighthouse Beach, or for the months she'd tried to hold on before that, determined to make amends, to make it work, until she couldn't try anymore. She'd thought she'd made progress, was on her way to living out the rest of her life, if not with happiness then at least without doing harm.

But that had all changed with Jess's wedding invitation. She'd taken a chance and it had torn her tenuous existence right down the middle.

So what now? Did she go or did she stay? She hummed that line while she sipped coffee and watched the rain.

Then she crammed a change of clothes into her backpack; she'd need them by the time she walked to the clinic. She put on her rain slicker and boots, pulled up the hood, tucked her head in anticipation of the rain, and went outside. Stupid idea. Nobody but the desperately ill would venture out on a day like this.

The clinic was bound to be quiet today.

They wouldn't need her.

There would be a lot of time sitting around doing nothing.

Clancy and Agnes and maybe even Ned would want to chat. She could make herself busy. The files probably needed organizing.

But you could chat and file at the same time; filing wasn't brain surgery.

She reached Main Street. She could turn right and give meaning to why she was standing out in the rain. Or she could be the coward that she was beginning to see she was and turn around and go back home.

While she was standing there a familiar Range Rover drove past. Stopped. Reversed. Stopped. The passenger window lowered.

Ian Lachlan leaned over the passenger seat. "Need a ride?"

Lillo nodded and got in.

They sat looking at each other for a few seconds.

"Where to?"

Lillo shrugged.

Ian waited.

Someone honked. Ian pulled the Rover to the side of the street.

"I just let Ned off at the clinic. Convinced him not to ride when he could get a lift."

Another silence.

"Were you going there?"

Lillo shrugged. Started to thank him and get out, but he stepped on the accelerator and the Rover shot forward. He didn't turn back toward the clinic but drove straight, up the road to his office and home, the place that had once been her home. She knew where they were going, she just didn't know why.

It was a place she didn't like to visit. Not because she was envious that Ian owned it now. She hadn't wanted to return there; she was happy in the cottage. Ian's house held many good memories. Too many good memories.

She didn't really want to go there now. A few weeks ago she would have demanded he stop and let her out. Might have even jumped out of the car if he'd refused. But last week was a dim memory and what seemed like logic then no longer seemed to make sense now.

So Lillo sat back, letting the metronome sound of the wipers calm her, let her fate and Ian Lachlan take her where they would.

The house appeared dimly through the sheets of rain. Wavering and indistinct like a melting picture, a remote dream.

Ian stopped the Rover at the front steps and reached across her to open the passenger door.

She smiled. Was that his attempt at chivalry? Maybe he was afraid she wouldn't get out and he'd be stuck with her. Would serve him right.

"The doors have been sticking lately," he said, and got out of the SUV.

They ran up the steps to the porch, where they dropped their rain gear and went inside.

"I haven't had time to do much with the decor."

"No, you haven't," Lillo said, looking around. The once-cozy living room, crowded with the plush overstuffed furniture, the sofas and love seats, reading chairs and ottomans her parents loved, was gone. Today an old couch and a big club chair and ottoman were placed around the fireplace, now just a gaping box surrounded by quarry-cut stone and looking like it had never seen a stocking hung with care in its life. But it had. Many of them. Twice a year: once in December for the family and local friends and once for Christmas in July, when campers added their stockings to the collection.

She tried to imagine Ian as a little boy hanging his stocking, and failed.

"You want to change? The bathroom's in—never mind; you know where it is."

"Thanks. I'm fine." She was beginning to wonder why she was here. Why he thought she'd want to come, and why she hadn't stopped him.

"I can make tea—or something."

"No, that's okay."

He shot his fingers through his hair. It was wet from the rain and it was left sticking up in shiny dark spikes.

He walked to the fireplace, back to the couch where Lillo had just sat down. He looked down at her. She looked up at him, wondering what was happening. Outside, the rain continued to fall, enclosing them in this slightly chilly, barren room.

He sat down. "Ned says you're fucked up."

She was so shocked that for a second she couldn't even react. Then her first response was to slug him.

She did.

He didn't even try to protect himself.

"Sorry," she said. "A case of shooting the messenger."

He nodded.

"Do you think I'm fucked up?"

"I guess that's what some people would call it. I get it."

"What would you call it?"

He shrugged, and for a moment Lillo saw utter defeat in that taciturn face.

"I don't know, but you better get rid of it while you still can."

"How? How do you get rid of your demons, Ian?"

"On a good day, one demon at a time."

"And on bad days?"

"I've never wanted to cope more in my life and I don't know how to get there, so I suggest you figure it out before it's too late. And you end up like me."

"I feel like maybe it's already too late."

He shook his head. "Don't let it be." He stood. "I have to see to the animals. Then I have to go out to Hansen's for feed. Stay as long as you want. Or I can drive you home."

She watched him go. Taking care of the animals, taking care of her in his own way. She knew he was right; she wished she could help him, but she knew she had to help herself.

Chapter 18

"For crying out loud, Diana, you've been pacing all morning. Come get a cup of coffee and sit down."

"I'm floating in coffee," Diana said, but she dropped the curtain across the front window. Water was gushing down the path toward the cottage, there was no sign of the rain letting up, and she was about to miss her daily ride with Ian. Actually, eleven o'clock had come and gone. Did he expect her? Had he given up on her? Did he even notice she wasn't there?

She went over to the kitchen and took a cup from Jess.

Jess scrunched her eyebrows at her. "You're not really thinking about going over to the stables, are you?"

"Well, the horses do need to be fed and the stalls mucked out."

"Gee, I wonder how Ian managed without you for so long? Oh man, you've got it bad."

"'And that ain't good,'" Diana countered.

Allie's head appeared from behind the fridge door. "That is the saddest song I ever heard."

Diana and Jess just looked at her.

"Duke Ellington, right? Nina Simone? My mother loved her."

"Lost me," Diana said.

"'I Got It Bad,'" Allie said, bringing out two apples and a bag of English muffins. "We're going to have to make a food run soon."

"What about I got it bad?"

"It's the title of a song. A real tearjerker. I'd play it for you if I could pick up a signal."

Diana put down her cup. "Not in this rain." She wandered back to the window. It was not letting up and she wondered if it was true. Did she really just want to ride or did she have it bad for Ian Lachlan?

"Well, if you're that worried about the horses, maybe you should tromp through this downpour to check it out." Jess grinned. "And arrive looking like a drowned rat."

"I'm not that desperate," Diana said.

"Good," Allie said. "But I'm that hungry. Jess, is there anything else for lunch besides apples and English muffins?"

"Ugh," Diana said. "Do you think somebody in this town delivers?"

"In this weather? I doubt it."

Jess opened a cabinet and brought out a jar of peanut butter. "Mac probably has some wonderful soup simmering on the stove. Do you think that's where Lillo is?"

Diana turned from the window for the umpteenth time. "Who knows? I can see the keeper's cottage from here, but we might as well be on a deserted island . . . in the rain."

"She's got it bad," Jess said.

"Looks like it to me," Allie agreed.

"I'm standing right here," Diana said, and went to retrieve her coffee cup. She leaned her elbows on the pass-through counter. "There's not even a radio here. Not that there's a station to pick up."

"I noticed that," Jess said. "There's that old television in the corner but no cable. So you can forget Netflix."

Diana strode across the room, opened the cabinet below the television. "Oh great. An ancient DVD player to go with the ancient TV covered with dust and not one damn DVD."

"That's so weird. We used to watch movies all the time."

"You still do," Diana reminded her.

"I know. Total escapism." Jess sighed. "But can you blame me?"

"No. But I'm beginning to understand. Maybe they're in the unused bedroom."

The three of them looked at the closed door of the bedroom.

"I'm not sure we should go in without asking," Allie said.

"Why not?" asked Jess. "That's where she got the wineglasses from."

"And I have a hankering to see that *Horse Whisperer* movie," Diana said.

"Yep," Allie said. "She's got it bad."

"I'm sure she would have it," Jess said. "It was our favorite. About overcoming adversity. And it was Robert Redford. A young Robert Redford."

"That settles it." Diana walked over to the door of the bedroom, turned the knob, and opened the door. "Holy shit."

"What?" Jess hurried over, Allie right behind her.

They crowded behind Diana and peered inside.

"It's like hoarder city in there," Allie said.

"It is." Diana would have never taken Lillo for a closet hoarder, the rest of the cottage was very orderly and not overfurnished. There were no stacks of old newspapers, no boxes of parts of things that would never work, but inside this room was a mountain of stuff.

She could see a bed beneath cardboard boxes, some neatly taped and stacked, some open and shapeless, filled with castoffs.

Jess and Allie nudged her inside. Diana didn't really want to go; she was feeling a little sick. There were bookshelves crammed with books and other stuff, a closet whose door wouldn't close. It was packed with dresses and suits. Good quality, Diana could see even from where she stood. So why had Lillo had to borrow clothes for the wedding?

"Look at this," Jess said, peering into one of the boxes.

Diana and Jess joined her.

"They're medical books," Jess said, barely above a whisper.

"She said she'd planned to go to medical school but it hadn't worked out." Jess pulled out a red leather folder. Opened it. "She didn't just *plan* to go to med school. She graduated with honors." She looked at the others. "I don't understand. Why isn't she practicing?"

Jess closed the folder and placed it back in the box. "I think maybe we should leave."

"Too late now," Diana said. "There's no way we can pretend we didn't see this. I mean, I can get pretty messy and I've been known to let my shoes pile up in the bottom of the closet, but this isn't normal. It's like she dumped everything in here and never touched it again. Look at the dust."

"And the damp," Allie added. "It's like a dead room."

"Or like somebody whose life is permanently on hold."

"Oh, stop it," Jess said. "You're just being gothic. There's probably a perfectly good reason. She moved back and didn't have time to unpack."

"Jess, she said she'd been back a year or more." Diana looked around the room. Definitely gothic. "And what the hell is that stack of boxes? They look like—"

"—presents," Allie finished.

"That doesn't make any sense," Jess said. "Why would anyone get presents, then just leave them in the boxes?"

"Maybe because of this." Diana lifted a poster away from the wall. It was an enlarged photograph, printed on foam board. She'd seen one like it not too long ago. At Jess's engagement party. A photo of the happy couple that everyone signed with their best wishes. And a big printed HAPPILY EVER AFTER KYLE AND LILLO across the top.

"Oh my God," Jess said. "That's Lillo."

"That about covers it," Diana agreed. "Good-looking guy." And Lillo looked . . . glowing. It was the only word for it.

"But Lillo isn't married," Allie said.

"Guess it didn't work out. Some of us should know about that." Diana eyed Jess.

Jess leaned in to get a better look. "She didn't say a thing about it."

"Maybe she didn't want to rain on your parade," Diana said. "And then . . . maybe it just didn't come up."

"And she didn't return the presents?" Allie said. "That's odd."

"And not like Lillo," Jess said. "She must be devastated."

"Or thanking her lucky stars."

"Diana, you don't mean that."

Diana shrugged. She didn't know what to believe.

Jess sniffed. "Here she is taking us into her home after a broken engagement, and I didn't even sense something was wrong. I've been totally self-absorbed."

"I have, too," Allie said.

Diana gave it up. "Okay, me three. But it really isn't our business unless she wants to share. Besides, I see the DVDs." They'd been hiding behind that damn engagement poster.

Allie grabbed Diana's arm. "If we bring them out, she'll know we saw this."

"She's going to know anyway. It's not like we can pretend we didn't see any of it. We're going to have to fess up. But until then, Jess, see if you can find the damn movie."

Jess squeezed past them to look through the pile of DVDs. "It's right on top." Her voice cracked. "She probably brought it out to watch, all alone."

"Stop it. Let's get out of here."

The three of them reached the door at the same time and squeezed through.

"Like three sardines." Diana shut the door behind them. "That would have been laughable if it wasn't so pitiful. Put in this movie, and it better be worth it." She pulled one of the chairs around to face the screen.

Jess turned on the television. "It is." She opened the cover. "You'll be crying ten minutes into it, so don't diss it." She looked over her shoulder. "Chairs, please."

"You sure you know how to work that thing?"

"Some people still use DVD players," Allie said.

"Luddites," Diana groused.

Jess fumbled with the controls of the DVD player. "Can somebody turn on a light? I can't even see what's what in the gloom." The tray opened. "Never mind. Got it."

"Yeah, yeah," Diana said. "Watch what you're doing or you'll drop it and step on it and then where will we be?"

Jess popped the DVD into the disc holder, pressed the button to close it. "See. It all came back to me in a flash. Like riding a bicycle."

Diana and Jess moved the writing table out of the way and pulled over two more chairs while Jess fiddled with the connections.

"Stupid place for a media center," Diana said.

"Something tells me Lillo doesn't watch television at all."

The screen brightened, turned blue.

"There's no remote," Jess said, and leaned over the player to press play. "Now, no snark," she demanded, and sat down between Diana and Allie. "I wish we had popcorn."

After several seconds of black, the movie started. It only took a few seconds for Diana to realize it had nothing to do with horses or handsome men. It wasn't even a movie.

It was a homemade video—a party—an engagement party with Lillo and the man on the poster, Kyle, opening presents, laughing and kissing and everyone having a great time.

Diana could do nothing but watch. Like the proverbial train wreck, and she knew when this one hit, it was going to be nasty—still, she didn't get up to turn it off.

"This isn't the movie," Allie breathed.

"They look so happy," Jess said. "What could have gone wrong?"

"We shouldn't be watching."

But no one got up to turn it off.

And then it was too late.

The door opened. A gust of rain and wind blew in—and along with it, Lillo. The other three froze, the party video playing behind them. The door shut. Lillo had stopped inside the entryway, shucking off rain gear. Then she really stopped, stared past them to the TV screen.

Jess found her voice first. "We didn't know, I swear. We were looking for *The Horse Whisperer*. We thought it might be in the storeroom. We didn't mean to snoop."

"It's true," Allie said. "We just wanted to watch the movie. It was in the *Horse Whisperer* case; we didn't notice until it started playing."

Jess stood and turned toward Lillo. "We're so sorry."

Lillo shook her head.

"You didn't get married."

Lillo just shook her head.

"What happened?"

Lillo looked from one to the other. Took a shuddering breath. "I killed him."

WHEN LILLO HADN'T shown up by eleven o'clock, Ned knew she wasn't coming. But he held out hope for another couple of hours. Then he got mad.

"She's a selfish, self-involved, stubborn—"

Clancy handed him a sandwich. "Doesn't do any good to be pissed off."

They were breaking for lunch. It had been the first thing Clancy did on his return: close the clinic from one to two for lunch.

"Then what will do some good?" Ned unwrapped the sandwich. "What's this?"

"Mac's chicken cacciatore BLT. You should have come over last night."

He should have, but he'd been too riled up. Lillo was really getting to him this trip. "How long can she keep up this stupid self-imposed exile? It's stupid."

"So you said."

"And counterproductive."

"Goes without saying."

"Can't you do something?"

"I've tried. Like you said. She's stubborn. And she's still hurting."

"I get that. I do. It's just like she won't let herself move on. She was rocking it the day she came to help out. Then zip, nada."

"Maybe she realized she liked it too much."

"Then she should go back to it."

"Well, you can't force her into it. And we have patients to see. I'll take the next one; you finish your sandwich."

Ned finished his sandwich wondering if he would ever be as accepting and even-tempered as Clancy. It was great for instilling a sense of safety in your patients. Ned was pretty good with his patients, but it was like all the goodness in his bedside manner tended to go south in his personal life, when his impatience and temper took over.

He went down the hall to tell Agnes he was ready for the next patient.

She called out Will Clayton and his sons. It was time for the boys' annual checkup. Tommy, eleven, the town hellion and his brother Alex, eight-year-old hellion-in-training. No wonder Clancy had been willing to take the first appointment.

Will Clayton came into the exam room, dragging Alex. There was no sign of Tommy.

"I don't wanna!"

"Hush up, now. You just be polite and say hello to the doc."

Ned had known Will for years. A single father who worked two jobs off island. That left his boys a lot of time to get into trouble, and get in it they did. He was tempted to say something about Tommy's attacks on Bobby and Joey Trader, but he knew it would go nowhere. Will was barely keeping his head above water.

Today he looked like he might drown.

"Couldn't find his brother anywhere. I just hope he's not down at the marina in this weather. He just can't get enough of them boats."

"Is Tommy down by the boats, Alex?" Ned tried.

"Don't know."

"Probably knew he needed his DTP booster," Ned said. "Climb up on the table."

"Nooo! I don't wanna shot!"

Will grabbed him as he tried to slide to the floor.

"And you're not going to get one. But I do have to prick your finger."

Will kept hold of him while Ned examined him. Nothing untoward showed up on the cursory examination. He probably had iron, vitamin D, and a few other deficiencies. Ned would prescribe vitamins and the father would either forget to buy them or he'd buy them and they'd forget to take them. But barring any serious illness, they'd muddle through.

Ned checked the boy's heartbeat, his blood pressure, his reflexes. He took blood. He'd given up trying to get kids to pee in a cup.

"All right, you're done."

"I wanna sucker."

"Alex," his father admonished. "Sorry, Doc, just can't seem to drum any manners into neither of them."

"You do the best you can. Alex, if you ask Ms. Agnes very nicely, she might give you one."

Alex slid off the table and pulled his father toward the door.

Will held back. "You go over there by the door and wait for me," he said. "I need to talk to Doc Hartley for a minute."

Alex stuck out his bottom lip, but he went to the door and stood facing it, resting his forehead against the wood.

Ned wondered if he spent a lot of time with his face to the wall. Ned would have used more drastic tactics. Though he wasn't sure what. He wasn't planning on having any of the little buggers himself.

"I'm at my wit's end with these two. They're out of control and I know it. People are always complaining about them. Alex over there is only eight, how can an eight-year-old get into so much trouble?"

By following in the footsteps of his eleven-year-old brother, Ned thought, but he wouldn't say it. He knew Will was doing what he could do and didn't have the family or the county services he needed to make ends meet and raise two healthy, well-behaved boys.

"You don't have anybody who could watch them while you're at work? They've just got too much time on their hands."

"Don't I know it and idle hands are the devil's—"

"Have you talked with Sada over at the community center?"

"I did, but there's only her most days. And they pick on the other kids and she told me not to bring them back until they learned to behave."

Will's shoulders slumped. "They don't even want to go back there. And I can't trust them not to get in trouble. My own flesh and blood. And don't go tellin' me to get a wife. Won't no woman look at me twice when she knows I have these two."

Ned couldn't help but laugh. "I don't think a wife is necessarily the answer to your situation." Though at this point it couldn't hurt. "Boys need a routine. They're better during the school year. Right?"

"A little, but even there it's gettin' worse. They're good boys, just took a wrong turn somewhere. I'd stay home with 'em if I could, but somebody's got to earn a living."

"Let me think about it. Maybe Sada can enlist some guys to play ball with the kids or something." God knew there were plenty of retired and unemployed old geezers who could oversee a few kids. But getting them to do it was a whole different ball game.

He passed Clancy in the hall as he was walking Will and Alex back to the waiting room. Clancy nodded at Will and rolled his eyes at Ned as he passed by.

Ned left the two Claytons in Agnes's capable hands and took the next patient.

Maybe Lillo could help Sada out with the kids, put her in

charge of games and finger painting. He smiled with satisfaction. If *that* didn't drive her back to medicine, nothing would.

LILLO WANTED TO push past the three women who were staring at her in horror, in disbelief. Rip the DVD out of the machine and throw it into the ocean. But it was one of her few testaments to a happier time. She'd stored it in that movie case because she thought it would be safe there. Away from prying eyes when she still lived in her apartment, when she still had friends and colleagues, before their sympathy and support turned to questioning, then to suspicion. Before they pulled away and avoided her at the hospital.

But Lillo had known this could happen. Maybe she welcomed the discovery, just to feel something besides a dull familiar ache for whatever she used to be. Once she'd said yes to their flight from Jess's wedding, let them stay at her cottage, it had probably been inevitable.

She'd seen the same look on her friends' faces before. That initial horror. And she could predict exactly what would happen with her houseguests, too. They'd want to hear her story, and she would have to tell them because it was stupid not to. They'd sympathize, tell her it wasn't her fault. But their sympathy wouldn't last, and just like the others, their curiosity would change to doubt, their compassion to contempt. The distancing, the looks and whispers, the hurrying past would start all over again and nothing would ever change.

She might as well send them packing now. Except the rain was still coming down—not as heavily as before, but it would be a while before it cleared up. And someone would have to drive them somewhere to get a rental car.

In the meantime, she might as well get the whole sordid thing over with, and then she'd burn the contents of that godforsaken room. She should have done it a year ago. She should never have brought any of it back in the first place.

Jess was the first one to move. She stepped toward Lillo then stopped.

And Lillo's heart, what was left of it, broke. She turned and ran blindly for the door. She didn't know where she'd go. To Mac's? Wait it out until they figured out how to leave? But Mac wouldn't help her, wouldn't make them leave.

Back to Ian's? If only she could go back to that house and start again. Make different choices. Stay on the island and run the camp like her parents did before her. Like they'd hoped she would do. Until it finally gasped its last breath and succumbed completely to the rich Ivy League camp down the road.

Back to before she left for Jess's wedding? If she'd refused to go, she'd be waiting the rain out, with only one thought, wondering if the tomato stakes would hold. But that wasn't true, was it? She never had just one thought. Wherever she was, whatever she was thinking or doing, there was always, always, the underlying knowledge of the lives she'd destroyed, including her own.

She turned the knob, yanked the door open only to have it slam shut again.

Diana's hand pressed against the wood. The weight of her body keeping it closed.

Of course, it would be her.

Lillo wrenched at the knob, but the door barely gave as Diana leaned against it.

"Our bad," she said. "We're sorry. If you want us to leave, we will."

What was the point? Too late to pretend like it didn't happen.

"Or you can come sit down and tell us what really happened. Because I can tell you right now, none of us think you committed murder."

Chapter 19

D id you?"
Lillo shook her head, a small jerky movement that reminded her of a dog drying off.

"So why are you trying to escape?"

How could she answer that? She couldn't. It was just too complicated. So she just shrugged.

"Well, it's a stupid idea. It's pouring rain out there. So you might as well come on back and enlighten us."

Before Lillo could do more than shoot a panic-stricken glance at the door, Diana took her by the shoulders and guided her back to the couch. She could have gotten away, run back to the door; she didn't think Diana would try to stop her twice. But she really didn't want to run; like Diana had said, where would she go?

She sank down on the cushions.

Jess immediately sat beside her. Allie hesitated, then sat on her other side, virtually trapping her between them. Diana pulled over a chair to face her.

Like an inquisitor, thought Lillo.

"Spill," Diana said. "I have a feeling it's about time." She frowned. "Definitely not your ordinary town."

Lillo laughed. It surprised them all, but she couldn't help it. Diana could make her laugh at the most inappropriate times. She knew she was about to spill her guts, she could feel the words coming, and she just didn't have the strength to hold them back, so she stopped trying.

"It was stupid. A stupid thing to do. We were both residents at Holy Name Hospital. In surgery. We should have been more careful. We were always careful. But we were happy and on the cusp of success. The top two students in our class and the top two surgery residents that came out of that class.

"We were going to be married. Practice side by side. The best of the best. Unstoppable together. We were going to do great things. We were both up for a big grant. We were competing, but as long as it went to one of us, the other would be happy.

"There was a picnic on the beach, a bonfire, hot dogs, marshmallows, beer. Not healthy but fun.

"He challenged me to climb the palisade. I knew I could beat him, but I agreed. Everyone egged us on. He jumped up and ran toward the cliffs. I ran after him.

"We started together, with everyone yelling advice and having a great old time. I made it to the top easily. And turned around to gloat." Her voice cracked.

Why was she doing this? How many times would she be made to relive those final minutes? Picking at it to keep it festering. Hoping it would scar over and gradually fade away. But she knew that would never happen.

Jess moved closer to her and she felt claustrophobic. How did you tell someone who cared about you that you didn't want their compassion. It just made things worse.

And suddenly she was there again, standing on top of the

palisade, looking down at Kyle, who was looking up at her. He was laughing, too, even though they were both competitive, and she knew it galled him that she'd made it to the top first. It didn't matter that she had years of being a camp child in the out-of-doors. He was from Chicago and she'd easily beaten him up the side of the cliff. And she couldn't help but gloat a little.

She shouldn't have laughed at him.

"So you're standing at the top gloating and . . ." Diana looked her squarely in the eye. She wasn't going to let Lillo off the hook. Who the hell did she think she was?

But Lillo went on. "He started to slide, but he was laughing, too. And I called him City Boy just as the earth gave way beneath his feet and he was sliding down the side.

"Someone screamed. He landed on his back, but he was still laughing.

"I couldn't believe it, he looked so silly lying there in the dirt laughing. I yelled, 'You're such a klutz.'"

She gulped in air. "And then he stopped laughing, looked at me with this look on his face, like surprise, and closed his eyes.

"I thought he was acting at first. And told him to man up. But he didn't get up or open his eyes and I knew something must really be wrong.

"I slid all the way down." It had been the fastest and slowest descent of her life.

"A few people came over from the campfire to see what was going on. A couple even tried to rouse him. They knew the drill. We all did. Someone called the EMTs.

"He wasn't breathing, so I started CPR. It was a good twenty seconds before someone noticed the blood oozing from behind his leg. He'd fallen on a broken limb and it severed the femoral artery. It didn't occur to me to look until it was too late.

"I should have noticed earlier. I should have checked him for external wounds first. But I didn't. I just knew he wasn't breathing and I didn't think properly."

"Understandable. He was your fiancé. You were traumatized," Diana said. "It sucks, but it's understandable."

"Understandable? I was laughing at him while he died."

Something like a cry escaped from Jess and she threw her arms around Lillo. Lillo wanted to push her away. She didn't want to be comforted; she wanted to go back to the past.

Jess hugged her tighter. Lillo felt suffocated. "Why didn't you tell us? We've been imposing on you, and I've been so self-absorbed about my own misspent life I didn't even think about what had happened to you all this time. I'm sorry. I should have kept up."

On her other side, Allie put a tentative arm around her shoulders. It felt like prison. Diana was the only one who didn't try to console her and she was still blocking Lillo's path of escape.

"You tried to save him, you couldn't have done more; from what little I know, he probably bled out before you even reached him."

"Diana!" Jess admonished. "Have a heart."

"Just saying."

"She's right," Lillo said, thankful for the dose of reality. "He probably did. And intellectually I get that."

"But it still hurts," Allie said.

"Yeah."

"Is that why you quit medicine?" Jess asked. "Nobody could blame you for not trying."

"Oh, they didn't," Lillo said, wishing she could just get away from them. But she never would now. They'd made a place for themselves in her life, whether they realized it or not. Even if they left this minute and never returned, Lillo knew her life would never be the same. "At first.

"And I didn't quit, not right away. I went through the motions. I went to lectures, did my rounds at the hospital, saw my friends on occasion.

"But after a while, once I came out of the numbness, I noticed my colleagues weren't the same. A little cooler than they'd been before. The looks that passed between them when they thought I wasn't watching. The whispers in the cafeteria, the glances in the operating arena.

"As if they didn't trust me anymore."

"That's terrible."

"Oh, it wasn't overt, not really, but it got to the point that I could never walk into the hospital, the staff room, or anywhere without wondering what people were thinking.

"Some people didn't even try to hide what they thought."

"And what was that?" Diana asked.

"That I didn't try to save him, maybe even let him die because we were both up for the same fellowship."

"Nobody lets someone die for a grant!" Allie exclaimed.

They all just looked at her.

"At first it was just a few, but you know how it is. Where-there's-smoke kind of thing. After a while it felt like everyone thought I was incompetent, maybe even a killer. I guess maybe I began to believe it myself.

"Then—" She broke off, tried to laugh, but what came out of her mouth sounded like the wounded animal she was. "They awarded me the fellowship, even though I had told them to withdraw my name.

"That was the end of things. I could see it on everyone's face, what they thought of me. The resentment, the distaste. I couldn't do it. I just couldn't, so I quit and came home." She tried to smile but it hurt her face. "And here you find me.

"So you see, Jess, you didn't need me to save you. I couldn't even save myself." Lillo's face twisted as she tried to fight away the tears, the pain, the waste of it all. It was useless. The tears fell, not flowing tears, but big fat ugly ones that dropped into her lap like water balloons.

"I didn't know," Jess said. "I'm so sorry."

Lillo tried to pull away but Jess held firm.

"But none of that was your fault. It was the reaction of stupid, insecure, mean-spirited people. God, I know them. And I know what they can do to you. It makes me so angry. They wrecked your career."

"No, I pretty much did that myself. My parents sold their camp and our home to send me to medical school and this is what they got."

"Is it too late to go back?" Allie asked.

"I couldn't."

"Why not?"

"I'm already a year behind. And the story will just go around again. And it will be the same looks and the same . . . just the same everything."

"Don't you miss it, though?" Allie asked.

God, how she missed it. "I do. I tried not to, but . . ."

"That's why you wouldn't help out at the clinic," Diana said. "It's like a dangling carrot that you think you can't have . . . maybe think you don't deserve."

"You should have been a shrink instead of a geek," Lillo snapped.

"Not me." She was looking at Lillo with an odd expression Lillo couldn't read.

"You're really annoying, you know that?"

Diana bared her teeth.

"And that fake nah-nah smile is annoying, too."

"Too bad you can't rustle up some of that attitude for the ass-hats that ostracized you."

"What if they were right?"

Diana shrugged. "You're the only one who can answer that. I think it's happy hour." She stood and wandered into the kitchen.

Jess and Allie sat as if they were stuck to the upholstery.

"She didn't mean that," Allie said.

"Yeah, she did," Lillo said. "And she's right."

"No," said Jess. "Those people are just bullies. Subtle maybe, but just as mean as if they'd chased you and poured soda in your hair. And I should know."

"Don't let it get maudlin while I'm gone," Diana called from the kitchen.

Jess clutched Lillo's arm. "You have to stand up to those people. You stood up for me my whole life, and the other kids, too. Now you have to stand up for yourself."

"Why?"

"Well . . . because if you don't . . . you'll end up like me."

Before Lillo could even frame an answer to that, shouting erupted from outside.

"Kids," Diana said. "I recognize the pitch of their precious little voices from yesterday. Ignore them."

"It's sounds like they're fighting." Jess jumped up and ran to the door. Allie followed her.

"Now, suddenly, she grows a pair," Diana said. "Jess, maybe you should just let them have their fun."

"Fun? They're probably picking on that poor little boy from the other day."

"Bobby," Diana said.

Lillo looked at her in surprise.

"I heard the whole story yesterday at the stables. Many times.

Each telling more lurid than the last. Though, maybe we should kibitz. At least the rain seems to have stopped."

Lillo went outside gladly. Sad but true, she welcomed the interruption. A couple of bloody noses was par for a summer day around here. But unraveling her life in front of an audience had left her depleted.

Jess was already outside. Hands on her hips, looking around.

"They're probably on the beach near the jetty," Lillo said.

Diana gave Lillo a woeful look. It made Lillo laugh; *bless her.*

Jess started across the sand, shaking her fist, Allie at her heels. "You stop that right now. Stop it!"

"You gotta love her," Diana said.

"Diana and I'll cut them off at the jetty, they'll run that way," Lillo called after Jess.

"You seem to know a lot about this," Diana said as they walked quickly up the path to the parking lot.

"Fistfights and hasty retreats are major means of communication around here. Children and adults alike."

They reached the jetty and the group of boys just as Tommy Clayton pushed Bobby's older brother, Joey, into the wet sand. It was a bedraggled group; they must have been hanging out in the rain all afternoon. Lillo knew them all. There weren't that many families with children left in the town.

Joey pushed to his hands and knees, but two of Tommy's friends pushed him down again.

Behind them, Jess appeared like an avenging petite-sized Valkyrie. Grabbed them both by the back of their shirts and yanked them away.

"Damn, did hell just freeze over?" Diana asked.

Jess pulled Joey to his feet. He wriggled away from her and grabbed his brother's arm.

"C'mon, Bobby. Let's go home."

Joey's nose was bleeding and Lillo knew she should take them both inside and clean them up before sending them on their way. But she also knew better than to interfere with juvenile pissing contests. It was something that Jess should have remembered. Intercede and it declared open season on the underdog.

Bobby yanked away. "Don't wanna. Wanna go in the boat."

Joey grabbed him again. "Tommy ain't gonna take you in his boat. He wants to be mean to you."

"Nuh-uh. He said I could be in the gang, and he's gonna let me break into the lighthouse with them. He said. Didn't you, Tommy?"

"Sure I did." Tommy smiled one of those hateful smiles kids learned either from their bully parents or from watching too much network television.

"He's lying to you. He ain't gotta boat."

"Fuck you! I do, too," Tommy screamed, and lunged at Joey.

"Man, I didn't even use that kind of language until I was an adult." Diana strode over to the two fighting boys. Leaned over, pulled them apart, and held them at arm's length. She shook the one in her right hand. Tommy. "You know what we do with thugs like you on the streets of New York?"

"What?" Tommy drawled, and tried to jerk away.

Diana just grasped him more firmly.

Everyone, including the other boys, watched raptly.

"We hang them upside down until their eyeballs pop out."

Tommy's eyes narrowed. But he bit his lip. "No, you don't."

"No? I can demonstrate right here. Your friends can watch. Jess, Allie, come give me a hand."

Two of the boys took off. Diana and Tommy had a brief stare-off, then suddenly she let go. "Beat it, kid." Tommy took off after the other two.

She turned to Joey and Bobby. "News flash. Those guys aren't your friends. If you want a ride in a boat, ask Ian to take you in Mac's rowboat."

"Would he do that?"

Diana looked over their heads to Lillo. "Sure he would."

She let go of Joey. This time when he grabbed Bobby, Bobby went willingly. She made a show of flinging sand off her fingers.

"That's awful," Allie said. "You've probably scarred them for life."

"Hopefully," Diana said, inspecting one of her nails. She looked at the other three. "Oh, really, girls. You're still living in an *Anne of Green Gables* world. Kids these days are raised on *Hitman: Sniper* and *Street Fighter*. I should know. I make apps and I know what sells."

Allie craned her neck to see the retreating boys. "Should we just let them run off like that? Shouldn't we call their parents?"

"And say what?" Lillo said. "'Your kids have been fighting again'? Unfortunately I have to go with Diana on this one. Most of the kids are left to their own devices for the summer. And it's either television or hanging outside waiting for something to happen. What usually happens is they get into trouble."

"What about the community center?" Jess asked as they started back to the cottage.

"You saw it: there are no programs, no one to even manage them. During the school year, they have someone to watch them and make sure they get their homework done until their parents come get them. Some of them just sneak off between the bus and the door to the center. Life in these United States."

"That just isn't right. There should be a camp."

"There *was* a camp," Lillo reminded her. And got a painful stab of sadness for her trouble.

"I know and it was a great camp, but I meant a day camp."

"You want to volunteer to run it?"

"Huh. Is there anything for dinner?"

They went inside; Jess, Allie, and Diana migrated toward the kitchen. Lillo headed for the DVD player. While the others were rummaging in the fridge and cabinets, Lillo ejected the disc. Held it long enough to make herself feel sick, then placed it back in the case.

"The cupboard is bare," Jess said, looking into the fridge. "Should we invite ourselves to Mac's?"

"Doc Clancy is taking Mac out to dinner," Allie said. "I think he's going to push her on the cataracts thing. Here's those vegetable sticks from the other night."

"No thanks." Jess opened the fridge again.

Lillo eased past the others and opened the bedroom door wide enough to slip in and return the DVD to obscurity.

Diana was waiting for her when she came out again. "Anything besides pizza in town?"

Lillo jumped. Closed the door. "There's Mike's Bar. Decent burgers, but don't expect fancy."

"Burgers sound good."

Lillo tried to ease past her.

"You know you're going to have to face that room someday."

"I know, but not today."

MIKE'S WAS JUST around the corner from Main Street. It had been a pharmacy in better days and still had the original dark wood and well-worn floors. The original soda fountain had been restructured into a serviceable bar, with stools and a mirror behind, only now instead of serving sodas and banana splits, it dispensed beer on tap, a variety of bottled beers, hard liquors, and a handful of wines, none of which would live up to Allie's standards.

"Well, this is rustic," Diana said, looking around the semi-darkness of the bar.

"A nice way to put it," Lillo said. "We can go back to Sal's."

"No, this is great."

Diana sidled up to the bar, where Mike Growalski was talking to two old fishermen. Mike was a stocky guy, with a jovial personality when he wasn't arguing football or the state of the local economy.

Mike looked over Diana's head. "Well, if it isn't Lillo Gray. I was beginning to think you weren't going to bring your friends. You woulda broken my heart."

"We've only been here a few days and we've been busy."

Diana perched one hip on a barstool. "I'll have a dirty martini, Grey Goose."

Allie and Jess climbed on stools beside her.

"I got Stoli."

"I'll have one of your microbeers."

"That I can do. How 'bout you gals? I hope you all aren't expecting me to make you fancy drinks all night. 'Cause one of my two waitresses called in sick, so I'll also be your friendly server as well as bartender. Could take some time."

Lillo opened her mouth, but Diana cut her off. "How 'bout *four* microbeers?"

Mike grinned at Lillo. "I like her attitude. You can bring her back anytime. Have a seat, I'll bring your beers over to the table."

They started toward a table just as the door opened and Doc and Ian came in, creating gridlock in the middle of the floor.

Jess glanced at Lillo and Diana. "Hey, guys, we're just getting a table. Would you like to join us?"

Lillo wanted to kick her. But she just smiled—tightly.

"Love to," Doc said. Ian looked away, probably trying to

decide if he could make it out the door without someone stopping him. But he stood his ground and the women detoured
to a larger table and sat down. Lillo made sure to place herself
between Allie and Jess. She was still feeling sick and weak from
the girls' discovery about her. They seemed to have forgotten
about it, and maybe to them it wasn't a big deal.

Of course, they didn't have to live with it. And after Lillo
had tried so hard to hide it away . . . Her past. Her fail. Her
loss.

"I was hoping to see you today," Doc said as he passed by the
back of her chair.

"Well, here I am." She concentrated on unrolling her paper
napkin from the silverware.

"Ian said you got rained out."

"Yes."

"C'mon. Don't act so glum. I was just trying to be friendly."
He took a seat on the other side of Jess and didn't look Lillo's
way for the rest of the night. So she ate her burger in relative
silence, though she noticed that Ian was actually talking to both
Allie and Diana and almost looked like he was enjoying the
conversation.

They had reached the end of their meal when Howie and the
guys came in and headed for the bar.

They ordered beers then pulled up extra chairs to the table.

"Man, has this week gone fast," Howie said.

"A week?" Allie said.

"A week . . . tomorrow." Diana frowned and called Mike
over. "Another round?"

Mike went off to get the beers.

Tomorrow, Lillo thought. It had gone fast. And was rapidly
coming to an end. After today's confession, she should be anxious to see them go. But she wasn't. Even with all the angst that

seemed to surround them, she felt lighter tonight than she could remember feeling for a long time.

A week ago she hadn't even seen Jess in years or met Allie and Diana. And now? For the first time in a long time, Lillo felt she had friends. Friends outside of those in Lighthouse Beach whom she'd known all her life.

She looked at Allie, who was seriously listening to something Nando was saying, and wondered if she was thinking about her husband. Lillo really didn't think about Kyle as much as she thought about what had happened to him. And that surely wasn't right. But The Tragedy and his absence were so tangled up in each other that it was hard to separate her feelings. She wasn't sure if she was lonely without him, or lonely without medicine.

The familiar pain radiated through her. Her standing over him, both of them laughing, then . . . then one of them was gone. She'd lost precious minutes—or maybe it really was only seconds—standing there on the ledge; lost even more as she tried to revive him, not realizing his femoral artery had been severed.

If only she had seen it earlier, if he hadn't been laughing like nothing had happened, though she knew that often a victim is unaware of the severity of a wound until it's too late. If only she'd been faster, had seen the blood. If only they hadn't dared each other to race to the top, if they hadn't gone to the bonfire, if it had rained that day.

If only . . .

Allie leaned over and whispered in her ear. "I'm going for a walk with Nando. I'll be back later."

"Oh," Lillo said, surprised by the interruption of her thoughts.

"Is that okay?" Allie asked, looking worried.

"It's great."

"If you guys leave before we get back, I'll just come to the cottage. Can you spot me dinner until then?"

"Absolutely, take your time, have fun," Lillo said, and real-ized they were still talking in whispers.

Allie pushed her chair back and she and Nando left. Lillo watched them, but surreptitiously. So did Jess and Diana, but no one said a thing or called attention to their leaving. Howie was just finishing a story about a late-night emergency call from a girls' dorm that led to a blackout and the triggering of a fire alarm and the hilarity that ensued. Lillo doubted if he or the other guys even noticed Nando's absence.

Chapter 20

Lillo awoke sometime in the middle of the night; she'd been waking up off and on ever since she lay down. Sometimes groggily, as waves of regret roiled through her. Regret for her past, for her failings, for telling her friends the awful truth. Sometimes shaking, or holding absolutely still, forgetting for a moment where she was, thinking Kyle was lying beside her still, or that she was sleeping on a cot in the residents' room at the hospital. Then she would revisit Kyle's death, her fall from grace, her acceptance of it, until she drifted off again. This time she awoke with a start, aware that someone was walking across the floor.

She stiffened. She always locked the front door, a habit she'd picked up in college. Then she remembered she'd left the door unlocked because Allie hadn't returned when they'd all gone to bed. Lillo didn't move but listened as the steps tiptoed down the hall and went into the bathroom.

She groped for her phone. After three A.M. Well, good for Allie. She hoped she would find happiness. As for Lillo . . . she just wanted to find sleep.

Everyone seemed a little tired when Lillo padded over to the kitchen the next morning. She sat down and braced her elbows on the counter while she watched Jess and Diana work, team-like, making the coffee.

Jess glanced over her shoulder. "We have three eggs, half a loaf of bread, and a package of bacon I found in the freezer. We're going to attempt French toast." She yawned, narrowed her eyes at Lillo. "Is that okay?"

"Sure."

"Then *what*?"

"Nothing."

Jess turned and leaned on the pass-through counter. "That's not a nothing face. What gives?" Her expression changed and she reached across the counter and pulled Lillo's hand toward her. "You're not upset with us about yesterday and finding the DVD and butting into your life, are you?"

Lillo shook her head. "No. It's just . . . nothing."

"You wish we hadn't and now you don't know how to go on from here?"

Lillo pulled her hand away. "Is that coffee ready yet?"

Jess took a mug out of the dish drain and poured Lillo a cup, but instead of handing it to her, she held on. "Do you?"

Lillo thought about it, but mainly she was just awed by Jess. Since Jess had come to Lighthouse Beach, Lillo could see glimpses of the person she had become, or at least said she'd become during college and her years working in Manhattan. She was fun to be around, had managed to shed her insecurity. In the old days, faced with the slightest confrontation, she would back off, but today she was standing across the counter looking Lillo dead in the eye. Waiting for an answer.

"How do you do it?" Lillo asked her.

"Do what?"

"We kidnap you from your wedding, after the mother of all confrontations with your parents, drive to the back of beyond, where you're living without any of the creature comforts. You sent your father's goons packing. Before, any of these things would have sent you into a downward spiral."

"You really want to know?"

Lillo desperately wanted to know, not just for Jess but for herself. Because she was getting near to bottoming out and she didn't know what the hell to do to stop it.

"Practice." Jess finally pushed Lillo's coffee over to her, and lifted her own cup. "You only knew me as the sad kid who would gradually peek out of her shell as the weeks went by only to succumb to her former life each August. My parents had the advantage of time in those days. I'd start believing in myself and they'd snatch me away from those dangerous waters before I could understand what I could be. What I really was. But that changed in college. I spent more time without them than with them. And I began to live as that other me, the summer me, all the time."

She put her mug down. Looked into its center. "I used to pretend I was you."

"We used to pretend we were sisters," Lillo corrected her.

"I said that, but I wanted to *be* you. To live here. To have your parents for my parents. Mac as a neighbor. By the time I moved to Manhattan to work, I was spending almost all my time away from the family. More time being a productive independent woman than the Parkers' disappointing daughter. I started becoming the person who I imagined myself as. Not you. Each time I had to reconnect with my parents, it got a little easier to return to that person I'd become."

"Then how did you end up about to marry what's-his-name?"

"James. They swept in like something from *Harry Potter*, all of them, the sibs, all of them. It was a done deal before I even heard about it. I'd gone out with him a few times, not realizing it was just part of the hostile takeover. Megabucks and corporate power on the table, and me the pawn.

"They all applied the pressure, stayed in my face, and I caved. It's like an alcoholic or a drug user. One misstep and I was screwed. I knew it, but I just kept being sucked down, and I couldn't get out of it by myself." Jess stopped, blinked furiously. "I needed my posse. And you came through."

"We're *your* posse, Lillo, if you want us to be. I got my life back; you can get yours, too, if you want it. If you let us help."

"Well, thanks, but I've got a life."

She watched Jess shrink and could kick herself for causing that little twist of pain even for a second. "Sorry. I've got to get dressed and get over to the clinic. They need files filed. Floors mopped."

She started to stand but Diana stopped her. "Look, we're reaching the end of our vaca. I've got to get back to work, Allie needs to see her kid, and Jess . . ."

"I'm working on it," Jess said.

"And Jess has to do something she won't tell us about."

"Your point being?" Lillo asked while kicking herself for asking.

"I think we should help you clean out that storeroom. We'll send the presents back or give them to Goodwill or the community center. We'll toss whatever's holding you down. And rearrange the rest so that the space is livable."

"I'll do it. I just haven't had time."

Diana fisted her hands on her hips. "A year? It will take us an afternoon, and you'll be glad we did it when it's done." She dropped her hands. "There may be a few tears involved. But hell, that's what your friends are for."

"Don't you have something better to do on your week off than to clean my house? Weren't you going to a spa?"

"Look, I've—we've—all had a better time than we would've had at Jess's wedding or at a spa. Why not let us do this? Besides, if we don't, when we all come back for a visit, Allie and I will still be sleeping in the same room, and she snores."

"She doesn't!" Jess exclaimed.

"Not really, that was just an excuse. Best I could do on short notice."

"Diana's right, Lillo; look what this trip has done for me. You might as well take advantage of Team Road Trip while you have us. It'll be fun."

"Like a root canal. I have to go to the clinic." Lillo stood and hurried to the back of the house to retrieve clothes from her bedroom. She'd go to the clinic and she'd stay there until they closed. When she finally came back to the cottage, they'd have to have dinner, and besides, it would be too dark to carry stuff outside. She took her clothes into the bathroom, showered, changed, and grabbed her rain poncho and boots from the closet, then left the house with a "Don't touch my things while I'm gone."

She was immediately engulfed in a thick layer of fog. She'd be lucky to find her way across the parking lot without losing her way, wandering out to the jetty, and falling into the depths.

"Ha, wishful thinking." And knowing she was acting like an ungrateful bitch and hoping her friends would see through her and still be there when she returned, she hurried toward town and the clinic.

"WELL, SHIT," DIANA said, passing a plate of French toast and bacon to Jess, across the counter, where she'd gone to sit after Lillo's dramatic exit. "Eat," she said. "I didn't spend the morning playing Suzy Homemaker to have everyone turn down my poor attempts."

"I should've minded my own business," Jess said, making no effort to even pick up a fork.

Diana picked it up and handed it to her. Picked up her own. Looked down at her plate. "God, this looks awful."

"It looks delicious," Jess countered.

"What's burning?" Allie croaked from the hall door.

"You sound like a foghorn," Jess said.

"In keeping with the situation," Allie said. "You can't even see the lighthouse from here. Would a ship have been able to see its light through this kind of fog?"

"Not my area of expertise," Diana said. "Let's just say I'm glad not to be a ship dependent on it today. Want French toast?"

"Oh, that's what that is," Allie said, snagging a piece of bacon off Jess's plate.

"Hey," Jess said, and took a piece from Diana's plate. Diana reached across to the opposite counter and placed the whole platter of bacon between them.

Allie made herself a plate and coffee and carried it around to sit beside Jess.

"Where's Lillo?"

"On her way to the clinic. In a huff," Diana added. "Jess put it to her."

"I did not. I was trying to be helpful."

"What happened?" Allie asked.

"First tell us why you sneaked back in the middle of the night last night?" Jess said. "And I hope it's X-rated."

Allie sighed and smiled. And Diana wondered, *What the hell?*

"I went for a walk with Nando. We talked . . . about everything."

"And . . . ?" Jess encouraged.

"And he kissed me . . . a few times. And then he walked me home."

"Holy mother, for crying out loud, did you—"

Allie shook her head. "It was awkward."

"Awkward?" Diana rolled her eyes. "It's a simple process of tabs and slots."

Jess slapped her hands over her face. "Diana."

"Well, it is. You guys are such prudes."

And listen to me, Diana thought. Talk about awkward. She couldn't wait to get to the stables each day. Was in a constant state of indecision while she was there, and left wondering what had, or more to the point, *hadn't* happened. At least Allie had gotten kissed.

"Really, people, who ever heard of four single women taking a road trip and not one—let me repeat—not one of them gets laid."

Jess and Allie both turned on her.

"You mean you really *are* mucking out stables and horseback riding?" Jess asked.

Diana covered her eyes with her palm. "It's so humiliating. I think I'm losing my touch."

"Well, in your defense, I think that man has issues."

Diana gave her a look. "All men have issues. Usually to do with size. I may be wrong, but in this case I don't think that's it."

"What happened after I left?" Allie asked, reaching for the syrup.

Jess shrugged. "We had another round of beers, Doc and Ian left, we stayed a few more minutes, and then we left."

"I swear I felt like spring break at the beach," Diana said, "though it's getting hard to remember that far back."

"Oh bull," Jess said. "You've been to the stables twice now."

"Three times if you don't count the first day, when he practically ran me off with a shotgun."

"He has a gun?"

"No, that was just an expression." At least she didn't think Ian had a gun, though on second thought, he probably would have to. So he could put down wounded animals and things. The French toast was beginning to get to her stomach.

"Well, if the fog doesn't lift, you'll be stuck mucking out stables all day."

Allie's eyes rounded. "Don't you dare go out riding in this, you could go off a cliff or something."

"Same goes for you, no motorcycle rides." Diana smiled wickedly, she hoped. "Maybe just curl up with a certain CPA-mechanic and . . ."

"Well, we did talk about maybe doing something today, but he has work to do. And I don't want to neglect my friends."

"Oh hell, I'd drop you guys in a New York minute to get a quick one in the hay."

"Not hay," Jess said. "You don't know who's been sleeping there."

"Or is still sleeping there," Allie added.

Diana barked out a laugh. She really did love these nutcases. "I have no intention of deserting you. Besides, I told Lillo that we were going to meet back here later and help her clean out the storage room."

"You didn't."

"Yep, I did." Diana stretched. "It didn't go over really well."

Jess leaned on her elbow. "And then I told her . . . Hell, I don't even know what I said, but she bolted. We may have done more harm than good."

"Maybe, but we're cleaning out that storeroom whether she gets back or not."

"Diana, we couldn't. You wouldn't."

"Look, how much longer can we stay? . . . Wait—that sounded weird. I'm having a great time, but I have to get back to the office."

"And I need to go home," Allie said. "Last time I called home, I told them that I wanted to take care of Mac's eye situation, but I'd try to catch the red-eye Sunday night."

They both looked at Jess. "Well, I seem to be unmarried, unemployed, and familyless. Is that even a word?"

"You can always come work—"

Jess held up her hand. "I know, and I may, but I sort of have an idea . . . that maybe I'll stay on here for a while longer. Work on some ideas about stuff and things."

"Oh my God. That was vague even for you. Must mean there's a dynamite idea percolating in that convoluted brain of yours."

"Maybe. Anyway, I hate to see you go, but I'll be around to hold down the fort, as they say."

"Have you told Lillo?"

"I haven't mentioned it. But if she needs her space back, I'll stay at Mac's."

"You really *are* working on something, aren't you?"

"Maybe. Thank you for making that delicious breakfast. I'm going to drop by Mac's for a minute, and see if she wants to come here for dinner."

"Or invites us to her place," Diana added.

"Or invites us there. Then I have to go into town."

"Why?" Allie asked.

"Well, I'm getting these 'someone is trying to get into your bank accounts' notices. Must be dear old Dad. I changed the passwords, but he probably already has his hackers on it. So I need to get to a secure server and change my passwords again. Then get on to the bank and freeze all activity. Which can be a bitch. I'm hoping no one is using the computer at the community center."

Diana sighed. "It's come to this. Dial-up. What they need here is connectivity."

"Tell me about it. But it's worth it if I can keep my father busy enough not to come galloping here to disrupt everybody's life."

Diana gave her the look her horse metaphor deserved.

"You think he'll send those men again?" Allie asked.

"Oh, definitely, if he can't get to my money."

"I'm sure he cares about more than just your money."

Diana and Jess looked deadpan at her.

"Or not," Allie reluctantly agreed.

"Not," Diana said. "I'm sorry, Jess, but you know it's true."

"Yeah, I do. And the really sad thing? He doesn't really care about my money. He doesn't need it. He just needs to be the winner. And you know, now that I've finally given in to the truth—the real truth—not his version of it, I feel ridiculously fine about it."

Allie looked like she might cry.

"It's all right, Al. My brothers and sister and I lived in luxury, had a mother who usually loved us. And plenty of nannies who did for real. And I've realized, now that I've had time to think, he didn't love any of my siblings either. They were just possessions, just like me. They're still shackled to the company store. I'm free at last, free at last. It's empowering."

"Great," Diana said. "Do you feel empowered enough to stop at the liquor store and carry all the bottles back in the fog?"

Jess laughed. "I love you. And absolutely. I'll pick up wine and provisions if you'll make a list." She checked her watch. "It's after ten and I have to make another stop after the center, though I have a feeling everybody will be running late today."

She headed down the hall to get dressed.

"You might as well go, too, Diana," Allie said. "I can see you're chomping at the bit to get to the stables."

"What a fetchingly descriptive phrase." Diana snapped her teeth and tossed her head. "What about the dishes?"

"I'll do them, then I'm going to curl up with a book and look out the window to where I can't see a damn thing, not even the lighthouse, and—"

"Wait for the studly CPA."

Allie immediately grew serious. "Nothing is going to happen."

"Why? Time's a-wasting, girl. Seize the day, while you have the chance. And go home happy." She went to their room to put on her last clean pair of new used jeans.

Allie was at the sink when she came out. "You'd better put a jacket on over that sweatshirt. The weather can get raw."

"How do you know?"

"I'm from California, land of fog and damp."

"I thought you were the land of sunshine and movie stars."

"Movie stars, yes; sunshine, I think, is Florida. Take mine. It's on the peg by the door."

"You may need it."

Allie flashed a smile. It transformed her face and Diana suddenly realized it was a younger smile, a smile she'd grown accustomed to in school but hadn't really seen since they'd reconnnected this week.

Damn. She didn't want to admit it, but there was something weird about this town. It made you feel different. Believe in odd things. Caught you off guard, which was not a smart place for Diana Walters, CEO of a cutting-edge tech company, to find herself. Not a smart place at all.

The wet and the cold and the fog hit her the moment she stepped out of the cottage. Damn. They weren't kidding when they called it pea-soup weather. This was ridiculous.

She was ridiculous. To go out walking in this weather, to stumble blindly up a country road in the cold and damp just to muck out some stables. Yeah, keep believing that one and she'd be sitting around the fireplace all winter with Lillo Gray, ex-physician.

So why wasn't Lighthouse Beach working out for her?

She tripped over something in the road, realized she'd wandered onto the shoulder, where branches and other stuff had been brought down by the storm. She eased back to her left, felt the firm pavement under her feet. Realized she might have trouble seeing the sign to the stables. It was hard enough to see it in the sunlight.

She slowed down, peered into the denseness. It was like a smoke machine in a theater gone berserk and pumping noxious fumes over the audience as the curtain rises. The coughs and teary eyes that follow. Only this fog didn't lift and it wasn't noxious and it didn't disperse, just hovered in the air, unmoving.

Had she missed the turnoff? It was impossible to tell. How long had she been walking? Her heart stuttered and she berated herself for her moment of fear. If she didn't find the turnoff soon, she'd just turn around and go back to the cottage. It wasn't like she was lost in the woods.

It came upon her like the roll of doom. She heard it, but before she could identify it or figure out its direction, it rose over her, barely lighter than the fog itself.

She threw up her arm to protect herself, but the scream died in her throat. She was knocked to the side; recognized Loki's whinny as she hit the ground; heard the scrambling of hooves. But she couldn't see a thing.

"Jesus! Where the hell are you? Don't move." Ian's voice.

Diana froze, tried to tell him where she was, but her landing had knocked the air out of her. She gasped, wheezed. "Here," she croaked.

She could see the white shroud moving above her and then something kicked her thigh.

"Shit." Ian's face came into view, eye level, two inches away. *"Are you fucking crazy?"*

He was screaming at her. Music to her ears. She started to laugh.

"It isn't funny. I could have killed you. I could've—" His voice broke and his face moved away. She was alone in the mist.

"Do not leave me," she ordered. She'd meant to order, but it might have sounded like a plea. The fog was doing odd things to her voice.

"Just don't move." Ian's disembodied voice echoed around her. Where was he?

She could hear him mumble and realized he was talking to Loki, not her. She tried to stand.

"I said don't move."

"Sorry, I thought you were talking to the horse." She giggled, stifled the sound. She freaking giggled. What the hell was wrong with her? She hadn't giggled even as a child. She took a deep breath. Pulled herself together. Hauled herself to her feet and came nose to chest with Ian Lachlan.

It was a good place to be, she decided.

"What are you doing out here?"

"Coming to the stables. Why are you riding in this fog?"

"I—I almost ran you down." His voice sounded weak, breathless.

She swore he was shaking.

Damn. Sometimes a girl just needed to act. She slipped her arms around his waist and managed to find his mouth with hers. Not bad aim, when you couldn't see shit.

And then she stopped commenting, stopped analyzing, gave up, and gave in.

Chapter 21

Lillo reached into the carton and pulled out two more boxes of swabs. The clinic was quiet and virtually empty. The fog was keeping people away. They'd seen only three patients since she'd arrived. And all three of them had walked.

With nothing to do, she had decided to rearrange the supply cabinet. Anything to keep from thinking about this afternoon. Had she really agreed to throw out the stuff in the storeroom? *Throw it out?* Was she nuts? Her whole life was in that room.

No, Lillo thought, her whole *past* life. Her whole life was here.

Not here in the clinic but here in Lighthouse Beach. Maybe she would have to get a steadier job than emergency gardener, handyman, grocery shopper to the infirm.

But people *left* the island to get jobs. She didn't even have a car. She'd sold it along with whatever wasn't waiting for her in the extra bedroom.

She was such a mess. *Pharmaceuticals salesman?* Oh, right, no car. She could buy a secondhand clunker, but with what money? Borrow Mac's van? Then what would Mac do?

Waitress at Mike's?

Hell, what was she thinking? She'd just racked up a quarter of a million dollars in tuition to be a waitress? "Hi, Mom and Dad, how's Florida? I got a new job, working at Mike's."

She could barely force herself to make her once-a-month call as it was. Let several of their calls go by before she answered the phone. She was consumed by guilt. She'd never known what that phrase meant until the first time she'd talked to them after her return to Lighthouse Beach. She'd thrown up after she'd hung up.

She'd taken their love, their support, their money, and betrayed them with her failure.

Clancy came into the room with his coffee mug. "You gonna hold that box of swabs all day? Have you even moved since the last time I came in for a refill?"

Lillo hastily put the box in the cupboard. "Yes." She opened the door wider to show him the nearly filled shelves.

Clancy shook his head. "Very neat," he said, and walked toward the door. Turned when he got there. Opened his mouth and Lillo braced herself. But he just shook his head again and left the room.

Even Clancy was disappointed in her. Well, stand in line. No one was more disappointed in her than she was. Not just because she'd lost the man she loved, or her profession, or all the friends and colleagues she'd had pretragedy. But because she believed in her failure.

She hadn't at first. At first, she'd known that what happened wasn't entirely her fault, that emotions had made her slow on the uptake. It was her fiancé, for heaven's sake. He'd been laughing and then he'd stopped. She didn't automatically start sorting through the list of possibilities as she slid down the palisade.

She was screaming his name. Refusing to believe and panicking. She'd panicked and Kyle was dead.

She reached for another box of swabs; it crumpled in her hand. It wasn't even the self-doubt that had driven her home. It was the doubts of her peers. She was culpable, but so were they. The looks, the whispers. The snippets of overheard conversation. They'd subtly but insidiously broken down what little self-confidence she'd had left. Maybe it hadn't been intentional, but they'd been ruthless. And she'd let them do it to her. And now she had nothing left.

She gulped back a cry. Pushed the box back into shape and put it on the shelf with the other boxes. Supplies she would never have the right to use. She'd known this for the last year. And yet today, with the fog shrouding the light, pushing into the windows and creating a suffocating bubble of remorse around her, she saw, for the first time, that she wasn't alone in her downfall.

If she hadn't let her guilt wear her down, if she hadn't let the suspicions get to her, if she hadn't let Kyle die, if she had never left the island in the first place, she'd be happily running a fat camp for kids like Jess. Jess, whose own life had almost been ruined by her inability to stand up for herself. To resist the motives of others. Who still didn't know what she was going to do with her future.

Lillo shut the cabinet door. She hadn't been needed in the examination rooms since she'd arrived. Maybe she should just go home. Give herself a minute to confront her storage room before the others dismantled it.

Because she was going to let it go. Somehow. All of it. Sever the final ties to her life and let it go.

She blew out air. Stretched her neck, and went out to see if she was really needed at all.

"We're rescheduling all nonemergency visits until tomorrow

and Saturday," Agnes told her. "The fog is hanging around like an obnoxious relative. Not safe to drive in unless you have to.

"We're sending Doc Hartley home. He'll be on call; you might as well catch a ride with him if you want to leave. But I hope you'll be able to come back tomorrow, when we'll really need you."

Lillo was surprised at the disappointment she felt at being sent home. That was dangerous. Because it wouldn't do to start getting comfortable. Clancy and Ned would be gone next week. She and Mac and the rest of the town's inhabitants would go back to life without a working clinic. Maybe some internist or nurse prac would retire and be looking for a place to settle down.

Fat chance. People moved away from Lighthouse Beach; they didn't settle there.

"I guess I will go. Call my cell if you need me."

Agnes blinked and Lillo realized what she'd just said.

"Are you and Doc Clancy both staying?"

"For a while longer; then I'll put everything on call forwarding."

"Well, be careful in this soup."

"You too, hon. Ask Doc for a ride."

Lillo gave one of those noncommittal chin lifts and went to get her things.

"DAMN," NED MUTTERED as he saw Lillo. He'd been on his way to tell her about the change in plans and offer her a ride home. The way she was headed for the back door, it looked like Agnes had gotten to her first.

He grabbed his jacket off the peg, clapped his pockets to make sure Ian's car keys were there, and hurried after her.

He didn't know why he kept trying to fix her. She didn't appreciate it. Actually, he was pretty sure she was beginning to hate him for it. But he couldn't stop. She was talented and selfless when she wasn't being a self-indulgent, self-pitying—ugh. What was wrong with her? The world needed her. People needed her. Hell, they needed her right here in Lighthouse Beach.

Mac had told him to lay off. That he was doing more harm than good. But he couldn't just sit by and let Lillo destroy herself. Ever since he'd known her, she'd wanted to be a doctor, ever since the days as a skinny ten-year-old hanging out at the clinic, begging to be allowed to put the supplies away and asking a million questions. She'd studied hard, was at the top of her class. Had a great future in front of her, until— Ned clenched his fist. He'd tried to avoid her, which turned out to be totally unnecessary because she'd been avoiding him. And she was much better at it than he was.

Still, if he believed in anything unscientific, which he didn't, he'd think that the fates were pushing them together. And the only reason for that was to get her to admit she missed medicine and then convince her to return to it, before she got so far behind she'd have to start over again and not just slip back into her residency.

"Hey, wait up."

She hesitated. "Now what?"

"Lunch?" He'd meant to ask if she needed a ride, but "lunch" came out instead. He was such an ass.

"Thanks, but apparently there's something I have to do today."

"What?"

"My houseguests have made plans."

"Oh." She was reaching for the doorknob. "You're not planning to drive anywhere in this fog, are you?"

Lillo gave him her "How stupid do you think I am?" look.

He knew it well enough. "Just asking. It isn't safe to be out." He sounded like a condescending asshat even to himself.

"Do you think you will ever stop acting like a . . . a . . ."

"Man?"

"Not the term I actually had in mind, but yeah, that too."

Bossy? Pushy? Overbearing? Probably none of those were strong enough, so he didn't even try. "I've got Ian's SUV. I'll drive you home. I mean—"

"I'll take you up on that offer."

She opened the door. He only had time to call out to Agnes that he and Lillo were leaving.

"Fog seems to be letting up some," Agnes called back. "But it's still dangerous, so be careful."

He reached past Lillo and held the door for her. "Well, that's good," he said. "Clancy's taking the first on-call and I don't want him out on the roads if the visibility is bad."

Lillo rolled her eyes. "Do you ever get tired of trying to run everybody's life?"

He turned on her, stopping her on the porch, and grabbed her by the shoulder. "What? Can't someone be concerned about a friend? That's what friends do."

She jerked away and started down the steps.

He ran after her before she could bolt. He was sick and tired of tiptoeing around her like she was some fragile figurine. She wasn't. She was tough as nails. Or at least she had been.

They reached Ian's SUV. He opened the door and pushed her inside before she could refuse to get it. He ran around to the driver's side and hopped in, started the engine, and backed out of the parking space.

Other than telling her to buckle up, he said nothing until they got out on the street. She sat slouched in the seat next to him, arms crossed protectively over her chest, not afraid, just sulking.

"What is wrong with you? Sometimes I don't even recognize who you are. What's happened to you?"

"I killed the brightest resident M.D. the hospital had had in decades."

"Second brightest." He shot her a defiant look; they both knew she was the top student in her class. "And you didn't kill him."

"I stood there and watched him die."

"Along with twenty other people."

"But I could have saved him."

"Doubtful. He probably bled out within seconds, before you even reached him."

"I stood there laughing while he died."

"It was an accident. Not your fault. Not his fault. There was nothing you could do. You know that. Somewhere your rational self—remember her? You used to think with it before you managed to shove it into a dark corner. That self knows what the facts are."

She shifted in her seat to look out the window. He stared straight ahead into the fog—on the alert.

"Tell that to my colleagues. They all knew I could have done more. Should have done. I couldn't go on day after day with them looking at me like I'd done it on purpose."

"What? That is so much bullshit. Is that why you're holed up here, out of sight, out of mind, because of what you think people are thinking? They're not. They gave you a grant for the next year."

"One Kyle should have had. The one that they changed to the Kyle L. Drummond Award to honor him. That was the last nail. I couldn't go on. I just couldn't."

"Okay, that might have been a little insensitive on their part. But that's their bad judgment. Not yours."

"Really? Imagine the response to that one. 'She killed her boyfriend for his grant money.'"

"You're making this shit up. You're just having a crisis of self-doubt. We all get it. Patients die. It's shitty. But it's what happens when you're a doctor."

"I'm not a doctor."

"Actually, you are, but time is running out on your license. You'll have to reapply and go through a lot of retraining if you delay this much longer."

"I'm not going back."

They'd reached the parking lot; he pulled alongside the cottage.

"Then do something else, something that doesn't involve triage."

She released the seat belt. "I'm going to clean out my closet. Thanks for the ride."

She reached for the door handle. He pushed the lock button. "Wait a minute. Will we see you tomorrow?"

"Probably not. I do have guests and they haven't seen any of the sights."

He frowned at her. "You know, if you're planning on staying on here . . ."

"I live here. Would you please unlock the door?"

"Live here; then maybe you'd consider keeping the clinic open."

"They need to find a nurse prac to run the clinic."

"So go back and get licensed as a nurse prac."

She stared at him, anger, revulsion . . . she wanted to hit him . . . he could read it as easily as if she'd said it aloud.

"I'm a surgeon, or at least I would have been."

"If you hadn't quit."

"You don't understand. Let me out."

"Sure I do. Shit happens. You learn to deal with it, or you quit."

"Well, we know what I did."

"Yeah, but it doesn't have to be permanent."

"Sure, now open this door."

"You know, you should really take a page from Ian's play-book. Do you know how hard it is for him to go out day after day, treating favorite pets, saving the livestock of people who fear him, avoid him, until they need him. He could have walked away. But he didn't. He lives in a personal hell and still manages to do good."

"Are you finished?"

"Yeah, I think I am." He jabbed the lock button.

She pushed the door open. "I know you think I'm a selfish bitch."

"No, I think you're a coward."

She slid out of the SUV, slammed the door, and for a moment disappeared into the fog. He could just see bits and pieces of her as she groped her way down to the gate.

Ned wanted to stop her and shake her, but mostly he wanted to kick himself. It was killing her to stay away from medicine, to live in this self-imposed exile from the thing she loved most. Or maybe it was just him. Maybe it was killing him to watch all that talent go to waste.

And they were right back where they always ended up, with her in denial and him pissed off.

For the briefest second he considered going over to Mac's, but she'd just tell him he was an insensitive clod or words to that effect. He'd spare himself that. He'd had enough of them both for now. He turned the SUV around and headed slowly up to the road to Ian's. Now there was someone who had taken his demons by the shorthairs and fought them daily, hourly, every moment of his life. And he'd managed to find a productive if solitary existence.

If Lillo wanted something to feel guilty about, it should be for sending the CEO to Ian. Ned knew her type, and if Ian slipped back into darkness because of her, he would never for-give either of them. You didn't flirt with someone whose sanity was balancing on the edge.

LILLO WONDERED IF Ned could still see her. Everybody was on her case. She couldn't go anywhere without someone calling her out about how she'd chosen to live her life. She groped for the gate, pushed it open. She could walk this path in the fog or in the pitch black of night. Here, she knew where she was, where she was going. And everybody should just bug off.

She'd go inside and tell the others that they wouldn't be cleaning out the spare bedroom, that thank you very much but it was none of their business. And where did that stop? Did she tell them to get out, that she didn't value their concern, that they'd only known her for a few days, except for Jess—Jess, who hadn't bothered to get in touch with Lillo until she needed her. It was all true. Wasn't it? It seemed true. She had been happy since she'd been back here, before they came, before Ned started poking his nose into her business again.

As she walked down the path she caught snatches of objects—the mailbox, a branch, a patch of sand. The fog was beginning to clear. But the way in front of her was as opaque as the clouds. She didn't miss the symbolism of that. Even nature was against her.

She reached the door to the cottage; her hand went straight to the doorknob.

She was first struck by how warm it was inside. She'd been oblivious to the cold, ragged weather until she'd stepped into the cottage. The lights were on, warm and welcoming. Allie was sitting in Lillo's reading chair—reading a book. She could hear the shower running.

"You're home early," Allie said. "Get a cup. There's a fresh pot of tea."

Lillo shed her raincoat and boots. Got a cup down. She'd wait until the others returned before she announced the change in plans. Right now a cup of tea was just what she needed.

"Want your chair back?"

Lillo shook her head, poured herself a cup of tea, and sat on the couch. The lighthouse rose out of the clouds like a beacon in a religious painting. She shook her head to clear her mind. The lighthouse was merely shrouded in fog, no different from all the other foggy days. She really needed to get a grip. At least the fog was lifting. Hopefully it would leave and stay away.

"How was the clinic?" Allie asked tentatively.

"Agnes rescheduled all nonemergency appointments and we shut down early. Ned and Doc Clancy are on call to make house calls. Who's in the shower?"

"Diana."

"She didn't go to the stables? They couldn't have ridden in this weather anyway."

"Oh, she went and came back. Gave me a look that dared me to ask what happened, went into the bathroom, and hasn't come out since. I'm beginning to worry about her."

"The water heater isn't that big, she'll get out when the water gets cold."

The front door opened and banged shut. "Thank God," Jess said, and leaned against the door.

Her hair was windblown above her pale face. She was carrying two heavy-looking plastic grocery bags, and her windbreaker was zipped up but bulged out in front like she'd maybe eaten several dozen doughnuts. Lillo hoped she wasn't swinging from near anorexia to the other extreme.

"I got wine and sandwich stuff. That's about all I could carry as I groped my way home." She unzipped her jacket and pulled out a thick cardboard accordion folder.

"What's that?" Lillo said.

Jess plunked it down on the counter and shrugged out of her windbreaker. "Is there more tea? Man, it's cold out there. What kind of beach weather is this?"

"There's more tea," Allie said. "Get a cup and tell us what's in the folder."

"Historical society records."

"What? Where did you get those?" asked Lillo.

"And why?" asked Allie.

Jess got down a cup and poured herself tea. "I got them from the historical society. OMG. Mac said the whole society consisted of two old men. 'Old' doesn't begin to cover it. And the 'society' is one room on the first floor of their house.

"Luckily they live two doors down from the liquor store or I would still be wandering the moors like Heathcliff, calling their names. Is Diana in the shower?"

Her answer was an expletive shouted from the bathroom. A sudden silence as the taps closed.

"Ran out of hot water," Lillo said. "You didn't answer the rest of the question. Why did you go to the historical society?"

"Because I'm getting an idea," Jess said. "And I want to do my due diligence. Though I may have to make a trip to Augusta. Where is Augusta anyway?"

"About forty or fifty miles northeast of here. What's this all about?"

"I'll tell you when I know." Jess glanced at her watch. "Looks like we're all back early. I missed lunch."

"I don't think any of us have eaten," Allie said. "I'll make some sandwiches."

The three of them were crowded around the kitchen counter when Diana emerged a few minutes later.

"Guess you didn't go riding," Jess said.

Diana lifted an eyebrow, snagged a bag of chips, and opened it by slapping her hands together. The top exploded with a loud pop. She reached inside and grabbed a handful. "I've always wanted to do that."

"I thought I heard horse hooves when you came back," Allie said. "That was nice that he saw you home."

Diana scowled at her.

"Or maybe not." Allie bent her head over the slices of bread she was spreading with mayonnaise.

Lillo and Jess made themselves useful. It was obvious Diana was about to explode from some emotion. It seemed to Lillo it wasn't happiness.

After a minute or so during which the only sound was the crunch of Diana eating chips, Jess said, "Okay, spill. What happened?"

"What happened? What happened?"

"I believe that was my question. What the hell happened? Why are you so pissed off? What did he do now, because we can be pretty sure it wasn't something the horses did."

Diana chewed and frowned.

"Spring more kids on you? Refuse to let you ride? Forgot you were coming and wasn't even there?"

"He kissed me."

Three faces turned to her in surprise.

Jess was the first to recover. "I thought you wanted him to kiss you."

"Not like that."

"Oh boy. Give us the blow-by."

Diana threw up her hands, walked away, came back again.

"He kissed you and . . ." Jess coaxed.

"Well, I sort of kissed him first."

"That's it. I'm declaring happy hour."

"It's only two o'clock," Allie said.

"It's five o'clock somewhere. We're on vacation, we're surrounded by fog, and Diana is acting like a lovesick teenager. I declare it's happy hour."

MAC HADN'T BOTHERED to open the gift shop that morning. There wouldn't be any tourists today. For one thing, they'd close the bridge to all but necessary travel. This was a real humdinger, a pea-souper. It kept everybody home who could stay home.

So she sat at the window looking out at the parking lot. She couldn't see anything. The window was like a frame on one of those modern paintings, just a stretch of gray.

That would be her whole world soon, she knew. It wasn't as bad as she'd feared. Not a brain tumor, not macular degeneration, not glaucoma. Cataracts. Easily fixed, they said. If you had the time, had the money.

Still, she'd have to go away to have it done and probably stay overnight. She could get someone to watch the lighthouse. Lillo would do it. But what then? What if something went wrong? The surgeon's hand slipped? What if she went blind anyway? Where would she go? What would happen to the lighthouse? What would happen to her?

And how would she pay for the operation? The doctor had said Medicare would pay for the regular lenses but he'd recommended the advanced lenses. And they cost several thousand dollars that she would have to pay. She couldn't afford that. She didn't have thousands of dollars to spare, she barely had enough savings to do one eye, much less two. And she depended on those savings to augment her Social Security.

Clancy said he would loan her the money. *Loan. Ha.* Neither of them believed that. He would give her the money. But it didn't do to give money to friends. It always ate away at friendships. She wouldn't risk it. Her friends were more important to her than being able to see, and maybe even more than the lighthouse.

"OKAY, SO I'M groping my way up the road, trying to figure out where the drive to the stables is. Was I nuts? I couldn't see shit, and I was tripping and stumbling like some too-stupid-to-live heroine in a bad horror movie." Diana took a sip of her wine.

"When out of the mist . . ." She laughed. "Sorry, it does sound like a horror movie."

"No, it sounds like a romantic fantasy," Allie said.

"Well, to be perfectly truthful, when I got over my initial 'What the fuck,' I thought it did, too. Fool that I was."

"Would you just get on with it?" Jess said.

"So out of the mist appears Loki, two feet from me. Ian reins him in, but he still knocks me to the ground. I wasn't hurt, but he throws himself from Loki's back—I'm making this up. I couldn't see shit . . . I don't know how *he* saw *me*; he could have stepped on me, except that I was already getting up.

"He pulled me to my feet, and I thought what the hell. So I reached up and kissed him." Diana made a growling noise, but Lillo thought it was more at herself for either succumbing to her desires, or maybe for telling the others about them.

"There was this moment of will-he-won't-he, but I'm telling you, at that moment I didn't care. Then he kissed me back. I mean, like *kissed* me. Not like 'Had a great time, I'll call you,' or 'I think you're hot, let's spend the night together,' or even like 'Thanks for last night,' but more like it was real." She'd been pacing in the small space in front of them but she stopped. "Ya know?"

Allie was the only one who nodded.

"And I was beginning to think . . . well, at that point I wasn't thinking, but all of a sudden he pulled away.

"I can't see his expression but I can feel the energy pulsing from him, and for a minute I think, 'Please don't be a psychopath,' then he grabs Loki's mane and throws himself back on the horse. I'm standing there feeling like an idiot and I can barely see him, and I'm thinking, 'What just happened?' and 'Just shoot me now.' He'd responded, really responded, and now he's sitting on his horse and I'm standing on the ground. Fucking crazy.

"Then suddenly his hand is there reaching down to me. And okay, I swear this is the truth. I took it and he swung me up behind him. Impossible. It would take fairy dust to get me up on a horse without a stirrup. But I was there. Sitting behind him. I swear.

"And now I'm feeling like a Disney princess about to gallop away to Happily Ever After with the prince to make passionate, searing-hot, satisfying love, and hoping he'll take me inside his house and not the stable. But whatever works.

"He took me home, all right. At a walk, not a gallop; I mean visibility was pretty nonexistent at that point. Between the kiss and the fog, I was totally disoriented, and when he stopped and told me to get off, I did, thinking, 'At last.' Only then he stayed on Loki's back, looking down at me. And said, 'I'm sorry, I can't. Please don't come to the stables anymore.' Then he pulls Loki around and they disappear into the mist.

"And it turns out I'm standing in the parking lot in front of the cottage. And I'm a total fucking asshat for even thinking it might not end this way."

Chapter 22

At first they just stared at Diana. It was the first time Lillo had seen her anything but assured and energetic, and she had a feeling that was the way Diana lived every day. A "Move over, world" attitude that Lillo wished she could emulate. Granted, she'd only known her for a few days—it seemed like much longer—but this apparent acceptance seemed at variance with the woman she knew. And from Allie's and Jess's silence, Lillo thought maybe they were seeing a different side of Diana, too.

Jess was the first to recover. "Wait! That's it? He drops you off and you go meekly into the house?"

Diana shrugged and picked up half of the sandwich Allie had handed her. "I'm not sure 'meekly' is an encompassing enough word to describe it."

"Pissed? Sad?"

Diana pulled a stray leaf of lettuce from between the two pieces of bread and let it drop to her plate.

"Disappointed?" Allie ventured.

"Keep going."

"Humiliated?" Jess cringed as she said it.

"Hmm. Getting closer." She was just looking at her sandwich, studying it like she might find an answer there. This was so not Diana.

"Rejected? Hurt?"

"Jess, maybe you should stop," Lillo said.

Diana glanced at her. "Good idea." She took a huge bite out of the sandwich, effectively ending the conversation.

Lillo wondered if she was imagining Ian's arm or possibly neck as her teeth tore through the bread and cheese and ham.

Diana had called herself several epithets because of Ian's rejection, but Lillo also imagined it was some kind of defensive safeguard against someone else doing it first. Was it possible that Diana, who seemed so self-assured, had been thrown off her game by a reclusive country vet?

Of course, Ian was a lot more than that. And it was probably better that Diana never found out the rest. Especially if, as odd as it sounded, she was developing feelings for him.

No, it would just be too weird. And could never work. And why was she even thinking stupid things like this? Girls' weekend was having an undue influence on all of them, including Lillo.

Diana tossed the crust of her bread on the plate. "So much for that. The sandwich was good, the day sucked, but to every fog a silver lining. We're all back early and we have the whole afternoon and evening to clean out Lillo's storage room."

"No." Lillo jumped up, sudden panic freezing her midmovement. "I mean, maybe I should take some time to go through things."

"Nope. This is the week for new beginnings. So get on board. You know what the Amish say."

"No, I don't," Lillo said.

"Well, I think it was the Amish. 'Many hands make light work.' And you've got your many hands for at least three more days, then I have to get back to work. So. Chop, chop."

Jess looked at Lillo, worried. About Lillo?

"Are you sure you want to do this?" Jess asked.

No, she was not, no more than she'd been sure about inviting these three women into her home. She was glad she did. But would she still be glad once they started deconstructing her life?

The three of them stood in a semicircle, ready to go to work, but not moving until they got the okay from Lillo.

Lillo's mouth was dry, she tried to swallow but couldn't get the muscles to work. She wanted to cry, but there were no tears. She wanted to run, but she stood in place.

Then Diana lifted her eyebrows. And the simple change of expression released Lillo from her indecision. Hell, call it what it was: fear. She was afraid of that room and its contents. She was afraid once she got rid of it, there would be nothing left. Nothing of her left.

"It won't be as bad as you think," Diana said as if she'd heard Lillo's thoughts. "We'll be gentle."

And Lillo laughed, again. Damn, Diana could make her laugh when she should be crying. It was just weird.

"All right, let's get it over with."

They walked as a group to the spare bedroom. Waited while Lillo turned the knob and pushed the door open. It was all there. Everything that belonged to the girl with a future. Bright and optimistic, going places, doing great things, loving with a great love.

That's what Lillo had thought it was, remembered it as, what it should have been, but today it was just a room with a bunch of junk. Old clothes, old books, old DVDs. An old life. They belonged to another time, another person.

She breathed deeply, let it out slowly through pursed lips. "Let's do this."

"Garbage bags," Diana said.

"I saw some under the sink." Allie left the room.

"And a Magic Marker," Diana called after her.

The other three crowded through the door. There was barely space to walk around the bed to the other side of the room. Diana began to weave her way through.

"Shouldn't we just start near the door and clear a wider path over to the other side?" Jess asked.

"No," Diana said, climbing over a pile of things that had toppled to the floor at some point in time. She stopped at the two stacks of boxes that reached up past the windowsill. "What is this stuff?"

Lillo swallowed. "They're my"—she cleared her throat—"engagement-party gifts."

"Shit. I thought so. Aren't you supposed to return gifts?"

"Diana," Jess warned.

"No, it's okay," Lillo said. "I've been through this stage already. Most have been returned. Some friends—at the beginning, when I still had them—contacted everyone. Some people had moved, and we couldn't reach them; others didn't want their gifts back. They sent back all that did want them. I think."

"So what do you want to do?"

"I don't want them."

"Not even this teakettle?" Jess said. "You could use a new one."

"None of them."

"Fair enough," Diana said. "Let's get rid of them."

Allie returned with a box of large garbage bags and three Magic Markers.

Diana tossed the teakettle to Lillo. She caught it, clutched it to her chest as if it were a family heirloom. But it wasn't. She'd never even bothered to open the box. Why was she holding on to the stupid teakettle, or any of the presents that cluttered the room? She didn't even remember what most of them were or who they were from.

And still she hesitated.

"Set them free," Diana intoned.

Lillo sputtered. It was as if every time she interacted with Diana, laughter forced its way out. "I hate it when you do that."

"What?"

"Make me laugh when I shouldn't. This is traumatic."

"Hell, there's no better time to laugh, if you ask me. Let's carry all these boxes out to the front door. We can decide what to do with them later."

"Not throw them away," Lillo said as panic rose inside her.

"The community center," Jess said. "I'm sure they could use these things or know families who could. You can take it off on your income tax."

"Yeah, as soon as I get an income," Lillo said. "But you're right. The center could use them, except the underwear."

"There's naughty underwear?" Jess started looking through the flat boxes.

"Later," Diana said. "We can try them on and dance in the moonlight—except from the looks of things outside, there will *be* no moonlight."

She was right. The fog had lifted, but it was still dark and overcast outside. And from the way the wind was roaring around the cottage, they could still be looking at some serious weather.

Lillo reached for her phone. No bars.

"Hey, pay attention," Diana scolded. "Jess, put the things that go to the community center on the right side of the door. Damn, I wish we had some big boxes. Allie, you'll have to label the trash bags: 'Trash,' 'Community Center,' 'Maybes,' and 'Keeps.'" She frowned at Lillo. "Only the important stuff."

Lillo nodded. She was so far into panic mode she didn't even know what Diana was talking about. Thank God Diana had taken charge. Lillo's knees were knocking so hard she could barely stand; she felt as weak as seaweed. She just hoped she was capable of carrying her share of the load.

Diana began parceling out the engagement gifts, and Lillo, Jess, and Allie carried them to the living room. Within a few minutes one whole side of the room was free of junk.

"Who knew?" Diana said. "Look at all the room you've got. Why did you keep this junk so long?"

Because it wasn't junk, it was her life. Her former life. Or maybe it wasn't. Lillo wasn't sure, but she felt a little bereft at losing all these things now.

Jess stepped close and put her arm around Lillo's waist. "Is it because you don't want to let go?"

Lillo bit her lip, her mouth twisted. "I guess."

"I know what that's like. Are you sure you want to go through with this?"

Lillo hugged herself, wishing she had a sweatshirt. She did, though. There was one folded on the bed. With her old college seal on the front. *Leave it, leave it,* she told herself. She'd just stay cold.

She grabbed a trash bag. The sweatshirt went inside, then the stack of tees and sweats beneath it.

"Don't you want to pick out . . . ?"

Lillo shook her head and pushed clothes into the bag until it was full. She pulled the red ties tight, knotted them, and hauled the bag out to the living room.

When a few more bags were carried to the front room and the bedroom was actually beginning to look like a bedroom again and not like Miss Havisham's wedding feast, Diana came into the bedroom with four beers. "Ten-minute guzzle break."

Diana passed around the bottle opener; no one suggested they leave the bedroom. Jess and Allie sat on the bed. Diana went to the window. Lillo just stood where she was.

The room looked fine. A little dusty and old-fashioned, but spacious enough. The closet was still filled with clothes and shoes and who knew what else. The bookshelves were half filled with books; most had been stacked along the hallway walls waiting to be boxed. There were two boxes of books stacked in the corner. Lillo couldn't keep her eyes from wandering to them. It was only a question of time before someone asked her about them.

She looked away. To the window. The day was gray. The wind was blowing sand across the beach. The tide was coming in and the waves were already lapping across the jetty, stirred up by the wind and an offshore storm. The jetty would be completely covered long before the water reached high tide.

Not exactly anyone's idea of girls' weekend at the shore. Well, they should have gone to Jones Beach if they wanted to sunbathe.

She wasn't being fair. No one had complained, not once. Not only had they not complained, they had embraced her friends, her lifestyle, befriended Mac, were helping Lillo spring-clean even though spring had come and gone.

What had started out as an intervention to save Jess from a terrible marriage had turned into something else. Something special. And what should have been the end of the story, saving Jess, had actually changed their own lives. Jess had a new start. Allie a chance to feel again. Diana? Who knew what that was.

Diana seemed to be the only one of them who had her shit together. Who could organize and be strong for all of them.

And yet she was drawn to Ian, there was no way to deny it. As impossible as it seemed, it had happened.

Diana put down her beer. "Okay, troops, almost done. One more time with feeling."

The hanging clothes came next. Lillo would have just gotten rid of them all. But no. Diana, Jess, and Allie pulled out each piece, scrutinized it, asked questions about it, then discussed it. Piece after piece: the jeans, the shirts, the suits, the dresses, the formal attire; each either went back into the closet or into a donate bag.

And Lillo just watched. Several times she'd almost said, *Keep that.* But she held her tongue and let them do away with her wardrobe like they'd done with everything else.

It looked like an enormous amount of castoffs, but when they were done, the closet was still filled, but not crammed with more clothes than she'd ever wear.

The bookshelves were filled but not overstuffed, with the DVDs on the top shelf and the biggest books on the bottom.

And finally, the only things left to deal with were the two boxes of books in the corner. Diana lifted out one of the heavy textbooks. "*Operative Dictations on* . . . I can't even pronounce it." She put it back and took out another. "*Diagnostic Pathology?*"

"Toss," Lillo said.

"Can't you at least resell them? They must have cost a fortune."

"They're probably already outdated." Lillo turned away. Looked out the window. Tried to pretend she was anywhere but here.

She was aware that no one was moving. She didn't turn around.

"Toss." It was the hardest thing she had ever said.

"Are you sure?"

Jess stepped close. "Lillo, no. You might need them again."

Lillo shook her head. "Toss." She turned back to the window. She'd let them carry the boxes out. She wasn't sure she could.

"Okay," Diana said. She hefted the top box into her arms and carried it out to the hallway. Nodded to Allie to do the same with the other. Jess just stood there looking at Lillo. Lillo stared at the sand, the waves, the lighthouse. It had signaled her home; it was beginning to look like she was here to stay.

Diana and Allie came back in.

"Looks like that's— Wait a minute, spoke too soon. It was hiding behind the boxes." Diana lifted a black nylon carrier bag and deposited it on the bed. "What the heck. It's got a lock. Have you been moonlighting for Brinks?" She pressed the clasp anyway and it opened.

Lillo whirled around. In her mind, she screamed *"NO,"* leaped across the bed, and grabbed the bag before Diana could open it. But she just stood there, paralyzed.

Once the lock was opened, Diana unzipped the bag, exposing the contents. And they all moved closer to stare at the objects inside. Even Lillo, who knew exactly what she would find.

"It's your medical bag," Jess said. "I didn't even know doctors still carried bags. I mean, do any of them make house calls?"

"No," Lillo said, thankful to draw the conversation away from her past. "This is for community-service rotation."

"Like a glorified first-aid kit," Diana said. She zipped it up and placed it back in the corner.

"Toss," Lillo said.

"It might come in handy someday," Diana countered.

Lillo didn't bother arguing, but walked around the bed, grabbed the handles of the bag, and carried it out to the hallway, where she placed it on top of the medical books.

When she retreated to the living room, Allie, Jess, and Diana were standing in the only cleared space between them and the front door.

"I think I'll call Sada and see if she can get someone to come over and haul this stuff away," Lillo said, and pulled her phone out of her pocket.

"Well, the fog *is* lifting," Jess said. "At least we'll be able to see to load her . . . does she have a truck?"

"Actually, she does, and she has help at the center on Thursdays, so she might be able to grab a couple of able-bodied men and come over soon." Because if Lillo had to look at the piles of her former life for much longer, she might go stark raving mad.

She had to go out to the parking lot to get a signal, but when she came back inside she had good news. "Half an hour," she told the others. "How's that for service?"

"Better than you get anywhere else." Diana looked at her watch. "Shall we start happy hour before she gets here?"

"Didn't we already start happy hour?" Jess said.

"Twice," Allie said.

"Like I've often said . . . third time's a charm." Diana grinned. "I'm thinking something pink and girlie."

SADA WAS BETTER than her word. Her gray pickup backed up to Lillo's gate twenty minutes later. Three strapping teenagers accompanied her.

Lillo came out to meet them. "There's a lot of stuff."

"Perfect. The one thing I have plenty of is space. I'll take anything you're getting rid of." Sada motioned to the boys and followed them to the cottage.

"Holy cow," she said when she saw the stacks of gifts and cast-off clothes. She looked at Lillo.

"These are gifts I never used. The rest are clothes I don't

wear, or stuff I don't need. Just throw whatever you don't want in the Dumpster."

"I'm sure we can use it all. Guys, take this out to the truck but be careful with breakables. You know the drill."

The young men spread out.

"Can we help?" Lillo asked.

"Looks like you're about to relax. You all take a load off. If we have any questions, I'll send out a yell."

"Works for me," said Diana. "I was thinking that since the fog is lifting we could sip and sup on the deck."

"Then you'd better start. Small-craft advisory is out," Sada said. "Gently, fellas." She shook her head.

"What does a small-boat advisory mean to those of us on land?" Diana asked.

"Just that there's a storm somewhere that's kicking up the waves. We might see some wind tonight. Just part of normal life. Don't put that on the bottom!" she yelled at one of the boys, and hurried away.

The rest of them donned sweatshirts and jackets and carried food and drinks to the porch.

An hour later, Sada stuck her head in the opening of the sliding glass door. "All done. I don't know how to thank you, Lillo."

"My pleasure. Do you have time to sit for a few?"

"Nah, I'd better get this stuff back while I still have my moving guys. But thanks. We'll have to get together soon." Her head disappeared and the door closed.

When Lillo went inside a few minutes later, the house looked like it had that morning. Maybe cleaner.

She let out a huge sigh that ended in a shudder. She felt Jess come up beside her and slip her arm around her waist.

"You okay?"

Lillo nodded. She wasn't sure if she was okay or if this was the beginning of her end.

Jess squeezed her. "You're going to be fine. I know you are. You just need to get your groove back."

Lillo smiled. They'd spent their childhoods bolstering Jess's self-esteem and now the tables were turned. Jess was supporting her. Life was weird. And sometimes good.

"This was a smart idea," Ned said as Ian set two plates on the table. Each was covered by a steak that extended over the sides.

"Yeah, the fog lifted just in time to grill."

"And we don't have to beg a meal off of Mac." Ned sliced his baked potato lengthwise.

"That too. When are those women leaving?"

Ned looked up. "I don't know. It was supposed to be a long weekend, but they don't seem to be in any hurry to leave. Does it matter?"

"I—damn, listen to that wind. Guess we better shutter the windows after dinner."

"Yeah, okay. You know if you'd thin out some of the damn trees, you'd wouldn't have so much trouble with the wind. Plus, you'd have a view of the ocean."

"Yeah, I guess."

"And you wouldn't have to worry so much about falling limbs."

"True."

"So why do you want to know when they're leaving? Is that CEO still annoying you?"

"No. Just curious."

"Ay, well, I don't know. Lillo's barely talking to me."

"I thought you two were getting along."

"For a minute. She pisses me off. Just sitting around here when she could be practicing medicine. But nothing I say changes her mind. I don't know why she has to be so damn stubborn."

"She's not stubborn."

"No? What would you call it?"

"She's afraid."

Ned put down his fork. "Neurotic, maybe."

"You don't get it. And I'm really glad for you. You've probably never felt paralyzing fear."

Ned had been scared plenty of times. But not so that it paralyzed him. He couldn't imagine Ian not being able to act. Was that what Lillo's problem was? And he'd called her a coward.

"It's not like fear that you get from something specific, like people are afraid of the water, or being in a car accident. It's not a thing you can describe, but it's always there, knowing that if you stop paying attention even for a blink of an eye, one split nanosecond, you'll be sucked into a black nothingness that has no end and no escape." Ian swallowed.

"You're not going to get trapped in any black hole."

"You still don't get it. It's not the fear of not being able to escape, it's the fear of not *wanting* to."

Ian was right. Ned didn't understand it. He'd never felt he was losing himself or his grip on the world. He was just an ordinary pragmatist, with an average grip on life. He was a good surgeon. But there were a lot of good surgeons. He did volunteer work with the hospital, but he knew that his reason, or at least his initial reason, for doing it was so that he'd have more freedom.

"I kissed her."

Ned jolted back to the conversation. "What? Wait. You kissed Lillo?"

Ian shook his head. "The CEO."

Ned put down his fork, leaned forward on his elbows. "Well,

good for you. When did this happen? I mean, it's none of my business, but . . ."

"This morning."

"We've been here all afternoon and you didn't mention it?"

"I wasn't going to mention it at all. It kind of slipped out."

"Okay, so you kissed her and . . . ?"

"Well, actually, she kissed me. I was so startled I just sort of kissed her back."

"When did you even see her? Don't tell me she came for a riding lesson in that fog."

Ian shrugged. "I'd had to go out on a call, you had the SUV, so I took Loki. Just up the road to Nehemiah Jensen's. I was coming back and I nearly hit her. I guess she was on her way to the stables but she'd gotten disoriented.

"If Loki hadn't sensed her and shied, I would have trampled her." He shuddered.

"Jesus, she didn't really think you would take her out riding in heavy fog?"

"I didn't ask."

"So, then you . . . ?"

"I jumped down to make sure she was all right. And I pulled her to her feet and she kissed me."

"Right, and then you kissed her back, and then she kissed you back and . . . ?"

"And I put her up behind me and took her back to Lillo's."

Ned turned away, turned back. He'd known from the get-go the CEO would be trouble, and as it turned out he'd been right.

"What was I supposed to do?"

Ned picked up his knife and fork, cut into his steak. Ordered himself to keep his mouth shut. *Stay out of it.* Best to let her leave without rocking Ian's boat, it was rocky enough as it was. "I don't know. Give her a chance. Make love to her knowing it's going to end in a couple of days and enjoy it for what it's worth."

"Shit, man. It's not like that."

"Aw, crap. What's it like, then?"

"Damned if I know." Ian speared a piece of steak and inspected it with more intensity than it deserved. "I don't think I've ever met anyone like her."

"That I can believe," Ned said. "Sorry, you're right. If you think you can't do casual, then you *should* stay away from her. To expect anything else is asking for trouble."

"I know, that's why I told her not to come back." Ian put his fork back on his plate. "God, I really told her not to come back." He shoved the plate away. "What else could I do?"

Ned stared at him. *Shit. Shit. Shit. Ian finally is ready to show interest in another being—let's call it what it is, a woman—and it has to be a loudmouth pushy business mogul from Manhattan.* He'd laugh but it was just too damn sad.

Chapter 23

L illo stretched as the morning sun poured through the window, bathing her in warmish light. A perfect day for sightseeing. A perfect day for not seeing Ned at the clinic. For Diana to get away from Ian.

She sat up just as Diana came through the front door.

"Where have you been?"

"In the parking lot talking to the car rental place." She rolled her eyes to the ceiling. "If my friends could see me now. Wait. They can." She twirled around and headed for the kitchen.

Lillo followed her over. "Did they have a car?" She'd never seen Diana quite so effervescent. Was she anticipating going home, or just pretending like she had forgotten all about riding and Ian?

"Yep; said we could pick it up this afternoon. Is the place far?"

"Not really, we'll just end our sightseeing tour in that direction and you can follow us back to the island."

"Great." Diana poured out two cups of coffee.

Allie and Jess showed up minutes later. Everyone seemed

bright and enthusiastic at breakfast. Maybe too enthusiastic? Lillo thought that in spite of all the drama, they'd had a good time. Maybe they were anxious to leave, maybe they weren't.

It didn't matter. Today they were just going to enjoy themselves. Without Ned. Without Ian, without Jess's parents or Allie's family. Just four girls on the lam. It would be fun.

In a few days they'd return home. Ned and the bikers would leave. Move on to the next town and the next until jobs and families called them home. And things on the island would settle down to the way they had been. Lillo would prepare the flower beds for fall, do the occasional errand, and wait for another Maine winter. Which normally she would look forward to . . . Maybe she'd take up knitting.

"What's so funny?" Jess asked, stretching over with the coffeepot to refill Lillo's mug.

"Nothing, you guys about ready to hit the road?"

"Almost," Allie said. "Should we take jackets?"

"Always in Maine. I'll just run over to let Mac know we're leaving."

A few minutes later they all climbed into the van and Lillo drove through town toward the bridge to the mainland.

"I thought we'd drive along the coast for a ways. There's some good shopping and several really good places to eat. Anything else you want to see or do?"

"Sounds great," Allie said.

"And it will be a day away from those little thugs," Diana said, gesturing to a group of boys standing on the corner.

As Lillo approached the intersection the boys stepped off the curb and into the street. Lillo slammed on the brakes.

The boys, looking studiously sullen, sauntered across.

"Or I may kill them first." Diana unfastened her seat belt.

"What are you going to do?" Allie and Jess yelled from the back seat.

The kids reached the front of the car. Tommy Clayton turned and smirked at them.

Diana rolled down her window and stuck her head out. "You sure would look funny with our bumper up your butt."

Several of the boys flinched and sped up. Tommy stuck his hand out to stop them, but they scurried across the street and he did, too.

"I can't believe you said that," Lillo said.

"Screamed it for the whole town to hear," Jess said. "Priceless."

"My nana always yelled that," Diana said. "And it always worked."

"Very effective," Lillo said. "I may have to borrow it sometime."

"Be my guest."

"He's only eleven?" Allie said.

"Yeah, I know," Lillo said. "Seven whole years before he leaves town and one of the younger ones takes his place."

The boys finally reached the other side of the street and Lillo drove forward.

"A vicious cycle," Jess said. "Hey, isn't that little Bobby with them?"

Lillo looked out the window at the boys walking up the middle of the cross street. "Looks like it. He's supposed to be at the community center. His mother works full-time and so does the father. Actually, they should all be at the center."

"They're going to grow up to be those old men sitting in the general store rocking and reminiscing about the good old days," Diana said. "Totally forgetting they were the little shits who grew up to be bigger and older shits."

"Thank you, Diana," said Lillo. "I believe we all get the point."

"Well, it's true. Once a bully, always a bully. Isn't that right, Jess?"

"Yep. Pretty much always," Jess said, turning forward in her seat. "These kids have way too much get-into-trouble time. They could use a good camp."

Lillo glanced at her in the rearview mirror. "Well, don't look at me. That ship has sailed."

Lillo took the eastern fork that would keep them close to the ocean. They drove in and out of woods, along cliffs, then dipped down to rocky beaches. They stopped at scenic lookouts, browsed through two quaint antiques malls, bought moose scarves in honor of their almost road trip, ate lobster rolls walking along the brick streets of an old fishing village.

Jess made Diana and Allie try homemade whoopie pies. They sat at a round picnic table chewing and licking marshmallow cream off their fingers while Jess reminisced about her days in camp, conveniently remembering the good parts and glossing over the majority of events that were anything but good.

Lillo smiled, inwardly amazed at how the past could take on the mood of the way you were feeling in the present.

"Didn't we, Lillo?" Jess asked.

"Didn't we what?" Lillo asked, brought back from her own reminiscing.

"Take the skiff out to the marshes and get stuck in the mud. It was so disgusting. We had to tromp through the mud, I swear it was like quicksand. And the smell. Ugh. I can still remember it."

Yeah, Lillo remembered. They'd both been given a good talking-to. Jess was sent back to her cabin to think about responsibility—carrying a huge care package sent by one of her mother's secretaries. Lillo was sent to scrub the drying mud from the boat.

Even then she hadn't resented it. It wasn't about punishment. It hardly ever was with her parents. It was about taking responsibility. Like they'd told Jess. Lillo had thought Jess would have learned more by helping to clean the boat. But they didn't dare treat the campers in any way that could be considered punishment. Many of the parents were of the same ilk as the Parkers.

Lillo's parents loved kids, loved the opportunity to share their enthusiasm for living a healthy life in a place they thought the most beautiful place in the world. They'd hoped Lillo would carry on their legacy, run the camp herself. But they'd sold it all.

Now they had no camp and no doctor. And hadn't seen their daughter in over a year.

A cloud passed over the sun. At first Lillo thought it was her changing mood, then realized it was the sky.

"We'd better get a move on. Looks like there's more weather coming our way."

They gathered up their trash and hurried back to the van. They left the coast and took a county road to the rental place, where Diana and Allie picked up their car, then followed the van to Lighthouse Beach.

This time when they crossed the bridge, no one commented on the sign that said their lives would never be the same. They were in two separate cars, already breaking up. About to go their separate ways.

When they reached Main Street, Diana beeped and turned left. Lillo continued to the town parking lot.

"Probably stopping for more wine and cheese," Lillo said.

"Ugh." Jess crossed her arms across her stomach. "I don't think I'll ever eat again. My stomach must have really shrunk." She sighed. "At last, Mother would be so proud."

"Are you feeling any qualms about your decision?"

"Nope. For the first time since that whole horrible wedding thing began, I'm actually enjoying myself, eating and drinking what I want, and I still fit into my clothes."

"It has only been a week," Lillo reminded her.

"I know. But I feel like I'm really in control of my own destiny. Well, you know what I mean."

"Yes, I do. And I'm happy for you."

"What about you?"

"What about me?"

"What are you going to do when Allie and Diana leave?"

"Go back to doing what I did before they came. What about you?"

Jess looked thoughtful. "I'm not really sure. And for once, that's a good thing."

Was it? Diana and Allie were already making preparations to go back to their lives. Jess didn't have a life to go back to. So did she have a plan? Or was she planning to stay?

NED GLANCED OUT the clinic window as he and Clancy and Agnes finished cleaning up the examination rooms for the day. They'd been here a week. There was more to do, but they were scheduled to travel to another town starting Monday. The group had decided to spend their two days off in Lighthouse Beach. They usually did. Clancy was born and raised here, and several of the guys had made real connections with their host families. And the new guys were always made to feel at home.

Ned had spent his teenage years here and he felt like his second family was here. He cared about what happened in the town. But as far as helping Lillo get back on her feet, time was running out. If she stayed out of her residency much longer, it would be a long uphill battle to go back.

Maybe she just didn't want to go back, didn't have what it took to be a surgeon. Maybe she just didn't care enough to fight for it.

Well, he'd give her space, spend a little time with Ian, and then hit the road. Summer was short enough without wasting it on someone who didn't want your concern.

The phone rang. Ned groaned. It always happened. An emergency on Friday just before you're leaving for the day.

While Ned and Clancy stood by, watching her, Agnes picked up the phone. "Lighthouse Free Clinic." At first she only listened, but Ned could hear a frantic voice at the other end of the line. She put her hand over the receiver and mouthed, "It's Lou Trader. Bobby's missing."

Ned looked at Clancy, who shook his head. Ned took the phone from Agnes. "Mrs. Trader. This is Dr. Hartley."

"Oh, Doc. We can't find him. I don't know where to look. And Flynn is off to work still."

"Okay, where are you now?"

"I'm at the community center. I came to pick him up. But they said he wasn't here. That he hadn't been here. But I left him here this morning. He's supposed to be here. Why ain't he here?"

"Mrs. Trader, Lou, take a deep breath. When did you last see him?"

"I dropped him off at the side door when I left for my job at the Laundromat. That was around eight thirty this morning. Sada's car was here and some others. I told him to go straight inside. I didn't go in with him 'cause we were running late. I should have waited." She started to cry.

"And Sada hasn't seen him at all?"

"Said he never came in, but I left him right there at the door."

"Did you search the building? Maybe he came in and fell asleep somewhere."

"We did. Twice. People are out looking around the neighborhood. And Sada's started the phone chain. I know that something awful has happened."

"Is Joey missing, too?"

"No, he had speech therapy on the mainland, the bus dropped him off at the community center afterward. He hasn't seen his brother since this morning. What could have happened to him?" She broke down completely and Sada came on the phone.

"Doc?"

"Yeah."

"I'm so glad I caught you before you left. I've called almost the whole list. No one's seen him. Least that they're saying. I'm having people meet and report to the center and expand the search from here. Mike and Sal are leading the search in town. Junior Nomes for the surrounding area."

"And is Mrs. Trader sure he didn't just go home?"

"Barbara Carroll volunteered to take Joey home and stay with him in case Bobby comes back. You know these kids, they're running off all the time. They usually return in time for dinner, but with the wind advisory, it could be dangerous if he's out in the elements. I just didn't think we should wait. I was hoping maybe you had seen him. I know he sometimes goes to ask Agnes for a lollipop."

Agnes's hand flew to her mouth. She shook her head.

"We haven't seen him today. What about the other kids? Have any of them seen him?"

"The ones we could reach haven't. It may be nothing, and I'll personally tan his hide if he's causing us all this worry for nothing. I—" She lowered her voice. "He's so enamored with that Tommy Clayton and his gang. I should have nipped that in the bud, but what can you do? I called the Clayton house but no one's home." Her next sentence was even quieter and sounded like she had placed her hand over the receiver. "I even have men searching down by the beach."

"We've got a little more cleaning up to do here. I'll call you when we're done, and if he hasn't turned up we'll join the search. If you hear anything call us here or my cell."

"I do give him lollipops," Agnes said. "But he didn't come in today. Oh dear."

"Don't you give it a thought," Clancy told her. "He's probably safe asleep somewhere. Totally unaware that everyone is looking for him."

"Probably," Ned agreed. "I wonder. Do you think he would have gone out to the stables by himself? I know Ian does equestrian therapy with both boys."

"He might. I don't know if he could remember the way; his directional skills are about on the same level of the rest of his skills."

"I'll call Ian and tell him to look out for him."

"You do that," Clancy said. "And then if you will, call Lillo, tell her not to let Mac go careening all over the place looking for the kid. Then we'll have a cup of coffee, finish cleaning the kitchen, and call it a night."

"Excellent idea." Ned punched in Ian's number.

LILLO'S CELL RANG, but when she picked it up, the call dropped. No one ever called her unless it was important. She walked out to the path in front of her cottage, hoping for a better signal. The wind was blowing like crazy. She tried to connect but couldn't.

She climbed up to the gate, to see if Mac's lights were on. A gust of wind hit her from the side and she staggered a couple of steps to regain her balance. They had wind all the time; this was baby stuff compared to the heavy winds.

Still, she should go check on Mac. Leave it to her to go check on the lighthouse and get blown off the jetty.

She'd started across the parking lot but stopped when she saw Ian's SUV turn into the parking lot. He stopped by Lillo and jumped out.

"Did Ned call you?" His hair was blowing around his face and his windbreaker was snapping like crazy.

"No, why? What's going on?"

"Bobby Trader's missing. Everyone is out looking for him. Sada's coordinating the search. She's sending some people down here to check the beach. Ned said to make sure Mac stays inside. He and Clancy are coming down when they finish at the clinic."

"Bobby? Lou's little one?"

"Yes. I thought he might have come down here." He wasn't looking at Lillo but was scanning the parking lot and beach around the cottage. And Lillo got a chilling visual of Ian on the lookout for hostile marauders. Every moment of inattention liable to be lethal.

"Come inside."

They fought the wind gust and practically fell into the cottage. Lillo threw her weight against the door.

"Damn, that's some wind all of a sudden." She turned around and was met by three startled faces.

"Bobby Trader is missing," she told them.

"You haven't seen him around here?" Ian asked. "Or any of the kids?"

"We were gone most of the day."

"We saw them this morning," Jess said. "But that was around eleven maybe? It was the same kids that were fighting down here yesterday."

"Down here? Bobby and Joey are not supposed to come down by the water."

"Well, they were here," Lillo said. "The others, Tommy and that crowd, are another story. We heard them fighting and went out to see. They'd knocked Joey down and were going at him. Until Jess intervened. Then Diana grabbed them by the shirts and lifted them off their feet."

She saw Ian flick a look at Diana before returning his attention to Lillo.

"Yeah, I should have knocked their heads together before I let them go," Diana said.

"Has anyone spoken to Will Clayton?" Lillo asked. "Maybe Bobby is with them?"

"They haven't been able to reach him."

"So maybe they're both missing."

"Are you sure Bobby was with them? They've been told to stay away from Tommy and that gang."

"Really?" Jess said. "Because it didn't do any good. His brother tried to get him to leave, but Bobby wouldn't go because of the boat. Tommy said he could go in the boat or something like that. And we saw them crossing Main Street when we were leaving this morning, and Bobby was with them. I didn't see his brother."

"You wouldn't. He has speech therapy off island on Thursdays. Bobby was supposed to stay at the community center. I guess he never showed up."

"You want us to check the beach?" Lillo didn't need to ask; Jess, Allie, and Diana were already gathering up outerwear. "What about the marina? Isn't that where Tommy's father keeps his skiff? Though not even Tommy Clayton would take a boat out in this wind, but they might have gotten stuck somewhere—"

"The lighthouse," Ian said. "Bobby's always talking about going in a boat." He threw his head back. "Not just going in a boat. Going with them in the boat to the lighthouse. I told him

I'd take him. I wasn't listening. It wasn't because he wanted to see the lighthouse, he wanted to be part of the group." He slammed his fist into his palm so hard that the sound echoed in the air and all four women jumped.

"Surely they wouldn't go to the lighthouse," Lillo said. "Mac is always running them off."

"I hope not." Ian spun around and headed outside, Jess and Diana at his heels.

"He'll be safe as long as he's inside, won't he?" Allie asked. "But what if he's hurt? He's just a little boy."

"He'll be safe," Lillo said. *As long as he doesn't try to get back.*

She grabbed her jacket off the peg by the door and followed Ian outside.

Ian had run ahead and was standing at the jetty entrance, scanning the lighthouse tower.

"I don't see any lights," Lillo said. "The kids usually bring flashlights."

She wasn't sure Ian heard her, he was so intent on the tower and the stormy sea that rose around it.

Then he started forward and she knew what he had in mind. "Ian, no. The water's already over the jetty. You can't get across, and if you drown, who will save Bobby? You don't even know he's in there."

He didn't hear a word she said.

"Ian! Stop! At least call Ned and have him send some folks down."

He jerked to a stop. "Sorry."

"Let's call Ned and see if he has any information, then we'll figure out how to get into the tower." She took him by the arm, afraid he would do something stupid. He had the most developed superego of anyone she had ever encountered. And she wasn't sure if he cared enough about his own safety or even his own life to make rational decisions.

And she knew that if he decided to cross the jetty, there was no way in hell she could stop him.

But he turned and they jogged single file down the path to Mac's kitchen. Mac was sitting at the table with a cup of coffee and surrounded by the smells of something delicious.

"Ned called. He told me to stay put until you got here. He and Doc are standing by at the clinic in case they're needed." Mac stood. "Let's go."

"No," Lillo said. "Think before you act. Both of you. First. Could they have gotten into the lighthouse? Is it locked? What about the windows?"

"You're damn straight it's locked. And I boarded up the windows from inside. Though I suppose if you brought a hammer you could knock them out. But why would Tommy take Bobby to the lighthouse? He won't have anything to do with the kid."

"Bobby said Tommy was going to let him in the gang," Lillo said.

"You think it was some kind of initiation?"

"I don't want to think that even Tommy Clayton would be that mean."

Mac gave her a look.

Ian turned on them. "If he's in there and tries to get out, he could be washed away, his body never found. Are you going to tell that to his mother and father?"

"We don't know that he's in there," Lillo told him.

"I'll get the lanterns." Mac headed for the storage closet.

"But don't turn them on," Ian told them. "If he sees the light he might try to come to us," said Ian. "And if he does . . ."

He'll be swept out to sea.

Chapter 24

It took less than a minute for Mac to hand out flashlights, then she snatched the lighthouse key ring from the nail by the door and they all followed her outside.

They reached the parking lot just as several trucks pulled in and came to a stop. Will Clayton got out of the first one. Sonny Dumas and his sons were right behind him. Will ran around to the passenger side and yanked his son Tommy out of the car just as Nando and Howie roared into the parking lot.

Lillo hurried toward Will. "Do you have Bobby?"

Will shook his head and thrust his son toward the group.

"Tommy here has something he wants to say."

Tommy didn't say a thing.

"Tell 'em." Will shook the boy. "Tell 'em."

Ian crouched down until his eyes met Tommy's. "Do you know where Bobby is?"

Tommy nodded spasmodically. "In the lighthouse."

"How did he get there?"

Tommy shrugged.

His father gave him a shove.

Tommy wrenched away. "He was always pestering us to let him hang out with us, to go in the boat, go to the lighthouse. Like we really wanted him or anything. He's nothing but a moron."

Will Clayton cuffed the boy so hard he nearly fell into Ian, who put him back on his feet.

Jess sucked in her breath. Lillo grasped her arm to keep her from interfering.

"And now he's out there with no way to get back to shore. If he tries he'll probably be washed out to sea," Ian said. "And that will be your fault."

"Whoa," Diana breathed behind Lillo.

Ian's voice was so measured, so free of emotion, that shivers ran up Lillo's back.

He seemed so detached that she was afraid it might be one of those instances of the calm before the storm. She'd seen it in the hospital in the psych ward; hell, she'd seen it in family members just waiting to hear the news of a loved one. Trying to hold it together until they snapped.

"You took him and left him there?"

"He wanted to go. And we thought it would be funny if we left him there. We were going back for him, but the waves got too high. I don't want him to die."

"You should have thought about that before you left him." Ian stood, shoved his flashlight into the waistband of his jeans.

But before he could make a move, Mac barred his way. "What are you doing?"

"What does it look like? I'm going after him."

"The waves are over the jetty. The wind is too strong. You can't make it on foot and a boat would crash. You'll have to wait until lower tide or the weather breaks."

"It's dark; he'll be scared."

"I know, but you're the only one he'll trust, and if you get swept away, he'll still be stuck there."

Ian grabbed the keys from her hand. "I can't leave him."

Sonny strode after Ian. "If you're determined, I got a winch on my truck. We can rig up a lifeline. Won't do much good on the way out, but if you can attach it to the lighthouse somehow, you'll have something to hold on to on the way back. It'll take just a couple of minutes."

"Okay, let's do it," Ian said.

It took more than two minutes to get everything ready. Sonny backed his truck up to the jetty, then fitted Ian with a utility belt with a walkie-talkie, a first-aid kit, and a Mylar blanket.

Ian clasped it around his waist.

"I'll attach the cable to you on your way out, not that it will do much good if you fall and hurt yourself. When you get there, attach the anchor to the lighthouse, oughta be a hook or an eye somewhere outside for the boats." Sonny attached one end of the cable to the utility belt, added a couple of rolled-up webbing straps and carabiners. "Use these on your way back, I'll keep the cable taut, but you're on your own until we can reach you."

Ian nodded.

"You sure you don't want me to go instead?"

"Thanks. But I'm the best one to go."

"Meaning he don't think his own life's worth a damn," Mac said under her breath.

"Well, he's wrong," Diana snapped.

"Hell, girl, we all know that. Why don't you take it on yourself to enlighten the man?"

"Maybe I will." Diana started to move closer to him, then decided against it.

They were all holding their breath. At least they still had a few hours before dark. Hopefully they wouldn't need that long.

Ian braced himself and stepped onto the jetty. For a heart-stilling moment, he swayed as a gust of wind nearly wrenched him from his feet.

He was weighted down heavily enough so that if he fell in the water, the undertow would pull him under before any of them could do anything to save him.

Lillo had lived in this fishing village her whole life and she knew steady wind or no wind were the best environments for rescue. But the erratic gusts could sweep a man away without warning.

Diana slipped in beside her. "Is this as dangerous as I think it is?"

"At least that."

"Why doesn't he just wait?"

"He's afraid that Bobby will find a way out and try to make it across the jetty by himself."

"Damn those kids. I would have gladly wrung their necks yesterday if I'd known what was going to happen today. The little shits."

"Pretty much." Lillo glanced over at Tommy, who no longer looked like a bully, but like a terribly frightened little boy. His father didn't look much better. Under constant stress, trying to make ends meet, raising two boys by himself. Refusing help because it wasn't macho to take a handout, not for any of the few services available to those in need. And content to blame everyone but himself for not succeeding. One of the ones who had held on to fishing even though the writing had been on the wall for a long time.

Not willing to let go of what he knew, the only thing he knew. Not willing to learn something new. Waiting for the world to go back to what he'd expected it to be. And letting his disappointment poison his own sons' lives. Maybe this would jolt him into doing something for them.

Everyone drew nearer together, watching Ian moving in slow motion over the rocks. Another car arrived. Lillo was vaguely aware of Lou Trader arriving with Joey and her husband, Flynn, but she couldn't take her eyes off the figure fighting his way toward the lighthouse tower.

And then the inevitable happened. He slipped, disappeared, and for a horrible second became a part of the landscape. The watchers gasped, leaned in, looking, praying, collectively willing him to get back to his feet.

He did, but by the time he reached the small island that served as the foundation of the lighthouse, Lillo's lungs hurt from not breathing. She gasped in air. She thought the others did, too.

Ian didn't go in immediately but searched for an anchor for the haul rope. Finally raised his hand to signal that he'd found one. Attached it, then signaled Sonny to test the connection. Sonny jumped back in the truck, slowly let out the clutch, and rolled forward. The rope snapped in the air, grew taut, then held.

Ian signaled the okay, turned his back on them, and after a few breath-held seconds, they watched him go inside.

The Traders had moved to the front of the crowd and were huddled together. Will Clayton and Tommy stood off from the others. And Lillo hoped for all their sakes that Ian and Bobby made it back and unharmed.

An eon passed with no one talking. Eyes fixed on the seemingly deserted lighthouse. Unexpectedly, a gust of wind would whip through, ruffling them like stalks of grass. At other times, a whisper would rise and die on the wind.

And they waited. Jess, Allie, and Diana had moved toward Lillo as they watched the rescue. Now they moved closer together, focused on the empty lighthouse door.

"What's happening?" Jess asked. "Can you see him?"

And then there was Ian standing in the door, Bobby in his arms.

Lillo's breath hitched. They hadn't considered that Bobby couldn't make it back across the jetty even with Ian's help.

"What's he doing?" Jess asked.

"Trying to connect his carabiner to the cable so they won't be swept into the water." He was having a hell of a time. He only had one free hand and the wind kept buffeting him, pushing him in one direction, then another. *Put him down,* Lillo thought. *Just for a second. Put him down or you won't make it.*

"Dammit, man, put him down!" Sonny echoed Lillo's thoughts out loud.

Sonny and three of the other men moved onto the jetty, blocking Lillo's view. They spread out along the base of the rocks to help Ian as soon as he got close enough.

Lillo moved over, trying to catch a glimpse of Ian and Bobby, but for what seemed an eternity all she could see were the backs of three waiting men. She saw the men surge forward. Someone cried out. Then they stepped back and Ian emerged between them, carrying Bobby, wrapped in the Mylar and clinging to Ian's neck.

The Traders surrounded him. Flynn Trader tried to take Bobby, but the boy cried and kicked and clung to Ian.

"Hey, Bobby, you okay?" someone from the crowd yelled.

"Bobby? Bobby?" Lou Trader whimpered; she held out her arms.

Bobby raised his head, looked at the group, then nuzzled into Ian and clung tighter.

"Bobby!" Flynn said, his voice shaking with emotion. "Go to your mama."

"Just give him a minute," Ian said. "He's cold and in shock." He whispered something to Bobby. Sonny got another blanket out of his truck and threw it over the Mylar one.

The Traders stepped closer to Ian, and for a split second Lillo thought they might fight to take Bobby away from him. Gradually, Ian managed to slip Bobby into Flynn's arms. The boy fought to get back to Ian, but Ian stepped away, and gradually he calmed and Flynn carried him back to their car.

"Thank you, thank you," Lou said, and hurried after them.

"Stop by the clinic and have Doc Clancy check him out."

She nodded distractedly. Ian followed them and stopped Flynn. "Take him to the clinic. It's important."

"Okay. I will." Flynn hesitated, nodded brusquely, and got into the car.

"He sounds pissed at Ian for saving his son," Diana said.

Mac rolled her eyes. "It's hard to give up your place as numero uno with your own blood. It took forever to get Flynn to accept the fact that Bobby has special needs. He hates everybody else knowing it. To his eyes it makes him a failure somehow. He knows Ian helps his sons, he just don't understand what Ian does and he's scared of him. Fool."

"Well, I thought he was amazing," Allie said.

"Amazing," Diana echoed. She was watching Ian watching the Traders' car drive away.

"Jeez, that was incredibly risky—they could have been killed," Jess said. "And an insurance nightmare, not to mention bad for my nerves. So the first thing on my new agenda is to build a handrail out to the lighthouse."

Mac snorted. "You and whose cool million?"

"It won't cost a million and it's my treat."

They all did a double take at Jess.

"What? Can't I build a handrail if I want to?"

"Do you have any idea what is involved?" Mac asked. "Drilling through jetty rock. Getting variances. Building to code. It'll cost a fortune."

Jess sighed. "In case you haven't noticed, I *have* a fortune. Several of them, actually. I think I can afford to build a damn rail. But if it makes you feel any better, we can do a fundraiser. Put up one of those tacky signs with a thermometer filling up with red. I've always thought they were so silly looking. I'm changing my mind."

"Apparently I'm not the only one feeling a little traumatized," Diana said under her breath. "I think our girl Jess just lost it."

"Or found it," said Lillo.

Ian walked slowly back toward Sonny, who went about extracting the utility belts and carabiners.

"Mighty fine work, Ian," Sonny said. The other men nodded; one clapped Ian on the back.

"Better get into some dry clothes. That water's pretty damn cold."

"Got some in the SUV. Thanks for your help. Couldn't have done it without you."

"Anytime you want to risk your fool neck, just give me a call first."

"What?" Diana asked.

"Manspeak for 'Thank you, you did great,'" Mac said.

"A new one on me," Diana said.

"'Cause you been hanging around those wussy New York types for too long."

Diana gave her a look. "Is that old-broad-speak for 'I'm an idiot'?"

"No, it's me telling you it's about time you had a taste of a real man."

"Yeow," Allie said.

"Man, I think Diana might be blushing," Jess whispered.

Mac paid no attention. "Sonny, you fellas want to come in for a beer?"

"Thanks, Mac, but we're gonna head on down to Mike's as soon as I get this equipment put away. Worked up an appetite. Ayuh. Have to leave the truck here until low tide so I can get my winch back."

Mac just waved good-bye. "Ian, you come on in and get a hot shower and change. I got brisket and scalloped potatoes in the oven."

Ian hesitated, then said thanks, grabbed his clothes, and walked past them. The others started to follow him, all talking at once.

Mac waved them off. "Just leave the man alone until he's comfortable again." And she trundled Ian inside.

"Comfortable?" snapped Diana. "He could be dead."

"Definitely blushing," Jess said.

"She just wants us to give him some space," Lillo said, "until he's cleaned up and relaxed. Let's go see if Sonny needs some help." Sonny didn't need their help, but Lillo didn't want Diana stumbling on to Ian going into or coming out of the shower. She had no idea what he would be like after the harrowing experience he'd just been through. She just knew he would need time to get back to the rest of them.

Before she even reached Sonny's truck, a black limo and two SUVs drove into the parking lot and came to a stop behind the other vehicles blocking their way.

"Are you fucking kidding me?" snapped Diana. "Hey, Jess. Daddy's here."

Jess, who had been studying the jetty, spun around. And froze. Allie stepped closer to her.

Lillo grabbed Sonny's arm. "We may still need you," she said, and nodded toward the cars; the limo driver was opening the back door. George Parker, dressed in his business-as-usual power suit, stepped out while four men, similarly but not as expensively attired, swarmed out of the SUVs.

Lillo stepped away from Sonny's truck. Sonny joined her and Diana was right behind.

But it was Jess who strode past them and stopped her father in his tracks. "So, what has you hying to the backwoods of Maine this afternoon?"

Lillo blinked. Jess wasn't waiting to take the offensive. And Lillo sent her every shred of good energy she had left after Ian's rescue of Bobby Trader.

"I'm your father and I've had enough of this juvenile behavior. We've been lenient so far, but enough is enough. You've cost us a fortune on this wedding. Which we had to cancel."

Hang tough, Lillo thought. *Hang tough.*

"Seems like you already tried to get to my money while I was gone. What? Did you plan to make me pay for your mismanagement of my life? Well, too little too late.

"Must have been a surprise when you found yourself locked out of my accounts, and don't bother trying to hack your way in. I'll save you the trouble: those accounts are empty. You've been stealing from me for I don't even know how long. Your greed is unsurpassable. Well, you're not getting my money."

Jess started to cross her arms, caught herself, and put them down by her sides. From defensive stance to one of strength.

"So tell your goons to get back in their spy cars and leave."

"You ungrateful bitch." Parker's hands were fisting and unfisting.

If he so much as touched Jess, Lillo would go for his throat.

"That would be me, yes."

"You'd better be careful before you think of crossing me."

"Why? You'll destroy me like you do your other enemies? You can try. I wouldn't expect less." Jess huffed out a bitter laugh.

Parker took a step toward her. Lillo saw movement by the gift shop, but she was afraid to turn her head to see who it was and risk destroying the delicate balance of Jess's power. She just prayed that whoever it was, Mac or Ian, they didn't interrupt. Jess was on a roll. It had been a long time coming.

Parker stepped toward his daughter, thrusting his chest forward in an unconscious display of intimidation.

Jess didn't flinch. "I'm thirty-two years old, and for most of those years I tried to rationalize what you did, how you treated people, trod on them, cheated them out of their wages and what you owed them. Because you could. You actually prided yourself on your despicable behavior, and I sat by trying to make myself think it wasn't so bad, because it's what all businessmen did.

"Well you know what? Not everyone acts so reprehensibly, there are actually honest businessmen, and you can sneer at them all you want, but they do good in this world and you're just a canker sore.

"You're my father. I wanted so much to love you, but I detest you, and I will not make excuses for you anymore. So go home, and sit in your big white house on the hill and congratulate yourself on being so fucking fantastic, and try to pretend that people actually respect you and look up to you. The only people who do are the ones you're stepping on.

"So go back to what you're doing; there's no hope for you. But I'm moving on to a better life. Get out of my sight, I never want to see or hear from you again."

"You better stop and think, girl. If I leave now, I won't be coming back and don't think I'll take you back later."

"Don't worry about that. I want nothing from you. You've taken everything you possibly could from me. Every shred of my self-esteem and self-worth, and spit on it, trampled it underfoot. I let you do it, I know. It's my fault, too. I let you demean me until I had nothing, nothing.

"At least I thought I had nothing, but I was wrong there, too. I have three friends who have loved me and cared about me more than you were ever capable of. And I've made more friends this week. I found a family here. Not with my parents and siblings but with total strangers. I don't expect you to understand. I just expect you to leave."

She turned, in the most determined movement Lillo had ever seen her make. The sun was just beginning to set and Lillo watched as it cloaked Jess in an aura of red.

Next to her, Diana let out a slow breath.

Lillo saw Parker move after Jess. He was going to grab her, and Lillo moved to warn her at the same time Mac stepped away from the house.

She lifted her shotgun; a shot rang out, shattering the air around them. But it wasn't Mac's—her gun was never loaded.

Then the world shifted to slow motion. Mac's arms flew to the side, the shotgun clattered at her feet, and she crumpled to the ground.

Chapter 25

Someone screamed. Lillo's ears were ringing, and she turned, aware of Ian flying past her, diving for the man whose arm was still outstretched. They stumbled back, and a second man pulled his pistol and hit Ian across the head. Ian dropped like a stone.

She was already running when she heard her name. Allie was kneeling over Mac, her face contorted, fear in her eyes. "Lillo!"

Lillo pushed her out of the way. "Call the EMTs. The sheriff. Doc Clancy and Ned are at the clinic."

She knelt over her old friend. Mac looked stunned, and was mumbling obscenities. Blood was pulsing out of her left sleeve.

Lillo found the seam and tore the fabric away. She knew immediately what she was looking at.

It was all happening again.

She swallowed the bile that rose in her throat. Folded her hands and pressed them into the wound.

Mac let out a howl.

"Sorry," Lillo cried. "I'm sorry." Mac would never last until Clancy or Ned got there.

She looked wildly around. "Jess, get my kit from the spare room. Oh shit. I gave it away. Oh my God! I gave it away."

Think. She had to think. She was applying pressure to the wound. She'd done it automatically, without thinking, but it wasn't enough, her hands were already covered in Mac's blood.

"No, you didn't. I hid it in the closet." Jess took off at a run.

Mac's eyes closed. Lillo couldn't let go in order to feel for a pulse. "Mac, can you hear me? Mac, respond, dammit! Stay with me."

She was barely aware of things around her, she was totally focused on Mac, keeping constant pressure on the wound while she waited a lifetime for Jess to return with her kit.

And Lillo prayed. Prayed that she could stop the bleeding, that Mac would hold on until a doctor arrived, the EMTs or Clancy or Ned—that she wouldn't have another death on her hands.

She knew stuff was happening behind her but she was in a bubble that held just her and Mac and a million fears.

Jess returned with the kit. Lillo gave her directions; she hardly knew what she said. She was on automatic now.

A crowd was gathering, she could hear the hum of their voices asking what had happened, but she couldn't turn around to see, not even for a second, a second could mean the difference between living or dying.

She heard a screech rise over the other voices, then the voices getting angrier.

And Lillo just kept praying, *Please, please, please.*

It took Diana a lifetime to react. It was crazy. The goon shooting Mac. Ian flying past her to attack the man. He was lying still on the ground. He was crazy, risking his life . . . again; he'd already risked it once that afternoon.

People were running down the hill from town. All hell was breaking loose. Sonny grabbed the man who'd shot Mac and threw him against the hood of his SUV.

"Don't move." He yanked his head back and slammed him against the car a second time. His colleagues moved as one, but Howie and Nando were there to stop them.

Mr. Parker stood on the fringe, demanding that someone call the authorities.

"You're in luck, mister," Howie said. "The sheriff just happens to be in town helping us look for a missing boy. Mighty convenient. He's on his way over."

Ian pushed to his hands and knees, propelled himself to his feet, swayed, then staggered in Mac's direction.

Diana caught him as he stumbled by. "Lillo's working on her. Are you hurt?" *Stupid question.* "Are you okay? Maybe you should sit down."

He didn't seem to hear her.

"Ian! Look at me!"

His eyes were unfocused, deep and as unreadable as a black hole.

They all heard the siren approaching. It split the air as the sheriff's car entered the parking lot and screeched to a stop. The sheriff jumped out.

Clancy and Ned jumped out of the back seat and ran to Mac and Lillo.

"Stop that man!" George Parker screamed, pointing to Ian. "He attacked one of my men."

The flaming asshat.

"Because your thug shot an old lady," Sonny said.

"It was self-defense. She was coming after him with a shot-gun."

"Bullshit. There ain't no shotgun."

Diana pulled her gaze away from Ian long enough to look toward where Doc, Clancy, and Lillo were kneeling over Mac. Craned her neck to get a better view. She didn't see the shotgun.

"Did anybody see any shotgun?" Sonny asked.

"I didn't see no shotgun," Howie said.

"Didn't see any kind of gun, 'cept what you folks are carryin' concealed," Sonny added.

The sheriff strode up to Parker. He was a good six two and at least two hundred and fifty pounds; he looked from Parker to Mac, lying white as ash on the pavement. And Diana's stomach rebelled. *God, please don't let her be dead.*

"This is a fishing village. We don't take to handguns around here. Causes too much domestic vi-o-lence. Ayuh."

"That's right," Sonny said. "Arrest these jokers, Sheriff. They were here last week causing a disruption, and now they've gone and shot Mac. I had my son go to the trouble of confiscating his weapon for you, Sheriff."

Parker brushed past him. "She had a shotgun and she was aiming at us."

The sheriff grabbed him by the shoulder, stopping him. "You just go stand over there out of the way until my deputy arrives. Then you can tell her why she shouldn't arrest all of ya."

"Let go of my men. We're leaving. You have no right to keep us."

"Name?"

"What?"

"What is your name?"

"George D. Parker. This is my daughter, who has been kid-napped."

The sheriff looked over at Jess. "Seems I heard something about that." He motioned her over. "Have you been kidnapped?"

"No, sir. It's just the ravings of a greedy old man."

"Old? Who the hell are you calling old, you ungrateful—"

"Well, if that's how you're in the habit of treating your own flesh and blood, no wonder she ran away. Miss Parker, are you over eighteen?"

"I'm thirty-two."

"Then I say she has a right to go where she wants." He turned back to Parker. "Why don't you go stand over there until I sort things out here? And Mr. Parker . . . ? Open your jacket, please."

"What?"

"You aren't carrying, are you?"

"I certainly am not."

"He has goons to do it for him," Jess said.

"Yes, Miss Parker. Why don't you come stand over here with the rest of us."

"They all have permits," Parker argued.

"But not," the sheriff said, "to shoot unarmed ladies."

"She was armed."

"That little old woman you just tried to kill? Hogwash. Lillo? How's she doing?"

Lillo didn't answer, but Diana—and she suspected everyone else—turned to see what was happening. Lillo was still kneeling by Mac. Doc and Clancy were standing over them. Why weren't they doing anything? Cold dread overtook her. Because they couldn't? Was it too late? Mac couldn't be dead.

Diana moved involuntarily toward them. Didn't stop until she reached the little group. She came to stand next to Ian, but her whole focus was on Mac, willing things to turn out good.

Lillo was still applying pressure to the wound as she wrapped gauze around Mac's upper arm.

It seemed like blood was everywhere. Lillo was so intense that Diana began to be afraid.

Lillo wrapped and pulled the gauze tighter, all the while keeping Mac's arm lifted in the air. "Take over," she pleaded.

"You're doing fine," Doc said.

"Fine," Doc Clancy added, but Diana could tell he was dying to attend to Mac himself.

They must trust Lillo. Or they wouldn't stand by with Mac close to death. Because it certainly looked like she might be. Diana had never seen anyone so devoid of color. She sure as hell hoped this wasn't one of those therapy-for-Lillo moments. Not with Mac's life hanging in the balance. Surely, if Mac was still in danger, or Lillo wasn't up to the job, they would take over.

But they just stayed there, huddled over the two women; Doc Clancy's hands braced on his knees, Doc Hartley crouched just behind Lillo's shoulder.

Diana could hear Lillo breathing. Each breath sounded like a sob.

Jess came up beside her. "Is she going to be okay?"

"I don't have the faintest."

"I'll never—"

"It's not your fault; don't even go there. It's your father's fault for bringing those assholes. But not yours and not Lillo's if Mac doesn't make it. Too much guilt floating around here today. It doesn't help."

"You're right. And I didn't think about Lillo." Jess covered her mouth with both hands. "I just assumed Mac would be okay."

Ian had gone to stand behind the two doctors, and Diana wondered why this town, so small and forgotten in the back of beyond, was so lucky to have three doctors like these men, even part-time.

Clancy stood, looked at Ian, then reached into Lillo's bag, pulled out an ice pack, and slapped it open. He handed it to Ian. "No arguments."

Ian raised it to the back of his head and winced.

The sheriff strode up to them. "Can she be moved? Thought maybe we could put her in my cruiser and meet the EMTs half-way."

Clancy nodded. Lillo finished wrapping the bandage and Clancy took over holding Mac's injured arm. The sheriff scooped up Mac like she was Sleeping Beauty. Clancy held her arm over her head and they walked slowly to the police car. Sonny was there to open the door, they got Mac in the back seat, and Clancy climbed in beside her.

Lillo stood. Turned. She was covered in blood, and Diana gagged at the sight. A few deep breaths set her to rights. Lillo stepped toward the police car as if she meant to go with them, but Doc stopped her. She turned around, looked up at him, and let out a sound like a drowning man gasping for air.

It was heartbreaking and bone-chilling and Doc wrapped his arms around her; held her tight while she stood stiff as a board. Inanimate. Until finally her body sagged, melted against him, and she began to cry.

"Shit," Allie said. Diana and Jess looked at her in surprise. "That was intense."

"It was," Diana agreed.

"She's going to be okay," Jess said. "Thank God."

"Well, don't relax yet."

Just then, two more cruisers arrived. A woman, who must be the deputy, got out of the first cruiser, followed closely by two men from the second car. They rounded up Parker's goons and escorted them to the two police cars. The deputy stopped at Jess's father.

"I demand to speak to my lawyer," Parker was saying.

"You'll have plenty of time at the station."

"You're making a big mistake," he said as she led him away.

"Not as big as the one you just made," Jess said, and hurried toward the police.

Diana made a feeble grab for her, but didn't really try to stop her. If Jess wanted to finish off the cretin who was her father, fine. And if she caved one more time, better to do it here and now, get it over with, and admit once and for all that she would never be free.

"Get out of my sight, I never want to see or hear from you again."

Parker laughed. "Fine."

"You don't need anybody, do you? Well, good for you, you won't be disappointed. I, on the other hand, plan to surround myself with good people who care about others and who stick up for what they believe, whose lives aren't consumed with rampant greed and acquisition, but who want to make the world a better place."

He snorted. Diana wanted to deck him where he stood.

"Think what you want of me or don't think about me at all," Jess said. "I no longer care. Oh, there's just one more thing. I know you have a habit of destroying your enemies, but don't even think about coming after my friends or this town, because if you do, I'll finish you."

Jess spun away from him. Found Diana. Took measured steps toward her, but she looked stunned. Diana wanted to run and hug her, but she resisted. The last steps would be the hardest and Jess needed to make them herself. So Diana waited for her to reach her.

They watched until the police drove away, then Diana grinned. "You just made my day."

Allie joined them and gave Jess a hug. "You were awesome, Jess. But could you really finish him?"

"Well, I could help." Jess shrugged. "I've been around him long enough to at least know where some of the bodies are buried. And if it ever comes to it, I'd be happy to testify against him."

"For someone so nice, you are one scary lady."

Jess smiled. "I think maybe I'm done with letting people walk all over me." She nodded as if agreeing with herself. "In fact, I'm sure I'm done. Now, did Clancy say anything about Mac's condition before he left?"

"Yep. She's stabilized. Lillo did something about the artery and stopped the blood loss. But she'll probably have to stay in the hospital a few days. And we're supposed to leave on Sunday."

Two days, Diana thought. So little time, and a shitload to do. But she needed to get back to work and Allie needed to go home.

She looked around. Ian was gone. Vanished. While the final scene played out, he'd taken the opportunity to slip away.

"Don't worry. We'll figure it out. But right now, there's something else I have to do." She struck off across the parking lot.

"Where are you going?"

"To see a man about a horse."

Chapter 26

Lillo couldn't get warm. Mac was going to be fine. Clancy had called from the ambulance, which had met the police car fifteen minutes out of town. Lillo had caught it in time. The bullet had nicked an artery. Mac was in surgery, but she'd be fine. She'd regained consciousness before she went in.

But Lillo just couldn't get warm.

Ned had brought her back to the cottage. Made coffee while she showered. Threw out her bloodied clothes and cleaned the bathroom while she changed into jeans and a heavy sweatshirt. Was waiting for her now, a mug of hot coffee in hand.

She wanted to be annoyed at him. Tell him to stop micromanaging everything.

Except when she'd need him to. She'd never been so glad to see anyone in her whole life than when Clancy and Ned knelt down beside her. But they wouldn't take over. She pleaded with Ned, but he just squatted there like some deaf and dumb gargoyle while she fought for Mac's life and hers.

She blinked back fresh tears. Why the hell couldn't she get warm?

She sat on a stool, reached across the counter for her coffee. Their eyes met as he handed her the mug, and she thought how much it was like looking at a nurse or an attending surgeon over their masks. Everything communicated with a look.

"Drink," he said. "I put in a lot of sugar. It should help with—"

"—shock," she finished for him. "I'm not in shock." The coffee splashed over the rim of the mug. She put it down.

Ned leaned on his elbows on the counter, moving him closer to her. "You were saying . . . ?"

"Why didn't you help me?"

"You didn't need me, and I didn't want to screw up the procedure."

"You could have helped."

"I could have. Would have if I needed to. But I didn't."

He moved back, came around the counter, and sat on the stool next to her. Put his arm around her. "You did good."

"I didn't want to." Damn, the tears were starting again.

"I know."

"You thought you'd teach me a lesson. You always—"

He grabbed her so fast her teeth rattled. "Let's get this straight. I'm not trying to interfere in your life. And if you think for a minute I would jeopardize Mac's life, any life, to teach you a lesson, or even to give you a crutch, you are dead wrong. I saw a competent surgeon, doing the job that needed to be done, and didn't interfere. That's the beginning and the end of it. So deal with it.

"You don't want to be a surgeon. Fine. But you're not going to stop because you feel sorry for yourself, not so you can sit around here planting petunias and acting 'poor me' while people who need your help are going without.

"If you're not willing to face death every day, don't. It isn't easy, as you've found out. No, I take that back, you only lost one and he wasn't even your patient. I've lost count."

"Liar."

He smiled, almost. "You're right. I remember every single one. So go be a nurse. Be a GP. Be a podiatrist, for Christ's sake."

Lillo's lip twitched. "A podiatrist?"

"Nobody ever died of a hangnail." He turned away. "Drink your coffee."

"You think I'm a coward, don't you?"

"I think I made that fairly clear. But I'm done trying to persuade you otherwise. If today didn't convince you . . . well, I'm no competition."

He walked into the other room, but he came back. "If you've finished your coffee, Jess and Allie are over at Mac's, tending Mac's brisket. And I, for one, am starving."

He found a hoodie on the peg and held it while she put in on, turned her around, and zipped it up.

"Do you get how annoying you are?"

He smiled for the first time. "Only to you. Most women enjoy the attention."

They went to Mac's. Lillo wasn't hungry, but she didn't want any more confrontations with Ned. She thought if she hesitated he would just wash his hands of her and would leave her behind. She didn't want to put either possibility to the test.

So they walked across the parking lot, side by side, not talking.

Down the path to the back of the gift shop. A ritual they'd almost lost today. Without Mac, there would be no gift shop, no lighthouse. No one else was interested in running it, keeping it up with practically no funding.

No one to talk to, listen to, to be a friend to. No reason for

Lillo to even be here. The camp was gone. Her parents were in
Florida.

Holy hell, it had been a long day. A long week, when she
stopped to think about it. She'd had more fun than she'd had
for a long time, and more heartbreak, too. It's what happened,
she guessed, when you let people into your life.

Ned opened the door for her. "Sorry, I can't seem to help
myself."

She stopped on the step. Impulsively reached up and kissed
his cheek. "You're annoying as hell, but I appreciate it."

"Uh-huh."

"When I'm sane."

"Ah." He walked in behind her.

The kitchen smelled like Mac would be there greeting them,
but it was just Jess, Allie, and Nando.

"Well, see you tomorrow, I hope." Nando nodded as he
passed them on his way out.

"We were making plans for that motorcycle ride tomorrow,
providing Mac is okay," Allie told them.

Jess lifted a roasting pan out of the oven. "I tried to get him
to stay for dinner but he didn't want to encroach." She took the
lid off the brisket. "There's enough for a crowd. Doc, I hope you
know how to carve this slab of meat."

Ned gave Lillo a sardonic look and went to get the cutting
board.

DIANA DIDN'T REALLY know what she was going to do once she
got to Ian's place. But she was used to thinking on her feet—not
that that was actually where she wanted Ian Lachlan.

He was turning out to be a lot of trouble, and normally she
would have taken the hint. But God, she just kept coming back
for more. He was just so damn intriguing. Always surprising,

and there was something about him that made her usual expectations go up in smoke.

This was not good. Or maybe it was. Besides, he had just accomplished two heroic acts. No one seemed surprised, hardly seemed to pay attention to him once Bobby was back on land. Didn't even try to help him off the ground when he attacked Mac's assailant. What the hell?

Is that why he had disappeared into the mist? Of which she noticed there was less and less. Thank God; she might never have found the way to the stables.

But she did find it and walked up the drive wondering what she was going to say to him. *I came to see if you were all right.* Of course, she could have called him. But it was too easy to get rid of someone on the phone or ignore their text. And Diana didn't intend to be ignored.

Between Bobby's rescue and Mac's brush with a bullet, her adrenaline was still pumping strong. This was as good a time as any to . . . to do something. And see what happened.

The house was dark, lit only by one porch light. She wondered if this was to save money or just because Ian didn't need to leave lights on. Was he sitting there in the dark? The man made her wonder about the dumbest things. She'd known him less than a week, only spent a few hours a day with him, mostly riding behind him or working at the other end of the stables. They'd barely talked, but something about him just spoke to her.

And she had to see what it was.

She didn't stop at the house but walked straight around to the barn. She knew that's where he would be. With his horses. With Loki. The lock was off the door to the barn. Still, she hesitated, suddenly feeling like a fool.

Well, hell, he'd been hit on the head. She'd just say she'd come to make sure he hadn't passed out and died. She slid the door open the least amount possible and squeezed through. It was dark, but the smell of hay and horse calmed her.

There was a dim light at the far end, a work light maybe. She started to call out but something stopped her. As she walked along the stalls, Clara and Pete came out to snuffle her. And she gave them each a stroke as she passed.

Farther down, Loki's stall door was open. Surely Ian hadn't taken him out riding. She hesitated. Listened. And heard Loki's snuffle. She moved silently toward them. Afraid to make a sound. Instinctively knowing that she was the intruder.

She lingered by the post then peeked inside. Loki was there, head bent down. Ian leaned against him, his arms spread along Loki's side, his head resting on the horse's shoulder. The two of them stood perfectly still.

Loki rolled his eye toward her but didn't acknowledge her presence in any other way. Did Ian know she was standing behind him?

He didn't seem to. Just stood there, his arms outstretched, his body pressed against the barrel chest of his horse. A communion. She'd seen him do something similar with the boys. *Soothing,* he'd said. *Self-soothing,* Lillo had called it.

So now what did she do? This was obviously something she shouldn't be witnessing. Something too private and fragile for an audience. Like Spider-Man without his web, Iron Man without his suit.

Diana knew how to take things by storm, flummox a roomful of app geeks, demand parity from HR, write a kick-ass superhero. But she didn't know what to do here. Her first instinct was to back away and quietly leave.

Like you walked away from those kids?

She couldn't do it then and she wouldn't do it now. So she stepped forward, softly, carefully, trying not to make a sound or disturb the newly laid hay with her bargain-store sneakers. She moved like a phantom she might create for a video game, until she was standing directly behind Ian. Slowly raised her hand, held her breath as she gently touched his back with a careful finger.

He didn't flinch . . . she wasn't even sure if he realized she was standing there. She carefully glided her hand down his arm, moving closer until her body was almost touching his. He was warm. Hot. As if he were burning from the inside out.

Loki snorted, shuddered, driving Ian and Diana closer. Until they were touching, body to body. Their arms spread along Loki's body like acolytes in some ancient ritual. She rested her cheek between Ian's shoulder blades, trying not to think about what would happen next.

Then Loki moved away. They both stumbled slightly. And Ian turned to face her.

"Why are you here?"

She didn't have an answer.

She just looked at him, every glib retort, every snappy comeback, any clever one-liner she'd ever said fled, leaving her mind empty and blank. She just knew this was where she wanted to be.

She told him so.

He shook his head. "It's no good. I can't do this."

"Can't do what?"

"This."

"What is this? Do you know? Because I'll be damned if I do."

He took her by the shoulders. Tried to move her away, but she stood her ground and thought, *What the hell.* She slipped her arms around his neck. Stepped into him.

He grasped her wrists. "I can't."

"Everything feels like you can," she said, pressing her body into his.

"Jesus, you're a stubborn woman."

"Just tell me what we can't do, can't be, can't whatever. I'm not even sure what we're talking about."

He pulled her arms away. "I'm not having this conversation standing in a horse stall." He slid past her and out of the stall.

She followed him out. "Fine. Let's have it somewhere else."

His head dropped back—exasperation? prayer?—then he hooked the stall gate and started toward the barn door.

Diana followed right behind him. She should just walk out of the barn and down the drive. She was going home in a couple of days and she'd forget about him. He was just a blip on her vacation radar.

She didn't know why she'd even gotten involved with him. They *weren't* involved. The *situation* might be involved, but they weren't. Much. Were they? Her need to know overrode her reason.

He stopped at the barn door. "God, please, just go away."

"Why?"

He pushed the door wider, stepped through, waited for her. She reluctantly came out and he shut and locked the door.

"I'll drive you home."

"I'll walk."

He kept walking.

"Or I could stay."

He stopped so abruptly she almost plowed into him.

"I've killed people."

"You too?"

"What?"

"Lillo killed—to her mind—the most brilliant medical student who ever walked, and until today she was convinced she had no right to live in his world."

"There's a difference between not being able to save someone and what I did."

"What did you do?"

"Diana, I can't."

"Do you know that's the first time you've actually said my name?"

He glanced at her. "I've tried not to."

"What? Say my name and I claim your soul?"

"You're out of luck. Mine deserted me years ago."

They reached the house and he started up the steps. She knew the best thing to do was to get the hell out, because this conversation was getting beyond weird. But she doggedly climbed the steps behind him.

He opened the front door.

Diana pushed him inside and followed before he could lock her out. "Aren't you being just a little melodramatic?"

He walked across the wooden floor into a modern kitchen with a massive wooden table, and Diana lost her train of thought for a second. He opened a modern fridge and took out two beers. "Okay, I'll give it to you, then will you leave?" He opened the beers and handed her one.

"Maybe." She followed him into the living room.

"I don't have a lot of furniture."

An understatement. The room was huge, the ceilings were high. It had a beautiful stone fireplace and wood paneling, like an old lodge house. Then she remembered that Lillo had lived here when her parents owned the camp.

Diana couldn't imagine it filled with overstuffed furniture and game tables, crowded with campers and their parents. Now there was one big couch, two stuffed chairs, and a couple of floor lamps.

She sat on the couch.

He stood at the fireplace. Took a long drink of beer. Pushed his fingers through his hair.

"How's your head, by the way?"

"Huh? Fine."

"Okay, you killed these people and . . ."

He put his beer on the mantel, scrubbed his face with both hands, picked up his beer again. "I was a part of this organization that worked with third-world villages to turn them into sustainable communities."

"Like planting crops and stuff?"

"That. And irrigation. We helped them set up filtration sites so they had clean water to drink, taught them how to build structures, take care of livestock, start a school."

"Got it. Sustainable. Hope for the future and everything."

"So sometimes it worked out; sometimes shit happened."

Diana decided not to ask.

"Some of these places are constantly at war. Tribal or terrorist. You either live in fear or live in hate. Or both. They hate anyone who has anything. Fear that what they have will be taken away. So they fight, tear down, destroy, kill."

"But you were there to change all that."

"Yeah. There were successes, but as often as not, when we left, some warring tribe would come in and attack and kill and destroy." He laughed bitterly. "The circle of life."

He drank some beer. Stared into the cold grate of the fireplace.

Diana braced herself.

"On my last project we were working in a little village in Somalia. These people were so enthusiastic, so ready to learn, could actually imagine their future. Then we got word that fighting was heading our way.

"We started evacuating as many as we could on the few vehicles we had. Trying to fortify as much of the village as possible. I released as many of the animals as I could get to, knowing they would all be slaughtered and they might have a chance of survival in the jungle.

"But they were on us before we could get everyone out. There was one jeep left and too many people. We were pushing as many children and women onto that jeep as we could, when the firing started. Those who were left tried to flee into the countryside; most of them didn't make it. The jeep had to pull out."

Diana held her breath. *Please don't be the story of the Titanic and you got on the jeep and left children behind. Please.*

"I was lifting a toddler up to his mother as the jeep pulled away and they shot the kid right out of my hands. I just snapped. I turned around, picked up the heaviest thing I could find, and started to fight back.

"I killed men that day. Men. Hell, half of them were hardly more than boys. The same age as Tommy Clayton, maybe younger. I killed them willingly, with hatred. At first with whatever came to hand and then with rifles I stole off the attackers' bodies.

"I'd sworn to do no harm. I was a committed pacifist, but I killed, out of sheer anger, all day long. I just kept killing. It was hopeless. And I just kept killing."

"But you survived."

He laughed bitterly, a heartbreaking sound even to Diana, who thought of herself as a hardened case.

"Did I?"

And there it was, and Diana's heart broke for this man she barely knew, but loved.

"We held them off until reinforcements arrived from the fighting someplace else. They drove them away finally, but everything was destroyed—the irrigation system, the crops, the huts, the cistern, half the population lay dead or dying.

"We had one doctor on staff; I helped where I could. But we treated our own tribe first. Left whoever belonged to the attacking tribe for last. Some died while they lay there ignored, crying out for help."

"Well, not to sound uncaring, but they should have thought of that before they attacked you."

He tried to smile, shook his head. "It's the way they live, always so close to the edge of extinction, natural, man-made, it's what they do."

He breathed, a painful rattling sound that made Diana's own chest hurt.

"So now you know. So I want you to go, get away, leave me alone."

But she couldn't move; she just sat there forming words that wouldn't be spoken. She knew she should step away, leave this man to his overwhelming guilt and disappointment in himself. At least give them both time; her to assimilate what he told her and try to make some sense of it, and him to find his way back to the place where he could live in peace.

Strangely, nothing he'd said had changed her feelings for him. She wasn't repulsed, she wasn't drawn any closer to him. Didn't condemn or condone. She wasn't really comfortable not taking a stand, whether it was for a just cause or against a bad app. She was a businesswoman first and foremost, but she knew how to care for people, and she cared for Ian Lachlan.

She stood, but she didn't leave. She went to the fireplace, stood facing him, stood there until he was forced to look at her. "What happened to the village?"

He looked at her as if she'd sprouted horns.

"We returned, salvaged what we could, the higher-ups decided it was in too volatile an area to rebuild, so we said good-bye, left them with nothing, with less than they'd had before, and we were sent to the next project. That was the worst of all. I'd rather kill again than see those people's faces in my dreams."

"You gave them hope."

"And it was killed."

"Maybe this time they'll have the tools to rebuild themselves."

"You? An optimist?" He huffed out a painful laugh. "They were attacked again. This time both sides had automatic weapons supplied by some first-world nation—Russia, the U.S., maybe both. The village was totally destroyed. Those who managed to escape walked fifty miles to the refugee camp just across the border. Those who made it, I guess, are still there, will probably die there."

She stepped closer, crowding his space, looking for an emotional opening into that defeated spirit.

He looked away. "For a moment they had a future. Hope. And then it was gone." He turned back to her and the bleakness in his face made her want to cry. "Losing hope is worse than never having any hope at all. Now please, if you have any feelings for me at all, go away."

She touched his cheek. "No."

He flinched away. "I'm broken, Diana, I can't be fixed."

"I don't believe that."

"Believe it; nobody can fix me, not even you. There just isn't an app for that."

Her hand slipped around his neck, pulled him closer. "That's a challenge I can't refuse." And she kissed him.

Chapter 27

It was actually going to be a perfect beach day, Lillo thought. She pushed the comforter away and sat up on the couch. Someone had opened the sliding glass doors to the deck to let in fresh warm air. Yep, a perfect beach day.

Too bad she felt like she'd been hit by oncoming traffic. She rested her elbows on her knees and lowered her head to her hands as reality began to seep in. Bobby in the lighthouse. Mac being shot.

She reached for her phone. Nothing had come in during the night. Not since Clancy had called to say the surgery went great, and Mac was awake and demanding to be brought home. That was a good sign. It had been close. Oh God, how close.

Jess sat at the breakfast bar, yawning and squinting at the screen of the new, doubly protected, unlisted-number, waterproof cell phone she'd bought on their sightseeing excursion.

"I defy anyone to try to hack into my phone," she said as Lillo padded over to the counter to pour herself a cup of coffee. "Did you hear from Clancy this morning?"

"No. But I'm sure he would call me if things weren't going well. I'll give him a call when I'm fully awake."

"Allie and Diana are awfully quiet this morning."

"I'm not sure Diana came home at all last night," Lillo said, joining Jess at the counter.

"She didn't," Allie called through the bedroom door.

"Sorry; didn't mean to wake you," Jess called back. She looked at Lillo. "You think Diana and Ian . . ."

Lillo shrugged. "Stranger things have happened. Maybe this is just what needed to happen. The immovable meets the unstoppable."

"Diana *can* be persistent, in business and in matters of the heart."

Lillo put down her mug. "You don't think her heart is involved? Already?" She wasn't worried about Diana. She wasn't sure Ian could withstand the siege.

And where the hell would it lead, except to disaster?

"Well, it's after ten," Jess said. "Do you think we should be worried? I mean what if she didn't stay over and she's lying hurt somewhere in the woods?"

Allie padded into the room. She was wearing boy boxers and a Bob the Builder T-shirt. Her hair was about as crazy as long hair could get. "She called. It was late. She said she was fine, and she'd be back someday."

"Aw, crap," Lillo said. "I don't guess she mentioned how Ian was."

"Nope. I started to ask, but she hung up."

"Do you think he left a necktie on his doorknob so Doc would know he had company?" Jess asked.

Lillo sputtered coffee. She hadn't considered that Ned would be there to witness the seduction, maybe not firsthand, but . . . would he intervene? "Really, Jess? I don't think he owns a tie."

"I can hardly wait to hear all about it."

"Huh," Allie said, and zombie-walked to the coffeepot.

"Why don't you go back to sleep? We've got nothing on the agenda," Lillo said.

Lillo's cell rang.

"Hopefully," Jess added, and Lillo ran outside to take the call.

She was back two minutes later. "That was Clancy. He's going to try to get Mac released this afternoon, since she's giving everybody hell. He said the duty nurses were bribing him to bring her home."

"Oh dear." Allie poured herself a cup of coffee. "Though that's good; she must be okay or they'd never release her even if they wanted to. I was hoping to see her before I leave. And I really have to leave tomorrow."

"Then this will be perfect," Jess said. "Wish you didn't have to go, but a girl has to do what a girl has to do."

"Right." Allie parked herself on the third stool and they all looked forward into the kitchen.

"It feels like we're sitting at a diner counter," Jess said. "Too bad the old luncheonette burned down. You would have liked it."

The front door blew open and Diana appeared in the doorway.

"Too early for dramatic entrances," Allie said.

Diana softly closed the door. "Okay, I'm a little embarrassed. I have a confession to make."

"I need another cup of coffee," Lillo said. "I'll bring the pot."

"So it's like this. I seduced your vet. I wouldn't take no for an answer. He took a while to convince that hell wouldn't freeze over, or maybe that hell wouldn't devour us in one fell swoop. He's a complicated man."

"Did—" Jess began.

"It was exhausting. I mean, getting him to say yes. Though

now that I think about it, he may not have consented. I don't think he'll take me to court." She smiled a canary-eating smile.

Lillo thought boardrooms must quail before that smile. She knew she felt a frisson of unease just watching. She wasn't sure she even liked Diana very much at this moment. "I hope you were gentle with him," she said in her most sardonic voice.

Diana gave her a tight one-shoulder shrug. "Totally out of my hands. Well, not totally, but you know what I mean. Coffee, yeah, that would be good."

Lillo waited for her to pour herself a cup. "So what now?"

Diana was no dummy. She knew she was in unknown territory with Ian. Why had she acted on her feelings if she was leaving?

Diana held the cup in both hands but didn't drink. "That . . . is an unknown."

"That's pretty damn selfish."

She gave Lillo a questioning look. "Afraid I'll use him and spit him out when I'm done?"

"Something like that."

"Well, actually, I don't blame you. It certainly is my MO, but I may be in big trouble here. Somewhere during the night my seduction shifted to something much scarier."

"He didn't get dangerous," Allie said.

"Not in the way you mean."

"Then what? I don't get it."

"Me neither, girlfriend. Me neither." Diana wandered out onto the deck and sat down on a deck chair. The other three looked at each other, then followed her out and sat in the remaining chairs.

The sun was warm, like their first day in Lighthouse Beach.

"Ah," said Allie, "a perfect ending to a week that has been totally wonderful . . . crazy."

And upending and frightening and almost tragic, Lillo thought, and closed her eyes to the sun.

"I'm not walking away," Diana said.

Lillo turned her head to look at her. "Was that directed to me or are you trying to convince yourself?"

"What? For someone whose life is so totally fucked up, you're judging me?"

Lillo thought about it. She wanted to be offended, but Diana was right. "Guess it takes one to know one."

"Touché."

"I guess we're a little overprotective of each other."

"He's a grown man; he can take care of himself."

"I know, but—"

"But none of us can really take care of ourselves by ourselves. It helps to have friends." Diana batted the air with one hand. "God, listen to me. Next thing you know, I'll be having us all holding hands and singing 'Circle of Life.'"

"I doubt it," Jess said. "So are you going to ride today?"

"I don't know. It may be too much of a good thing."

"Ha!" Jess jumped from her chair. "You're scared."

"Am not."

"Are too."

"Dee-Two."

They both started laughing.

Lillo just watched in stupefaction and a kind of admiration. Friends. Their little rituals. Their private silliness. She missed that. She had Mac and Ian, and Doc when she wasn't fighting with him, Sada, and even Barbara. She loved them and trusted them, but it wasn't the same.

But she hadn't realized it until this week.

Part of her wanted life to go back to BRT, Before Road Trip. A road trip that lasted one night before settling in here at her sanctuary, disturbing her life—a lot of lives. But would she really go back if given the chance? For the first time in a long time she'd laughed, had gotten close to women near her own age. Reminisced, told secrets. Felt human for a few minutes.

What was Lillo going to do when they were gone? Sit out another winter while she waited for spring planting? Eat stew with Mac while they listened for trespassers?

Jess sat up, frowning at Diana. "How serious is this? You can't stay here. I mean, can you?"

"Let's not get overexcited here. We just had sex between consenting adults."

"Diana—"

"Let me rephrase that. We had a . . . an interesting . . . amazing night together. I can't believe I'm saying this shit. We're getting to know each other. There's bound to be a learning curve. We'll work it out. Now let's leave it."

"What?" Now all three of them were looking at her.

"'Work it out'? He's not a glitchy new operating system." Lillo didn't know why she was so mad. She should be glad for Ian if this was what he wanted.

"She didn't mean it that way," Jess said.

"Sorry," Lillo said. "It's none of my business."

Diana laughed. "Well, that's a first. Everything seems to be everybody's business around here. First it was Doc."

"Doc?" Allie asked. "When did you see him?"

"He's staying with Ian. I tried to sneak out while Ian was still asleep." She cut a look at Lillo. "I needed time to think. But no such luck. I thought for sure I heard Doc leave for the clinic before I crept downstairs, but no. He was in the kitchen waiting for me.

"Let me tell you. I was ready for awkward with Ian. Those first mornings-after usually are. This was much worse."

"Yeah, he *can* be a bit of a buttinsky." A trait that Lillo was beginning to appreciate.

"At least he'd made coffee. Then he gave me holy shit. Jeez, I don't know why everybody is so protective of Ian. He's drowning in . . . in . . . kindness and protection. It's so enervating. He freaking talks to horses instead of people." Diana held up her hand; it was the one holding her mug and coffee flew into the air. "I'm not saying that's a bad thing, but hell. Let him try to get out of his comfort zone before it suffocates him."

"You're suddenly an expert."

"No. I'm not. And I realize it might be a pretty scary experiment."

"You're planning on conducting some kind of long-distance relationship after one night?"

"Maybe."

"Oh shit," Jess said. "You really are."

"'Fraid so."

"It's kind of amazing." Allie had been pretty quiet until now. Everyone's focus switched to her.

"What is?" Diana asked. "Me actually thinking about a relationship?"

"Not just that . . . but think about it. A week ago we had just run away from Jess's wedding. All of us had . . . I don't know . . ."

"If you say 'issues,' I may have to hurt you." Diana grinned at her.

"Issues," Allie said, and grinned back. "No, really, think about it. Jess was about to give her life over to the Parker corporation, Diana was setting the world afire with cutting-edge apps, but already divorced twice. Me, refusing to believe I could still have a life. And Lillo . . . well, Lillo came riding in like the cavalry and yanked us all out of that.

"Now look at us. Diana is actually being serious about a man. And a relationship. Heck, when was the last time you ever heard *that* word on her lips."

Jess tapped her chin with her finger, an over-the-top gesture of thought. "Um, 2012?"

"Thanks a lot," Diana said.

"And Jess stood up to her father. And by the way, stood up for bullied kids everywhere." Allie fist-pumped the air.

"And got Mac shot for it," Jess said.

"That is not your responsibility."

"I know, but he never would have come if I hadn't been here."

"Maybe, but someone else would have if Mac kept brandishing that shotgun the way she did. Somebody needs to take it away from her."

"I think someone did," Diana said. "Because there was no shotgun to be found by the time the sheriff arrived."

"Well, I hope they threw it in the ocean."

"Agreed," said Jess.

"But on the other hand," Allie said, "if Mac hadn't gotten shot, Lillo would have never known that she could save a life either." She shot Lillo an apologetic look.

"Seems like there should have been an easier way," Lillo said.

"Maybe, but things happen for a reason and—"

Diana jumped up. "If *you're* going to start singing 'Circle of Life,' I'm outta here."

"I wasn't."

Diana sat down.

"You can sing anytime you want," Jess said. "But for now, I plan to sit out here all day until Mac gets back. But I'm getting into my swimsuit and slathering on the sunscreen."

"Sounds like a plan," Diana said. "What about you, Lillo? Up for an afternoon of sunbathing?"

"Hmm?"

"We're going to sit out and get a tan. You in?"

"Yeah," Lillo said. "But first I'm going to run over to Mac's and make sure she has everything she needs."

"Why don't we all go?" Jess said.

"No, that's okay, you guys prepare to laze. I have a few things I need to do while I'm there. Just start the girlie drinks chilling. I'll be back."

"If you're sure."

"I'm sure. There's not that much to do." Plus, she needed time alone. Stuff was happening. She was just getting used to having people around and soon they would be leaving—Jess, Allie, Diana, and Ned and the other guys. No sooner had she gotten used to this new situation than it was all beginning to unravel. She didn't want to be the one left with the tangled mess that was her life. But she wasn't quite sure she had a choice. Maybe it was time she asked for advice.

"STOP FUSSING." MAC tried to push Clancy away, but she was weak as water. Damn, this was not fun. She was tempted to climb back into that stupid, comfortable hospital bed and take another one of those pills.

But if she let the lighthouse go, if she let anything go, she'd turn into an old woman, rocking on the front porch.

She did sit in the wheelchair they insisted she use. She sat, complaining yet grateful, though she'd never tell Clancy. She was surprised she was still alive. Didn't remember much about what happened, except that she knew she had to do something to help the girls.

So she did what she always did. Grabbed the shotgun. Big mistake.

Clancy said Lillo had kept her from bleeding out. Well, it was worth it if it helped Lillo get back to what she loved.

Damn, she was tired.

They rolled her out to the sidewalk. "That's an ambulance."

"No, it's an ambulatory care van."

"Same thing."

Clancy's face appeared before hers. "You thought maybe I was gonna take you home in a sidecar? This is what we got. Be thankful."

She was. How did she get to be so tired? She had thought when she finally got her butt to a hospital or clinic, it would be to fix her old eyes. Now she was going to have to come back again for those. But for now she just wanted to get home. "Humph."

"What are you humphing about?"

"Getting old."

"Beats the alternative."

"I knew you were going to say that."

"Then why did you say what *you* said?"

"Aw, heck, help me get in that thing."

"You just sit. Let them earn their pay."

The back of the van opened and lowered. A cabana boy in a white uniform rolled her onto the loading dock, raised her and the chair, and placed them inside, where Mac didn't get to lie down as she'd been hoping, but had her wheelchair strapped to the floor with her in it. Clancy sat on one of the bench seats, which Mac guessed were reserved for the ambulatory passengers. He folded his hands over his middle, which Mac noted was getting a little paunchy, and closed his eyes. If he fell asleep on the way home, she'd figure out a way to get out of this contraption so she could kick him.

"Enjoy the ride," Clancy said.

Fat chance, Mac thought as they pulled out of the hospital parking lot. But a few minutes later they were passing under the trees down a road that was taking them home.

Home . . . she'd be fine when she got there.

WHEN LILLO FINALLY made it back to the deck, it was afternoon, the other three were in their swimsuits, and drinks were being passed around.

"Where have you been? I was about to come get you," Jess said, handing her a glass.

"Sangria?"

"We thought it only fitting," Allie said. "Sort of bookending the road trip. Besides, we figured we better use up the fruit before it went bad."

"Good idea."

"So what took you so long?"

Lillo sipped her drink. "Oh, this is good."

Jess frowned at her, but didn't ask again. And that's exactly what Lillo wanted. She wasn't even sure of what she'd done. She just knew she'd done it.

Chapter 28

Half the town was waiting in the parking lot when the ambulette brought Mac and Clancy back. They were carrying balloons and homemade cookies, flowers, and a banner that said WELCOME BACK MAC.

How word got around so fast was a mystery. Then again, it was Lighthouse Beach.

The only person who was missing was Ian, and Lillo wasn't sure if that was intentional or if he hadn't yet heard about Mac's return.

"Lord, it's a parade," Mac mumbled as Ned hurried over to help Clancy roll her off the lift.

A cheer went up.

"Just wave and smile, you old grump," Clancy said. And Lillo heard the happiness and relief in his voice. He might grumble, but he and Mac went back a long way, and neither he, nor any of them, were willing to give her up yet.

Allie, Lillo, Jess, and Diana gathered up all the well wishes, took the banner that the community center children had made, and carefully carried it all into the house. The crowd dispersed and headed back up the hill to town.

More than once, Lillo caught Diana looking up the road toward Ian's place.

"He's probably out on a call," she said. "Was he expecting you? You should go on. We can manage here."

Diana shook her head. "Maybe he needs some time."

Maybe, thought Lillo. She just wished Diana hadn't waited until the eleventh hour to jump into bed with the man. Though that wasn't fair. She'd only been here a week. Any earlier would have been just as bad. She just hoped it all worked out.

Mac insisted on sitting up instead of going straight to bed. She was a little loopy from the drugs the hospital had given her for pain, but she wanted to hear about everything that had happened after she'd been whisked away.

They gave her the edited version of the sheriff taking Parker away, Jess giving him what-for.

"Sorry I missed that." Mac's eyelids drooped a bit. "And where is Ian? Did they hurt him very much?"

"No. He's tough," Ned said. "The sheriff said he had to come in and make a statement, but everyone gave him an earful, so there wouldn't be any problem. After all, he was just defending a defenseless old woman."

"Who you calling old?"

"You," Clancy said. "And if we have to go to court, which I doubt, you'll act like an enfeebled, weak-minded biddy and you don't know anything about a shotgun."

"Where *is* my shotgun?" Mac looked around.

"Hopefully washing up on the Norwegian coast by now."

"Ian's fine. He's out on a call," Ned said. "He called the clinic before he left. Said if he didn't get back today in time, he'd come by tomorrow first thing."

"And what about the rest of you? I feel like I've been gone an age. Are you all off tomorrow still?"

Diana moved closer. "I'm afraid so. Allie has a flight to California and I've neglected my business for as long as I dare."

"Of course, you need to go. And it's been a pleasure to have you all here. You must come back. How about you, Jess? Leaving with Diana and Allie?"

"Well, actually," Jess said, "I thought I'd hang around here for a while. If that's okay with you and Lillo. I have some ideas about putting the lighthouse in the black—and using those kids to do it. If you think it's a good idea."

"I think it's an excellent idea."

Clancy heaved himself out of his chair. "Okay, that's enough excitement for one evening. Mac, it's time you rested."

He trundled everyone out the back door. And said good night.

The women walked back toward the cottage without speaking. Lillo lagged behind with Ned. "Is Ian really on a call?"

"Yes."

"You didn't—"

He cut her off. "Interfere? No. So Jess is staying?"

"First I've heard of it, though she has been working on something she wouldn't talk about for the last couple of days. Maybe she does have an idea."

"I hope she's not staying out of guilt."

Lillo gave him a look. "Stop it. Believe it or not, we'll all try to bumble along without you. You're leaving tomorrow, too?"

"Tomorrow afternoon. Our work here is done, for the moment, and they're expecting us in Zed's Landing."

"Are you taking Clancy with you?"

"No. He'll stay around until Mac's on her feet. Actually, the only way they'd let her out today was if he promised to stay with her."

"Nice to know people in high places."

"I guess. Well, good night. Maybe I'll see you before I go. We're out of here at four."

Lillo followed the others into the cottage, where she and Jess watched while the other two packed.

Lillo kept casting surreptitious looks at Diana, but she was looking as stoic as the Sphinx.

They took food and drinks out to the deck and sat while it grew dark. The breeze was nice and kept the bugs away. They finished the last bottle of wine.

No one seemed to have too much to say.

And Ian never made an appearance.

And the sun set on the "Flight from Kennebunkport" road trip.

Sunday morning arrived way too soon.

Mac and Clancy came out to see Allie and Diana off. There were hugs and a few tears, and promises to visit.

Diana didn't mention Ian and Lillo wondered if she would ever return to Lighthouse Beach.

"I THINK THE sign is right," Allie said as she and Diana drove up the hill toward Main Street.

"What sign?"

"The one at the edge of town. 'Welcome to Lighthouse Beach, Life Will Never Be the Same.'"

"Yeah, it got that right."

"No, really, I mean look at us, what we were like before we came."

Diana raised an eyebrow.

"Don't give me that look; we've all changed. Jess finally stood up to her family. I'm ready to face my future."

"And what about Lillo? Now that we're gone, is she going to click her ruby slippers together and say there's no place like home?"

"I don't think she's found home yet."

Diana slowed down at Main Street to let a truck pass. Looked right for a last good-bye to the clinic, Mike's Bar, the consignment store. To the left toward the road that led to Ian's. Straight ahead of them lay the fork where they would continue left on their long trek to Boston.

Diana suppressed a sigh. "You think she'll ever leave?"

Allie looked back to where Mac, Jess, and Lillo stood watching. "I don't know. I hope so."

"So what about me? I'm the same as when I came."

"No, you're not."

"Am too."

"Prove it."

"How?"

"Look to your left, then keep driving."

Diana looked. Ian was striding down the road, looking like thunder. She shoved the car into park and got out. Managed not to run to him like some slo-mo movie with a soundtrack. They stopped when they were inches away from each other.

"Where have you been?" she asked.

"At the llama farm. Didn't Ned tell you?"

"Not precisely. Does this mean we're not over?"

"Sort of up to you."

"I say yes. I will be back. Maybe not every weekend. But you could actually come to Manhattan sometimes. But we can talk about that down the road."

Down the road. Was she nuts? What about three's a charm and that's why she was taking no more chances with men? She'd only known him one week, but who knew? Ian was unlike anyone she'd ever known. It could be a disaster; then again this one might stick. You never knew until you tried.

"WELL, I GUESS that's it," Mac said. "Just us chickens now."

"Chickens?" Lillo and Jess said together.

"Just an expression," Clancy said. "Not casting aspersions on anyone's valor."

"Come into the house," Mac said. "Clancy will make us some soup, and Jess can tell me about these wild plans she's been cooking up."

Jess and Lillo were happy to comply. The cottage would feel empty with Allie and Diana gone.

"So this is what I'm thinking," Jess said as they sat down at the table and Clancy ladled soup and cut fresh bread. "We can't depend on tourists to sustain the lighthouse, so we'll make it a part of the foundation."

"I like how you throw this 'we' person around," Mac said. "And what foundation?"

"The one I'm going to set up for you. And before you start harping on not taking my money, it won't be all mine. We'll set it up as a nonprofit."

"A nonprofit lighthouse. Guess that's better than a lose-money lighthouse."

"Hush, woman. Eat your soup and listen to her." Clancy put a pitcher of lemonade on the table and sat down. "Please proceed, Jess."

Jess grinned. "The lighthouse will be the symbol of the foundation's antibullying program."

Mac stopped eating to gape at her. So did Lillo and Doc.

"We'll get the troublemakers and the special needs, the bullies and the bullied, together, have a program where they have to work together. Learn to respect their differences and their similarities."

"How?" asked Mac. "And who's going to run this program? I don't know anything about teaching kids."

"You don't have to. We'll start with volunteers. When I was at the historical society the other day, I mentioned the idea to Jed Emerson. He said he'd be willing to run a boat-building program. And he knows some retired coach around here who he might get to run some sports activities.

"And I know there are plenty of handy-type people in town to oversee the kids in their first 'Lighthouse' project. Restoring the lighthouse itself. Once they have a personal investment in it, I guarantee the vandalism will stop." Jess sighed. "At least for the most part."

"You think they'll actually participate in it?"

"You know what they say: Build it and they will come."

Mac raised a skeptical, but hopeful, eyebrow.

"Mac, it's only been a few days; give me some time to work out the logistics. I can make it work."

"I'll drink to that," said Clancy, and lifted his glass of lemonade to her.

Lillo joined in.

"Yeah, I expect you can do whatever you set your mind to," Mac said, and lifted her glass. "Here's to the Lighthouse Beach Foundation and to Jess."

IT WAS ALMOST four when Lillo heard the first motorcycle arrive in the parking lot. Jess was sitting at her writing desk working out the plans they'd been discussing at lunch. Lillo was pacing her tiny kitchen and dreading the next few minutes.

Jess glanced over to her. Lillo ignored her. Her heart was

pounding so loud she was afraid she might not hear the others arriving.

"Well, are you at least going out to say good-bye?" Jess put down her pen and stood. "I am."

"I am, too." They met at the front door. Lillo's thoughts were ricocheting off her brain. Her throat was tied in several knots.

Jess opened the door. "Well?"

"You're right." Lillo spun around and ran down the hall to her room. Grabbed the backpack she'd packed that morning after Allie and Diana had gone. Just in case. She raced down the hall. Jess stepped aside and pushed the door wider.

All the guys were there, revving up and ready to drive away.

"Ned!" she called. She was weirdly out of breath.

He was on his bike, at the head of the pack, helmet on and ready to go. He flipped up the visor.

"Zed's Landing is north of here, isn't it?"

"Yes."

"Do you think I could hitch a ride as far as Doctors Hospital?"

He just stared at her for a minute.

"I've got an appointment with my old adviser. No promises."

"Get a helmet."

She shrugged into the backpack, reached in the hard case for the extra helmet, and climbed on behind him. "You sure you don't mind?"

"I can't think of anything I'd rather do. Hold on." He revved the engine and they sped away. Doc "Harley" and his ragtag band of merry do-gooders. And one hitchhiker trying to find her way home.

Acknowledgments

The writing of this story was a road trip in itself—mentally, physically, and emotionally. Much appreciation to the historical and restoration societies and preservationists up and down the coast, beginning with the Absecon Lighthouse folks in Atlantic City who were the first stop on this journey.

As always, many thanks to Kevan Lyon and Tessa Woodward, Elle Keck, and my whole William Morrow team. They're the best.

Gail Freeman, who always seems to know that one elusive fact that I need but can't quite put my finger on . . . and Google has never heard of.

To my Girls' Weekend Away friends, Nancy, Yvonne, and Irene, who when I say, "I wonder if there's a . . . ," they say, "Get in the car, we'll go see." Thanks for your help turning thought into action.

There's a saying that a picture is worth a thousand words, but life experience can certainly create chapters worthy of discovery.

Reading Group Guide

1. Why do you think Lillo decided to attend Jess's wedding when it would have been easier and safer to stay home? Why was it so important to Jess that she come?

2. Are Lillo, Allie, and Diana the catalyst Jess needed to make the break that would finally let her find herself? Or was she just using them because she wasn't strong enough to do it on her own? Did it work? Will Jess continue to grow? What do you think about depending on others to help you? Will she ever be able to reconcile with her family? Should she even want to?

3. And what about Lillo? Do you think she would be able to straighten out her life without Jess, Allie, and Diana? Or would the "specialness" of Lighthouse Beach alone eventually help her find her way?

4. Do you think Lillo is punishing herself for what she sees as her own shortcomings? Is it guilt that prevents her from going back? Why do you think she let her perception of

what others thought about her, whether true or not, drive her away from a profession she loves?

5. What about Diana and Ian? Do they have a chance together? Why would two people apparently so different be drawn to each other?

6. Ian says he's a broken soul who can't be fixed. Do you believe that some people can't be "fixed," not because they're violent or greedy but because their life beliefs have been so damaged? Is Ian one of those cases of the higher they fly, the harder they fall? Can Ian be fixed?

7. Allie and Mac seem to bond in this short time. They are both bound as well as nurtured by "place"—Allie to the vineyard and her family, Mac to the lighthouse and her way of life. Are these kinds of ties good or restrictive? What have these two women learned from their unexpected encounter?

8. Why do you think Ned Hartley (Doc) takes such an interest in Lillo? Is he just the buttinsky know-it-all she sometimes accuses him of being? Or is it something deeper?

9. What would cause someone to choose itinerant medicine over an office and hospital? Is it really as simple as freedom and a motorcycle? What else might be the reason for this kind of life?

10. Lighthouse Beach, like so many small towns, seems to be limping along, tied to the past and uncertain about its future (like many people). Do you think the townspeople of

Lighthouse Beach will survive? What are the different ways they are responding to this situation? What about the next generation?

11. The sign to Lighthouse Beach says WELCOME TO LIGHT-HOUSE BEACH, LIFE WILL NEVER BE THE SAME. Do you think certain places and communities can actually change a person's life? Are those places really "special" or "magical," or are they just ordinary places that are perceived differently by different people?

BOOKS BY
SHELLEY NOBLE

LIGHTHOUSE BEACH
A Novel

BEACH AT PAINTER'S COVE
A Novel

FOREVER BEACH
A Novel

WHISPER BEACH
A Novel

BREAKWATER BAY
A Novel

STARGAZEY POINT
A Novel

BEACH COLORS
A Novel

ALSO AVAILABLE • E-NOVELLAS BY SHELLEY NOBLE

Stargazey Nights

Holidays at Crescent Cove

Newport Dreams: A Breakwater Bay Novella

A Newport Christmas Wedding

Available in Paperback and E-Book Wherever Books Are Sold